As a child, reading t... sowed the seeds for ... career. Using her ex... medical romances v... and heroines to fall in love with is a dr... true. Colette lives in a beach house in Australia in her daydreams, but in reality, she lives in the heart of England, just about as far from the sea as it is possible to be in the UK but very close to the home of Mr Fitzwilliam Darcy! As well as writing, she practices yoga, which she isn't bad at, and French, which needs much more practice!

Kate MacGuire has loved writing since forever, which led her to a career in journalism and public relations. Her short fiction won the Swarthout Award and placed third in the 2020 Women's National Book Association writing contest. Medical romance has always been her guilty pleasure, so she is thrilled to be writing novels for Mills & Boon's Medical Romance line. When she's not pounding away on the keyboard Kate co-runs Camp Runamuk with her husband, keeping its two unruly campers in line in the beautiful woodlands of North Carolina. Visit katemacguire.com for updates and stories.

Also by Colette Cooper

Nurse's Twin Baby Surprise
Wedding Fling to Forever

Also by Kate MacGuire

Resisting the Off-Limits Paediatrician
City Doc for the Single Mum

Discover more at millsandboon.co.uk.

MILLION-DOLLAR BABY DOC

COLETTE COOPER

BUMP IN THEIR ITALIAN FLING

KATE MacGUIRE

MILLS & BOON

All rights reserved including the right of reproduction in whole or in part in any form. This edition is published by arrangement with Harlequin Enterprises ULC.

This is a work of fiction. Names, characters, places, locations and incidents are purely fictional and bear no relationship to any real life individuals, living or dead, or to any actual places, business establishments, locations, events or incidents. Any resemblance is entirely coincidental.

Without limiting the exclusive rights of any author, contributor or the publisher of this publication, any unauthorised use of this publication to train generative artificial intelligence (AI) technologies is expressly prohibited. HarperCollins also exercise their rights under Article 4(3) of the Digital Single Market Directive 2019/790 and expressly reserve this publication from the text and data mining exception.

® and TM are trademarks owned and used by the trademark owner and/or its licensee. Trademarks marked with ® are registered with the United Kingdom Patent Office and/or the Office for Harmonisation in the Internal Market and in other countries.

First published in Great Britain 2026
by Mills & Boon, an imprint of HarperCollins*Publishers* Ltd,
1 London Bridge Street, London, SE1 9GF

www.harpercollins.co.uk

HarperCollins*Publishers* Macken House, 39/40 Mayor Street Upper,
Dublin 1, D01 C9W8, Ireland

Million-Dollar Baby Doc © 2026 Colette Cooper

Bump in Their Italian Fling © 2026 Kate MacGuire

ISBN: 978-0-263-41984-9

02/26

Printed and Bound in the UK using 100% Renewable Electricity
at CPI Group (UK) Ltd, Croydon, CR0 4YY

MILLION-DOLLAR BABY DOC

COLETTE COOPER

MILLS & BOON

For my beautiful daughter, who lit up my life
from the first moment I saw her.

CHAPTER ONE

'I NEED SOME help here, please!'

Dr Maddie McArthur swung round, the urgency in the man's voice as he strode powerfully through the paediatric emergency room with a young child in his arms kicking adrenaline into her bloodstream. Maddie could see immediately that the child, around five years old, was in a seriously bad way.

'Over here,' she called, indicating to the child's father to place his son onto the trolley bedside them. 'I'm Dr McArthur, one of the paediatricians. What's happened?'

'Asthma,' he replied, stripping off his jacket and throwing it over the back of a chair.

Maddie reached for a mask from the grab board, placed it over the little boy's mouth and nose and turned the high-flow oxygen to one hundred per cent.

'He's in status,' continued the boy's father, rolling up his shirt sleeves, 'cyanosed, exhausted and making poor respiratory effort. His mum's following with the baby.'

Maddie was a little taken aback at the boy's father's knowledge and use of medical terminology, but often parents of children with a chronic illness became experts in that particular condition so it wasn't entirely unusual.

'Salbutamol nebuliser, please,' he continued. 'Where are the blood gas syringes?'

Maddie had already squeezed the bronchodilator into the

nebuliser and automatically nodded towards the resus trolley at the side of the bed as she reached for a cannula to slide into the little boy's arm.

'Second drawer down.' She checked herself. This man was more than just a knowledgeable parent. 'Sir, are you a doctor?' Parents weren't allowed to treat their own children and, hard though it was, she couldn't allow this man to treat his child.

The man glanced up to the monitor as one of the nurses who'd rushed over quickly attached the leads. Flashes and alarms immediately registered the child's worrying vital signs.

'Sats eighty-eight; resps forty-four; heart rate one fifty,' he announced, apparently ignoring her question. 'I'll do the blood gas from the right radial artery.'

'Woah, just a second.' Maddie reached out towards him, halting him, her hand hovering over his forearm. There was no way she was going to let this man treat his son. 'You have to stand back and let us do this—you know you can't treat your own child.'

He stared at her and, just for a moment, there was a flicker of confusion in the bluest eyes she'd ever seen. And then he smiled—a wide, warm smile, lighting up his face and lightly creasing the outer corners of his eyes. He held out his hand towards her. Maddie looked at it and back at him.

'Will Lawrence,' he said. 'I'm not the father, I'm the new paeds consultant—starting today. Sorry.' He grimaced but his eyes still twinkled. 'I should have introduced myself.'

'Oh.' She let him take her hand, feeling suddenly off balance as concern turned to confusion and then everything registered, falling into place. 'Yes, maybe you should've.'

But he'd released her hand, taken a syringe from the drawer and his dark head was bent once more as he took blood from the boy who wasn't his son.

'This is Mum,' said India, one of the paediatric nurses arriving in the cubicle, her arm around a terrified woman who was clutching a brown teddy bear and a blue inhaler in one hand and the handle of a pushchair in the other. 'Violet.'

'I thought he was getting better from his cold,' said Violet, her eyes darting between the staff and her blond-haired son, who lay barely conscious and barely breathing on the bed. 'His wheezing had eased today.'

'What's your son's name, Violet?' said Maddie gently.

'Noah,' she replied. 'Is he going to be okay?'

'We're doing everything we can for Noah,' said Maddie. 'You did the right thing bringing him in.' She addressed India. 'Chest X-ray, please.'

'Can someone take this to the gas analyser, please?' Will Lawrence held a small syringe. 'And bring the results straight back to me.'

'I can do both,' said India, picking up a tray for the syringe. She glanced at Maddie, a question in her eyes.

'New consultant,' explained Maddie, and India's eyebrows rose.

'Can you bleep the on-call paeds anaesthetist, please?' said Maddie, turning to Jake, the second nurse. 'We need them down here asap, just in case.'

'On it,' he replied, his eyes widening in obvious approval.

'Sats unchanged,' said Will, studying the monitor. 'We may need to intubate.' He pulled a stethoscope from the pocket of the jacket he'd slung over the chair, bending to listen to Noah's chest.

'Blood gas results,' said India, handing a printout slip to Maddie, who'd recovered enough to take them from her.

'Thank you.' Maddie studied the figures—they were as she'd feared but still her heart sank. She glanced at the new consultant…who *should* have introduced himself well before he did and well before she'd ordered him to step back. He caught her look, read it and reached for the equipment on the grab board behind him, as if her brain had broadcast the blood results directly into his.

'I'll intubate,' he said. Had he also mind-read her simmering irritation at his failure to identify himself sooner?

'Vic is the anaesthetist on today,' said Jake, reappearing. 'He's stuck with a patient at the moment but said he'll be over as soon as he can.'

'Could you bring a ventilator in, please?' Will Lawrence was laying out the intubation equipment, flicking on a laryngoscope to check the light worked.

Maddie glanced at the monitor. Noah's oxygen sats were holding—he'd need intubation before long if things didn't improve pretty rapidly. Will Lawrence was right to prepare.

'Sats are holding,' said Will, following Maddie's glance to the monitor, 'but respiratory effort is poor. Magnesium infusion?'

'Yes,' replied Maddie. Just what she'd been about to say. She turned to India. 'Can you draw that up, please?' Will Lawrence was obviously competent—so why was she bristling?

'Sure,' said India. 'Check it with me, Jake?'

'We should consider intravenous salbutamol too,' said Maddie. Had she voiced that to say it before he did?

'You read my mind, Dr McArthur.' Will smiled and then turned to the resus trolley. 'Which drawer?'

'Third one down,' replied Maddie, tearing open a syringe and taking the vial of drug from him as he handed it to her. Reading each other's minds was helpful in clinical situations like this, but not so great if he could tell how annoyed she was with him and definitely not good if he could sense how inexplicably those eyes of his had made her stomach do an annoying somersault.

'We're going to give Noah some of the same medicine he

has in his inhaler,' said Will, addressing Violet, 'but we'll give it into a vein so it acts more quickly.'

'Do whatever you need to, Doctor,' said Violet, clutching the teddy bear to her more closely.

Will smiled then glanced at the monitor, turning to Maddie. 'We should have seen a response by now. We've maximised medical treatment and I think the benefits of ventilation outweigh the risks now, do you?'

'Agreed,' said Maddie, unable to disagree but somehow wishing she could. 'I'll intubate if you can give the drugs, do cricoid pressure and the ventilator. The drugs are in a pack in drawer three.' Will Lawrence had literally strode in, taken over and demanded her immediate attention—expecting her to somehow know who he was without an introduction. He might well be impressively clinically competent but he hadn't exactly got off on the right foot.

'We need to pop Noah to sleep so that we can let a breathing machine take over his breathing for a while,' he said to Violet. 'Would you like to stay or would you prefer to have a seat in the waiting room? It's completely up to you.'

'Can I stay with him?'

'Of course you can,' said Maddie. 'It all looks and sounds a little scary with all the machinery and alarms but it's all helping Noah. Just try to ignore the machines and the noises. Have you got any questions?'

Noah's mum shook her head. 'Just make him better... please.'

'Chest X-ray?' A radiographer arrived and an X-ray was taken. Maddie brought the image up immediately—Will looking over her shoulder, standing just a little closer than she was prepared for and definitely closer than she could ignore.

'No pneumothorax,' he announced.

'That's a good sign,' said Maddie, looking at Violet and smiling, moving away from him.

Violet nodded and smiled back weakly, burying her nose into the teddy.

India returned with the ventilator, which Will turned on, adjusting the settings, casting his eyes over the line of equipment, making sure everything they'd need was within reach. Once the procedure was started, there was no going back.

'Dr McArthur is going to take over Noah's breathing,' said Will to Violet. 'Once he's asleep, she'll guide a small tube into his windpipe and attach it to the ventilator, which will breathe oxygen into him. Anything you want to ask?'

Violet shook her head.

The monitor began to alarm, making Maddie and Will glance up at it. Noah's oxygen sats had dropped. Will, who was nearest, reached out and silenced the alarm, looking at Maddie, quickly masking the concern in his eyes. There was no time to lose now. Noah had failed to respond to medical treatment and although there were risks involved in putting the little boy onto a ventilator, if they didn't, he could stop breathing altogether. Will Lawrence had proved himself competent up to now but this was where his capabilities would be tested. If he could handle a rapid sequence intubation with as much ease as he'd shown so far, she might have to consider forgiving his less than ideal entrance into the department.

'Induction drugs and cricoid pressure, please.' Maddie took her eyes off Will only when he'd nodded and moved into position, picking up the syringes of anaesthetic and muscle relaxant.

'Drugs are in,' said Will, flushing the IV line. Maddie quickly positioned Noah's head to open the airway, turning on the light to view the vocal cords, sliding the laryngoscope into his mouth, then, without removing her gaze, holding out her palm for the endotracheal tube, which Will placed into it. She guided it down into position quickly.

'We're in. Remove cricoid pressure, please.' But Will had

already done it, had the ventilator circuit tubing in his hand and attached it to the endotracheal tube she'd just placed in Noah's throat. If there was a definition of something going like clockwork, this had been it. Rapid sequence intubation was a procedure that needed to be completed swiftly and it had been as though she and Will had been one mind, working together. He'd anticipated her every move and she couldn't help but be impressed.

'Sats improving and air entry all areas.' Will pulled his stethoscope from his ears, looking up at Maddie, intense blue eyes locking onto hers, smiling at her—a wide, genuine, approving smile. 'Good job, Dr McArthur.'

Maddie managed a small smile in return, her stomach flipping again, throwing her off balance.

'Quite a start for your first morning, Dr Lawrence.'

'Am I too late?' Vic Hazelwood, paediatric anaesthetist, strode in, surveying the scene. 'Looks like you've done the hard bit.'

'It was a straightforward intubation,' said Maddie. 'Noah's sats have improved and his heart rate is beginning to settle. Have you a space on PICU?' Getting little Noah a bed on the paediatric intensive care unit was paramount. He would receive one-to-one care there and be monitored minute by minute.

'We've one patient being stepped down to the high dependency unit shortly,' he replied. 'We can take Noah in about half an hour, if that's okay?'

'We can manage him here in the interim, no problem,' said Will, slipping his stethoscope back around his neck. 'I'll do another blood gas now he's on the ventilator.'

Vic turned to him, a frown creasing his brow.

Will held out his hand. 'Will Lawrence, new paeds consultant. It's my first day.'

'Pleased to meet you, Will,' replied Vic, shaking the proffered hand. 'Maddie isn't easing you in gently, then?' He grinned. 'I can take over here if you two need to crack on with other patients. I'll keep in touch with PICU and let you know when the bed's ready.' He turned to Noah's mum. 'Come and have a seat here with me and we'll both keep an eye on Noah, shall we?'

'Shall we go and get you set up to work here officially?' said Maddie, washing her hands at the sink.

'I guess we should,' replied Will, pulling paper towels from the dispenser on the wall. 'I don't want anyone else almost throwing me out of the department for being an impostor.' He grinned and Maddie's stomach flipped again. She looked away, her annoyance with him notching confusingly higher.

'The consultant's office is this way.' She indicated a corridor just off to the left. The new consultant strolled beside her, his jacket hooked over one finger, slung over his shoulder, looking entirely relaxed—which was more than she was. He should have told her who he was straight away—instead he'd almost let her publicly humiliate herself by confronting him only to have him calmly announce who he was afterwards.

She stopped by a storeroom door and opened it, leaning in and placing her hand on a shelf that was piled high with folded scrubs of various colours and sizes. She turned around to face him, immediately regretting it. Not for the first time that morning, her heart rate kicked up a notch. His intense blue eyes had already caught her off guard. But now, forced to scan his body to determine the right-size scrubs to select from the shelf, she found her breath catching too.

He towered above her, broad-shouldered, slim-waisted and undeniably well muscled beneath his crisp white shirt and tailored trousers. Everything about him was honed, composed, perfect. She drew in a breath, willing her pulse rate back under control. He was about the finest figure of a man she'd ever seen—and that was with his clothes on. She turned away, pretending to rummage through a pile of navy scrubs. Dear Lord, she hadn't noticed those things about a man in a long time.

'Long leg, medium-waist trousers and forty-two-inch chest for the top,' he said, behind her. She turned to face him, noticing one dark eyebrow rise and his lips curve towards a smile. 'To save you guessing.'

Maddie swallowed. She'd guessed right. She reached for the scrubs, pulling them from the shelf and placing them in his outstretched hands, letting the door to the storeroom close and continuing down the corridor.

'You'll need to get logged in to the IT systems; do the induction, then get your ID and security swipe card. It'll be the afternoon by the time all that's done and you can see patients...officially.' She raised an eyebrow as he held the door for her to go into the office first.

'After you.' He followed her in, looking round. 'Any particular desk I should use?'

Maddie pointed to the desk on the right. 'That's yours.' She pointed to the other desk. 'And that's mine.'

Will glanced between the two desks. Each had a monitor and keyboard—bare, functional, exactly as she liked it.

'Very minimalist.'

'I don't like clutter,' she replied, bracing herself for a comment. The room had the personality of a paper clip but she'd grown up owning almost nothing and still lived in the same frugal manner even now. Spending money on anything that wasn't strictly essential didn't come naturally—which meant that quirky pen pots, colourful desk calendars and unnecessary trinkets had never adorned her desk. Family photos hadn't either, but that was for entirely different reasons.

Will grimaced but his eyes sparkled with good humour. 'I'm not exactly known for my tidiness but I'll try not to scandalise your workspace.' And he smiled that smile again—

easy, confident. It lit up his already striking features. With his raven-dark hair, neatly trimmed stubble and eyes that twinkled when he looked at her, he was dangerously handsome. But it was the dimple in his cheek when he smiled that undid her. It was the last tick in the box on the checklist of most handsome man in the world.

But she didn't trust handsome—handsome lured you in, chewed you up and spat you back out again, which was exactly why she was going to ignore the way her heart rate annoyingly picked up every time he locked his eyes onto hers. Was that why she felt so out of sorts around him? Because he was so attractive and had made her look at him as she hadn't looked at a man for a long time?

'Have your desk however you want it,' she replied. 'I'm not precious about it.' She pulled a large file from a drawer, handing it to him. 'Everything you need is in here. Come back onto the unit when you're changed and all that's done and I'll show you where to get your ID and security clearance from. I'll nip back to see how Noah's doing.'

She needed to breathe—she was responding to him as if she fancied him. What on earth...?

'Great, thanks, Maddie.'

'No problem—see you later.' She closed the door with a click, leaving the new consultant to himself, grateful to step away so she could gather her thoughts. It was a relief to finally have another consultant working with her to share the load and Will Lawrence had already proved he was well worth the long wait the recruitment process had taken. He was sharp, competent and empathic—clearly someone everyone could work well with. But she really didn't want to appreciate him in any other way—in the way she had since his dramatic entrance with Noah. She'd just got her life back on track after kicking Andrew out of it—it had taken a while and she still bore the scars but at least she hadn't cried herself to sleep lately, and the self-worth her ex had so successfully destroyed had begun to peer out from under the rubble of their so-called relationship.

Will Lawrence, with his sharp suit, darkly handsome good looks and breath-taking physique might well have made her heart skip a beat but she wasn't going to put herself in a position where someone could shame her again. He was a highly competent doctor and a very welcome addition to the department—that was all.

Guilt tugged at her. She'd been short with him and not because he'd neglected to introduce himself—it had been because she'd noticed him and hadn't wanted to. She swiped her security card and the door to A & E swished open. She'd be nicer to him later—it wasn't his fault he'd made her want to look into his piercing blue eyes for longer than was wise.

Will made his way to A & E. The new employee induction had been as dull as ditchwater, as he'd expected, but he'd sped through it, eager to return to the department and to his new colleague, Maddie. Her baby-blue eyes had alighted on him with alarm as he'd rushed towards her with Noah in his arms, then with concern as she'd realised the seriousness of the little boy's condition, followed by conflict as she'd thought he was ill-advisedly treating his own son and lastly with relief and gratitude when the crisis had been over. Such a plethora of emotions in such a short space of time and beautifully played out across her delicate features. He'd wanted to say to hell with the induction and to get to work straight away on the unit with her. But he hadn't gone to all the trouble of leaving the only life he'd ever known at the other end of the country to fall into another, no doubt ill-judged relationship as soon as he arrived.

Scarlett.

She still had the power to turn his insides to ice.

It had been over a year since he'd discovered her lies.

He'd pieced it all together, confronted her calmly. She'd denied everything at first—she'd had too much to lose by admitting it, hadn't she? But the evidence had been undeniable and in the end she'd confessed. What he hadn't expected was the venom in her reaction when the truth came out. It had cut him deeper than he'd cared to admit. But it had taught him a lesson—he wasn't ever going to risk going through it again. Not for anyone.

'I'm official now.' He rested his arms on the counter of the nurses' station. Maddie looked up and those big blue eyes alighted on him once more, recognition registering in them before she broke into a warm smile, the first real smile she'd given him and one that surely no one on earth could have resisted smiling back to. He needed to be careful. He'd spent the first six months after Scarlett's devastating revelations skulking around, feeling sorry for himself. In the second six months he'd behaved like a bear with a sore head, taken a sabbatical from work and trekked, or rather stomped, his way around South America, making some decisions about his life. Decisions that had led him to York Royal Infirmary.

Will had done a little research on his colleagues before taking the position. One of the colleagues he'd read about had been one Dr Maddie McArthur, who'd graduated from Cambridge and risen through the ranks at warp speed. He'd been keen to see her at work and hadn't been disappointed that morning when she'd swung so effortlessly into action when he'd swept in with little Noah in his arms.

'You've done your induction already?' she replied, glancing at the clock on the wall.

'I have,' he said. 'Passed with flying colours. IT have set me up on all the systems here and I bumped into India, who showed me to the ID badge office. So, I'm ready to begin... officially this time.'

Maddie smiled. 'Perfect. Well, there's a seventeen-year-old in cubicle four who Jake triaged a few minutes ago. I was just about to go and see him myself but if you're free, you could start with him, if you like?'

'Sure, what's he come in with?'

'Sounds as though he's had a seizure,' said Maddie, a grimace flattening her lips. 'Mum says he dropped to the floor as he was about to leave for college this morning. That's all I know at the moment.'

'Okay, I'll go take a look.' The other interesting piece of information he'd read about Maddie McArthur was that she'd specialised in paediatric neurology—one of the most challenging sub-specialities there was—and she'd just given him a probable neurology case to go and deal with. Vic Hazelwood had been right—she wasn't easing him into his new job gently. In fact, he'd been thrown right in at the deep end.

Not that he minded—he loved his job. He hadn't needed to become a doctor and earn a living that way, of course, and he'd surprised his family when he'd announced his intention to do so. Money from his shares in the family business had helped him start up his own medical tech company and he'd already had a few million in the bank by the time he'd enrolled in college. But, as he'd hoped, becoming a doctor, having a real-world job, had saved him in more ways than one over the years. He didn't need the money but he needed what his job as a doctor did for him—keeping him grounded and in touch with real people, giving him a purpose other than watching his bank balance go from strength to strength and his share prices rise.

'Let me know if you need anything,' said Maddie.

'Will do,' he replied, glancing around for cubicle four.

'Eleven o'clock,' said Maddie, a smile playing on her very full lips.

He swallowed. The photos online really hadn't done Maddie McArthur justice.

Stop it.

'Cubicle four,' she explained, smiling and pointing towards it.

He turned and finally spotted cubicle four.

'Ah, thanks, great…got it.' Hopefully he hadn't looked at her like a lovesick puppy. He paused before the curtain at the cubicle, calling to Jake to ask if he could go in. This was his fresh start, a new beginning away from the world he'd grown up in—a world that had slowly eroded his trust. When you had millions—multimillions—in the bank, you learnt that not everyone around you was there out of love or loyalty. Scarlett had taught him that lesson in the harshest way imaginable. And although he loved his large family dearly, he'd needed to get away from that world to a place where no one knew anything about him—his past, his real self, who he really was. All that needed to remain buried. Keeping that secret—protecting his truth—was the only way he could begin to move on.

CHAPTER TWO

'ONE MORE ESSENTIAL thing you need to do on your first day is add your name to the brew list,' said Maddie as Will strode towards the nurses' station. 'You don't want to be left out.'

'Brew list?' His dark brows drew together. 'I have a very real fear of missing out on anything so, please, fill me in.'

Maddie smiled, standing up. 'Come with me, I'll show you. How did you get on with the young man in four?'

'Mathew—sounds like he had a tonic clonic seizure, which spontaneously resolved after about a minute, witnessed by his mum, who's with him,' replied Will as they walked down the corridor. 'No previous episodes; he's otherwise fit and well; observations and blood sugar are normal. Neurological examination is grossly normal and there's no obvious head trauma. I've ordered an MRI scan and an EEG to see if there are any focal lesions in the brain.'

'Any history of drug or alcohol use?' Maddie pushed open the door to the staffroom.

'His mum's present,' said Will, 'so I can't be certain he's telling the truth. I'll ask him when she's not there.'

'Sounds good to me—we'll see what the tests show.' She pointed to a notice on the wall. 'Add your name to that so that whoever's making drinks knows your brew of choice.'

'Ah, of course—*brew* as in cuppa. If I needed reminding that I was in the north, you just reminded me.'

'Coffee, black, no sugar,' said Maddie, watching as he

wrote. 'Very southern. Not a pumpkin spice latte?' She smiled at him.

'Oh, is that an option?' said Will, his tone heavy with mock innocence, his pen hovering over the paper. 'I'll change it if it is.'

Maddie laughed. 'I'd leave it as black coffee if I were you, otherwise the staff will start talking about you.'

'We can't have that.' Will slipped his pen back into his pocket, his eyes locking onto hers, dimple creasing his cheek as he smiled. He really was very good-looking. It wouldn't be long before he was snapped up by someone and became the talk of the hospital grapevine. Unless...

'Are you married?' The words tumbled out of her mouth before they'd risen to the level of her consciousness and she was shocked herself at hearing them being spoken by her own voice. 'Sorry, I... I just thought...it's probably one of the questions people will ask...with you being new and...' Her voice trailed off and it was all she could do not to screw her eyes closed and hope that when she dared to open them again, he wouldn't be there. She'd been about to say 'so good-looking' but thankfully had realised what her errant mouth had been about to do.

'Divorced,' he replied lightly, 'and not aiming to repeat the process. So, if anyone does ask, you can let them know I'm not on the market...please.'

Maddie looked at him. He was grinning and relief washed over her. He wasn't on the market. Good.

'Same here,' she replied, almost in triumph.

He raised his eyebrows in a question.

'As in, not on the market,' she clarified.

'I see. Well, I know what the hospital grapevine is like when someone new starts,' he continued, 'so I'd rather be upfront. What is it about hospitals that makes them so gossipy?'

'I know,' agreed Maddie, rolling her eyes. 'Well, I've got some blood results to check, so I'm going to get back.' She was very aware that her own love life, or lack of, was occasionally a topic of debate amongst staff. Her best friend, hospital neurosurgeon, Aisha, kept her informed if there was any tittle-tattle about her, but Maddie had no intention of providing the gossip mongers with any material. Anyway, there was no material to provide. Maddie's love life was non-existent and that was exactly how she wanted it to be.

Just as Will Lawrence did, by the sounds of it. And that little snippet of knowledge was so welcome she almost sighed with relief. All she had to do now was remind herself of that every time he locked those seriously blue eyes on her, daring her to gaze into them.

It was a short walk back to the paediatric emergency department, with Maddie explaining who the few people they met en route were. Will's presence was met with more than obvious approval from the women and very obvious green-eyed disapproval from one of the male senior surgeons, who clearly saw Will as a potential rival. But Will greeted them equally with warm genuineness—no flirting back and no testosterone-fuelled sparring. He didn't have any reason to do either, did he? His dark good looks, impressive stature and jawline that could have been chiselled by an Italian Renaissance sculptor were enough to render other men invisible. And he wasn't on the market.

But as he walked away from the nurses' station to go and see his next patient, her eyes, despite herself, strayed from the back of his dark head to take in the broad width of his square shoulders then downwards to his slim waist and to the very firm butt, hugged by the navy scrub trousers that fitted perfectly over it. She dropped her gaze, focussing on the log-in screen without seeing it, as though she'd been caught looking at something she shouldn't. She hadn't looked at a man in that way since…

Andrew.

And she wasn't putting herself through that again…not in a million years. Why she'd ever thought she was good enough for him in the first place still confounded her. If she'd learnt anything at all from the start in life she'd had, it had been to know her place and remember who she was and where she'd come from. She'd been dismissed by others all her life, constantly having to prove her worth, always living in fear of the judgement of others. So why had she ever thought she'd be worthy of someone like him?

She'd known not to trust anyone who had money. So why she'd thought, even for one second, that getting into a relationship with high-flying, privately educated, holiday-home-in-Aspen Andrew was ever going to end in anything but tears, she had no idea. He'd lived in one of Notting Hill's grandest villas, apart from in the summer when the family went to their house in the South of France and in the winter when they stayed in their ski lodge in Colorado. His father was a high court judge and his mother a very successful barrister, for goodness' sake. So why had she been so surprised and devastated when he'd refused to take her home to meet them? Because she'd allowed her silly heart to fall in love with him and that had prevented her brain, which should have known better, from thinking rationally and stopping her in her tracks.

She sighed and closed her eyes momentarily before entering the ward. Well, she wasn't ever going to make that mistake again. It was doubtful she'd ever meet anyone who'd had quite the same dysfunctional upbringing she'd had, but what she knew for sure was that if she was ever going to be able to trust anyone again, it was going to be someone who'd had a more normal life and might value her despite her very chequered background. It would definitely not be someone with wealth.

***

'No focal lesions or structural abnormalities on the brain,' said Maddie, standing just to the side of where Will sat and peering over his shoulder at the MRI images on the screen. He hadn't asked her to review the images. *Was she just interested or was she checking up on him?* 'Did you manage to speak to Mathew privately to ask about drugs and alcohol?'

'He denies both,' replied Will, glancing up at her as she straightened up, disturbing the air between them and giving him a breath of her ocean-fresh scent, 'and I believe him. I think he's a good kid. He wants to study medicine actually.'

'Has he been studying hard recently?' asked Maddie. 'Burning the midnight oil?'

'I asked that,' replied Will, a stab of indignance piercing him at her question. 'He says not.'

'And neither Mathew nor anyone else around him has ever noticed any other signs that could have been seizures—staring, twitching, visual disturbances, loss of awareness, odd tastes or smells?' Maddie folded her arms.

'None of the above,' said Will, 'and nothing that appears to have been a trigger either. Did you get your blood results back?' He might be the new boy, but didn't need checking up on.

'Yes, thanks,' she replied. 'So what's the plan?'

Really?

'He's had an unprovoked first seizure so medication isn't warranted. I'm going to keep him overnight…perhaps do a sleeping EEG. That okay?'

'Sounds like a plan,' said Maddie. 'We can't make a diagnosis from one seizure. I'd do an echocardiogram too just to rule out any cardiac cause.'

'Yes, I've arranged an echo.' *As if he wouldn't.* 'I'll go and explain to them what the plan is.' Will pushed his chair back and stood.

'Do you mind if I come along with you?' said Maddie.

He frowned. *Why? Didn't she trust him?* She was a neuro specialist but Mathew's case wasn't exactly difficult.

'Because he's a neuro patient?' he asked.

'No,' she replied easily. 'You mentioned he's interested in studying medicine and I have a bit of an interest in supporting potential medical students, that's all.'

'Okay,' he said slowly. 'As long as you're not testing me.'

As she was testing him not to look at her in the way he had been all morning—as if she were the blue-eyed, blonde-haired picture-perfect girl next door. He was glad she'd asked if he was married, even if it had conjured a very unwanted flash of Scarlett into his head. Setting out his stall from the beginning was best—he was off the market, determined to stay that way and the more people who knew about that, the better. Maddie was stunning and seemed lovely with it, but he wasn't ever going to trust another person with his heart again. It had begun to mend after being torn apart once—it wouldn't withstand it a second time. No, his heart was firmly locked away and he'd long since lost the key. It was safer that way.

'Not at all,' replied Maddie.

But she was, she just didn't know it. She was sending his senses into overdrive. This wasn't what he'd moved away from home for. He'd moved away to create distance from the only life he'd ever known—a life he'd always feared would consume him and almost had. Moving to York had been about hiding who he was—living the life he hoped would help him to find out if he was worth knowing without his wealth. The family countryside estate, the mansion in Kensington, London, the apartment in New York, private jets and helicopters—they were nothing without also having people around you who cared, loved you even. The wealth had lured Scarlett into his life—Scarlett, who'd fallen in love with his money and not him and who'd finally admitted it…to his face…all but destroying him.

They made their way to cubicle four, Will introducing Maddie to Mathew and his mum.

'So, we'd like to keep you in overnight, if that's okay with you,' said Will. 'We may run some more tests to see if anything shows up.'

'It must be epilepsy though, mustn't it?' said Mathew's mum, worry etched on her brow.

'Not necessarily,' replied Will. 'A number of conditions and circumstances can cause a seizure—we need to do a little more investigation.'

'Dr Will tells me you'd like to study medicine, Mathew,' said Maddie. 'Have you applied to any medical schools yet?'

Mathew glanced to his mum, who looked down at her hands.

'I'd like to,' he replied, 'but it's tough to get in and…well, I'd just like to work in care of some kind really—you know, help others in some way. It doesn't have to be in medicine. I mean, everyone plays a part in a hospital, don't they, from porters to surgeons?'

'They do,' said Maddie. 'We're all small cogs in a big wheel, but if you can get the grades and feel you want to be a doctor, then you should follow your heart.'

Will watched the three of them. Mathew's mum looked suddenly saddened, glancing up at her son and then back down at her hands. Mathew himself wore a braver look on his face but had a sadness in his eyes and Maddie… Maddie's blue eyes suddenly had an earnest intensity in them as she spoke to Mathew. She'd mentioned having an interest in helping potential medical students—this clearly meant a lot to her.

'Maybe,' said Mathew, dropping his gaze.

'If you've got any questions about studying medicine or what it's like to be a doctor, just ask me,' she said. 'I'll be around on the ward tomorrow.'

Mathew looked back at her and nodded. 'Thank you, Dr Maddie.'

'I'll pop up to the ward later,' said Will, pushing the cubicle curtain aside, 'to see how you're doing.'

'Thanks, Doctor,' said Mathew's mum, a smile lifting her face. 'We're very grateful.'

'That was kind,' said Will as they made their way back to the nurses' station, 'offering to chat to Mathew about med school.'

'It can be difficult for kids sometimes to get access to someone to talk to, can't it?' she replied. 'Not everyone knows a doctor they can just call up and get careers advice from. There are kids out there who'd make great doctors but don't have the exposure, the contacts, the access to decent education sometimes and who never get the chance to fulfil their potential—I hate to see that.'

'It's true,' replied Will. 'Not everyone has the same chances in life that we've had and if we can give something back, then we absolutely should.'

He smiled at her but Maddie didn't smile back. Her delicate jawline had set and she had a determination about her suddenly, her baby-blue eyes all steely resolve. It was such a sudden and unexpected change in her that he was momentarily taken aback.

'Maddie!' A middle-aged man in a dark pinstriped suit and shoes you could see your face in approached, smiling widely at Maddie. 'Just wanted to invite you to a barbeque at *Chez Johnsons* on Saturday. The new outdoor pool is finally complete and Fiona and I are having a bit of a pool-warming, as it were, to celebrate.'

'Ryan,' said Maddie, turning towards him, her smile returning, 'this is Dr Will Lawrence, our new paediatric consultant.' She gestured towards Will. 'Will, this is Mr Ryan Johnson, one of the orthopaedic surgeons who specialises in paediatric trauma.'

'You're invited too,' said the surgeon, shaking Will's proffered hand heartily. 'Three o'clock onwards. Maddie has the address. Oh, and no need to bring a bottle—we stocked up the wine cellar when we were in Italy a couple of weeks ago. Welcome to York Royal Infirmary, Will. I'm sure we'll be seeing a lot of each other. Anyway, better dash, I've got clinic in minus two minutes—the clinic sister will be tutting at me all afternoon.' He bellowed a laugh, turned on his heel and walked away as if he expected applause.

Will glanced at Maddie. Her eyes were closed and her lips, naturally full and usually with a perfect little cupid's bow, were pressed thinly together. She opened her eyes, letting out a long breath, raising her eyebrows as she caught his look.

'He's a bit of a whirlwind, isn't he?' said Will.

'That's one word for him.' Maddie sucked in a breath. 'He's a very good surgeon but...'

Will watched her as she pondered her next words, her head a little to one side making her blonde ponytail swing into view.

'He knows it?' suggested Will.

Maddie's mouth twisted as she wrestled to find the right words.

'Actually, I'm not going to cloud your judgement,' she replied decisively. 'Go to his "pool-warming" and see what you make of him.'

'I'm not sure I'm free,' said Will. He'd come to York to work, not socialise. Work was his safe space—the place where he was just a doctor and not a multimillionaire who was rich pickings for people who wanted to use him for their own ends. Besides, working with Maddie was already making him doubt the strength of his own convictions—what would being at some pool party do to his already spiralling senses? Spending time with Maddie outside work was tempting—but it was way too tempting, because every time he looked into those eyes, he realised he didn't anywhere near trust himself to keep to his own promise not to get involved with anyone.

Maddie smiled. 'And there's clue number one.'

'What do you mean?'

'He didn't wait for a response from either of us, did he? Didn't check if we were free or not.'

Will thought for a second. 'Come to think of it, he didn't.'

'He assumed we'd both be delighted to be invited and wouldn't even consider not going. He also assumes we're desperate to see his new swimming pool in the grounds of his huge house.' Maddie pursed her lips. 'Except that I'm not.'

'Ah,' said Will, 'don't you go either, then.' Great, he was off the hook. No tempting pool party with Maddie in some pretty little summer dress to make him want to look at her for longer than was advisable.

Maddie sighed. 'As I say, he's a very good surgeon and we do a lot of work with him so, for the sake of a couple of hours of having to pretend to have pool envy, it's worth it to keep relations with him good.'

'Right,' said Will, his heart sinking. 'So I should probably go too, then.' Was that a question or a statement? He didn't have to go but this Ryan guy clearly expected them both to and Maddie obviously felt that maintaining a good work relationship with him was important.

'No, don't go if you don't want to—you're new and can probably say you're still busy moving in or something, but I suppose I'll have to.'

'I'm not going to risk getting caught bending the truth— I'll go. And as you have the address, will you be the navigator if I drive?' *Where had that come from?* But really, in the interests of forging a good work relationship with this Ryan guy, it was probably the sensible thing to do. It had nothing to do with seeing Maddie outside work.

He shook his head. *Who was he kidding?*

CHAPTER THREE

'IT'S KIND OF you to come in to help this morning.' Maddie slid into a seat beside Will at the nurses' station on the ward. 'You really didn't need to.'

'Purely selfish,' he replied, grinning but still concentrating on the screen in front of him. 'I didn't want you to have a last-minute excuse not to go to the barbeque at *Chez Johnson* because you were too busy.'

Maddie's hand flew to her chest and she feigned a look of deep shock. 'As if I'd ever pull that one!'

He turned to face her, logging out of the screen, still grinning. 'Something tells me you just might have. Anyway, I wasn't risking it.'

'You smite me, Dr Lawrence. How can I ever forgive you?' She put her forearm to her brow like a black and white movie star, making Will laugh just as his pager bleeped.

'It's A & E,' he said, picking up a phone and dialling the number. 'Weird, they don't know I'm on shift this morning.'

Someone clearly answered his call.

'Hi, it's Will Lawrence, you paged me? Mathew Parker? Yes, I treated him a few days ago—he was admitted after having a seizure but all investigations were normal so he was discharged home with advice and a diary to keep a note of any symptoms. I'm reviewing him in clinic in another week.'

Maddie's heart rate rose. *Please don't say he's been admitted again.*

'Oh no, how is he?' Will looked at her, biting his lip. 'I'll be right down.' He put the phone down.

'What's happened?' said Maddie.

'Mathew's had another seizure. He's fallen against a French window and out onto a paved patio. He's got some minor lacerations but a significant one on his head. *Damn it.*' He ran his hands through his hair.

'I'll go down and see him.' Maddie got to her feet. 'It's me on duty so they should have paged me anyway.'

'It's okay, I'll go and see him, you carry on here.'

'We'll both go,' said Maddie. 'We're almost done on the ward anyway and Chris will be here soon to take over.'

'You really don't need to,' he replied. 'I'm quite capable.'

'I know,' said Maddie, 'but I'm done here and he's a nice kid.'

They headed down to A & E, Maddie swiping her security card to open the doors to the department. Will seemed unusually quiet. Did he feel bad about Mathew?

'Most clinicians these days don't instigate anti-seizure meds after only one episode,' said Maddie as they headed through Minors. 'The general consensus is that it's better to watch and wait than unnecessarily medicate.'

'I know that,' said Will, a little sharply, glancing around and striding towards a nurse who was nearby. The nurse pointed and Will headed for the cubicle she'd indicated. Maddie followed, catching hold of his arm before he reached the cubicle, beckoning to him to stand aside.

'Wait,' she half whispered. He seemed distracted, tense—he needed to know he'd done the right thing. Colleagues had to support each other.

His eyebrows drew together in a question.

'It was a first seizure,' she said, her voice low, 'tests were negative and there had been no previous absence seizures. In my opinion, you were—'

'Right not to prescribe anti-seizure meds,' he cut in, blue eyes meeting hers, reading her mind again. 'Thanks for confirming. Shall we go in?'

Fair enough. Will Lawrence clearly didn't need the confirmation.

Seventeen-year-old Mathew Parker was sitting semi-prone on an examination trolley, his mum sitting in a chair in the corner of the room and a nurse was dressing his more minor wounds. He smiled apologetically.

'Hey, Mathew, how are you doing?' said Will. 'You couldn't stay away from us, then?'

'What can I say, Dr Will, Dr Maddie? I missed you both.' Mathew grinned. 'But if there's a next time, can I please not be put into a room with crazy pink unicorns painted all over the walls?'

'I'll make a note of it,' said Will, glancing round and grimacing. 'So, can you tell me what happened this morning? What can you remember?'

'I can remember coming downstairs to get breakfast and then finding myself lying on the patio covered in glass. What happened in between, I have no idea.'

'I see,' said Will. 'I'm just going to have a look at the cut on your head first and then we'll go through the same questions and tests we did the other day, is that okay?'

'Sure,' said Mathew. 'Will I need stitches?'

'Let's have a look,' Will replied.

'I'm all finished with the smaller cuts,' said the nurse, 'so you're welcome to have this dressing trolley if you'd like?'

'Great timing,' said Will. 'Thanks.'

'I'll assist,' said Maddie to the nurse, smiling. 'Thank you.'

'Great, thanks,' the nurse replied. 'I'll go and write the care plan, then.'

Will donned gloves and inspected the wound while Maddie tipped a sachet of sterile water into a pot.

'It looks as though we'll get away with glue,' said Will, dipping gauze into the water and cleansing the wound. 'It's stopped bleeding.'

'Great.' Maddie smiled at Mathew. 'No needles.'

'So why would you choose glue over stitches?' asked Mathew. 'Are there criteria for using each?'

'Great question,' replied Maddie. 'Glue is better for a number of reasons, particularly in younger children, because there's no need for needles or sedation and it's a whole lot less scary having a cut glued back together than having it stitched.'

'Are there any types of wounds you can't glue?' said Mathew.

'Deep wounds involving multiple layers of tissue or if it's likely to become infected or is in a highly mobile area, such as on a joint or the hands, then it's better to use traditional stitches.' Maddie tore open a tube of glue, dropping it onto the sterile field on the trolley.

'That makes sense,' said Mathew. 'So an uncomplicated head wound is ideal for gluing?'

'It certainly is,' said Maddie, smiling at him. 'I think we have the makings of a doctor here, Dr Will.' But he still seemed out of sorts—as if it was bugging him.

'Definitely,' Will replied, dropping the used tube into a clinical waste bag. 'There you go, all done. We'll need to admit you to the ward again and we may need to start you on some medication this time.'

'I was hoping not to have any medication,' said Mathew, dropping his gaze. 'It might affect my studies.'

'We'll find the right medication for you, Mathew,' said Maddie, 'and we can talk about some strategies to help with studying. There's no reason this should stop you from going to medical school.'

Mathew glanced at his mum, who was gazing at the floor.

'I don't know if I want to go to med school,' he replied,

'but I'd like to do well in my exams, whatever I decide to do afterwards, just to prove to myself that I can do it, you know?'

Maddie nodded, smiling at him. The young man's eyes had a sadness about them even though the words he was speaking were positive and determined. Something wasn't quite right. When she'd spoken to him about being a doctor the other day on the ward, he'd been full of enthusiasm, asking intelligent, pertinent questions as he just had about his wounds. Now he seemed almost to have changed his mind. *What was different?*

'How long will you need to keep Matty in for?' asked his mum.

'Just a few days probably,' replied Will, 'to start the medication. We'll get him up to the ward shortly.'

'Thank you,' Mathew's mum replied. 'You've both been very kind.'

Maddie smiled at her. 'I'll go and give the ward a call while Dr Will finishes up here.' She turned to Will. 'That okay?'

'Mmm hmm,' he replied, not looking up and continuing to pack away the used instruments.

'Right.' She pulled the curtain aside, frowning as she made her way to the nurses' station. What was wrong with him? He was blowing as hot and cold as Mathew was about studying medicine. Well, she was nothing if not determined. She'd get to the bottom of whatever it was that was bugging both of them.

Maddie spotted Will at the nurses' station as she made her way back towards the cubicle. He was talking on the phone.

'The number on the back of the card is three, zero, seven,' he said. 'Tell the driver to wait at the paediatric A & E entrance, please. The name is Parker.'

He looked up as she approached.

'Just ordering a taxi for Mathew's mum.' He put his credit card back into his wallet, stuffing it into his pocket.

Why did he look as though he'd been caught with his hand in the sweetie jar?

'On your own card?' she asked.

Will shrugged.

'She asked Mathew to call on his mobile but you know what the signal's like down here, so I said I'd call on the hospital landline.'

He didn't need to pay too though, did he? She lowered her voice. 'Don't feel bad about this. It isn't your fault. You did the right thing in not prescribing medication the other day.'

'You really don't need to keep telling me that, Maddie—the more you say it, the more it makes it sound as though you don't believe your own words. I'm quite happy with my treatment plan for Mathew.' He pushed his seat back and stood. 'I'll go and tell them the ward's ready.'

Maddie held up her palms, her eyes wide.

'Do I owe you an apology?'

Will turned back around.

'I don't know, do you?'

'I sort of feel as though I do but I'm not sure what for.'

Will sighed.

'I know neuro is your thing, Maddie, but you don't need to check up on me treating a pretty straightforward case like Mathew's.'

'I just wanted to make sure you knew that it wasn't your fault Mathew had another seizure—you seemed edgy about what had happened.'

Deep blue eyes held hers and she was sure she wasn't breathing. Why was she reacting to this man in this way? She didn't want this.

'No apology needed, then,' said Will, 'apart maybe from me for jumping to the wrong conclusion.'

'I wasn't testing or checking up on you and I'm sorry if I

gave you that impression,' said Maddie, an apologetic smile on her lips. 'Are we good?'

'Sure,' said Will. 'We're okay.' He smiled, but not in that way that made his eyes sparkle and her legs turn to jelly and she wasn't sure whether she was relieved or a little disappointed.

Maddie walked to the stairs to go back up to the ward, glancing back to see Will slip back into the cubicle. He was just feeling bad about Mathew getting injured—which said a lot about him as a man. Will Lawrence was proving himself to be a huge asset to the team. He was a complete people magnet and everyone thought he was the cat's pyjamas. He was an excellent clinician too, which was why she got on so well with him.

But was that why she'd been looking forward to the dreaded pool party ever since he'd agreed to go too?

She drew in a breath. Not really.

Not at all, Maddie McArthur.

The reason for Ryan's pool party becoming something not to be dreaded was much more to do with the fact that Will Lawrence ignited every nerve ending in her body every time he even glanced in her direction. And she really wasn't at all sure that was in any way wise.

Ryan Johnson was obviously extremely pleased with his new outdoor pool, which sat in the grounds of his large house in one of York's very affluent areas. Will watched the surgeon, greeting guests, taking them to the bar by the pool and talking animatedly about the trials and tribulations of finding a builder and a designer and the maintenance of filters and water-quality testing.

He smiled. The outdoor pool at Brockley House, his family home, had provided him and his many siblings with hours of fun growing up and still did, especially as there were nieces and nephews now to join in. But his father hadn't had a grand opening when he'd had it built nearly thirty years ago and certainly wouldn't have dropped heavy hints about how expensive it had been, as Ryan Johnson had to him and Maddie. Maddie had tried to appear suitably impressed but, although she'd smiled widely, her smile, usually so warm and genuine, hadn't quite lit up her eyes as it usually did. In fact, he'd been sure he'd seen her struggling not to let them glaze over and she'd definitely stifled a yawn as Ryan had extolled the virtues of taking an invigorating early morning dip in his pool before work.

'Canapé?' One of the catering staff approached them with a platter of dainty morsels and he and Maddie took a couple each.

'I might need to go for a pizza when we leave here,' said Maddie in an undertone, looking at the tiny works of art on her plate.

'Just keep going back for more,' said Will, grinning. 'That's what I do at events like this. I mean, a loudly grumbling stomach, complaining it's hungry, doesn't help when you're trying to make polite conversation, does it?'

'Definitely not.' Maddie glanced around furtively and lowered her voice. 'Although I'm not sure how much more polite conversation I can take. If I hear Ryan or Fiona mention "balancing chemicals" or how the property market around here demands an outdoor pool once more, I just might accidentally drop one of these little bites of cardboard into the water to see how quickly Ryan can run to the pool house to fetch a net.'

Will nearly choked, bringing his forearm to his mouth as he held a plate in one hand and a half-eaten canapé in the other.

'That's wicked,' he managed, 'although, if I hear any further mention of how the solar-panel pool cover cleverly allows sunlight penetration while retaining heat, I might just do the same.'

'I can see you looking longingly at it,' said Ryan, approaching and nodding towards the pool with a satisfied grin. 'I can pass on the pool company details if you'd like to join the pool owners club.'

Maddie's eyebrows rose.

'Sure,' she replied, a hint of a smile playing on her lips.

'And how about you, Will?' Ryan continued.

Already got one…in fact it's about twice the size of yours. But that fact wasn't about to be shared. In fact, he wasn't sharing any information about his former life—least of all his enormous wealth. That was one of the very things he'd wanted to leave behind. And he had the distinct impression that Maddie would be about as impressed by his bank balance as she would be if Ryan handed her a pool brochure for bedtime reading.

'I'm in one of the riverside apartments in the city centre,' he replied, 'so no room for one there, I'm afraid.'

'Ah, well, maybe one of these days, eh—something to aim for. I've promised James over there that I'd give him the details so please excuse me. Help yourselves to canapés and I can recommend the Chianti—tart cherries, dried herbs and a hint of smoke.' He put thumb and forefinger to his lips before striding to a small group nearby.

'I have no words,' said Maddie, blinking slowly.

'I have a few,' replied Will. 'Not that would be suitable for polite conversation though. He's a little full of himself, isn't he?'

'*Something to aim for.* Why do I suddenly feel like a ten-year-old being given careers advice?' Maddie rolled her eyes.

'I can't imagine,' replied Will, lifting his brows, meeting her gaze. She was clearly mildly annoyed—the slight narrowing of her eyes gave that much away but there was mirth in them too, a mischievous twinkle. He smiled. 'You wouldn't really throw a canapé in his shiny new pool, would you?' It was a naughty thought but one that did have an appeal. Ryan would be horrified. And suddenly *he* felt like a ten-year-old—but in a good way.

Maddie clearly couldn't suppress a smile. She tried but her lips quivered briefly as though resisting before surrendering to a radiant beam. Her cheeks blushed like ripe apples and her eyes glittered with merriment. She was beautiful. She looked every inch like someone who ought to be at a high-class poolside party. The light summer dress she wore showed off her petite frame, the fabric fitted over feminine curves but floating as it progressed to her knees, the light breeze making it ripple gently. She'd released her hair from its usual ponytail and it hung loosely around her shoulders, the sun catching it—a cascade of golden waves.

It was exactly why he'd had second thoughts about coming. Being around her at work was tempting enough. But here, outside the clinical confines of the hospital, it unsettled him. He'd known it would. And he knew full well that was why he'd snapped at her earlier about questioning his treatment plan for Mathew.

'Are you daring me, Dr Lawrence?' One raised eyebrow challenged him. *Daring her?* It was tempting. But she was the one daring him. Daring him to forget the lessons he'd learned. Daring him to want to look at her for longer than was rational. Daring him to consider wondering if he might ever begin to think that trusting someone again might be possible.

'Not if we want to keep the best paediatric orthopod on side, Dr McArthur.' Which was the reason he was there. Not because he wanted to take every opportunity he could grasp to be in her company.

She tilted her head to one side, making the silver drop earring she wore come to rest on her neck, the one on the other side hanging, catching the sunlight.

She grinned. 'Spoilsport. Let's try this cherry, herby, smoky Chianti, then, instead. We don't want to get into trouble with him.'

But Will was already in trouble. He'd accepted the dare of looking at her, of wondering just how soft those golden waves might feel and realising how envious he was of that silver earring grazing the curve of her neck. But that would have to be as far as the dare went because he wasn't going to risk it going any further. Maddie McArthur was a colleague and he wasn't on the market.

CHAPTER FOUR

Maddie sensed there was something going on as soon as she walked onto the paediatric ward that morning. There was a highly unusual hush and a small huddle of staff just outside the sister's office watching something or someone intently. *What was it?* Lou Beresford, the nursing sister, glanced in her direction, put her finger to her lips and beckoned her over. Maddie crept softly towards the group as Lou pointed down the ward. They were watching Will Lawrence, crouched before a little girl who looked to be around five or six years old and who sat on a beanbag, beaming, as they had a silent conversation in sign language. They were both clearly fluent and enjoying each other's company and, inexplicably, Maddie felt the swell of tears behind her eyes.

'Isn't it sweet?' whispered Lou, not taking her eyes off them. 'Hayley was admitted during the night with breathing difficulties. She was born profoundly deaf. Her mum was with her but we've just sent her home to get a couple of hours of sleep. I was about to book a sign-language interpreter when Will turned up saying he could sign. He's been with her ever since.'

'Great skill to have,' whispered back Maddie, 'and as much as I agree that it is sweet, we can't really stand watching them all morning.' And if she stood watching them any longer, her heart just might melt that bit more towards her new colleague, which was more than a little disconcerting and definitely something to be avoided.

'Very true,' said Lou. 'Come on, team, stop gawping at Dr Gorgeous and his new friend—back to work.'

The group of staff disbanded, all with glassy eyes and warm smiles. Maddie took a last glance at Will and his little charge. He was pointing to something in a book and looking confused. Hayley laughed, shaking her head at him and clearly putting him right about something. Maddie made her way to the nurses' station. What a wonderful thing to be able to do, communicate with a child who probably found so few people she could communicate so easily with. Where and why had he learned the skill? Perhaps she'd ask him later.

Sister Lou had called Will Dr Gorgeous and she was right. He was undeniably handsome but he was lovely on the inside too. Of all the paediatricians in the world who could have taken up the vacant post at the hospital, she was glad it had been him...wasn't she? He'd made a positive impact on patient care already; every single member of staff seemed to like and respect him and his work ethic was remarkable. There was a 'but' though.

A really big 'but'.

She was spending far too much time looking at him and way too much time thinking about him and what he did to her insides every time he was anywhere near. It was unwelcome... ridiculous really. She had to stop looking up every time he walked past—people were going to notice. They'd start talking. And that was the last thing either of them wanted. Maybe it was just because he was new...and jaw-droppingly handsome, with his maddeningly blue eyes, that easy, devasting smile and those lean, infuriatingly perfect muscles.

Maybe, in time, she'd get used to those things and her heart would stop picking up its pace at even the thought of them.

Maybe.

Maddie wanted to see how Mathew Parker was. Technically, he was Will's patient, but the young man had been treated by both of them when he'd been admitted a couple of days ago after having had his second seizure. Will had commenced him on anti-seizure meds and she had no need to monitor him from that point of view herself.

What she did want to do was talk to him about his possible application to medical school. Something bothered her about his fluctuating interest in medicine and she wanted to find out why he seemed so hot and cold about it. Something didn't stack up and, although his situation clearly wasn't exactly the same as her own had been, it had occurred to her that perhaps his shifting attitude had something to do with the affordability of going to medical school. Maddie hated to see the potential of young people go to waste. Will's words came back to her—*not everyone has the same chances in life that we've had*. If only he knew.

Maddie had left school and become a carer in a hospital, never believing someone like her could go to university and having been completely unable to afford it anyway. Watching the doctors, nurses and other professionals had been both inspiring and hard. She'd so desperately wanted to gain a professional qualification but there had been no way of being able to afford it. By a stroke of luck, she'd once cared for a university professor—an elderly woman who, to Maddie's surprise, had shown her genuine kindness and taken an interest in her. At first, Maddie hadn't known what to make of it—adults, in her experience, only paid attention when they were scolding her or demanding something. But after a time, she'd grown to trust the professor and had found herself opening up—sharing her dreams for the first time with someone who'd actually listened…and hadn't made fun of her.

The professor had taken Maddie under her wing and eventually she'd got into university to study nursing because of her. Very quickly, Maddie had been taken to one side by one of her nursing tutors, who'd suggested she might want to study medicine instead, and Maddie hadn't been able to believe two things—firstly that she had the ability and secondly that now two people in her life had noticed her and believed in her.

'Mind if I join you?'

Maddie looked up at Will, shading her eyes from the bright sunshine and squinting.

'Of course not,' she replied. 'I'm just grabbing a quick bite and getting some vitamin D in the sun before clinic.'

'Same.' Will sat down, setting his food box on his knee. He peered into her box. 'What are you having?'

Maddie shifted a little away from him on the bench, placing her lunch bag between them.

'Just a salad with a bit of smoked mackerel thrown in. You?'

'Leftover pizza from last night,' he replied, with a guilty grimace. 'You win the healthiest lunch of the day competition.'

Maddie laughed.

'How's your new friend Hayley getting on? She's a little cutie.'

Will pressed his lips together. 'Not sure, actually. Mum brought her in last night saying Hayley had stopped breathing in her sleep but by the time she got to hospital, she appeared fully recovered. She's absolutely fine this morning—no foreign body in the airways, chest X-ray is clear, obs and bloods all normal. I'm going to keep her in for a couple of days and we'll see if she has any further episodes.'

'Do her tonsils and adenoids look okay?'

'Nasopharyngeal structures all completely normal.'

'Hmm, that is a strange one, then. Perhaps something will come to light over the next day or so. I spoke to Mathew earlier, by the way; he seems to be tolerating the anti-seizure medication.'

'He does,' said Will, sipping from his cardboard coffee cup. 'Yes, he said you'd had a chat with him about the med school entrance test. He was very fired up, revising when I left the ward.'

'He was very enthusiastic this morning when I spoke to him,' said Maddie thoughtfully. 'He tends to blow a little hot and cold with wanting to study medicine though, don't you think? It's a bit odd.'

'I think I might know why that might be,' replied Will, with a grimace. 'I was explaining to him earlier about carrying on with life pretty much as usual with epilepsy but with a few modifications—no dangerous sports like climbing, scuba, no driving for a year, managing screen time, dealing with stress, that sort of thing and he went very quiet.'

'Being diagnosed with something like epilepsy, even though it's usually very manageable, is still a lot to take in,' said Maddie, 'and he's got a lot on his plate with trying to get into medical school; it's tough at the best of times.'

'And even tougher if you have to look out for your mum.'

Maddie frowned. 'In what way?'

'He didn't have chance to go into any detail,' replied Will, 'because his mum arrived on the ward. But what he started to say was that he has to "be there for her". What he means by that I don't know but it sounds as though he has some kind of caring role.'

Maddie's eyes were full of concern. She put her finger to her lips thoughtfully for a moment before speaking.

'We have to help him,' she said, her tone determined. 'He's such a bright kid, we can't let him slip through the net. I've got a few pre-medical-school students that I'm mentoring at the moment so I'm pretty busy with them but I could manage one more.'

'You mentor kids *before* they get into medical school?'

'A few.' Maddie packed away her lunch box.

'As well as the usual *actual* medical students?'

'Yes, I enjoy it and I can't bear to think that there are young people out there who have what it takes to be good doctors but, through no fault of their own, usually because of poverty, poor access to good education or sub-optimal parenting, never get the chance to reach their potential. It's criminal and it happens way too often.'

Will stared at her, taken aback by the sudden steely vehemence that had hardened her usually warm, soft features. This clearly meant a lot to her…for some reason.

'So, I sort of take them under my wing,' she continued, more softly, 'and try to give them what they wouldn't otherwise get…a bit of a helping hand.'

'Wow,' said Will, staring at her in admiration, 'that's so generous.' *And so heartfelt.*

Maddie smiled but lowered her gaze, hitching her bag onto her shoulder and standing. 'I should get to clinic.'

Will checked his watch. 'I guess I should too.' Holding his last sliver of cold pizza between his teeth, he shoved his container back into his backpack, which he slung over one shoulder.

'I actually don't think Mathew will need much coaching, to be honest,' said Maddie as they walked across the grass towards the outpatients building. 'He's very switched on. We had a quick look at a past paper this morning and he worked out some of the answers really quickly. So although, with the other students I've got at the moment, I'm already pretty busy, I think I'll manage Mathew too.'

'I wonder if Mathew's biggest barrier to medical school will be what's happening at home,' said Will. 'Perhaps getting to the bottom of that might help.'

'Maybe so,' Maddie agreed. 'As you've already started

that conversation with him and he's confided a little, do you think you could pursue it further with him?'

'If you'll allow me, I might be able to do a little better than that.'

'How so?' said Maddie.

'Well, you seem pretty busy with the students you're already mentoring...would you let me mentor Mathew?'

Maddie stopped walking and looked at him.

'It's quite a commitment,' she cautioned. But Will could see the hope in her eyes. Her idea to mentor disadvantaged teens to reach their potential was a wonderful one and he wanted to be part of what she was doing. Anyway, he was better when he was busy. It stopped him from slipping back into the darkness of the last few years, when his wife—the woman he'd expected he'd spend the rest of his life with—had turned his heart to stone.

'Why don't we discuss it more after clinic?' he replied. 'You can tell me about some of the kids you've mentored and what exactly it entails.'

'Okay,' said Maddie, walking again, 'if you're sure?'

'We could go for dinner after work and you can tell me everything I need to know.'

'Sure,' said Maddie, slowly, as though she wasn't sure at all.

Neither was he—but that didn't seem to stop him. Somehow, he kept finding reasons to be around her—kept speaking words his brain hadn't fully vetted. As if some other, trouble-making part of him had made the decision way before his common sense caught up.

'Great—if there's somewhere you know that's good, you can choose.'

'I know a little place by the minster,' she replied as they reached clinic. 'This is me and your rooms are a little further down the corridor on the left. Good luck.'

'Thanks,' he replied. 'See you later.'

Will was looking forward to his first clinic at York Royal Infirmary. He enjoyed the buzz of a busy clinic, the huge variety of different cases—all puzzles to be thought through and worked out. And now he had the bonus of meeting up with Maddie afterwards to discuss joining a project that had such merit and one that might just give him something to think about other than the reason he was in York at all.

'Afternoon,' he said cheerily to the staff at Reception. 'I'm Will, the new paeds consultant.' Things were looking up. Not that he was looking forward to meeting Maddie for any other reason than finding out more about the mentoring. Not in the slightest.

CHAPTER FIVE

'JUST A TAP water for me, please,' said Maddie as she and Will stood at the bar of The Admiral pub in town.

'You're a cheap date.' Will grinned then turned to the barman to place their order. Her gut twisted.

The last person to have called her cheap had been Andrew, but there had been plenty before him who'd said or thought the same. In a way, she couldn't blame them because she'd been the very definition of cheap, hadn't she? Right from birth when she'd had nothing but the towel her mother had wrapped her in before placing her in a cardboard box and leaving her on the steps of the hospital. She'd been given the first name of the nurse who'd found her and the second name of the doctor who'd first checked her over.

Maddie McArthur. Female. Foundling.

She still had the tiny identity bracelet they'd placed on her, with the words that defined her. It hadn't said 'unwanted' or 'cheap' but that had been all she'd known growing up. Her identity, her upbringing, such as it was, had followed her everywhere even though she'd tried hard to shake it off, forget it even. She'd come a long way—getting into Cambridge on a scholarship to study medicine had made her begin to believe in herself and passing exams year after year until she'd qualified had, little by little, built on that self-belief. Thinking about her birth mother and why she'd abandoned her had slowly pervaded her thinking less and less. Until the letter had slipped through her letter box a few weeks ago.

'Shall we sit by the window?' said Will, a drink in each hand. 'We can see the minster from there.'

'Sure,' said Maddie. 'Have you been inside the minster yet?'

'I haven't, but I really must one of these days.'

'It's beautiful,' said Maddie, sipping her water. 'It was built in the sixth century, which is why it's called a minster and not a cathedral. The stained glass is extraordinary. Do you know what you're having?' She picked up one of the menus from the table and glanced through it. Will did the same.

'Well, last night's left-over pizza has definitely worn off so I'm in need of something substantial. The sizzling kebab sounds nice. How about you?'

Automatically, Maddie's gaze sought out the cheapest item on the menu. Old habits were hard to break. Growing up with nothing meant you spent every single penny carefully and even though now Maddie had a good salary and secure job, breaking the habits of a lifetime didn't come naturally.

'I'll go for the tomato and basil soup,' she replied, closing the menu and reaching for her drink.

'You are a cheap date,' said Will, laughing. 'You can push the boat out a bit, if you like. It was pay day yesterday, wasn't it?'

'It was,' replied Maddie, 'but the soup sounds nice.' Eating out at all was still a little indulgent. Her first ever meal in a restaurant hadn't been until she'd been at university and she still regarded dining out as a treat.

'Fair enough,' said Will. 'So tell me more about the mentoring. What started it? How long have you been doing it? How do you get to meet kids you want to mentor? What do you actually do with them?'

Maddie sat back in her seat, holding up her hands as though in surrender.

'Whoa, is this an interrogation?' She laughed.

'Just keen to hear all about it,' said Will. 'Sounds like a great idea.'

Maddie relaxed back into her seat. Talking about her programme put her in her happy place. She told him about Juliette, her first mentee, who'd been a patient she'd looked after during a house job. Her mum had been a single parent and couldn't afford to send her to university. She'd helped them to access some financial support and taken Juliette under her wing.

'By doing what exactly?' said Will, sitting back as the waiter set down a loudly sizzling skillet.

'Entrance exam preparation; interview practice—and just being on the end of the phone whenever she needed a hand at university.' Everything Maddie had needed and never had herself at that age.

'She got into med school?'

Maddie smiled. 'Of course.'

'Wow,' said Will, 'well done, you.'

'It was all down to her own hard work. It's much harder to succeed if the odds are stacked against you and they were definitely stacked against her back then.'

'As they seem to be with Mathew,' said Will.

'What did he tell you?'

'Not much,' said Will, 'but I pushed him a bit on it, asking him what his mum thought about him going off to university. He tried to change the subject by asking about his medication but when he realised that I wasn't going to be put off, he said that she needed him at home.'

'Did he say why?'

'I don't know for sure but I'm determined to find out.'

'We'll work on him between us,' said Maddie, dabbing her napkin to her lips and setting it down. 'How's the kebab?'

'Nice, actually.' He glanced around the pub. 'I didn't expect much—I mean, it's not The Ritz, is it?—but the food is good.'

'Who needs The Ritz when you've got a good old British pub? I used to think I wanted to be whisked away by a millionaire to Paris for lunch—I read too many fairy tales growing up—but I grew out of that idea when I realised that being a millionaire and being a decent human being aren't necessarily the same thing.'

Will glanced at her, sharply, the slightest crease between his brows.

'You don't think much of millionaires, then?'

'People who are well off are usually full of themselves and think they're better than anyone else, don't they?' She wasn't going to tell him about Andrew and how she'd begun to believe that maybe she was good enough for someone like him…how sweet talk and honeyed lies had lured her into his bed and made her fall in love with him. She should have trusted her instincts; remembered everything she'd learned growing up.

Dealing with so-called carers in kids' homes and landlords who knew exactly how to take advantage of vulnerable young girls had taught her not to trust—particularly those who had power and money, like the landlord who'd told her she wouldn't have to worry about paying her rent, that if she didn't have the money, there were other ways to pay. She'd had nowhere else to go that night but fear had made her pack her few belongings into the small suitcase she'd carried around from place to place over the years. She'd walked out and taken refuge in a homeless shelter that night, never returning.

'Not everyone with money is like that though,' said Will, setting his glass back down on the table, watching her.

'Of course not,' said Maddie, her head to one side, thoughtfully. 'I mean, Ryan "outdoor pool" Johnson doesn't think he's the bee's knees at all, does he?'

'Point taken,' said Will, grinning. 'I'll remember not to whisk you away to Paris for lunch any time soon, then.'

'Definitely not,' she replied, responding to his smile too easily as had become the norm, a flicker of awareness kicking her heart rate higher. It was maddening that he did that to her. The more she tried to resist the pull of him, the more aware she became of the way her whole body seemed to flame in his presence. She didn't want this. She knew better.

'I should get going,' she said, pulling her bag from the back of her chair and standing.

'Oh, really?' Disappointment flickered in his eyes—just for a second and it pulled her in even further. She was right to go—this was getting far too dangerous.

'I've got some paperwork to do.'

'I'll walk you to your car.'

She waved him away.

'I'm only down the road. See you tomorrow.' She walked away from him, tempted but not daring to look back because, although she didn't want to be drawn inexorably towards him, there was a part of her that didn't want it to stop.

'I'm just about to take Jodie's wound dressing down if you want to check it after,' said Jake, popping his head around the door of the office on the ward.

'Thanks,' replied Will, glancing up and smiling at the nurse. 'I'll swing by shortly and take a look before you redress it.'

Jake gave a thumbs up and disappeared.

Will reread the email he'd just read several times before—something about new arrangements for car-parking permits on the hospital site. He didn't have much time for lifeless memos at the best of times and he certainly didn't this morning, not after the dinner with Maddie last evening. Her quip about people with money not being decent human beings had stuck with him, looping round in his head ever since.

Where had she got that idea from? Past relationships? If she really meant what she said, it was just as well she didn't know the truth about him. She'd have dismissed him outright, lumping him in with them. Not that he planned on telling her, or anyone, about who he really was. But if he'd needed any more reason to keep the truth buried, her words had given him one.

'Morning, all!' Ryan Johnson's booming voice left no one on the ward in any doubt that he'd arrived. Will glanced out of the little window in the office, which had a view down the ward.

'Morning, Mr Johnson,' replied India.

'Maddie around?' he continued.

'She's around somewhere,' the nurse replied.

'Excellent.' He waved a brochure at the nurse. 'She wanted to know about the outdoor swimming pool company we used—we've had one installed in the grounds at home, you know—so I've brought one for her.'

'How lovely,' said the nurse. 'Try bay one—most of Maddie's patients are in there.'

Will watched as Ryan Johnson stalked towards bay one, a man on a mission armed with his glossy brochure. He smothered a grin, imagining Maddie's response to being hunted down for such an honour. He could see her now—politeness personified, smiling serenely while inside composing a symphony of profanity that would turn the air blue.

He logged out. He'd done enough admin for one day and he needed to check on his patient's surgical wound. Leaving the office, he went to bay three, washed his hands at the sink and reached for a paper towel, wondering how Maddie was dealing with being offered the chance to join the pool owners club.

Unable to stifle a grin, he threw the paper towels into the bin but a movement to his right caught his eye and he glanced to the corner of the room where the curtain of an empty bedspace definitely moved. The tips of two small blue pumps were the tell-tale sign that a child was hiding behind it. He smiled and, taking the two steps to reach the curtain, he eased it aside, bending down to face the hide-and-seek-playing child. But instead of his eyes alighting on a young patient playing peekaboo, he found himself staring at the slim waist of someone who was definitely not a child or a patient. He straightened up and stared into two baby-blue wide eyes that held a stern warning.

Maddie. A finger to her lips and a sharp, silencing stare told him in no uncertain terms not to reveal her hiding place.

'Who are you playing hide and seek with?' he whispered.

'Ryan. Shh, go away,' she hissed back.

He didn't recall a patient called Ryan.

'Which one's Ryan?' he whispered back.

Maddie put her palm to her forehead.

'The surgeon,' she hissed, shooing him away. 'Go.'

'Ah, that Ryan.'

'Yes, I just heard him down the ward telling everyone he'd brought a damn pool brochure for me. Go away, you're drawing attention.'

The laugh was halfway to leaving his mouth but her steely warning glare stopped it in its tracks. Clearly now wasn't the time to find the situation hilarious, even though it was. 'Naughty,' he whispered, wagging his finger at her. 'See me after school.'

Maddie's eyes narrowed and he straightened his features, trying to look serious.

The unmistakeable, booming voice of Ryan Johnson getting louder made Maddie stiffen. The surgeon was humming a tune as he approached the bay—clearly still on his quest to find Maddie. Will glanced at her. Five more seconds and he'd be in the bay and they'd be caught, awkwardly half hidden in the corner of the room. But Maddie clearly didn't want to be caught and, grabbing his arm, she yanked him behind the curtain and out of sight.

Pressing her finger to her lips, she glared a warning to him as the curtain settled around them like a cloak. But it wasn't the steely glare in her eyes that had made his stomach tighten. It was how close they suddenly were—closer than they'd ever been. Her body aligned with his in the narrow space. They weren't quite touching but the air between them crackled. Their eyes met and, for a breathless moment, it felt as if they were about to cross the line…as though they'd moved in for a kiss. It was all he could do not to dip his head and taste the lips he'd spent far too long looking at, thinking about.

'Must be in bay four.' Ryan's voice, a few feet away, talking to himself.

Maddie stiffened, the slight movement enough to cause her hand to brush his—the accidental contact was soft, fleeting, but it sent a jolt through him all the same.

Her eyes flicked to his, startled—he got it—he wasn't going to reveal their hiding place. They didn't exactly look innocent, pressed together behind a curtain.

Footsteps moved away, the humming fading.

'Do you think he's gone?' Maddie's voice was a whisper.

'Sounds like it,' he replied. Was he sorry? Sorry he'd have to move away from her, lose the scent of her, being so close he could have kissed her? His heart was hammering so hard in his chest, he was surprised it hadn't given away their hiding place.

Maddie looked at him sheepishly.

'Thank you,' she said.

'Pleasure,' he replied, drawing in a breath, not trusting himself to say anything more. Not trusting himself to stay behind the curtain a moment longer without the need to kiss her overwhelming him.

'I couldn't face him this morning,' said Maddie, her voice still lowered.

'How come?' said Will, peering out. 'Coast's clear.' He pulled the curtain aside and stepped out, relieved but missing her proximity all at once. Maybe his heart would stop trying to hammer its way out of his chest now.

'He's obnoxious, overbearing and odious,' she replied, stepping out from behind the curtain. 'I only put up with him at all because he's good at doing what he does, otherwise, I'd avoid him entirely.'

'Fair enough,' replied Will, one eyebrow arched, his eyes glinting with amusement. 'You don't usually actually hide from him, though.'

Maddie shot him a look, her lips pressing into a thin line. She sighed.

'I've just got a lot on my mind right now, that's all.'

'Anything I can help with? If you're busy, perhaps I can take a patient or two off your hands.'

'That's kind,' said Maddie, softening. 'It's not workload—it's more of a personal thing.'

'I'm a good listener.'

Maddie smiled and something like a thunderbolt hit him right in the centre of his abdomen. Her smile was pure joy, lighting her eyes with kindness and touching his soul so suddenly and unexpectedly that for a moment he couldn't respond. But he hadn't moved halfway across the country to fall for someone. He'd left his home to hide from the reality of his life, to live normally, without the trappings of wealth and everything that went with it—being unable to trust anyone, the resentment from others, being treated differently. And the biggest, hardest, toughest lesson of all—that money most definitely couldn't buy you love.

'I mean it,' he managed. 'If you need to talk, I'm happy to listen.' Hell, he was happy just to be with her. But he was on dangerous ground. He had a secret to keep and one that, knowing the little about Maddie that he did know, wouldn't chime well with her. Maddie seemed to have a problem with people who had money and he had more money than he could ever spend.

'Thank you, Will.' She slipped past him. 'I'm a little late for a finance meeting. See you later.'

'Sure, see you later.'

Will pushed the bed-space curtain back into place neatly against the wall, his heart beginning to slow its pace. He could have kissed her behind that curtain. He'd wanted to kiss her. But where would that have led? She could have slapped him, for a start. But something in her eyes, the way they'd lingered on his own, had told him she wouldn't have done that—something had told him that maybe she'd wanted it too. He ran his hand through his hair and held the back of his neck. They hadn't stepped over the line then but the air between them had definitely changed.

He shrugged his shoulders to his ears and stretched his neck right and left, easing the tension in them. He noticed a folded piece of white paper on the floor under the curtain and bent to pick it up, unfolding it. If it was patient information, he'd need to make sure it didn't get into the wrong hands. It was a letter and the heading on it was of the bone marrow donation registry.

Dear Ms McArthur,
It is now two years since your stem cell donation and your recipient has requested contact with you. Any contact would be via the transplant centre initially. If you would like to make contact, we...

Will stopped reading. It was private. Maddie had been a stem cell donor. *Why didn't that surprise him?* Maybe this had been what she'd meant when she'd said she hadn't been able to face Ryan just then—this was the personal matter she'd mentioned. Perhaps she was considering whether or not to have contact. It was indeed a huge decision. He folded the letter back up and slipped it into his pocket. He'd give it back to Maddie later. Maybe that was what was on her mind. But all *he* could think about was how hard he'd had to fight not to ruin a perfectly good working relationship with one impulsive, ill-judged kiss. Because for a few heart-stopping moments, he'd nearly done it—nearly closed the inch of space between them—nearly let desire win.

And he wasn't at all sure he'd be able to stop himself if there was a next time.

CHAPTER SIX

'Maddie,' called Jake, holding a phone aloft in his hand. 'Call for you—it's Will.'

Maddie took the phone, mouthing thanks to Jake, her heart skipping. The finance meeting had almost put her to sleep—what had kept her awake had been replaying the events of earlier in her head, being so close to Will she could barely breathe without touching him, brushing his hand with her own and sending a jolt up her arm, the way his eyes had darkened when they'd locked onto hers. She'd thought for one breathless moment that he'd been going to kiss her.

She wasn't sure whether she was relieved or disappointed he hadn't.

Probably both.

And that was the problem.

'Hi, Will, it's Maddie.'

'Hi,' he replied. 'I'm down in A & E with a two-year-old with pneumonia. I know you were thinking of discharging Noah today—if you review him and decide to, could you let me know? I could do with a bed for this little one here.'

'Sure, I'll go and review him now and call you back. Is that okay?'

'Brilliant, thanks, Maddie. I'll stay here with Mathilda and her social worker until I hear back from you.'

Maddie put the phone down, her heart sinking. *Social worker.* That was never good news—it meant that the toddler

Will was looking after had care needs and she knew only too well how that could affect a child. Most of the care staff she'd known growing up had been at best simply too overworked to care much or, at worst, slimy toads of men who believed they could get away with completely inappropriate behaviour.

Noah, the little boy who'd been rushed into A & E in Will's arms on his first morning, had done well and was fine to be discharged home. He'd needed some intensive physio and antibiotics but his parents were more than capable and more than happy to look after him now at home. Maddie never ceased to be amazed at how fantastically well some parents adjusted to life with a child with a chronic condition. When your own mother hadn't been able or even wanted to adjust to life with a child at all, it seemed remarkable to Maddie that some parents were so incredibly strong and exceptionally devoted.

Her own mother had only gone as far as wrapping her in a thin towel to protect her. She'd left no clue as to her own identity—no way that her baby could even begin to trace her if she'd wanted to when she'd grown up. As a child, Maddie had made up stories about her. Some of them were fantastical, like the one where her mother was actually a princess who'd fallen in love with a prince from a foreign land—someone the king and queen had forbidden her to have contact with—and her mother had been forced to abandon her baby or be disowned. When she'd told her social worker, they'd laughed at her and told her not to be silly. It had hurt her at the time but the social worker had been right, of course—she'd just had a silly, overactive imagination or maybe a wish that, one day, her mother might show up and tell her she'd made a huge mistake in abandoning her.

But that had never happened.

Her birth mother had clearly not regretted what she'd done all those years ago on that night in the middle of June. And Maddie had put her dreams of a heart-warming reunion to the back of her mind—locked away where the year upon year of disappointment couldn't hurt her any more. She didn't need her birth mother, not any more. And she hadn't wondered about her for a long time.

Until now.

Until the letters.

The letters had dragged it all back. The first one had been consigned to the back of a kitchen cupboard a few weeks ago and to the back of her mind…mostly. The one that had arrived that morning had unmuted the conversation in her head—should she respond? What could be the consequences if she did? She fished in her pocket for it, then tried the other pocket. Nothing. A chill crept up her spine as her heart picked up its pace.

Where was it?

She replayed the morning.

The finance meeting. She must've dropped it there. Her heart froze. What if someone found it—and read it? It contained information she didn't want to share—because it would lead to questions she couldn't…didn't want to answer.

She dialled Will's number on her mobile as she headed down the ward, speaking to Jake as she neared the nurses' station.

'I've just discharged Noah, in the side room,' she said to the staff nurse, who nodded, 'and Will is admitting a two-year-old with pneumonia from A & E into that bed—could you prep it for me, please?'

'Consider it done,' said Jake.

Will answered the phone.

'Will, I've discharged Noah. Mum and Dad are happy to go straight away; he doesn't need any meds from pharmacy so the bed will be available for your patient in the next fifteen minutes or so.'

'Great, thanks for that,' replied Will. 'How was your meeting?'

'Meeting?'

'Finance, wasn't it?' said Will.

'Oh, yes, tedious as usual,' she replied. 'Got to go back there, actually. Catch you later.' Maddie hung up, quickening her footsteps. The longer she took, the more chance there was of someone else finding the letter…and reading it…and that might lead to awkward questions she'd tried to avoid all her life.

The meeting room was empty save for the cleaner, who was emptying bins and straightening chairs.

'You haven't found a letter on the floor anywhere, have you? It would have been addressed to me, Maddie McArthur?' She was a little breathless.

'No, sorry. I'll let you know if I do though,' said the cleaner, emptying a small waste basket into a black bin sack.

'Thank you.' The letter couldn't fall into anyone else's hands. She'd never told anyone about the donation—it would only have given rise to questions about her family. And she couldn't answer questions about people who didn't exist.

Was it a family member she'd donated bone marrow to?

Did she have any siblings who might also have been a match?

What did her parents think—they must have been proud?

She couldn't answer questions like that because she didn't know the answers—because she didn't have a family and, in her experience, people simply didn't understand what that meant or felt like.

'Actually, would you mind if I had a look through the bins before you take them away?' said Maddie, desperation gripping her.

'Well, I need to get them down to the waste centre before I finish at three,' the cleaner replied doubtfully.

'I'll take them,' said Maddie quickly. 'You get off and I'll take the bags down when I've looked through them.' The letter had to be here somewhere. 'Please?'

The cleaner pursed her lips and sighed.

'I suppose so,' she agreed, 'but don't forget, because if my boss checks in here and the bins haven't been done, he'll have my guts for garters.'

'I promise I'll take them,' said Maddie, clasping her hands under her chin. 'Promise.'

'Fine,' said the cleaner, slotting a long brush back into her trolley before ambling out.

Maddie heaved a sigh of relief. There were two large sacks of rubbish to go through. Reaching for the one nearest to her, she untied it, kneeling down on the floor, hoping that the letter would somehow be obvious.

It wasn't.

She peered into the second sack. It contained plenty of screwed-up balls of white paper, some orange peel and half a tree's worth of brightly coloured Post-it notes. But not a neatly folded letter addressed to her from the bone marrow registry asking her if she'd like contact with someone who could well turn out to be someone she was related to.

A link…to her past and the mother who'd abandoned her.

She wasn't old enough or wise enough to make a decision on whether she wanted to find a long-lost family she'd once dreamt about, invented fairy tales about…and eventually forced herself to forget. Finding a spare black bin sack, Maddie began to methodically transfer each item from the full one into it, unfurling each screwed-up sheet of paper and checking it wasn't the letter she so needed to find. But each time it wasn't the letter, the need to find it became more urgent and her speed increased as each small disappointment grew, until disappointment turned into frustration and Maddie realised she'd stopped checking each piece of paper properly.

'Damn it.' She'd have to check again. Closing her eyes, she took in a long, deep breath, placing her hands on her hips and filling her lungs before breathing out slowly.

'Calm down, for goodness' sake.'

But the deep breath and sage self-advice did nothing to cool the burning knot in her throat. Rising panic clawed at her.

No one else could find it.

No one could see it.

No one could ask the questions she couldn't answer, unearthing her past, one she'd tried to keep buried—a past none of her colleagues had any idea about. To them she was Maddie McArthur, paediatric consultant, Cambridge graduate, one of the youngest ever appointed to her post. Successful. Capable. Respected. She had worth.

They didn't know the girl she used to be—the one who'd grown up in poverty, whose dreams of becoming a doctor had been impossibly out of reach. The girl who'd been dismissed without a second glance. That part of who she'd been had been locked away and she intended to keep it that way. She'd built her life refusing to allow the aching absence of love define her…but it still felt fragile. No one could know her truth—she didn't want pity, sideways glances, hushed whispers. And more than anything, she didn't want to be judged…not any more. She had to find the letter, avoid the questions. She couldn't be exposed like that.

The moment Will opened the door to the meeting room, he knew what Maddie was doing. Her head jerked up as she must have heard him enter the room and her blue eyes met his from under her long lashes.

'I was just helping the cleaning lady,' she said. 'She needed to leave early.' She bit her lip, looking like a toddler who'd been caught with her hand in the cookie jar. He smiled, fishing the letter from his back pocket, walking towards her, holding it out.

'Is this what you're after?'

Maddie stared at the folded paper and then back to him and her expression changed, a frown creased her brow and her full lips flattened into a line. She took it from him, her eyes narrowing.

'Have you read it?'

'No.' And immediately he regretted lying. 'Actually, I did read—' he began.

'Tell me you didn't,' she cut in. Her blue eyes, usually so soft, warm and full of humour, were ice. 'Tell me you didn't read a private letter addressed to me.'

'The first couple of lines,' he replied, 'just to check that it wasn't confidential patient information. I stopped reading when I realised it was yours and I've kept it safe until now.'

Maddie unfolded the letter and looked at it, scanning the text, her expression thunderous panic. Why was she reacting so strongly?

'Please don't be concerned that I'd tell anyone else about it because I won't. I can understand you might want to keep your stem cell donation a secret but, honestly, it's an amazing thing you did. You should be proud.'

Maddie stuffed the letter into her pocket, got to her feet and began to tie up the bin bags.

'I just don't want anyone to know,' she replied, not looking at him. 'I don't want to answer any silly questions, that's all.'

'Fair enough,' he replied. 'So are you thinking you'll accept contact with them?'

'You see,' snapped Maddie, dropping the bag and placing her hands on her hips, 'questions.'

'Whoa,' said Will, raising his hands in surrender. 'It was an innocent enough question—you don't have to answer. Okay, do you want a hand to take those bags to recycling?'

'I can manage,' she replied, tying the second sack then picking them up, one in each hand. She walked to the door using her elbow to dip the handle, pushing it open, and tried to walk through. But the heavy fire door began to swing shut, trapping the second bag. 'Damn it.'

Will walked to the door, opening it, but the second bin sack had ripped and balls of scrunched-up paper littered the floor. Maddie stared at the mess.

'Brilliant.'

'Let me help,' said Will, stooping to pick up the paper balls and bits of orange peel. 'Look, I'm sorry I read a bit of the letter but I was only trying to ascertain what it was—if it had been patient information—'

'I know,' cut in Maddie. 'You'd have needed to take care of it. Well, it wasn't patient information, it was a personal letter and I'd be grateful if you never mentioned it again, okay?' She stared at him, blue eyes glittering with annoyance, challenging him to refuse, but there was something else too—a flicker of fear. Her anger was a shield but what she was protecting herself from, he didn't know.

'Never…not to anyone. Are you sure you don't want a hand?'

'I'm sure.'

And she was gone.

What was so important about that letter? It was more than making a decision about meeting her recipient. She was hiding something.

Well, so was he.

It looked as though both of them had secrets—parts of their lives they'd rather stayed hidden. And although he really wanted to understand what had shaken her so deeply, he wasn't exactly in a position to expect her to tell him the truth, was he?

He was hiding so much from her.

He was hiding from so much himself.

He didn't want to think about what had brought him here, even though he was beginning to be grateful it had. What were you supposed to do when you thought the woman you'd married, promised to share your life with, build a family with, lied to you, crushed you, made you wonder what the hell you'd ever done that was so wrong you deserved to be treated the way Scarlett had treated him?

She'd lied every day they'd been married…before even.

Lied that she'd wanted his children.

Lied when she'd been crying in his arms, pretending to be distraught when she hadn't been pregnant, all the time knowing she was on the pill.

The joy he'd felt that time she'd told him she'd thought she was pregnant had been overwhelming. He'd lifted her, swung her around—they'd laughed and cried, he'd thought, with happiness—he'd ordered that hamper of baby clothes and he'd held them up in wonder at how tiny they were.

She'd made a fool of him. She'd been laughing at him. She'd never wanted his children—never intended to have them.

He braced his hands against the wall—he didn't need its support; he was stopping himself from punching it.

So, no, he wasn't sure what you were supposed to do. All he did know was that he wasn't, ever, going to allow the same thing to happen again.

CHAPTER SEVEN

Entering the paediatric intensive care unit invoked the same feelings in Maddie every time she walked in. It was an odd blend of apprehension, hope and wonder. The PICU was home for varying lengths of time to some of the most vulnerable patients in the hospital and, generally, staff either loved it or hated it.

Maddie loved it. She loved the highly controlled atmosphere of the place and the hugely impressive level of care each young patient received at the hands of the extremely dedicated team of staff. She loved the intensity, the fact that situations could be so quickly changeable and that, in response, staff were challenged to be their very best. It could be at once exhilarating and heartbreaking and it was the teamwork that made it happen and kept you sane.

'How is Annabel this morning?' she asked, peering into the incubator that was currently home to her two-day-old patient. Annabel had been born at full term but had been found very quickly to be suffering from TTN. Transient tachypnoea of the newborn was a common reason for admission to the PICU and was due to the baby being unable to clear the foetal fluid from its lungs, causing respiratory distress.

'Observations have been stable overnight,' replied the staff nurse with a smile. 'She's been behaving pretty well.'

'Her respiratory rate has settled.' Maddie slid her stethoscope from around her neck, placing it in her ears. 'Let's have a listen to your chest, little one.' TTN was usually self-limiting and, with the right supportive care, babies had an excellent chance of recovery. The challenge was making the correct diagnosis in the first place and instigating the appropriate treatment quickly.

'Breath sounds are normal,' said Maddie. 'I think we can increase the feed as protocol and reduce the oxygen.' She smiled, sliding her finger into Annabel's tiny palm. The baby responded perfectly by grasping her finger. 'Are Mum and Dad around?'

'They went to the kitchen to make a coffee,' said the nurse.

'I'll go and update them. Nice when you can give good news, isn't it?'

'It is. Mum will be relieved as she's been worried that bonding with Annabel might be affected.'

'Thanks, Amy, I'll go speak to them now. Bye bye, Annabel. Let's hope we can discharge you tomorrow.'

Maddie made her way down the unit, through the older children's area and towards the relatives' kitchen. It had been a good morning so far but it was never a good idea to tempt fate, not in medicine.

'Morning.' Will stepped out from behind a cubicle curtain as she walked past.

'Morning,' she replied, stopping in her tracks at his sudden appearance. They hadn't parted on the best of terms yesterday when she'd refused his offer of help with the bin sacks. She'd felt a little guilty later on at home. He'd only read the first line or two of the letter—she'd probably have done the same—but it had been enough that he'd started to ask questions. It had been a scenario she'd dreaded—being questioned and not having the answers to keep the truth hidden. Did she trust him to keep it to himself? Not to probe any further?

'How's it going?' he asked.

'I'm just on my way to tell some parents of a newborn with

TTN that their daughter is doing well and is likely to be to be discharged from the PICU tomorrow.'

'Nice to be able to give good news, isn't it?'

A smile found its way to her lips. Him reading her mind was becoming a habit.

'It is. How's it going with you?'

Will looked back towards the bed he'd just stepped away from.

'Four-year-old Olly was involved in a road traffic collision last evening,' he replied, with a grimace. 'He has a significant subdural haematoma, which the neurosurgeons are hoping to operate on this morning.'

Maddie looked over at the little boy. He looked so small and vulnerable surrounded by the banks of monitoring equipment, syringe drivers, drips and lines, but he had one of the best paediatricians she knew looking after him.

'Who's operating?' she asked.

'Aisha Doyle Anand.'

'She's great,' she replied. 'He's in good hands there.'

Will bit his lip.

'Look, I'm sorry about yesterday...the letter. I won't say anything to anyone, you know, and I understand why you were annoyed—it's a private matter and deciding whether to meet a donor recipient is a big deal. If ever you want to talk it over, I'm more than happy to listen.'

He looked at her with kindness and genuine concern and suddenly she didn't know why she was holding back. Because she'd never shared feelings with anyone? Because no one had ever been really interested enough? Even Andrew, the ex who still occasionally pervaded her thoughts, the man she'd idiotically thought she might have loved once, who had claimed to care, had only ever skimmed the surface and had, in the end, only ever been interested in her for fun...and sex. She shuddered involuntarily and Will reached out, touching her arm.

'You okay?' he asked, his gaze gentle and searching, as though he was trying to understand what she needed.

'Someone must've walked over my grave,' she replied. She smiled but knew it wasn't her usual wide, warm, relaxed smile and she knew exactly why. Maddie hadn't ever been the sort of woman to lay her soul bare—hell, she'd never been able to trust anyone enough. Everyone in her life had always been transient, flitting in and out of it depending upon which school she'd been sent to, which foster family, which care home. Most of the people in her life had only been there because they were being paid to be…not because they cared particularly. But here she was, contemplating talking to Will about something she'd never wanted anyone else to know about.

'There's no rush to decide, you know, Maddie. You don't need to get a reply out to them but I meant what I said—if you want to talk it over, I'm more than happy to.'

'I'd like that.' The words left her lips before she'd realised she was about to speak them.

'Good,' said Will. 'Later?'

She started, momentarily thrown off balance. That was quick.

'I'm not going to get time today. I'm meeting Ellie later on, one of the students I mentor.'

Will nodded. 'Yes, the one who's just about to sit the entrance tests for med school?'

'We've only got two more sessions before she sits them, so I don't want to miss any.'

'No, of course not,' said Will. 'Would you mind if I joined you? A bit of practice before I mentor Mathew?'

There was no getting out of it now—but did she want to get out of it?

'I'm meeting Ellie at 7 p.m. at the tea room in the Shambles. If you turn up about fifteen minutes or so later, that'll give me time to tell her about you.' This was one of those situations that snowballed and Will was doing the pushing.

'Okay, it's a date. I'm going to get back to the ward to do a round before clinic this afternoon. Catch you later.'

'See you later,' said Maddie watching him as he swiped his card at the end of the unit to exit. How had that happened?

'He seems to have that effect on everyone.' It was the unmistakeable lilting Irish accent of Aisha, her friend and one of the best neurosurgeons she'd ever met. Aisha wore her green theatre scrubs, her arms were folded and one wry, slightly accusing eyebrow was raised.

'What effect?' she asked, straightening her expression and making sure she definitely didn't look as starry-eyed and taken aback as she felt.

'Oh, you know,' said Aisha, 'people staring at him in adoration.'

'Do they?' *Yes, they did and she was very well aware of it.*

'Well, he's very good at his job, has impeccable manners, has time for everybody and is great craic…and he's very slightly handsome too…isn't he?' Aisha's eyebrow rose impossibly further.

'Is he?' said Maddie.

'Just a wee bit.' Aisha grinned. 'Single too, I believe.'

'And that's relevant because…?' asked Maddie, also folding her arms.

'Because,' said Aisha, conspiratorially, 'so are you…and he's nice.' She nodded towards the door Will had just left from.

'Well, we can't have his ears burning, can we, so shall we change the subject? Are you taking Olly to Theatre now?'

'When they've finished prepping him, aye,' Aisha replied, 'which means that, in the meantime, you can tell me how you're getting on with Dr Gorgeous.'

'Yeah, he's very good, extremely competent.' She was aware this wasn't the information Aisha was digging for. 'Great with the children and the parents.'

'And the staff, Dr McArthur?'

'Stop it,' said Maddie, grinning. 'I'm not on the market and neither is he.' And that was exactly what she needed to keep repeating to herself.

'Maybe you should be on the market,' said Aisha. 'It's been too long, Maddie, and I don't think Will Lawrence will stay single for very long—not according to what I'm hearing. It would be criminal to let a man like him slip through the net. If I wasn't already happily married…well, I would.'

Maddie's mouth dropped.

'Aisha, Olly's ready for Theatre.' One of the resident doctors, Brigid, poked her head around the cubicle curtain.

'Aye, right,' replied Aisha. 'I'll head on down there and get scrubbed, then, thanks.' She turned to Maddie. 'Saved by the bell, but we'll continue this conversation another time.'

'Good luck,' said Maddie, smiling to her friend but relieved she had to leave. Aisha's suggestion that Maddie should snap Will up as though he were a prize was ridiculous. Will wasn't available and neither was she. They were good colleagues and maybe friends. Aisha's excitement about the possibility of them getting together was heading nowhere…at all.

But, in his own words, they had a 'date' later, didn't they?

She tutted to herself. It had been a turn of phrase. And neither of them wanted to date. So what was that butterfly doing fluttering its wings in her stomach? Whatever it was, it wasn't to be mistaken for anything other than the very welcome prospect of the beginning of what could be a pleasant and supportive friendship.

Will spotted Maddie and Ellie as soon as he walked into the tea room. They were seated at a white-clothed table in the corner, deep in conversation. A large china teapot decorated with dainty flowers and a heavily laden three-tiered cake stand stood on the table between them, along with three cups on saucers. It was like a scene from *Alice in Wonderland*.

'Hi,' he said, approaching them and giving Maddie a quick smile before addressing Ellie directly. 'I'm Will Lawrence, good to meet you.'

'Hi,' said Ellie, smiling warmly. 'Good to meet you too. We ordered tea. I hope that's okay?'

'Perfect,' he replied, drawing out a wooden chair and sitting down. 'This is for you.' He held out a brown paper bag, which Ellie took, slightly shyly.

'Thank you. Should I open it now?'

'If you like,' he replied. 'I couldn't resist having a snoop around the magical potions shop a couple of doors down. I saw this and thought it might help with your application to medical school.'

'Oh, wow,' said Ellie, lifting a beautiful blue glass bottle with intricate elven script and a crystal stopper out of the bag, turning it in her fingers, gazing at it.

'It's for good luck, so they tell me,' said Will. The potion bottle had been available in other colours but something had drawn him to the blue one. It contained a swirling, iridescent liquid as though it held a bound spirit. It was quite mesmerising and suddenly, seeing Maddie, he knew why it had called to him—it matched her eyes.

'It's beautiful,' said Ellie. 'That's so thoughtful, thank you.'

'You're very welcome,' he replied. 'Now, what goodies have you got on there?' He nodded towards the cake stand, which was laden with tiny sandwiches, mini cakes and tarts and scones with little pots of jam and clotted cream.

'Just a few things to keep us going for the next hour or so,' said Maddie, smiling at him. 'Tuck in.' She lifted the teapot. 'Tea?'

'Please, and I am actually hungry—clinic was non-stop and I didn't get a break of even a minute.'

'The perils of being a consultant,' said Ellie.

'Worth it though,' he replied, lifting a sandwich from the bottom tier of the cake stand. 'Don't let me put you off.'

'Oh, I won't,' Ellie replied with a grin. 'I wouldn't let Maddie down now.'

The hour passed quickly and once the plates and the teapot were empty Maddie announced that Ellie was more than ready for her interviews. The three of them left the little teashop, Ellie heading home. Will and Maddie wandered along the narrow thirteenth-century cobbled street with its medieval timber-framed shops and their jettied, overhanging floors. York's famous Shambles was pure higgledy-piggledy charm and Will vowed to return to explore more of the quaint, intriguing, darkened shops. In minutes they reached the waterfront with its outdoor bar areas busy with people enjoying the early evening sunshine and city cruise boats speckled with tourists enjoying the sparkling river.

'My apartment's just along the Esplanade,' said Will, nodding in front of them.

'Very nice,' said Maddie, looking impressed. 'They cost a pretty penny along there.'

'No room for a pool though.' Will grinned.

'You're clearly not in the same league as Ryan, then.'

'Obviously not.'

'It makes you a nicer person,' said Maddie as they walked. 'Having money only ever seems to make people want even more of it. It turns people into greedy, materialistic monsters who think they can buy anything and anyone and treat other people like second-class citizens.'

'You think so?' *Did she really think that?*

'I know so. Take Ryan—he's a good surgeon but I can't bear how he goes on about his latest purchases all the time. Did you hear him bragging about picking up his new car at the weekend?'

'I did overhear him saying that he was going for a spin in his new car on Sunday. What's he getting, did he say?'

Maddie stared at him.

'Don't show him you're interested, for goodness' sake, he'll bend your ear for hours. I don't know what he's getting, I'd switched off after he'd said something about "high performance" and "top of the range".'

'Nice,' said Will, looking impressed. 'I wonder what it is.'

'You're kidding me.'

'What?'

'Don't tell me you actually care what gas-guzzling monstrosity of a vehicle Ryan's splashing his cash on this week?'

Clearly, he wasn't meant to be impressed. He wasn't, he just quite liked cars and had a couple of vintage ones that he loved tinkering with—and there was the Ferrari, of course.

'Just mild curiosity,' he replied, with a shrug. 'It's quite interesting to see how the other half lives.' *Where had that come from?* He *was* the other half. In fact, he was at the very high end of the other half. But Maddie wasn't going to be in the least bit happy about finding that out, was she? And he wasn't about to tell her.

Maddie rolled her eyes.

'It's shallow. People who put material things above being decent human beings are monstrous. Money, in my opinion, is the root of all evil.'

Somehow, her absolute certainty and the grim determination of her words prevented him from questioning her belief. There was a certain truth in her words but she wasn't entirely correct. *He* was a decent human being, despite his wealth. *He* cared. On the other hand, Scarlett *had* turned into a greedy, materialistic monster because of her need for money. Although he had the distinct feeling that she'd always been that and he'd just not seen it.

'I'm glad you don't think I'm in Ryan's league, then.'

Her smile returned. 'Your good-luck potion was a nice thought.'

'Couldn't resist that little shop,' he replied. 'It was like walking into a wizard movie.'

'Ellie was touched.'

'She's great. I think she'll do well in interview—her intelligence is evident and she shows great communication skills, empathy and confidence without being overconfident. She has a straightforwardness about her that is really appealing.'

'I think she'll do well… I hope so. She's had a rough ride but she's resilient. I think she'd be a great doctor.'

'How come she came to be brought under your wing? How did you meet? Was she a patient like the girl you told me about before—Juliette?'

'No. In fact, most are through schools. I have contacts in a few of the schools in the city—they get in touch if they have a student who's bright and interested in medicine but has issues that might cause them to struggle with achieving their grades or accessing higher education. It can be financial constraints or responsibilities like being a carer. Ellie's academically extremely able but was struggling to achieve grades in exams. It turned out that she's a carer for her mum who has MS and just didn't have the time to revise. We accessed small packages of care for her mum to give Ellie more time for coursework. I've also tutored her for medical school entrance exams and interviews and arranged work experience placements.'

'Nice,' said Will.

'Do you think you still might want to mentor Mathew?'

'I've got some news on that score,' said Will with a sigh. 'I had a chat with him earlier.'

'Shall we sit down and you can tell me what he said?' Maddie stopped by one of the wooden benches that was set back from the riverside.

'Actually, my apartment is right here. Would you like to come in for a coffee?'

Maddie looked doubtful. 'I think I've had enough tea to sink one of those cruisers.'

'No coffee, then,' said Will. 'We can talk without drinking coffee...if you like.'

'Actually, I've always wondered what the riverside apartments are like inside—I remember them being renovated a few years ago. They used to be warehouses.'

'Come on up, then.' He tapped a keycode into the door pad, holding the door open for her to go in first. 'Evening,' he called to the concierge who sat behind the desk.

'Good evening. Post for you.'

'Thank you.' Will took the pile of post and walked to the lift, pressing the button for the fifth floor at the top of the building. Maddie would be the first visitor to his new home. Unexpectedly, nerves kicked in. Was it because she was the first to visit his apartment or because she was a woman or because she was Maddie? He knew the answer. He liked Maddie...a lot. There had been a time when he wouldn't have thought twice about inviting an attractive woman back home, but things had changed. He'd learned some harsh life lessons thanks to Scarlett and he wasn't about to risk going through anything like that again.

But Maddie wasn't Scarlett. Maddie wasn't the sort of woman who'd lie...especially about something as important, as sensitive, as life changing as the lies his ex-wife had blithely told. Scarlett had known how important family was to him.

His large, loving family: brothers and a sister who were so close and parents whose marriage was the kind others admired—happy, devoted, unshakable. His childhood had been filled with warmth, laughter and a strong sense of belonging. He'd grown up believing he'd have the same happy for-ever marriage—that he'd be surrounded by children he could raise with the same love and stability he'd known.

Scarlett had known all that.

She'd told him she wanted the same.

But she'd lied...and he'd found out too late.

His fists clenched but practice had enabled him, still not without some difficulty, to unclench them swiftly.

'Go through to the lounge,' he said as he opened the door. Maddie stepped in, slipping off her shoes. He followed her in. She went straight to the huge glass window overlooking the river and gasped.

'Wow, what a view.'

It was. Will stood at her side. The evening sun was still warm through the glass and sparkled on the river below—the low-rise city beyond the river was dominated by the huge medieval minster, its spire reaching skywards, the ancient, mellowed stone of which almost glowed in the light.

'I've not seen it from above before,' said Maddie, in wonder.

'It's a gorgeous city, isn't it? Are you settling in okay? Finding your way around?' She turned to him, the sun on her hair making it shine. They weren't as close as they'd been behind the curtain but they were close enough that he could catch a trace of her scent—fresh and increasingly familiar. His skin prickled and his nerves were taut. Being this close tested him.

Keep it light.

He took a step away from her, pretending to look at the city from another viewpoint.

'I've still got a lot of the city to explore but what I've seen so far, I love.'

'If you'd like a guided tour, I can show you the highlights some time.'

'That'd be great, thanks. Are you sure I can't get you a drink?'

'Maybe just a cold water, please.'

'Okay, I'll be right back.' Will went to the kitchen and filled a glass with water, taking a long drink. He didn't need to feel nervous around Maddie. She was nothing like Scarlett. Maddie would never have lied to her husband, telling him she wanted a family while secretly remaining on the pill. She'd never have dragged them through the sham of putting them both through fertility tests to keep up the lie, fake disappointment and heartbreak over pregnancies that were never even possible.

And she would never, ever, have let him believe that she might have been pregnant that time, allow him to go out and buy baby things, knowing all along that she wasn't. Had she been laughing at him when he'd got emotional as he'd held up that tiny white baby onesie—knowing he had a dream she'd never intended to make real? The thought that she had had haunted him in ways he couldn't begin to put into words.

Maddie wouldn't do those things.

They were things Scarlett had done.

She'd lied to him.

To get to his money. That was all she'd wanted—the wealth, the lifestyle, the financial security. And she'd thought she'd secure herself a future by promising him what she knew he wanted. When, after months of tests and retests and when he'd confronted her with the facts in the boathouse at Brockley, she'd admitted what she'd done and told him, in that cold, detached way, that she'd only ever wanted him for his money. His world and his future had imploded.

There was no one else like Scarlett, he was sure, but the scars ran deep. He was never putting himself in that position again.

And that was the reason his gut had tensed right after the moment he'd invited Maddie into the apartment. Maddie was a stunning woman. She was lovely in every sense and although inviting her in had felt easy and natural, the moment he'd done it, an alarm had rung in his head. He didn't want to get close to anyone.

Or did he?

He leant against the sink. His head was saying one thing but his body was saying something entirely different.

But Maddie was a colleague who was fast becoming a friend and he'd been straight with her from the start—he wasn't on the market. So her being in the apartment wasn't anything other than two friends and colleagues spending time together. *So, chill out, Lawrence. Stop reading things into this that aren't there.* He took another drink and filled a glass for Maddie.

Friends and colleagues.

But their almost kiss still lingered in his mind—the way she'd looked up into his eyes, holding his gaze, the light, unintentional graze of her hand against his. It had been intimate and it had caught him off guard.

He hadn't wanted intimacy.

But almost kissing Maddie hadn't felt like a mistake. It had felt natural—worse, it had felt right. And her reaction to him having seen her letter had shown a raw vulnerability, making him instantly want to protect her—from whatever it was the letter had meant to her. But she needed protecting from him too—from his messed-up, locked-away, impenetrable heart. He walked back into the lounge and handed her the glass of water.

He needed to listen more carefully to his head and ignore how his body reacted to her.

'So, I was going to tell you about my chat with Mathew...'

'Thanks,' said Maddie, taking the glass from him. She didn't need a drink but the idea of cool water had suddenly seemed a good one—although the heat simmering beneath her skin had nothing to do with thirst and everything to do with finding herself in Will's apartment, alone with him. 'So what did Mathew say to you?'

'He's effectively a carer for his mum,' said Will, with a grimace. 'Sounds as though she has some kind of anxiety disorder, which has gradually got worse, to the point where some days she's not even getting out of bed.'

'So she's reliant on him and he doesn't want to leave her to go to university.'

'Exactly.'

'We can get help for her,' said Maddie. 'He can't suffer because of something that's entirely treatable and his mum shouldn't have to suffer any more either. Does Mathew think she'd accept some help?'

'He says he's suggested going with her to see their GP lots of times but that she's always refused to go. It sounds to me as though he's resigned himself to staying at home to look after her, but I've offered to speak to her and see if I can't persuade her to accept some help for his sake, if not her own.'

'Has he agreed you can speak to her?'

'He said I can try,' said Will, 'but that he didn't hold out much hope. I'm going to speak to the community outreach team in the morning to see what they can offer.'

'We have to find a way to help them.' Maddie placed her glass on a side table. 'Mathew has such promise—I'll be damned if I'll let it go to waste.'

'You really care about this, don't you?'

Maddie realised her fists were curled at her sides and released them. Of course, she cared—how could she not? These kids were her—underestimated, overlooked, insignificant. If everyone had stood back and no one had ever given her a chance, where would she be now? Not here, not living her dream and working as a doctor, that was for sure.

'They just need a bit of a helping hand, that's all, and we're in a position to do that—we have a responsibility.'

But it was more than that—more than a responsibility—it was a need she had deep inside her to save others from almost falling, the way she almost had. It was about grabbing their hands before the world taught them they didn't matter.

'We do,' said Will slowly, thoughtfully. He took a step towards her, his eyes not leaving hers. What was that look? Admiration? Approval? Desire? Her heart pounded against her ribs. The air between them was suddenly charged. He lifted his hand, hesitating before brushing a strand of hair from her face, his fingers grazing her skin.

She didn't move.

Didn't breathe.

He leaned in, just slightly…just enough…as something hovered in the air between them, his breath on her lips. How easy it would be to move towards him, close the gap. He wouldn't stop her, she knew that much. It was something they both wanted, that was clear. But something else was clear too—it wouldn't stop at a kiss. Crossing that line would break something open—it would unleash a deeper need.

And then what?

That wasn't something you could take back.

Her body ached to close the inch of space between them, but something wouldn't let her. It wasn't that she didn't want to taste those lips…she did. But that was what scared her… she wanted it too much.

She took a step back. So did he.

Neither of them spoke.

Neither of them was ready.

Not yet.

Maddie lowered her gaze and reached for her glass of water, taking a sip.

'I should go.'

There was a flicker of something in his eyes and he gave a small nod.

'Of course.'

He wasn't questioning her. She turned to leave, walking back out into the hallway and slipping her shoes back on. He didn't follow but she could feel his eyes on her. He was letting her go but part of him didn't seem to want to.

CHAPTER EIGHT

'Hi, I've come to review, erm…'

Maddie looked up from her seat at the nurses' station. A woman wearing a dietician's uniform and a frown stood scrolling on her phone.

'There it is,' the woman continued, 'a Mathilda Darlington.'

Mathilda was Will's patient—the two-year-old who'd been admitted with bilateral pneumonia a few days ago and who'd since been found to be dangerously underweight for her age. She'd been admitted by her social worker, who, Will had told Maddie, was seriously concerned for the child's safety at home as her mother was dependent on alcohol and drugs.

'She's in side room three,' replied Maddie. 'She's Dr Lawrence's patient. He's down at the bottom of the ward if you wanted to speak to him.'

'I spoke to him on the phone earlier,' the woman replied, 'so I know the score, thanks—failure to thrive due to living with an alcoholic, drugged-up mother who clearly puts her own needs above her daughter's. Poor little mite. She'd be better off being in care. Doesn't stand a chance, does she? I don't know why people have kids if they're going to treat them like that. If she wasn't wanted the poor thing would have been better off if she'd never been born.'

Maddie stared at the woman, speechless, her words landing too close to home.

'Everything okay?' It was Will.

'Dr Lawrence?'

'That's me.' He smiled but his smile didn't reach his eyes, Maddie noticed. 'You're here to review my patient Mathilda?'

'Yes,' she returned. 'I'll go and review her charts and suggest a feeding regime.'

'That would be great,' said Will.

'You okay?' he said to Maddie as the dietician strode down the ward.

'Yeah, fine,' said Maddie, 'you?' She'd gone back to the notes she'd been typing and didn't look up. The dietician hadn't meant to sound so cold, she was certain, but her words had been a sucker punch. Shouldn't Maddie have been born either? Her mother hadn't wanted her. Would it have been better if she hadn't been born? Was that what other people thought too?

'I've just booked sleep study tests for Hayley,' he replied. 'Going by the book, she could be discharged because since her admission there have been absolutely no signs of any breathing difficulties but my gut just won't let me discharge her yet.' He frowned, rubbing the back of his neck.

Will's five-year-old patient, Hayley, had become a firm favourite of the ward staff in the week since she'd been admitted. The little girl had been teaching some of them sign language and, with some tuition from Will too, some of the staff were able to have some conversation with her and Hayley was thrilled.

'What's bugging you?' Maddie asked him. Clearly something was.

'Fancy a coffee?' he asked. 'I'm sure you're due a break and I wouldn't mind running this case by you…if you don't mind.'

Maddie looked up. He *was* concerned and just because they'd nearly kissed twice in the last week and she'd wondered way too many times what might have happened if they had, she wasn't going to let that come in the way of being able to discuss a patient. In fact, maybe if they spent more time together, working alongside each other and not almost kissing, the better chance there was of the electric tension between them going away. Maybe then she could stop looking at his mouth.

'Okay, let's grab a coffee and take a walk in the sunshine.'

The air was summer warm with a light breeze and as the main lunchtimes were over, the garden outside the ward was deserted. Maddie sat down on the bench that encircled the oak tree, which gave a little shade and a lovely dapple of sunshine through the softly rustling leaves.

'So, tell me about Hayley—what's worrying you?'

'I'm not sure I even want to verbalise it.' Will ran his fingers through his dark hair. 'It sounds so extreme.'

'Talk me through Hayley's presentation rather than telling me your concern directly,' said Maddie, 'and let's see if we come to the same conclusion; then you're not swaying me.'

Will looked solemn. He opened his mouth to speak and then changed his mind, chewing on his lip instead before inhaling deeply and meeting her concerned gaze.

'Okay, so here are the facts. As you know, Hayley was admitted a week ago by her mother, who described an episode of severe breathing difficulties during the night. On admission she had no shortness of breath, wheezing or respiratory symptoms of any description. Her obs and bloods were normal. On examination, her respiratory tract was entirely normal—no enlarged tonsils or adenoids and no foreign bodies. Her echocardiogram was normal so no cardiac cause either.'

'Right,' said Maddie slowly, 'so you've eliminated all the most obvious causes. Could it have been a night terror or panic attack?'

'Possible, but she denies having had a bad dream and doesn't show any signs of anxiety.'

'Go on.' Maddie watched him. He was clearly struggling with this and she was beginning to understand why.

'I mentioned discharging Hayley this morning to her mum, Dana, and it was her response that stopped me.'

'She was reluctant to have Hayley discharged?'

'More than that,' said Will, his lips pressed into a line. 'She told me that in her sleep last night, Hayley had an episode where she stopped breathing.'

'Did she call for the nurses?'

Will shook his head. 'She said it was brief, that Hayley started breathing again and that she didn't want to disturb her.'

'Hence the sleep studies.'

'Exactly.'

'What's the relationship like between them?' asked Maddie.

'It would seem to be good—they're comfortable in each other's company. Dana seems devoted to Hayley, spends a lot of time with her, in fact, barely leaves her side.'

Maddie's eyes met his and, in that moment, she knew they were both thinking the same thing.

'It's a perplexing presentation,' said Maddie, 'and really, you've eliminated any medical cause.' She wasn't going to spell out what she thought. Will needed to come to his own conclusion and verbalise his opinion without her influencing him. It was a big deal, to accuse a mother of Munchausen's syndrome by proxy or FDIA, as it was also known—a rare mental health disorder where a parent or carer exaggerated or deliberately caused symptoms of illness in a child. It was a form of child abuse that most doctors never saw in practice and Maddie had only ever seen once.

'I'm just concerned I'm missing a treatable medical condition,' he replied, raking his hand through his hair.

'You've ruled out the symptoms being caused by a foreign body, an infection, asthma, an anatomical disorder of the respiratory tract, a cardiac cause or by an anaphylactic or stress-induced reaction. There's no reason to suspect sleep apnoea but you've ordered sleep studies because Hayley's mum, on hearing you were thinking of discharging her, described a further, unwitnessed episode of apnoea, which she didn't report to the staff on the ward at the time. Do you have a differential diagnosis?'

Will bit his lip.

'The presentation doesn't make sense,' he said slowly.

Maddie shook her head.

'You know you're not missing a treatable medical condition in Hayley, Will.'

'No. It was her mum's response that raised the red flag.'

'I agree,' said Maddie.

'I'll have to report it to the safeguarding team. If it is a case of Factitious Disorder Imposed on Another, it does look as though we've caught it early, at least.'

'And if Dana is able to acknowledge what she's doing, there's a chance that psychological treatment would be successful.'

'True.' Will smiled, that cute dimple dinting his cheek, drawing her eyes to it. 'Thanks, Maddie.'

'You'd worked it out already.' She returned his smile, her heart skipping when he didn't drop his gaze, increasing its rate when a moment later he still hadn't. His eyes held hers, smiling, glittering.

And then they changed.

They darkened.

And her heart hammered in her chest. She could hear the chirping of the birds and the distant hum of a lawnmower—she could feel that she still held the cardboard coffee cup, warm in her hand, but all she could see was Will's darkened blue eyes looking into her own...for far longer than they ever had before. Her breathing deepened. Colleagues didn't look at each other this way. She dropped her glance to her lap—she couldn't afford to gaze into his eyes because she couldn't afford to find herself wanting something she'd already told herself she didn't want.

'Thank you for working through that with me,' said Will. 'I owe you one.'

'That's what colleagues are for.' But they weren't just colleagues, were they? They had something much more—something as yet unspoken, unacknowledged, unactioned—a silent pull, drawing them towards each other.

'My offer still stands if you want to talk about your letter.'

Yes, they'd become more than colleagues. They'd become friends. That was the sort of offer a friend made. Did she want to take him up on it? Tell him about her dilemma? Anything more than that?

'It's not straightforward.'

'Have you had any anonymous contact with them before?' he asked.

'I had a thank-you card about six months after the transplant, but because the two years is up, it means that both parties are allowed to have the anonymity lifted and can find out whatever each person wants to tell about themselves—names, addresses, their whole life story if they want to...even meet up in person.' She dropped her chin, her fingernails suddenly demanding attention.

'And you're not sure you want the recipient to know who you are?'

'The HLA was a fifty-per-cent match.'

'Wow,' said Will, 'that's pretty high—the human leucocyte antigen match is usually only that high in siblings.'

Maddie looked up at him, biting her lower lip, her eyes

holding his as though trying hard to impart some unspoken knowledge.

'Do you think you may have found a lost relative?'

'It's possible, isn't it?' Maddie gazed at him. *Did she want to carry on with this?*

'Does anyone else in your family have any idea who it might be? A family member who'd lost touch or moved away?'

These were the questions she'd tried to avoid answering—why no one should have seen the letter. But she'd wondered what it might feel like to open up, share her story, expose this side of herself. It had always seemed terrifying, too raw, too risky...something she'd avoided at all costs. But now, with Will, the fear wasn't there. Instead, there was something else—a strange, welcome calm as if, somehow, she knew it was going to be fine. How could that be? How had she found she could trust this man when she'd never trusted anyone?

'Do you know your family, Maddie?'

She blinked and the tears she hadn't known were there overspilt as she shook her head.

'None of them?'

'No,' she whispered, 'I'm a...' Her voice cracked. If she told him any more there'd be no going back.

He placed his hand on her arm, resting there, gently—an anchor telling her he was there. He tilted his head, searching her eyes. And there was that look again—kindness, concern, softening her further. She lowered her gaze, unable to watch his reaction—she feared pity almost as much as she feared judgement. She'd spent her whole life unable to trust—but she wanted to trust. She could trust Will.

'I was a foundling.'

But he didn't speak, or gasp, or tell her how awful that was. He just stayed with her, his hand steady on her arm... present, solid. She could trust this man. She looked back at him.

'I never knew my parents. I grew up in care…children's homes, the occasional foster home—nothing permanent. I was left on the steps of a hospital in a box—I don't even know when my actual birthday is. I had no way of tracing them and they've never tried to find me—so I forgot about them until…'

'Until the letter,' he finished for her.

'I don't know what to do, Will. I've lived all my life on my own. Do I want to meet someone I'm related to after all this time? Someone who didn't want me? I don't know what to feel about this. What should I do?' Tears welled in her eyes but strong arms gathered her to him and she buried her face in his chest.

'You don't have to do anything you don't want to and you don't need to decide anything quickly. There's time. We'll work this through.'

The tears fell—tears that had been held back for far too long. But somehow, with him, it felt safe to let them fall. And as they did, he held her—with a quiet strength, grounding her. She didn't want to leave the shelter of his embrace—it felt right, safe, as if she belonged there. But she couldn't stay there, could she? She pulled away from him, even though every part of her wanted to stay exactly where she was.

'Sorry,' she sniffed, a watery, apologetic, shaky smile curving her lips. 'I don't know where all that came from.'

'A childhood trauma? Thoughts that you've probably managed all this time by not thinking about them suddenly resurfacing?' He sighed, tucking a stray lock of hair that had escaped her ponytail back over her ear. 'I can't imagine what you've been through, Maddie, but I'm here if you want to talk, about any of it, any time. You're not on your own.'

'Thank you.' Her smile widened and she held his gaze, feeling herself falling into it. It had felt right to trust him but, suddenly, she didn't trust herself.

***

'We should go back in.' Maddie adjusted her ponytail, smoothing it back so that no one would be able to tell it had been disturbed.

'I guess we should.'

Will was glad he'd been able to take out of his voice and words the anger that had surged through him at her revelation. How could any mother abandon her baby, not knowing or being able to ensure they were safe? A mother's instinct was to protect her baby with her own life if need be. In order for children to flourish, feeling safe and secure, loved, wanted and cherished were vital growing up. Maddie wouldn't have known those things. How she'd become the successful, accomplished, amazing woman she was now was incredible to imagine. What must she have been through?

He'd held on to her, allowing the sobs to wrack themselves out of her until they'd begun to subside, stroking her hair, keeping her warm and safe until she'd fallen silent and her body had relaxed. He'd felt her palms on his chest as she'd pushed herself back, away from him, and looked up into his eyes. A little of their brightness had returned but he wasn't going to forget the vulnerability he'd seen in them, nor the strength of the fierce protectiveness towards her that had flooded through him as he'd held her and remained with him now. The tiny spark of the Maddie he'd known up until then— the successful, strong, resilient Maddie—had reappeared after she'd opened up and exposed her vulnerability to him and, inexplicably, had made him want to protect her even more.

'So what date do you celebrate your birthday?' he asked, needing to lighten the tone before they got back to the ward.

'The sixteenth.'

'Of this month?'

'That's the day I was found,' she replied. 'I've no idea if it's my actual birthday.'

'That's Saturday.'

Maddie smiled.

'It is.'

'Are you doing anything…to celebrate?'

'I stopped hoping a millionaire would whisk me away to Paris for lunch a long time ago.' She smiled as she dabbed her eyes with a tissue. 'No, I've nothing planned.'

'Can we do something? Together?'

She looked up sharply.

Will smiled. 'Don't look so horrified—as friends, and I'm not offering lunch in Paris.'

A small, hesitant smile curved her lips and lifted something in his chest. It shouldn't have meant so much, but it did. Making her smile had started to feel important to him—more important than he wanted to admit. But there were tears in her eyes again.

'Hey, don't cry.' He touched her hand. 'I just want to do something nice to celebrate another year of your life…whether it's the actual day you were born or not.'

'Definitely not in Paris?'

'Absolutely not.'

CHAPTER NINE

Will packed the picnic hamper he'd hastily bought that morning with items from the bakery, fresh fruit and a bottle of chilled champagne. Where the idea had come from, he wasn't entirely sure. But doing nothing to celebrate another year of Maddie's life hadn't been an option.

But doing something together? The words had left his lips without having had permission from his head. His heart had stopped as he'd waited for her reply and he still didn't know if that was because he'd been in shock at his own probably wholly inappropriate request or because of the tears welling in her eyes even as she'd fought to control them.

He snipped the price tag from the rolled-up picnic blanket. Asking her to come out with him today, as weird a question as it had seemed to both of them, had actually lifted them from what had happened before. He couldn't begin to imagine the life she must have lived as a child—it would have been the polar opposite of his own, which had been filled with the love, laughter and fun of his large family. As a child, he'd never questioned that he'd been loved. There had always been someone there he could turn to, play with, get advice and support from. It was why he'd always imagined he'd have a large family himself one day. Not that that was ever going to happen now.

He made his way downstairs, nodding and raising his hand to the concierge on his way out. It was a perfect summer's day and he made his way along the river path towards the park. He spotted Maddie at the large wrought-iron gates before she saw him. She wore a pale-yellow dress and had on a large brimmed straw hat, which cast the top half of her face into shadow. She was watching a line of parents and children queuing at the ice-cream van.

'You can have one after lunch if you like but not before.' He lifted the picnic basket and smiled. 'I'm not taking you to Paris for lunch, I've brought Paris to you, *mademoiselle*.'

Maddie laughed.

'Merci, tu es tres gentil.'

The picnic area was near to the tennis court and Will unrolled the blanket, laying it on the ground as the distinctive sound of tennis balls being rallied over the nets popped in the summer air.

Will shook out the blanket and they sat down. Opening the basket, he set out white china plates and glass flutes, followed by boxes of variously filled croissants, baguette, a bowl of strawberries and a selection of cakes and pastries that looked like little works of art. 'Champagne?'

'Yes, please.' Maddie picked up one of the flutes as Will eased the cork from the bottle with a dull pop and filled her glass with the pale golden bubbles before filling his own.

'Wow,' said Maddie. 'I'm not sure where to start. What a spread and, yes, it's all very French—it looks delicious.'

Will passed her a plate.

'Start wherever you like—if you want cake first, have cake—I won't judge.' He smiled, pleased to see the warm smile on her face in return. The idea for a Parisian birthday picnic in England had, so far, been a good one, even if it had occurred to him out of nowhere. He could have taken her to actual Paris for lunch, of course—in his private jet—if he hadn't had the distinct feeling that she'd have objected.

Anyway, whisking her away to actual Paris wasn't something friends did, was it? Paris was a city for lovers and they weren't that.

'I had my first mentoring session with Mathew last night,' he said, picking up a strawberry.

'How did it go?' She popped a strawberry into her mouth.

'Really well, I think. We talked generally about what it's like at medical school and had a look at ones to apply to. He told me how he and his mum were getting on with the counselling.'

'I'm so glad she agreed to go to family counselling,' said Maddie, picking up a pink macaron. 'I wasn't convinced she would. So often, people just can't see they have a problem and don't think they need help even when it's obvious to everyone else that they do.'

'Poor Mathew had been coping with her anxiety disorder for so long that her increasingly debilitating phobias had become almost normal to him. But when he'd started talking to her about how he wanted to go away to university, she'd become even worse and he knew he wasn't going to be able to leave her on her own.'

'It'll be a while before they see any tangible improvement from the counselling,' said Maddie, 'but hopefully, Mathew can see there's light at the end of the tunnel and really start working towards his goal of becoming a doctor.'

'I hope so.' Will emptied his champagne flute. 'Imagine having to parent your own parent.'

'I can't imagine.' Maddie held her glass out for more champagne as Will poured.

He stopped mid-pour and looked at her.

'Sorry, I said that without thinking.'

'It's okay. I don't expect you to watch what you're saying all the time just in case you offend me because of my slightly unconventional upbringing. I don't even think about it most of the time.'

'Unless I ask dumb questions about the date of your birthday.'

'Or I get letters asking if I'd like contact with someone who could well be related to me.' Maddie smiled before taking a sip from her glass. 'There will always be times when I'm reminded that my mother didn't want me—I can't bury my head in the sand and pretend that didn't happen so, please, don't feel the need to tiptoe around me in case you say the wrong thing.'

'So can I ask if you've thought any more about making contact with your recipient?'

'I have, actually.'

'And?' Will's eyebrows rose.

'And I still have no clue.' She took another drink, looking at him from over the top of her glass, her eyes twinkling with humour.

'We should do a list,' said Will decisively. 'Pros and cons. That's what I do when I have a dilemma.'

'The pros and cons all depend on who my stem cell recipient was.'

'Whether they're a complete stranger or an actual relation.'

'Exactly. If the recipient is a stranger who happens to have a very well-matched HLA, then the pros are easy—you meet someone who you helped out and it's all very nice. The cons are zero.'

Will shifted his position on the blanket, lifting the empty strawberry bowl back into the basket.

'But if they turn out to be a relative?'

'It's a whole different ball game.'

'What's the worst fear?' said Will. Articulating that gave at least a starting point from which to begin working on a problem, he always found.

Maddie drew in a long breath.

'That I find my mother and that she rejects me again.'

'So,' said Will slowly, 'humour me here...what if you do find her and, actually, she doesn't reject you?'

Maddie smiled wryly.

'And she tells me she didn't want to abandon me, but she had to because she was a princess who'd fallen in love with a handsome servant boy and her father, the king, had threatened to lock her up in a tower in the castle for ever if she kept the baby?'

Will's eyebrows rose and the pastry he'd begun to lift towards his mouth hovered inches before it.

'Too far-fetched?' she asked.

'A little, maybe. Where did that come from?'

Maddie smiled.

'Growing up, I made up many stories about why my mother left me on those steps, but that one was my favourite. I guess it says something about me—that I'm a little melodramatic perhaps.'

'I think it makes perfect sense—your young mind couldn't begin to understand how a mother could leave her baby so it had to work out a reason that didn't involve it being either her or your fault—the servant boy, the king and the tower story renders both of you blameless. You were left at the hospital through no fault of either of you.'

Maddie tipped her glass, drinking the last of the champagne.

'I made it up because the truth was too hard to acknowledge. My mother didn't want me and still doesn't. If she did, there are ways now of tracing people—it wouldn't have been hard. So, yeah, my young mind made up a story I could go to sleep with, I guess.'

Will's heart ached for her. Her smile was brave but her eyes betrayed a deep sadness. Even after all those years, what had happened to her still hurt. Understanding why she might be reluctant to be rejected again wasn't difficult.

'I can't imagine, Maddie, that's so hard.'

'Enough about me. Tell me about your childhood. Do you have brothers, sisters?'

'Both,' he replied. 'Older and younger—I'm somewhere in the middle.'

Maddie relaxed, leaning back on her elbows, her legs stretched out in front of her.

'How many of you are there?'

'Seven.'

'Wow. Was that wonderful or a nightmare?'

'Both,' he repeated, laughing.

'I can't imagine.' She looked up at him, smiling at having repeated his own words. 'I always wanted a large family when I grew up. I guess it appealed because it would be the opposite to what I had… I'm not sure I'd go as far as seven though.'

'Pros and cons,' he said, closing the lid on the basket and facing her, on his side, leaning on one elbow.

She had her eyes closed and had flipped her sunglasses over them. Her face was turned upward towards the sun, elongating her throat, and her hair had fallen over her shoulders behind her, the ends of it touching the blanket. Suddenly he saw her surrounded by children, playing and laughing in the sunshine. She'd be a wonderful mother and he wanted her to experience what he'd had growing up—encircled within a loving family. *But who would give her those children?* Unexpectedly, he realised he didn't want any man to give her that.

Why not?

His breath caught in his throat.

Because he wanted that man to be him?

Maddie let out a long, contented sigh.

'What a perfect day,' she murmured, her eyes still closed behind her shades.

'It's a gorgeous day,' he replied, watching her. He didn't want another man touching her. *He* wanted to be the one who would trace a finger lightly from her lips and down her neck. His throat tightened.

Maddie opened her eyes and he started as though he'd been caught doing something he shouldn't...like looking at her.

Like seeing her as more than a friend.

As though he wanted her.

'I don't mean the weather.' She sat up, looking down at him, smiling. 'I mean because you made my birthday so special.'

'Paris in England...to celebrate that you're in the world, regardless of the day you were born.'

She removed her shades and soft baby-blue eyes looked into his own, her smile widening slowly. He was sure she didn't mean for it to be seductive but his stomach tightened just the same.

'Thank you for this, Will.'

'For not taking you to Paris?'

'Exactly that.' Maddie leant towards him, pressing a soft kiss to his forehead—gentle, brief but enough to stir something deep inside him. How what happened next happened, he wasn't sure, but when he lifted his head, somehow, his lips found hers. They were warm, soft and the fullness of them yielding against his own tightened every muscle in his body and for a moment, a sweet, out-of-this-world moment, nothing else existed.

She pulled away, slowly, but his gaze locked with hers and his breathing stopped as his mind swirled with possibilities. She didn't look shocked...or horrified. She looked at him steadily, as if she was trying to work it out too. *Did she want more? Did he?*

Yes.

No.

'I think the champagne's gone to my head.' She sat up straight and laughed, lightly.

He felt giddy too but it wasn't the champagne. He could still feel her lips on his. He hadn't meant to kiss her, at least not then. But it had been inevitable, hadn't it? Something that had been building between them for weeks in every look, every touch, every almost kiss that had gone before.

And now she was looking at him and he didn't know what to do with that. There was a part of him, a reckless part, that wanted to kiss her again but there was another part telling him how complicated this could get, how fragile she could be and how she deserved better. He had too much to hide and he wasn't going to mess her up with his secrets. But the truth of his feelings for her was impossible to ignore.

He wanted her.

He wanted more than a kiss.

Maybe she did too.

And that scared the hell out of him.

'I seem to remember I promised you an ice cream.' His brain was scrambled but had thankfully thought of something to say that wasn't entirely ridiculous.

'I think you did.' Maddie got to her knees and began to pack the remaining picnic items back into the basket, busying herself.

Will reached for the empty champagne bottle just as she did, their fingers touching. They both held on to it, looking up at the same moment, their gazes clashing.

If the park had been empty…

What?

He'd kiss her again.

But it wasn't…and she lowered her gaze, let go of the bottle, placed her sunglasses back over her eyes and stood.

And the moment was gone.

CHAPTER TEN

WILL'S AFTERNOON SHIFT in the paediatric A & E had been steady so far but that had just changed with the arrival of nine-year-old Rajesh. The little boy had worrying neurological symptoms and Will needed an MRI scan to help determine the cause. But his little patient's condition was causing symptoms that included cerebral irritation and it was making him extremely restless.

'India, can you stay with Rajesh and monitor heart rate and blood pressure again, please?' he asked. 'We're going to need to sedate him for the MRI.'

'Of course,' the senior nurse replied, sliding a pillow between Rajesh and the side of the trolley to protect the boy's flailing arms.

Will strode to the nurses' station, pulling his phone from his pocket and scrolling to find Maddie's number. She answered straight away.

'Everything okay?' she asked.

'I've got a nine-year-old in A & E with signs of increased intracranial pressure since this morning. There's no way to get a definitive diagnosis without an MRI but he's not going to be able to tolerate one without deep sedation. Would you mind popping down here to give me a hand, you being the resident neuro expert?'

'Actually, I've got Vic Hazelwood on the ward somewhere. Hold on one second.'

She was definitely avoiding him. Over the last few days since the picnic...and the kiss, there had been an awkwardness between them—a shift in the dynamic. She'd hidden it initially as they'd walked through the park but she'd quickly decided that it had been time for her to get home to prepare some mentoring sessions. And since then, she'd studiously avoided him. Perhaps they should talk...if he could get her alone any time soon.

'Hello? Will?'

'Hi,' he replied into the phone.

'Vic's kindly offered to come down to assist.'

'Great, thank you.' *No question—she was dodging him.* 'What time are you working till today?'

'Oh, erm, I'm not sure yet.'

Well, that was deliberate vagueness if ever he'd heard it.

'I wanted to catch you before you went home.'

Silence.

'Maddie?'

'Yes?'

'Can we talk?'

'Not right now.'

'I don't mean now; I mean after work.'

Silence. They really did need to talk.

'I'll be up there at six... Maddie?'

'Okay.'

'See you later.'

He ended the call, slipping the phone back into his pocket, picking up the landline and dialling the imaging department.

The kiss should never have happened. It had changed things between them and he wanted to change them back. He missed her company and friendship. What the hell had he been thinking, kissing her like that? He'd made a good friend in Maddie McArthur—a genuine friend—and for the first time in his life, he knew one hundred per cent that she was his friend because she had, somehow, found something in him that she liked that had nothing to do with his money.

And what had he gone and done?

Ruined it.

For a moment of desire, he'd potentially ruined a perfect friendship. The only perfect friendship he'd ever had.

And now, he had to try to turn the clock back and put it right.

Maddie glanced at the clock on the wall: 6:15 p.m.

Should she wait a little longer? Another five minutes? Did she even want to hang around to find out why he wanted to talk?

'Haven't you got a home to go to?' It was Chris, one of the other paediatric consultants, who she'd handed over to half an hour ago as he'd taken over the evening shift.

'I'm just waiting for Will to come up from A & E.'

'Oh?' The look on Chris's face told her she'd piqued his interest a little too much.

'He wanted to run something by me about a neuro patient in A & E,' she replied quickly, thankful to her brain for reacting swiftly...*with a lie*. Will wanted to talk about what had happened at the park...the kiss. The kiss that should never have happened but that had been heart-stopping. The kiss that had meant she hadn't dared to look into his eyes again because it had shattered the certainty she'd had that she didn't want to get involved.

'He didn't want you to go down there to review the patient?' Her colleague's eyebrow rose.

That would have been more usual. 'No, I think it was just a quick question he wanted to ask.' *Another lie*. Will wanted to tell her he'd made a mistake and she didn't want to hear it. Couldn't they just silently acknowledge it between them without having to say it out loud?

'Right,' said Chris slowly, in a 'whatever you say' kind of way. 'He made a good call with the mum with Munchausen's, didn't he? I'm not sure I'd have called it that quickly.'

'He did,' agreed Maddie, managing a smile. 'It was a tricky one.' Making a diagnosis of Munchausen's by proxy was huge and carried with it enormous physical, emotional and potentially litigious consequences for everyone involved.

'Every paediatrician's nightmare,' said Chris with a grimace.

'What is?' said Will, striding towards them, his rucksack slung over one shoulder, stethoscope still around his neck and his shirt sleeves rolled up. God help her, he was handsome.

'We were talking about Hayley.' Maddie met his gaze, not wanting to linger but being drawn in, reluctantly.

'Actually, I checked in with the psychiatric team earlier and her mum has been able to admit that she fabricated symptoms, so that's a good indication that successful treatment is possible.'

'Is that so?' said Chris. 'The condition is so rare that I've never actually seen a case first hand.'

'If someone is willing to accept what they're doing and to engage in treatment,' said Maddie, 'there's a much better chance that cognitive behavioural therapy will be effective.'

'You could have saved that little one's life.' Chris pulled in a deep breath, letting it out slowly. 'Not everyone would have spotted it and Hayley could have gone through years of physical and psychological harm. Nice one, Will.'

'I hope they're all okay,' said Will, his deep blue eyes concerned and not containing even a shred of pride.

'There's a good chance they will be,' said Maddie, smiling but still unable to meet his gaze. Will was one of the kindest, most thoughtful, genuine people she'd ever met—a lovely, caring doctor, deeply respected and who'd become a huge asset to the department. He'd joined her in mentoring some of the brightest but vulnerable young people in their community and…he'd brought her Paris in the park. It had been a gesture so thoughtful—a lovely, relaxing couple of hours… right up until the moment he'd sent her into a disorientating tailspin of confusion by kissing her.

'Well, I guess I've got patients to see,' said Chris. 'You two doing anything nice over the weekend?'

You two? Did Chris think they were an item? Or was he just digging? Heavens, it was almost as though he could tell they'd shared a kiss.

'Just the usual, for me,' Maddie replied. 'You?'

'Oh, we've got Ryan's pool company coming round to measure up and give us a quote,' said Chris, offhandedly. But Maddie didn't miss the way his squared shoulders and jutting chin gave him a sudden air of self-importance and she had to concentrate hard not to roll her eyes.

'Don't forget to invite us to the celebratory barbeque,' said Will. He appeared suitably impressed until she paid closer attention and saw the gleam in his eyes as he turned to look at her. 'I'm going to have to get one of these pools myself before I start feeling left out.'

'Me too,' agreed Maddie. 'I can't swim but I'm sure I can learn.'

'You can't swim?' said Chris, aghast.

'Never had lessons.' She'd never had anyone around who'd taken her as a child and as an adult it hadn't really crossed her mind.

Chris reached out and put his hand on her shoulder.

'If you want to practise, you can always come round to ours…when it's finished, of course.'

'Thank you, that's kind.' Maddie smiled at him, making sure she removed all trace of irony from her voice. She liked Chris, a lot, he was a great doctor, kind, good with the children—he had a reputation for telling jokes that made them groan. He'd been drawn hook, line and sinker into the social-climbing middle-class world of keeping up with the Joneses but he wasn't a monster, was he? Perhaps there was a little room in the world for people to have money and be nice too?

'See you next week, guys,' said Chris, heading down the ward.

'Well done,' said Will, placing his hand in exactly the place on her shoulder Chris had and looking at her with overly exaggerated sincerity.

'For?'

'Not punching him.'

Maddie smiled. The ice had been broken and she found herself being grateful to Chris for inadvertently facilitating it. Maybe she could forgive him his yearning for a garden pool.

'Can we go somewhere a little less public?' Will asked. 'The office?'

'Sure.'

Maddie's stomach lurched. It wasn't rocket science to work out why she had a fear of rejection and why she avoided it at all costs usually. But if Will wanted to apologise for kissing her and tell her it wouldn't happen again, she'd just have to suck it up, wouldn't she? She couldn't keep avoiding him for ever. He clearly needed to get it off his chest and she'd have to let him. Maybe then, they could get back to being friends without either of them needing to be concerned that they'd be tempted into blurring the lines of friendship again.

The moment their lips had met, a thousand questions had erupted in her mind—how it had happened, why it had happened, how she'd not wanted it, how she wanted it to happen again.

No.

Will was a friend, a colleague. Things had been awkward enough between them after one kiss, how would they be after another? Or after anything more?

Maddie drew in a steadying breath as they walked down the corridor. He was right, they needed to clear the air between them and she'd try not to take it as a rejection. They were grown adults and a silly, spontaneous kiss in the park shouldn't make things awkward between them. They could talk about this rationally and move on.

He held open the door to their shared office and she slipped past him, awareness flashing through her as she brushed past him.

She dropped her rucksack onto her chair and leant herself against her desk, pretending not to notice the more than obvious tension. Will did the same and faced her, a few feet away, leaning against his own desk. He lifted his gaze, meeting her own, and her heart hammered.

'How's it going with Mathew?' she asked, her nerve fleeing the scene and her resolve that this could be a simple conversation deserting her completely.

'The mentoring is going really well but that's not what I wanted to talk to you about.'

Maddie swallowed.

'Oh.' Her gaze shifted to his lips. The same lips that had been pressed against her own…lips that began to move as he formed words that stilled her heart.

'I'm sorry, Maddie.'

And there it was—the rejection she wasn't going to think of as rejection. Her heart dropped like a stone to her stomach.

'The picnic,' he clarified, mistaking her silence for confusion, 'well, more the kiss. It shouldn't have happened. Can we blame the sunshine and the champagne and…move on?'

It was what she wanted too, but how could anyone ever move on after being kissed by Will Lawrence?

'It's often an unscrupulous combination, sunshine and champagne,' she managed, a small, slightly awkward laugh coming from somewhere inside her.

'It's just that we'd been getting along so well and it's been a little awkward between us since. Could we get back to being as we have been...friends?'

'Of course,' said Maddie, her heart still beating far more rapidly than it should but also shrinking at the same time. *He was sorry he'd kissed her.* She'd been ready for it so why was that such a body blow? 'It was just the champagne.'

'Combined with the sun,' added Will, still looking into her eyes, his face, for the first time since they'd met, wearing an expression she couldn't fathom. She was used to seeing his concern, his humour, his kindness, but the expression he wore now was one she hadn't seen him wear before and she couldn't place it. It was somewhere between sorrow and...

Her breathing deepened.

It was somewhere between sorrow and desire.

Will stood upright and took a step towards her. Something rippled through her, heightening her senses, her lips parted, tingling as they had right after he'd kissed them.

'I value our friendship too much to let a kiss come in the way of it, Maddie.'

She nodded, her eyes not leaving his. He wanted her friendship. This wasn't a complete rejection...not really.

'Me too.'

'And we've both said we don't want to get involved.'

'Yes.' *So why was every nerve ending in her body screaming at him to take her into his arms and kiss her again?* It didn't make sense.

'So, we agree it was a mistake that we mustn't repeat?'

'For the sake of our friendship.'

'And because neither of us wants any commitment.'

The thought that suddenly flew into her head was as shocking as it was revelatory. They were consenting adults. Neither of them wanted commitment. *But they did want each other.*

Was there a way to have both? To satisfy the need she had to touch and be touched…risk free?

No emotional involvement allowed but everything else was on the table…or the bed?

'A kiss doesn't necessarily have to lead to commitment… It doesn't have to have strings attached.' Her words hung in the air between them—they'd been said and she couldn't take them back. *Had someone turned the heating up?* Will's eyes had darkened and Maddie knew the rising heat was internal. The air between them had shifted, bringing her senses alive—it was a warning and a pull all at once.

What was she doing?

She was acknowledging what had been between them for a long time. She was blurring the line between friendship and something much more dangerous—a line they'd drawn to keep themselves safe.

Friends. Simple as that. It was clean, easy, innocent.

What she was contemplating now had nothing to do with innocence. The clean line she'd drawn was blurring fast.

But what if it were risk free? No chaos. No aftermath. No consequences neither of them wanted.

It was possible. They were both sensible, rational people. They could talk to each other—keep emotion out of it. It didn't have to be complicated. It was lust—pure and simple. There was nothing complicated about that, was there? Was she trying to convince herself?

She hadn't wanted a man for so long.

She'd never wanted a man so much.

Her own words had shocked her as they'd left her lips, but they made an uncomfortable sort of sense. She trusted Will. She'd never trusted anyone more. Will didn't want to risk getting involved any more than she did. They were on the same page—dangerously so. She lowered her gaze for a moment and saw him swallow, his Adam's apple sliding in his throat, but, strangely mesmerising as that was, she needed to look into his eyes again and lifted her own, meeting them, recognition crackling in the air between them, robbing her of what little air she had left in her lungs.

'Maybe not.' His voice was low, his words deliberate. His eyes didn't leave hers. 'I value our friendship—I wouldn't want to lose it. But I'm not sure I'd want to stop at just a kiss, Maddie.'

'I value it too. We wouldn't have to lose it if we didn't want to. A kiss, maybe more than a kiss, wouldn't mean we couldn't also be friends. We both know where the boundary lies.'

Her heart hammered against her ribs as he took another step towards her, his eyes darkening impossibly further, his breathing deepening, his lips parting.

'Are you sure?'

She was sure she wanted him.

'We're grown-ups—we know what we want and what we don't.'

'So, if we obey the simple rule of keeping any strings out of it, I can kiss you again?'

She smiled slowly, looking up at him from beneath her lashes and nodding. It took every shred of self-control she had as he closed the last inch of space between them and she placed her hand on his chest.

'But not here.'

He closed his eyes, taking a long breath in, placing his hand over hers, holding it for a moment before looking at her again and removing her hand gently.

'Then let's get out of here,' he growled.

CHAPTER ELEVEN

THE WALK TO Will's riverside apartment, through the grounds of the hospital, along familiar streets busy with evening revellers and past the boats sailing by, had been in silence. A companionable silence but with a fizz of expectation sparking in the warm air, as though a sorcerer had followed them from the potions shop, casting spells that had crackled between them with sparkles of colour as they'd tried to ignore them.

Will held open the door to the apartment and she slipped past him, sliding off her shoes, standing in the entrance hall, waiting to be invited to go further. Years of being regarded as a second-class citizen had taught her many things, one of which was immaculate manners. People who looked down on you never had any hesitation in reminding you of your place in society if they felt you'd stepped out of line—often at the tops of their voices and using very choice language. So, Maddie had learned how she was expected to behave and it involved having the below-stairs politeness of someone who knew where she was in the pecking order of life.

Will dropped his keys into a dish on the hall table with a clatter. The hall was narrow. He was so close she could feel his warmth, inhale his spicy, earthy scent. She could have moved an inch and touched him.

'Would you like—?' began Will, his voice still low, a richness to it that made her skin prickle.

'No,' she cut in, meeting his gaze.

'No?' The blue of his eyes had darkened almost to black.
'No coffee, thank you.'

He inhaled deeply, still an inch away, his gaze locked on hers.

'Or tea,' she continued, her heart racing.

'Not thirsty?'

She shook her head. But she *was* hungry.

He dipped his head, placed one hand on the wall behind her, closing half of the remaining inch of space between them so that the simple act of breathing out caused her breasts to brush against his torso each time she did so.

'Maybe this instead, then.'

She closed her eyes as his lips touched hers lightly, as though the finest silk had brushed them. He pulled his lips away, just slightly, still close enough that his breath whispered over them making them tingle, wanting more.

'Are you sure about this, Maddie?'

She nodded. Right now, there was nothing she wanted more and it had nothing to do with champagne or the heat of the summer sun and everything to do with the raven-haired man with desire in his deep blue eyes whose lean, athletic body and incredibly kissable lips were a whisper away from her own. Her finger found the belt of his trousers and she pulled, so that, for the first time, their bodies made contact fully as his lips found hers once more. This time the kiss wasn't the brush of fine silk but was the burning hunger of a man who wanted her.

He placed his other hand on the wall behind her, enclosing her within the warm, earthy confines of his arms as her own hands found his hips, drawing him in further as he crushed her body against the wall, tasting her, exploring her mouth, the long anticipation from the silent walk they'd had suddenly unchecked, transformed into the reality of physical contact—the promise it held now in front of her in the form of Will, his strong, lean body and the need they had of each other.

Will took his kisses to her throat, one hand sliding from the wall, reaching around her back to unzip her shift dress, which she shrugged from her shoulders, allowing it to fall to the floor. His fingers found the clasp of her bra and in an instant that was on the floor too and she groaned when he traced his fingers over the curve of her breast and his thumb over her taut nipple, sending exquisite pleasure shooting through her entire body as, in the same moment, she found the buttons of his shirt, undoing them one by one before pulling it from his shoulders, tugging it from his wrists and casting it aside, somewhere on the floor.

She opened her eyes, needing to see the torso she'd up until then only explored with her hands. Smooth, strong shoulders, the muscles of a man who worked out, a fine smattering of dark hair across a broad chest that led her eyes lower to a perfect six-pack and the black leather belt of his trousers. She drew in a breath as he whispered her name, taking the lobe of her ear lightly between his teeth. He'd said her name a hundred times before but never quite like this—a delicious shiver shuddered through her as she turned her head, elongating her neck, giving him more of her skin to tease with his lips and his tongue.

Tracing his fingers down her body, he stopped at her hips, taking a firm hold of them and lifting her as, instinctively, she wrapped her legs around his waist, snaking her arms around his neck as once more their lips met and Will kissed her as she'd never been kissed...as though she was the most desirable woman in the world and he was greedy for her. His words about being just friends had never been said and all her objections to ever wanting to be with another man had never existed. It was him and it was her.

And nothing had ever felt like this.

Probably nothing ever would again.

They were friends.

This was lust.

They didn't want commitment.

His kisses slowed, lightened. He tugged at her lower lip with his mouth as he pulled away with a groan, looking at her before closing his eyes.

What?

'What's wrong?' *Had he changed his mind?*

'Condom,' he growled.

She smiled, placing her fingers over her lips.

'Oops,' she replied, 'you don't keep any in the hallway?'

Will grinned.

'Oddly, no, but come with me, I'm sure I can find one.'

Maddie hung on firmly, teasing kisses down his neck as he walked to the bedroom, carrying her, then placed her in the middle of a huge bed before rummaging in a drawer and finding what he was looking for.

He stood at the end of the bed looking for all the world as though he'd strolled off the set of a Hollywood action movie—smooth-skinned, broad-shouldered, effortlessly smouldering...and as if he wanted her.

'Where were we?' His eyes locked on hers as his hand went to his belt, undoing it, pulling it so it snaked through the belt loops with a seductive swish of leather against fabric, dropping it to the floor. A delicious shiver shot down her spine and Maddie pushed herself an inch backwards, further into the plump pillows behind her, as Will placed one knee on the bed and then the other, prowling towards her with a slow, unhurried pace, his eyes locked onto hers as her heart hammered against her ribs and every cell in her body ached with anticipation and a need for him to close the space between them more quickly than he was doing. She could see now where the dark smattering of chest hair led down to, through the narrow dip of his abs, disappearing into his shorts and meeting what had most definitely been aroused within them.

A slow smile lifted the corners of his mouth as she met his gaze and as he reached her, he placed one leanly muscled thigh either side of her, dipping his head, kissing her with the lightest kiss, kissing her again, more firmly as her own lips pressed his, telling him the time for caution was over. She wanted him. He took the hint, deepening the kiss, claiming her mouth as she threaded her hands up through his hair, pulling him closer, and in that moment she knew that was what she'd wanted from the first moment they'd met.

But then, he pulled back.

'If you're not sure about this, Maddie, I can stop… It might kill me but I could.' His voice was low and heavy, as though he struggled to say the words.

She traced a finger from his lips, over his darkly stubbled chin, down his throat and his chest, following the darkened route through the centre of his abs, stopping only as she reached the top of his shorts, lifting her gaze. Never had she seen desire in a man's eyes as she saw in his now and, suddenly, she was empowered… It was a completely new feeling and intensely erotic. This wasn't rejection.

She remembered his question. *Was* she sure? As she never had been. She smiled.

'Don't you dare stop now.'

It was all he needed. His lips were on hers, claiming the breath from her lungs as she wrapped her legs around him, sliding down the bed to be underneath him, reaching for his shorts, pushing them down, freeing his hard arousal between her thighs as he kissed his way down her body sending delicious but achingly tantalising sensations sparking through her as she allowed her fingers to explore his skin and the dips and contours of his muscles as they flexed and contracted as he moved over her.

'You're so beautiful, Maddie.' His words whispered over the skin of her abdomen as he made his way down, his breath warm, her thighs parting almost of their own accord, allowing him to explore where no man had ever explored in quite the way he was doing now.

He was taking his time. There was no rush to get to where he wanted to be. It had never been like this. It was exquisite and every movement of his lips and his tongue on her skin intensified the pleasure, building layer upon layer of delicious sensation within her as she gripped the sheets, balling them in her fists, her breathing rapid, her heart pounding, her hips arching up towards him. Something had to give and as a soft cry left her lips in surprise and ecstasy, it did and she spun out of control and into the pulsing, breathless release of oblivion.

Making love with Maddie was everything and more than he'd imagined it would be and it occurred to Will that he *had* imagined it, more than once and, looking at her now, resting against the pillows, eyes closed, breasts rising and falling with each still heavy breath she took, he realised that if she'd changed her mind when he'd asked her if she was sure about this, he'd never have got over it. He'd wanted Maddie from the first moment he'd laid eyes on her and he'd been kidding himself that he only wanted her as a friend. That was clear now.

She opened her eyes, taking a moment to focus on him, almost confused for a second. And then she smiled. A slow, sexy as hell smile curved her lips and a deep pink afterglow flushed her cheeks. She raised her hand, beckoning him to her slowly, and searing heat surged through him as he lifted himself over her and she hooked her legs around the backs of his thighs, drawing him closer. He didn't want to rush this but the need to be inside her was almost overwhelming. He dipped his head, claiming her lips—a different sweetness.

'Every inch of you tastes divine.'

She took his lower lip in her teeth lightly, tugging it, letting it go, kissing him again, deeply, taking his breath, deepening his need of her. Her hands slid to his hips and she gripped him, pulling him in towards her, his hard desire nudging the wet heat between her thighs. She drew in a breath, tightening her grip, and the knowledge that she wanted him as much as he wanted her was more than any man needed. She was sure and that was all he needed to know as, slowly, he drove into her, filling her inch by inch as his eyes locked with hers and they darkened and shone all in the same moment.

He stilled himself. If he hadn't, it would all have been over in an instant, but Maddie began to move, her hips rocking upwards towards him, her hands roaming his back, his shoulders, cupping the back of his head, her fingers twisting through his hair, along his jawline, over his lips, setting his skin alight. He closed his eyes, surrendering to her intensely erotic need for him and his for her, driving into her, the rhythm picking up, the end hurtling towards him, intense, inexorable, unstoppable.

Her voice came from somewhere, soft, urgent, abandoned. 'Will.'

It was enough. The cresting wave broke and he crashed over, arching back, eyes screwed shut, savouring every sensation rolling through him until, heart thumping, breathing deeply, aware somehow that the world had changed for him, he shifted to lie beside her, their bodies still touching down the length of their arms, finding her fingers and holding them.

Night had fallen when Will opened his eyes. The blinds were still open and moonlight slanted in through them and onto their naked bodies. Maddie had shifted her position at some point and was now lying on her side, her face towards him, still holding his hand. She still slept, her breathing soft and slow. She stirred, curling her legs in towards her, but slept on. The night had crept in upon them. Time had moved on. But he willed it to halt. He didn't want this night to end.

How had this happened? How had someone as amazing as Maddie McArthur *wanted* him like that? And why now was he gripped by guilt?

Because she'd trusted him...and he didn't deserve it.

They were colleagues who'd become friends...close friends...working together so naturally, supporting each other both inside work and outside. The chemistry between them, although definitely present from the first moment of their meeting for him at least, had grown organically because they liked and trusted each other. And for the first time in his life, he knew for certain that their friendship and what had just happened between them had nothing to do with his wealth. Maddie had become his friend because she'd found something in *him* that she liked. They'd made love and she was lying beside him now because she'd wanted *him*.

Money hadn't played any part in it. There wasn't even the slightest chance that what had happened this evening had been motivated by money or the desire to climb the social ladder and look for an easy ride to getting rich. Maddie had become his friend for entirely genuine reasons. Something deep inside his chest seemed to expand. This was what had been missing from his life.

But it had happened because he'd lied. She had no clue about who he really was—of the wealthy lifestyle he'd taken for granted growing up or of the even greater wealth he'd accumulated with the creation of his own successful business. Everyone in his life up until then had known all that about him and those who hadn't always reacted in the same way— with widened eyes and often the flicker of greed.

But Maddie, who'd trusted him with deeply hidden, painful secrets from her own past, knew nothing about him. And the lie sat between them, calling to him, reminding him that the choice he'd made was to blame for the heavy guilt sitting like a stone in his chest.

He glanced over at her again. She was looking at him and he wanted to remember this moment for ever.

'Are we still friends?' Maddie bit her lip but the glimmer in her eyes belied the bashful gesture.

His stomach tightened. 'I hope so.' But he didn't deserve her friendship. She'd trusted him and he was still holding everything back.

He should tell her.

'Perhaps a little more than friends?' Her eyes glinted in the semi-darkness and her lips curved into a mischievous, sexy smile.

'Friends with benefits?' He lifted himself up onto one elbow, facing her, unable to resist smiling back. 'It could work.' *If he kept to the rules and kept emotion out of it.*

'Should we try it?' She looked up at him from under long lashes, biting her lip again. But he wasn't fooled. There was a seductive smile in her eyes that told him that self-conscious and shy were the last things she was feeling right now and when she traced a line down the centre of his chest with her finger, her pretend innocence evaporated and his blood heated, firing every cell in his body into readiness for what he knew she wanted…him…just as he was and no ulterior, greedy, selfish motive to spoil it or hurt him.

What would happen if he told her the truth? That he was one of the wealthy elite she so distrusted? That he could buy her whatever she wanted—take her anywhere in the world—introduce her to people she'd only ever seen on TV?

He took hold of her fingers as they roamed their way over his chest, bringing them to his lips, kissing them.

She'd be horrified.

So even though the truth was only a breath away, he stayed silent.

And the stone in his chest grew heavier, settling deeper.

'Yes,' he said, 'let's try it and see what happens.'

CHAPTER TWELVE

MADDIE WATCHED WILL checking his bedspace as they awaited the arrival of the two young patients Ambulance Control had called through. He was so careful, so thorough and the way he so clearly cared about every patient warmed her heart. Working with him had been easy from the very beginning—from the first morning he'd strode in, calm, confident, in control, carrying Noah in his arms. But there had been an additional dimension to their relationship lately and one that was impossible to ignore—an extra beat of her heart when she spotted him across the ward. A flicker of awareness when he came to her side when she needed backup. She'd caught herself looking out for him in corridors, on the stairs, in the staffroom. His presence warmed her in a way that went beyond professional respect.

It made her heart beat that much faster.

It suffused her with a feeling of well-being...and of desire.

There were voices just outside. Their patients were arriving. She glanced at Will, an understanding passing between them. She didn't need to ask if he was ready—just as she didn't need to ask if he looked at her and wanted her. It didn't need saying. She knew.

The doors to Resus swung open with a thud as the trolley that came through made contact with them.

The paramedic lifted the semi-conscious six-year-old onto the bed and Maddie immediately attached the carbon monoxide pulse oximeter probe to his small finger, glancing to the monitor for a reading while attaching a high-flow oxygen mask. Both children were suspected to have carbon monoxide poisoning. The second crew arrived and Will raised his hand, beckoning them to his bedspace. The young child was in safe hands. Will wasn't only technically competent, he cared too.

The two brothers were stabilised and it became apparent that the effects of the carbon monoxide gas were reversing as the levels of oxygen in their blood began to slowly rise, their levels of consciousness improving and observations normalising.

'HDU are ready whenever you're happy to transfer them,' said India, replacing the phone.

Maddie smiled at the senior nurse.

'Perfect. Connor here will be ready once I've got this blood gas result back. How are you doing, Will?'

'Jack is doing fine,' he replied, meeting her questioning gaze with a smile that stilled her heart. 'Coming round nicely. Ready to transfer.'

India and Jake made preparations for the double transfer, loading portable monitors and oxygen cylinders onto the beds, changing the monitoring lines over, reassuring their patients. Two porters arrived. Maddie checked the blood results, reassuring herself that they were good to go.

'Okay?' said Jake, ready to kick the brakes off the bed.

'All good,' said Maddie. 'See you later, Connor.'

The young patient gave her a weak smile. He wasn't out of the woods yet. Carbon monoxide poisoning could have long-reaching effects, the evidence of which wouldn't be apparent for up to a few weeks. But the initial crisis was over and as the doors to Resus closed behind the transfer team, Maddie sank down in a chair in the once more empty room.

'They were lucky,' said Will, still at his bedspace and tapping notes into the tablet he held. 'Any longer in that house and they wouldn't have made it.'

'Connor's carboxyhaemoglobin levels were off the scale,' replied Maddie, leaning back into the chair, retying her ponytail. 'I'm concerned about the possible seizure he had. He could have a longer-term neuro deficit.'

'There were dysrhythmias on Jack's ECG,' said Will, 'and his cardiac enzymes were elevated. We'll need to review both of them for a while even after discharge but at least they've made it this far.'

Maddie closed her eyes, leaning back in her chair, her hands on her head. The young brothers had been left home alone. They'd also have to report to social services what had happened.

They.

She and Will.

Colleagues.

Friends.

Lovers.

They. A word that had taken on a new meaning when she applied it now to herself and Will. *They* implied togetherness, attachment, connection. There had been no *they* in her life before—not like this. And yet now it seemed entirely natural to link herself to Will in that together, attached, connected way. And there *was* a connection between them. It was undeniable.

It was there in the way they worked so intuitively together and in the companionable way they spent time in each other's company, the fun and laughter they shared…and in the way their bodies moved together, instinctively, perfectly, exquisitely. Maddie's pulse quickened, heat flooding through her from her core outwards. The sex had been incredible. How he looked at her ignited every fibre of her being, how he touched her and pleasured her, sometimes with such tenderness and other times with a hunger so intense it took her breath away.

And his words. He told her she was beautiful. No one had

ever told her that…ever. Will had told her until she'd lost count. And she was beginning to believe he meant what he said. Beauty was in the eye of the beholder, she knew that, but Will was the most genuine person she'd ever met and, incredibly, she believed him.

'Finished.' His voice made her glance over at him across the room. He placed the tablet on the locker, meeting her gaze, looking at her as if he knew her, making her breath catch in her throat. He knew her more than any other person ever had. He looked around the room. 'Looks like we're alone.'

She glanced around, unable to suppress a slow smile. Will leant against the wall at the empty bedspace. She'd seen that expression before…many times now and it still had the power to send a bolt of desire surging through her.

'So we are.' No one in the hospital knew that their friendship had skyrocketed to the next level. They were friends at work but it was a whole different story when they got home.

'Come here.' His voice was low, almost a growl, and his eyes had darkened in that way they did when she knew he wanted her.

She bit her lip, lowering her chin, looking up at him from beneath her lashes, fully aware of what that did to him, teasing him, seeing his eyes darken further as her nerve endings came alive.

'You come here,' she countered.

He pushed off from the wall and prowled towards her, his eyes fixed on hers, stopping in front of her, one leg either side of hers, bending forwards to whisper in her ear.

'I want you.'

Maddie craned her neck, whispering back.

'I know.'

His breath was warm and light on her skin as he replied.

'I can't wait to get you home.'

Maddie lifted her chin and traced a finger slowly over his

lips, Will catching it with his teeth, sucking on it until she removed it, replacing it with her mouth on his. Yes, they had a connection and yes, it was based on them wanting each other sexually, but sex with Will was like nothing she'd ever experienced before. *Was this how it was supposed to be?* In normal, trusting relationships where two people...cared about each other? She'd never had sex with a man who cared. Was that what the difference was? Will was the most caring, thoughtful, genuine man she'd ever met. Did he care about *her*? Dared she even begin to hope that?

Will groaned, ending the kiss, pulling away, his face agonised.

'How am I going to get through to the end of the shift now?'

Maddie grinned, tapping him on the end of his nose.

'Revert to "just friends" mode.'

'That's easier said than done.' Will stood up straight, drew in a long breath and stretched as if he'd just woken up, letting his head fall back for a moment before straightening up again and shaking his limbs out. 'Okay, okay. I'm going to go back out there and find a whole lot of patients and remain very, very busy for the next...' he glanced at the clock on the wall '...seven hours.' He groaned again, rolling his eyes.

Maddie laughed.

'Perhaps we should keep out of each other's way.'

Will held out his hand towards her.

'Come on, up you get.'

She slipped her hand into his and he pulled her up out of her chair. They'd get through the next seven hours as colleagues and friends but after that they'd go to either of their homes and lose themselves in the other, secret, next-level world they'd agreed to inhabit outside the hospital. It wouldn't last, it couldn't, and she didn't want to risk another relationship anyway, did she?

Will gave her the slightest wink as they left Resus and went off in different directions. No, she didn't want a relationship. But she was having to remind herself of that more and more and one of the few lines from literature classes that she remembered came to mind... 'the lady doth protest too much, methinks'. Perhaps Shakespeare was right. She'd been protesting quite a lot recently and, really, she was kidding herself.

Friends with benefits wasn't meant to be like this.

Weren't arrangements like this meant to have rules?

Keep it casual. Communicate openly. No emotions. No complications.

Was this what she had with Will? What she still wanted?

Just asking herself the question felt dangerous—like opening Pandora's box.

But being around him, touching him, being held by him—the way he looked at her with those darkened, full-of-promise eyes—the way she trusted him and knew she was right to.

None of that felt casual, unemotional or uncomplicated.

She was falling in love with Will Lawrence and the realisation slammed her heart into her ribs. She hadn't seen it coming but it was definitely there and she didn't know whether to embrace the warm glow the thought had given her or to run.

Will glanced at the text-message preview on his phone and frowned.

Bit worried about Leo. He's been getting headaches every day for a week now. What do you reckon it could be?

His nephew, Leo, was seven and the oldest son of Jonathan and Portia. He sighed. Why did people think you could make a diagnosis with practically zero information?

'Dr Lawrence?'

He glanced up at one of the junior nurses.

'Could you take a look at a two-year-old in three, please?

She's very pyrexial and tachycardic. She's had flu symptoms and I'm concerned it could be sepsis.'

'Sure, let's go,' said Will. 'Well done for spotting that and letting me know.' He tapped into his phone as he walked to cubicle three.

No idea from that. I'll give you a call in a bit.

Two-year-old Sonia kept Will busy for the next hour or so, after which a further hour was taken up with Dev, an eight-month-old with croup, and Martha, a nine-year-old who'd been found to have a dangerously low white blood cell count.

'There's a black coffee for you in the staffroom,' said Jake. 'Go and drink it.'

Will smiled at the nurse. Jake wasn't to be argued with, especially when it came to him making sure everyone took a break.

'Thanks,' Will replied. 'Very well timed.'

Pushing open the door to the staffroom, he saw that his black coffee was the last one remaining on the tray of drinks Jake had made. Maddie must have already been in and had hers. He sank into one of the armchairs, lifted the mug and took a long drink. It had been nearly three hours since he'd last seen her. She'd taken herself off to Majors and he'd gone to Triage.

The 'let's avoid each other' scheme wasn't working though. He'd been busy but she'd still been in his head, in the background, silent, smiling, keeping him warm. Maddie McArthur was the best thing that had happened to him in a long time… or ever, come to that. She was intelligent, funny, thoughtful, beautiful and…a friend.

He closed his eyes and her face swam into view, her eyes shining, her hair falling forwards half hiding them as she looked into his own with that look she gave him that heated his blood, her lips full, soft, parting slightly as she looked at him. He swallowed. He couldn't remember now which of them had first suggested the idea of friends with benefits. It had seemed like a good idea at the time. They were two consenting adults who desired each other. Neither of them wanted a relationship. What could go wrong?

He'd lied.

And he thought about that a lot.

He'd made a conscious decision to hide a secret. He'd had plenty of opportunity to come clean. He'd thought about telling her. The words had formed in his head any number of times when they'd been close, when he remembered just what she'd shared with him, how she'd trusted him...without question. He closed his eyes, hating himself. Maddie had been let down by so many people in her life—she was the last person who should have trusted him. But she had.

There was a part of him that wanted to tell her the truth.

But there was a bigger part of him that reminded him that his honesty would only hurt her.

What he had with Maddie wasn't sustainable, was it? They'd agreed on this whole 'friends with benefits' thing. And one day, sooner or later, she'd meet someone else—someone she did want to be in a relationship with—and then what? There was no point in kidding himself she'd want him long term when she decided the time was right to settle down with someone. Not when she found out where he came from, his past, his wealth—that he belonged to the very section of society that had hurt, abused, stigmatised and lied to her all her life. But he was too far down the line to suddenly admit everything now—and if he did tell her now, it would only hurt her...and finish them.

And contemplating that was unbearable.

His phone vibrated in his pocket. He fished it out, accepting the call. It was his brother, Jonathan, and he could tell immediately that something was wrong.

CHAPTER THIRTEEN

Maddie studied the X-rays on the screen, enlarging a section to inspect it more closely.

'No fractures,' she announced to India, who was looking on. 'Could you apply a sling to keep the weight off the shoulder? I'll write up a prescription for analgesia and do a letter for the GP.'

'Great, thanks,' replied India, smiling. 'I'll go and give them the good news.'

'Maddie?' It was Will and he was worried. Was it a patient?

'What's up?' she asked, smiling, pretending not to notice how her heart had skipped at seeing him for the first time in hours.

But he didn't return her smile.

'I've had a call from my brother Jonathan. My nephew Leo is unwell. I'm going to have to go back home to see what's going on. I just wanted to let you know as we were…' he lowered his voice '…meant to be meeting up later.'

'Oh no, what's wrong?' Maddie had heard about Will's large family. She wasn't sure she could remember everyone's names but Leo she remembered because Will had actually delivered the little boy at home when his mum hadn't been able to make it into hospital in time.

'He's been having headaches recently, apparently, but this afternoon had a seizure at school. Jonathan and Portia are on their way to A & E so I'm going to meet them there.'

'I'll drive you.' He was clearly shaken. She couldn't let him drive all that way on his own.

'*What?* No, it's fine.' But he wasn't—he looked distracted.

'You're worried, Will. You shouldn't drive while your mind's somewhere else—it's not safe. And if it's a neuro problem, maybe I can help?'

'I need to go.' He was already turning away. 'I said I'd get there as soon as I could.'

She caught his arm gently, making him stop.

'I get that, but I really don't think you should drive all that way on your own like this. I can come with you…we can take turns.'

Will dragged a hand through his hair, his jaw tight, his eyes on hers, betraying a turmoil, an inner battle she didn't understand.

'You can't.'

And then it dawned on her. Her and Will's 'situation' was a secret and it would raise eyebrows in the department if they both left early together. Maybe he hadn't told his family about her—he probably hadn't—there was no need—it wasn't as though they were serious.

She lowered her voice. 'Chris will cover what's left of the shift. It's not busy anyway and we can say I'm going with you because you want a neuro opinion—same with your family, if they ask.'

Will looked at her in a way he'd never looked at her before. His jaw was set, lips pressed together, his eyes searching hers as if he was silently asking a question he didn't want answered. It unsettled her. He was hiding something, shutting her out, but it was tearing at him.

'You can't come.' His voice was tight, his eyes determined but imploring. 'I'll text you when I get there.'

And he was gone, leaving her staring after him, open-mouthed. What the hell had that been about?

***

The London skyline came into view, the river Thames snaking through the city, its famous bridges branching over it at intervals, the familiar buildings reaching skywards, some new, mirrored and gleaming, others made of ancient stone. The family helicopter swooped, its rotor blades thudding overhead. Will's brother, Felix, was piloting and Will sat beside him as co-pilot.

There were only minutes left until they reached the hospital, having been given permission to land on the hospital helipad, but although the journey from York had been short, it had given Will time to reflect on his words to Maddie. He should have come clean by now. Told her the truth. He came from huge wealth—he wasn't just a doctor, he was also a multimillionaire shareholder in the multinational tech firm his father had started; he owned his own medical tech company and had, in her words, more money than he could ever spend. Keeping his secret from her had been bound to catch up with him at some point.

And today it had.

Right then hadn't been the time to explain everything to her and he knew he'd left her confused and—he screwed his eyes closed—he hoped against hope that he hadn't hurt her, but her eyes had told him that he had. *Damn it.*

'Good afternoon, Tower, this is helicopter LA 417 three miles south and inbound for landing. Request clearance.' Felix spoke to Air Traffic Control. Will needed to concentrate. The controller granted clearance to land and Felix headed due south as Will ran through the checklist. 'Roger, on final approach. Standby.'

The landing was smooth and the two brothers parked and switched off before heading into the central London A & E, where they were met by Leo's anxious parents. Leo was in the scanner and it was all Will could do not to head straight in there to find out what was going on, but, as he was a relative, it wasn't the right thing to do.

He wished Maddie were there. Not just because of her neuro experience, but because she'd have known exactly the right things to say. And she would have calmed him, too. Just her presence, looking at her, feeling her close beside him with her serenity, her grace. Somehow, all those things about her that he admired, that warmed him, infused into him when he was with her. And what he'd come gradually to realise in the last few months was that when he wasn't with her, he missed all that. And right now, it was magnified a hundredfold.

'Mr and Mrs Lawrence?' Will looked up. Three people walked into the waiting room—a consultant, her registrar and a nursing sister. His heart sank. Two doctors and a senior nurse weren't ever needed to give good news.

Dinner that evening was an unusually sombre affair. Almost the whole family were gathered at Brockley and when that happened, the result was invariably good-natured and generally loud chaos. Tonight, though, three of their close-knit clan were missing. Felix and Will had flown home leaving Jonathan, Portia and little Leo at the hospital. It had been left to Will to explain to the rest of the family that Leo's scan had shown a large tumour towards the back of the brain and that the surgeon was going to perform an operation that he hoped would remove it. The tumour was low grade, which was good, but was very close to the brain stem, which meant that the operation itself was high risk. They'd been given information about the advantages and possible risks of the surgery or not having surgery and been asked to decide if they wanted to go ahead with the procedure or not. It was a devastating decision to be asked to make and Will's first thought had been to turn to Maddie.

When he'd called her, she'd sounded a little cautious at

first, but when he'd explained what the situation was with Leo, she'd become instantly professional, talking him through the options, citing research, enabling him to think straight.

Lying in bed later that night, in his childhood bedroom, he looked out across the garden towards The Park—the children's name for the part of the grounds they'd played in the most. It contained the tree house, the rope swing and The Den. They'd spent hours out there during the long hot summers of their childhoods when school holidays had seemed to go on for ever and none of them had known what it was to have a broken heart.

Those of them that had married had been married in the gardens at Brockley House, including himself. Scarlett had insisted on poring over the photos of his siblings' weddings to make sure that hers was bigger and better. That should have been a clue, but he hadn't seen it. The term 'gold-digger' could have been invented for Scarlett. Was there also a term for someone who tore your heart out and made you feel worthless too? His worth in her eyes had been his wealth. Who *he* was had had nothing to do with anything. Without his money, he was nothing to her.

He'd worked out early on in life that if he didn't do something to prevent it, he'd be defined by his wealth for the rest of his life. The decision not to have his identity bound to the prosperity of his family and to study medicine had been one of his better decisions—it had given him a purpose he might otherwise not have found; it had saved him when Scarlett had ripped him apart; it had led him to Maddie.

Maddie knew nothing of his wealth and still they'd become friends. More than friends.

How much more?

Sleep was evading him. Walking over to the window seat, he sat down looking out into the moonlit garden. An owl hooted but there was silence otherwise. *What was Maddie doing?* He glanced at his phone sitting in the charger on his bedside table. Was it too late to call her? Would she even answer? He closed his eyes against the picture of her looking at him, confused and hurt, earlier. She hadn't understood why he'd spoken to her so sharply and why he'd declined her kind offer of coming home with him to help.

How could she understand? He'd never told her the truth. He'd been dishonest—not maliciously but because his truth had left him with friends he no longer trusted, a wife who'd shown him that money was more important than love and a life filled with people drawn to his status and his wealth more than to who he was himself. He'd grown up feeling loved and secure and Scarlett had brought it all crashing down around him, destroying his faith in other people and his ability to trust in anyone.

Leaving had been the obvious answer. Taking a long solo trip around South America had cemented in his mind that starting afresh, where no one knew him, was what he wanted. Keep moving on. Don't get close to anyone.

But he'd got close to Maddie.

And he hated himself for thinking he might have hurt her today.

Silver moonlight filtered through the leaves of the old oak tree, leading his eyes upwards to look at the moon—the same moon that Maddie was under. Was she looking up at it too, right now? Had he ever wondered that about any other woman?

He had to tell her the truth.

But what if she hated the truth?

What if she ditched him into the same slush pile as everyone else—all those she'd learned not to trust? He wouldn't blame her after what she'd been through. His fists clenched as the story she'd told him about the landlord at university came back to him—how he'd offered her an 'alternative' to paying her rent in cash, giving her the option to pay in kind instead, assuming she'd had no choice. The thought of that sleaze ball made his blood boil…if only he could go back in time and put that bastard in his place.

Will leant back against the coolness of the wall looking out over The Park. Life had been simpler back then when they had used to run around without a care in the world. It had become a world to be wary of…until Maddie. Maddie had breathed joy, fun and happiness back into his life. He took a deep, slow breath in and sat up. Once Leo's surgery was done and he was stable, he'd go back to York, back to work and back to Maddie.

He owed her more than he'd given her.

She deserved the truth—unfiltered, possibly unforgivable. Even if she hated it and him, he couldn't lie to her any more.

He'd tell her everything—who he really was, the past he'd buried, the wealth he'd concealed, the fortune he'd hidden from her. It was a huge risk that could shatter everything—a wonderful working partnership, a rare friendship and the respect of the only woman who'd shown him the difference between making love and simply having sex. But he couldn't remain silent, because doing that meant he risked losing something greater—the chance to give Maddie the respect she deserved.

Telling the truth might cost him everything but it was the only way to give back what Maddie had given him—honesty, trust and respect.

CHAPTER FOURTEEN

THE PAEDIATRIC WARD was busy, which Maddie was pleased about. It gave her less time to think about Will. He'd been back for two days and, after checking in on him to ask about Leo, she'd mostly managed to avoid him. His leaving at short notice had meant that the staffing rota had needed to be changed and that had meant, conveniently for her, that their shifts had opposed each other's for a while.

'Dana Morgan, Hayley's mum, would like a word.' Sister Lou Beresford placed her hand on Maddie's arm lightly. 'She's in the family room with Will.'

'Oh,' said Maddie, 'but Hayley was Will's patient, why does her mum want to see me?'

'I'm not sure,' said Lou, 'but Will just came out and asked me to see if you were free to go in for a chat.'

'Okay, I just need a minute to finish this.'

The functional development report she'd been writing up was complete, but Maddie needed a moment to think. She couldn't keep avoiding Will for ever, could she? It was his birthday at the weekend and before he'd cast her aside, roundly rejecting her offer to drive him home, she'd already made plans for a great way to celebrate it—just as he had for hers with the French picnic. She couldn't cancel it now; it wouldn't be fair on Mathew and Ellie. The two students they'd been mentoring between them both had good news and she'd invited them to Will's birthday lunch to share it. But that had been before things between her and Will had changed.

She tapped the keyboard, keeping the screen on, staring at it earnestly as though concentrating. She'd innocently offered to go back home with him to help. There was nothing wrong with that—friends would do that for each other. But he, clearly, hadn't seen it like that and it had made him put the brakes on—hard.

And she knew why.

Because he'd realised she was beginning to feel something they'd both pledged not to.

And it had made him want to back off. He'd put distance between them, literally, because she'd got too close. She couldn't blame him, could she? He'd been straight with her from the start—he didn't want a relationship and he'd thought she didn't either. That had been why he'd been able to agree to their 'friends with benefits' arrangement. It was supposed to have been a no-strings-attached understanding between two adults. Except that he'd sensed she'd overstepped the mark. She had to pull it back. If she didn't, she'd lose their friendship altogether.

She logged herself out of the computer and made her way to the family room down the corridor just off the ward, knocking on the door, entering at Will's invitation. Her stomach tightened at the sight of him looking up as she went in, his gaze meeting hers.

'You remember Dana,' he said, 'Hayley's mum?'

She found a smile.

'I do. How are you?'

'I'm being discharged from the hospital today, Doctor,' she replied. 'They're transferring me to St Martin's psychiatric unit to carry on my treatment and I just wanted to say thank you. I can see things much more clearly now and I know how you both helped Hayley and myself. I've still got a long way to go with my treatment, but my specialist says that I've got a good chance of having a full recovery thanks to you two realising what was wrong with me so quickly. So, thank you.'

'That's great to hear,' said Maddie, sitting down in a chair beside her. But Dana Morgan stood up.

'I don't want to take up any more of your time, so I'll get back to the ward. They're going to transfer me this afternoon. I just wanted to say thank you and keep doing what you're doing—you're a great team.' And with that, she was gone, leaving Maddie staring after her.

'I should get going too,' she said, standing. But it was only a stride for Will to reach the door first. He stood in front of it, barring her exit, looking at her with eyes she didn't want to break contact with.

He tilted his head. 'Are we still friends?' They were simple words but her heart stopped at hearing them again. They'd last been said between them right after they'd first slept together, when they'd been lying side by side, naked, sated. But they also signalled that maybe he thought they were no longer friends...because he'd changed things by rejecting her because he feared she'd stepped over the boundary they'd agreed on. She swallowed. It was a rejection—one she would have avoided if she'd played by the rules. And it hurt.

It was her own fault.

Don't let him see he's hurt you. She'd learned very early on in life that letting people see they'd managed to hurt you gave them the upper hand. She'd learned how to swallow her pride, mask her anger, hide her wounds. She'd done it all her life. It was almost second nature and she could do it now. Except being hurt by Will was a much harder blow and the nonchalant tilt of her chin, and cool denials she'd honed as a skill over the years and usually been able to fire like arrows back at an adversary, were suddenly difficult to summon. But if she could show him she was keeping to their rules, she might be able to save their friendship.

* * *

Will hadn't exactly expected a warm welcome back after how they'd parted but he'd hoped that perhaps he'd read too much into Maddie's coolness towards him. Maybe she hadn't heard the edge in his tone when she'd offered to drive him back home as the helicopter had been waiting for him. Perhaps she hadn't taken him turning down her suggestion that she might be able to help with Leo as a snub.

Who was he kidding? Of course, she'd noticed and of course, she'd felt hurt. He'd seen it in her eyes then and he saw it now, even though she was doing a reasonable job of pretending otherwise.

'Why would we not be friends?' She was throwing him a challenge. *Because he'd panicked? Because he couldn't take her back home because she'd have realised the truth...that he'd lied...over and over?*

'I wondered if I'd been a bit sharp the other day. I'm sorry, I didn't mean to be.' But he was ducking the question.

'It's your birthday on Saturday,' she said, her voice light, as though suddenly everything were okay between them. 'Are you doing anything? I've planned a lunch.'

Was someone playing ping-pong in his head? She'd avoided him for the last two days and now she was talking birthday lunches. No, he wasn't doing anything…not this year for the first year ever. Usually, every year, without fail, his family got together for each of their birthdays and made a huge event out of them. This year, with Leo being so unwell, it hadn't seemed appropriate to mention it.

'Nothing planned—a lunch sounds great, thank you.' Maybe it would be an opportunity to talk.

'Great, I'll text you the details. I'd really better get going now. I've got a mentoring session this evening.'

Will stood aside as she reached for the door, brushing her

wrist against his hip, making him want to hold on to it and pull her towards him.

'Have a good rest of the shift,' she continued, slipping through the door.

She hadn't answered his question as to whether they were still friends but her birthday invitation seemed to signal that perhaps all was not lost. He closed his eyes, taking a long breath, feeling a little lighter. There was still a light frost in the air but there was a chance that it might thaw.

All he needed to do now was fulfil his promise to himself.

Do the right thing.

Tell her...everything.

CHAPTER FIFTEEN

'There's a lunch booking under the name of McArthur?' said Will to the waiter, arriving at the reception of the restaurant Maddie had texted him the details of.

'Ah, yes, sir, follow me, the others are already here.'

Others? Plural? He followed the waiter, seeing Maddie immediately. She was laughing, her head thrown back, blonde hair falling over her shoulders, her eyes shining. It seemed so long since he'd seen her laugh like that, so freely, so relaxed. She was so beautiful when she laughed in that completely carefree way. His chest tightened. Guilt. It was his fault she hadn't laughed in that way for a while. It had been his lies that had hurt her. His need to keep secrets about his real life, pretend he was someone else—just a regular doctor and not a multimillionaire with homes dotted around the globe and a yacht currently moored in Miami.

'Dr Will!' Dragging his gaze away from her, he saw who the *others* were. Ellie and Mathew.

'Happy birthday,' they chorused as he took the seat offered by the waiter.

'What a lovely surprise,' he replied, beaming at them. 'What are you doing here?'

'It's your birthday,' said Ellie, her face shining, 'and we've got news for you.'

'News? Come on, then, tell me, tell me.' He glanced at Maddie, who couldn't disguise her happiness, and his heart swelled with pride for her. She'd done this. She'd taken these kids under her wing and given them the opportunity the world and their circumstances would otherwise have denied them.

'I passed the med school entrance tests,' said Ellie, her hands clasped in front of her, her voice almost squeaking with delight.

'With flying colours,' chipped in Mathew, smiling at her.

Will leant over, opening his arms, hugging her.

'Well done, Ellie, that's fantastic.'

'I think it was the magic potion you gave me that did it.' She grinned. 'Matt has news too.'

Will looked at Mathew. They'd spent many hours together preparing his applications to medical schools, making sure he'd had some good clinical placements from which to gain experience he could discuss on his applications, learning how best to study and manage his new diagnosis of epilepsy and his mum's anxiety disorder. Will was proud of the young man. He'd had a lot to contend with but had handled everything with stoic good humour and hard work.

'Don't keep me in suspense, Mathew.'

Mathew grinned.

'I've got five offers.'

Will's mouth dropped. Five offers from universities were amazing. He held up his palm and Mathew high-fived him.

'Congratulations. You so deserve them.'

'I couldn't have done it without you,' said Mathew. 'Thank you for everything.'

'Yes,' joined in Ellie, 'thank you to both of you. You're a brilliant team.'

That was the second time in the last few days they'd been told what a good team they were and it was true, they were, and it was amazing to work with someone he could work with so well, so comfortably. How stupid that he'd risked losing that.

He had bridges to build but she'd invited him out for his birthday and she was smiling. He'd take the opportunity to begin telling her the truth this afternoon, break it all to her. Gently. Little by little—maybe over a period of time begin to introduce the idea that he owned a company. Yes, he'd explain that first. The medical tech company he'd founded did some amazing research and development—he'd hired the very best engineers to work on some of the most challenging medical issues: developing wearable devices to enable remote patient monitoring to detect patient deterioration and instigate early interventions; creating AI algorithms that could analyse genetic sequences to enable correction of genetic conditions before they could cause damage.

She'd get that. She'd appreciate it, see he was doing something good—not just buying supercars and penthouses. Maybe, that way, she'd be able to accept it, realise that he wasn't like every other low life with money that she'd ever met. But that was all dependent upon whether she'd forgive him, whether she'd listen.

'That was a lovely surprise, thank you,' said Will as they left the restaurant. Mathew and Ellie had left a few minutes earlier to continue their celebrations in town, leaving Maddie and himself behind in a slightly awkward silence. Maddie had got up from the table and paid the bill quickly and they now found themselves back outside in the sunshine opposite the park. The park in which they'd had their first kiss.

'I'd planned it a while ago,' replied Maddie, 'before…'

'Before I'd been a complete idiot,' he finished. Now was as good a time as any to begin the slow process of revealing who he really was. He wasn't ready to go hell for leather and come straight out with telling her why he'd not wanted her at his family home, but he had to begin somewhere. 'Do you fancy a walk in the park?'

Maddie looked at him. *What was she thinking?* That he *was* an idiot? That she wished she'd never got involved with him?

'Okay.'

Adrenaline rushed through him. She was giving him a chance and he wasn't such an idiot that he wasn't going to seize it and make damn sure he didn't mess it up.

They found a bench near to the bandstand in the area of the park where larger events were held. The staff were clearly preparing for a concert or some event that evening and were hurriedly erecting traffic cones around the perimeter of the field and directing anyone who approached to leave the area.

'I think Mathew and Ellie might have found a good friend in each other,' said Maddie, her sunglasses over her eyes.

'They've a lot in common,' he replied. Unlike him and Maddie, but also a lot like him and Maddie. 'They'll be a good support for each other.'

Maddie rested back on the bench, her hands folded loosely in her lap. He could see even through the sunglasses that she'd closed her eyes, enjoying the peacefulness of the park—the sounds of summer birds chirping, the distant sound of faint laughter, children playing. And cutting through the stillness, the low, unmistakeable thrum of a helicopter in the distance overhead.

Will's phone rang. He ignored it. It stopped but immediately rang again, making his heart rate pick up. *Leo?*

'You should get that; it might be about your nephew.'

His phone stopped ringing but there was a text from his brother, Felix.

If you're still in the park, come to the events field by the bandstand. I'm setting the heli down there. Couldn't let you be on your own on your birthday bro! Leo is doing well and we decided to have a party after all.

What?

He looked up into the sky, shielding his eyes, locating the black helicopter in the distance. When Felix had texted him ten minutes ago to say 'Happy Birthday' as he and Maddie had been walking, he'd told his brother he'd gone to get some fresh air in the local park. That was how Felix had known where he was.

The helicopter came closer and the noise from the rotor became louder. He could see the registration number of the aircraft on its side—LA 417. The traffic cones weren't for a concert—Felix had requested permission to land and it had clearly been granted.

'Well, that's the peace shattered,' said Maddie, sitting upright and looking skywards. 'It looks as though it's going to land.'

It was going to land. And he was expected to walk over to it and climb aboard. *How the hell was he going to explain this?* So much for breaking the news to Maddie gradually.

'It must be a celebrity,' said Maddie, needing now to raise her voice to be heard over the sound, watching as the heli hovered overhead as the branches of nearby trees began to sway heavily in the downdraft and a flurry of leaves blew from the canopy. 'No one else would visit a park in a helicopter.'

Except maybe Felix, come to take him to a huge, over-the-top birthday party at their Grade II listed Georgian mansion in their hundred-acre country estate...with a swimming pool that Ryan Johnson would have been green with envy to see. The helicopter touched down, flattening the grass in a circle around it.

Think, Lawrence. His phone pinged. It was a text from Felix.

Landed.

As if anyone in the vicinity didn't know that.

Maddie sat forwards, lifting her sunglasses, peering at the aircraft, clearly curious to see who got out. The door opened and a dark-haired man jumped down wearing dark jeans, a white shirt and aviator glasses looking for all the world like the multimillionaire he was—Felix Lawrence, joint shareholder and CEO of Lawrence Enterprises. Will's brother.

Maddie shouted something to Will but he couldn't hear. She was thoughtful for a moment and then signed... *Who is it?*

Will signed back... *My brother.*

He didn't need her to sign back her response. It was written on her face and was something to the effect of...*what the hell?*

Maddie's knowledge of sign language had improved since they'd had little Hayley on the ward, but he knew it wasn't extensive enough that she would be able to understand his signed reply to explain why his brother had appeared out of the sky and landed a ruddy great helicopter in front of them. Nor would she understand him signing that he'd kept a pretty huge secret from her and that the undeniably wealthy man currently striding towards them was as undeniably wealthy as he was himself.

The rotors of the heli still turned. Felix must have been co-pilot and one of his other siblings was still in the aircraft. Felix stopped in front of them, Maddie looking up at him, her lips parted in shock. She looked from Felix to Will. There was no denying that they were brothers. They had the same dark colouring and, as did all the Lawrence boys, the same blue eyes and dimple when they smiled. And Felix was smiling now. Smiling and beckoning to them...both of them.

Act. Do something.

But his mind was blank. And then Felix, as older brothers often did, took charge, grabbing his arm and hauling him to his reluctant feet, then bending to speak to Maddie, cupping his hand and speaking into her ear. She nodded in response.

He'd clearly invited her to the party...and she'd accepted. Will watched as Felix offered his hand to Maddie, who took it, smiling, and stood as Will's mind whirled with the implications of what this meant.

It was as though they were in slow motion as the three of them walked to the helicopter in a line, sunglasses in place, looking like a scene from a mafia movie. Alistair was piloting and gave a thumbs up as Will climbed in before helping Maddie then picking his earphones up from the seat and putting them on, indicating for Maddie to do the same. They were now all on shared radio comms, which meant that there was no way he could explain anything to Maddie that the others wouldn't hear. There was nothing he could do but wait for this to play out, but soon enough they'd be landing at Brockley House. His plan to break things to her slowly was about to spontaneously combust.

'This is Maddie,' said Will over the radio. 'She's a work colleague—one of the paediatricians.'

'Hi, Maddie,' said both brothers, each introducing themselves.

'Hi,' she replied.

Will reached over and pressed a button on her headset, nodding for her to speak again.

'Hi,' she repeated and Will released the button. Felix had yelled in her ear above the sound of the rotors to ask if she'd like to go to Will's birthday party at home. She'd almost declined—Will had made it clear he hadn't wanted her there. But it had occurred to her that it might be a good opportunity to show Will that she knew where the boundaries were—that she hadn't, as he feared, got a little too close. She'd show him and his family that they were simply friends. She could manage that—pretend...to save their friendship.

'Everyone's waiting for you at home, William,' said Felix,

over the radio. 'We didn't want you to be alone on your birthday.'

'Although it doesn't look as though you were going to be on your own, bro,' added Alistair. She could tell he was smiling despite the fact he was sitting in front of her.

She glanced at Will and he caught her look, staring at her, his blue eyes a haunting fusion of sorrow, fear and regret... that she was going to meet his family after all? That they'd think she and Will were an item? He'd tried to prevent it, but it had been taken out of his hands by circumstances beyond his control. No wonder he looked so full of trepidation. He'd introduced her to his brothers as a colleague and she'd make sure that was all she came across to them as. She'd keep it light—as though they were at work...just friends...just as he wanted it. She could do that. She could make this better—heal the rift between them. It would all be fine.

She looked out of the side window. It was a gorgeous summer's day with barely a cloud in the sky. The thrum of the helicopters rotors was much more peaceful with the earphones, almost lulling, and Maddie watched the anatomy of the landscape below as they swooped over the Pennine hills and the flatter lowlands in the east, over towns and forests, lakes and rivers.

'Landing in ten minutes, folks,' came the pilot's voice over the radio.

Which airport would they land in? Or was he going to set the aircraft down in a park near the house? Will's hand touched hers, almost making her jump. She glanced at him and he handed her a scribbled note.

Don't judge me.

What did that mean?

He pointed out of the window as they began to descend into what appeared to be parkland below. She looked back at him.

Home, he signed with his hands as a huge country mansion came into view.

She looked back out of the window. *Home? Whose home?*

'There's the welcoming party,' came Felix's voice over the radio as a stream of people came out of one of the doors to the house and began waving up at them. Maddie's heart banged against her ribs. This was *Will's* home? *What the hell?* It was a stately home; the sort parents took children to on bank holidays. And there was a huge outdoor swimming pool.

An icy hand clutched at her heart. Of course he'd not wanted her to go back home with him when Leo had been ill. It was obvious now exactly why he'd been so adamant she didn't go with him. It had nothing to do with him having sensed her getting too emotionally close to him.

She wasn't good enough to meet his family.

He was ashamed of her.

Same old, same old.

Hot, angry tears prickled at the backs of her eyes and she swallowed hard. How had she been so stupid? It was Andrew all over again—he'd only ever been interested in having a good time. In his eyes, that was all she'd been good for...all she was worth.

That was why she'd never been introduced to his family. It had been why the invitation to spend Christmas with them that year had never come and why he'd spent the summer at their house in France without her too. When she'd asked about meeting his family, he'd made excuses, but when she'd pushed it, he'd finally, cruelly, given her the truth.

She wasn't like them.

And when she'd pressed him to be more precise... Maddie closed her eyes against the memory but his words came thundering back as though he'd said them only yesterday...

'They probably wouldn't understand your accent for a start.' He'd laughed as he'd said that.

'You're not from the same world. They'd want to know about your background; your parents, what profession they were in, and what the hell would you tell them? That your mother was such a low life that she left you in a box on the steps of a hospital not caring whether you lived or died? That she probably didn't even know who your father was?' Andrew's words had been factually correct, of course, but he'd used the facts of her past as ammunition, firing them at her like bullets.

'They wouldn't know what to do with you, Maddie. It'd be awkward. You'd just be an embarrassment.'

The bullets had hit their target, ripping into her, tearing her to pieces. Will's rejection of her, his desperate need to keep her away from his family, hadn't been with cruel words but they'd had the same effect. She was good enough for a fun time—end of.

She'd thought that with Will it had been different. But she'd walked into another situation where someone didn't think she was good enough. Just as she'd never been good enough to be fully accepted anywhere—school, gym class, for sleepovers, at medical school. Being abandoned by your mother, not having a father, living your life in children's homes, having to work two jobs to get through university and being an easy target for anyone to take advantage of didn't exactly make for easy conversation around the dinner table with people who only ever heard about poverty on the news.

Will raised his hands, signing, *I'm sorry.*

But staring into those deep blue eyes, always so enticing and persuasive before, wasn't enough to quell the anger and hurt she felt right now.

The helicopter landed with a soft thud and the rotors began to slow.

'Welcome to Brockley House,' said Felix, pulling off his earphones and turning around to face her. 'I'm sure Will has given you the low-down on the place and all its many inhabitants but I'll warn you now, our mother will regale you with more tales than you could ever possibly hope or want to remember.' He smiled, ruefully, then broke into a grin before unlocking the door and jumping down.

'Don't worry if you can't remember everyone's names,' said Alistair, placing his headset onto the dashboard and turning round so she could see him properly for the first time. He smiled, the Lawrence dimple evidence that he was definitely one of the brothers. 'We can be a little overwhelming at first when we're all together, but you'll get used to us.' He turned to Will, slapping him on the knee. 'Come on, little brother, there's a party waiting.' He pushed open the door of the cockpit on the pilot's side and jumped to the ground, leaving Maddie and Will in the back seats.

If there had ever been a time when Maddie wished she could have flown a helicopter, it was now. But as it was, she was trapped in a situation she had no control over and from which she couldn't escape. And Will was entirely responsible for it.

Or was he?

Was it all her own fault for being stupid enough to believe his lies…to trust him…to have fallen in love with him?

'I'm sorry.' She knew he was looking at her as he spoke but she couldn't look at him. She didn't want his apology. She just wanted to leave this nightmare.

'You lied.' Her voice was a whisper. It was all she could manage.

The door to her left was opened and she turned to see another man, who was also definitely a Lawrence brother, standing with his hand outstretched towards her and smiling, warmly.

'Welcome, I'm Hamish. Good to meet you. Let me give you a hand—it's a bit of a jump.' Maddie took the proffered hand, her heart hammering in her chest, her mind whirling, introducing herself as one of Will's work colleagues, and was led away towards the pool area, which was decked out in balloons and festooned with fairy lights, and to meet the assembled crowd, where she shook hands and was introduced to everyone.

'Come with me,' said Abigail, the youngest and only girl of the Lawrence children. 'You'll want a freshen-up after the flight.' She smiled, leading Maddie inside into a beautifully decorated, high-ceilinged room of pale green and white with a huge stone fireplace, bookshelves, tall palms and a shiny black grand piano in one corner. And Maddie had thought Will's riverside apartment was luxurious. She followed Abigail into the corridor beyond, where paintings hung in gilt frames along the long length of it—landscapes and portraits, still life and abstract art.

'Here we are.' Abigail held open the door. 'Can you find your way back, do you think?'

'I think so,' replied Maddie.

'Well, I'm sure William will come looking for you if he thinks you've got lost.' His sister smiled. 'He's seemed very happy since he moved to York. We've all been pleased to see it.'

'He's settled in very well in the hospital. He's very well liked by everyone.' Maddie hoped her voice didn't sound as strangled as it felt. Will was more than liked, he was admired by many, adored by others and respected by all. But what about her? That was easy, she knew how she felt about Will Lawrence—she'd fallen in love with him. But that had been when she'd thought he was the kindest, most thoughtful and genuine man she'd ever met. Before he'd lied to her.

Actually, that wasn't true. As it turned out, he'd lied to her all along...from the moment they'd met.

'See you shortly for champagne and birthday cake.'

The door closed behind Abigail and Maddie was alone in a large luxuriously appointed cloakroom, which had a row of coat hooks, two cushioned chairs, a framed mirror that filled one wall completely and two toilet cubicles with porcelain sinks and gold taps. After the din from the helicopter, the room was eerily silent. She sank into one of the chairs opposite the mirrored wall and took a deep breath. She could leave. If she could find another way out of this place, she could make her way home somehow...find a station and get a train. Or she could stay and face him...tell him exactly what she thought about the deceitful, dishonest, devious way he'd got her into bed.

Her instinct was to run. He'd lied to her...for months. She'd shared so much with him—being abandoned as a baby, the shame and humiliation of everything she'd faced growing up, the years spent climbing out from underneath the weight of that stigma. She'd told him about the unscrupulous landlords, the people who'd looked down on her, underestimated her, deceived her. And now he was one of them. Another in a long list of people who'd decided she wasn't worth the truth, didn't deserve care or respect—another person who'd made her feel unworthy of being loved.

She couldn't stay here—not where she wasn't wanted...not where the inevitable questions would be humiliating, where she'd cringe at answering them or appear rude for being evasive.

She opened the door and stepped into the long corridor. To the left was the pool, the way back—the way she ought to go. She turned right—there'd be another door, several probably, that she could escape from. She'd walk until she'd left the grounds, call a taxi, go to a station and get a train home.

No one would miss her, least of all Will. He'd be only too pleased she'd gone—it would save him the embarrassment. Hot tears prickled behind her eyes and she blinked them away. She wasn't going to cry over Will Lawrence—he didn't deserve it. He didn't deserve anything from her. She knew she'd have to face him again but if there was any way to avoid it today, she'd do it.

Right now, she hated him. Hated his easy smile, his practised charm, the way he'd lied without even blinking. If she ever saw his face again, it would be too soon.

'Maddie!' It was Abigail's voice. Maddie closed her eyes, her heart sinking. Caught red-handed. 'You're going the wrong way—it's this way.'

She turned around, faking a smile while disappointment dragged its way through her. Will's younger sister caught up with her.

'I thought you might not find your way back so thought I'd come and check. I'm glad I did now—you'd have ended up in the kitchens.'

Great. The kitchens seemed a much better option than having to go back and face the man who'd spent the last few months being charming and contemptuous all in the same breath—as though she was something he could play with, have fun with, lie to. She'd trusted him with so much and she hated that she'd done that—hated him for allowing her. She'd have to see this party through but the second she could get away, she would and after that…hell, she didn't know.

They worked together.

But there were other hospitals—and one of them would have to go.

CHAPTER SIXTEEN

WILL GLANCED OVER in the direction of his mother. She'd been talking to Maddie for a good ten minutes on the other side of the pool and he'd barely seen her draw breath. Lord knew what she was telling Maddie—probably childhood stories about when he'd got into mischief, not realising Maddie was past caring about any of that. Maddie looked comfortable enough but he knew full well that she felt uncomfortable in situations like this. He needed to go and rescue her but her last words to him before getting out of the heli and being confronted non-stop by his family since then echoed in his head.

You lied.

And what he'd seen in her eyes killed him.

Horror.

Betrayal.

Hurt.

He hated himself. Why had he ever thought it a good idea to lie about who he was? He looked around the pool, sparkling in the sunlight, surrounded by his family. His childhood home stood huge and imposing as the backdrop to the birthday party they'd organised. This was who he was but he'd tried to deny it...deny those he loved.

Why?

Because the wealth had almost destroyed him.

'Attention, everyone.' It was Felix and everyone fell silent. 'I've got Portia and Leo on FaceTime and they want to say hi.' Felix held up a laptop and everyone moved towards him, standing in a huddle, waving and calling 'Hi', firing questions, talking over each other as they always did, laughing, taking the laptop to show Leo the cake and the balloons. How could he have wanted to deny that these people belonged to him? Hell, they *were* him. He should have told Maddie about them from the very beginning.

But his new life in York had been about anonymity, hiding who he was, finding out if he, Will Lawrence the person, was worth something without his family connections and wealth. Never really knowing if your friends were your friends because of you or just your money had always been a part of his life. His father, followed by his older brothers, had learned that and always told him to choose his friends carefully. But people could be devious, especially when ruled by greed, and it wasn't always easy to work out who was genuine and who wasn't.

Scarlett had been the devil in disguise, a wolf in sheep's clothing. He'd fallen for her lies, been duped by her flattery and supposed adoration when the only thing she'd really adored had been his wealth.

Maddie laughed at something. He glanced over at her. She was kneeling down on the grass playing giant 'four in a row' with Toby and Bella, two of Rory's children. She looked entirely comfortable, in her element, radiant. She wouldn't have chosen to be here in this environment—it was his fault she was. And yet, she fitted so easily—smiling the smile that tightened his stomach, warming a place in him he'd thought had long since been sealed off.

'Now there's a smile I've waited a long time to see again.' Will's mother nudged his arm, coming to stand next to him. He looked down at her, putting his arm around her shoulders, giving her a light squeeze. 'She's nice.'

'She is.'

'Not at all like Scarlett.'

He looked at her quizzically.

'She's not in the least bit impressed by all this,' she explained sagely, waving her hand dismissively towards the house, the grounds, the pool, 'but she adores the children. She has her priorities right, I'd say.'

Will looked back at Maddie, who was now standing and held two-year-old Bella on her hip, laughing as four-year-old Toby did a silly dance for them. His mother was right, as usual, and he knew for certain that Maddie wouldn't be in the least impressed by the size and grandeur of Brockley. In fact, she'd positively loathe it because as far as Maddie was concerned wealth equated to corruption, exploitation, inequality and unfairness.

'She does,' he replied.

'Exactly what you need, then.' His mother gave his arm a squeeze. 'I'd better go and check she doesn't need rescuing from the terrible twosome. We don't want to put her off ever coming here again.'

Everyone seemed to have assumed that he and Maddie were an item and looking at the scene in front of him right now, with almost the whole family gathered around, eating, drinking, laughing, chatting, he could glimpse a world where they really were. She looked as though she belonged here. If he pretended for a moment, he could walk up to her now, slip his arm around her waist and spend the rest of the day by her side—laughing, talking. She'd tilt her face to his with that knowing, longing look, full of promises. The kind of look that said 'I see you and I want you'. They'd be connected, secretly, in a way no one else would notice. But he'd feel it in every glance, every brush of her hand. And later, as the sun sank lower in the sky, he'd lead her up to their room…not as some sort of fun-only casual arrangement but as something real.

And the thought of that filled him with a sudden, aching warmth.

He didn't want to deny it any longer.

The whole 'we're both consenting adults with no strings attached' arrangement hadn't worked out in quite the way he'd intended, had it?

How had he not seen it sooner?

The emotions, forbidden in the terms of their agreement, had crept in, catching him off guard.

It hadn't been just about sex for a long time.

It had become much more. Something real. Something he could ignore no longer.

He was in love with her. And he didn't know what scared him more—realising that or knowing that he might have realised too late.

Idiot.

He watched her chatting easily to Imogen, his sister-in-law. Maddie laughed in that way he loved—when she threw back her head as though she didn't have a care in the world.

No one would guess it now to look at her, but she was mad as hell with him. His stupid lies had cost him a wonderful friendship. It was hell not being able to talk to her when all he wanted to do was apologise. Since Felix and Alistair had landed the heli in the park, there'd been no opportunity to explain. He needed to talk to her and he wasn't going to wait a moment longer.

Felix called to Imogen and she spoke a few words to Maddie before slipping away to join his brother. Now was his chance. But Maddie was walking away from the pool and heading around the side of the house. He lengthened his stride and caught up with her as she rounded the corner.

'Maddie.'

She continued walking, ignoring him.

'Maddie.'

She stopped, shielding her eyes from the sun as she looked up at him.

'Can we talk?'

She looked back at him, cool and unreadable—the laughter of a few moments before gone.

'Please, Maddie.'

'I'm not sure what there is to say.'

'I need to explain.'

Maddie sighed, lowering her eyes. He wanted to lift her chin gently, coaxing her eyes back to his, but, although touching her had become so natural, he knew that the simple gesture would be unwelcome.

'Maybe we *should* talk,' she replied, 'clear the air—we're still going to have to work together, after all.'

'Let's get away from the house,' he said. 'This way.'

He knew exactly where he was going. A quiet corner of the estate, away from the music and the voices, where they wouldn't be disturbed. He'd never taken another woman there—it contained only happy memories and was untainted, free from ghosts. It was somewhere he could try to sort out this unholy mess. She seemed only to be interested in trying to salvage their work relationship. Well, it was a start, but he wanted much more than that and if there was any chance that could happen, what he said in the next few minutes would either give him a shred of hope or extinguish it altogether.

'We used to play in this as kids,' said Will as they approached an old tree house that had been built into a huge Douglas fir tree.

'It's bigger than some people's houses.'

She was right. Maddie hadn't known what it was like to have a family or a home of any size. It was hard to imagine.

They climbed the wooden stairway that led the way to a veranda, encircling the house itself in the branches of the tree. The canopy provided a little dappled shade, the light breeze playing with the leaves making the sunlight flicker and dance. He signalled for her to take a seat in one of the two log chairs. He had been an idiot—made a terrible error of judgement—and now he needed to win back her trust because if he didn't, he'd regret it for the rest of his life.

'I'm sorry, Maddie.'

'Is that all you've got?' Her eyes were glacial. 'You *lied* to me.'

He closed his eyes momentarily.

'I know... I'm sorry.' But sorry didn't scratch the surface. Maddie deserved more—the full explanation about Scarlett's soul-destroying deceit and friends who weren't always friends for the right reasons. 'I should have told you—I wanted to—I was going to...but not quite in the way it turned out.'

She stood and went to the edge of the veranda, looking out over the fields.

'You should...months ago, but I understand completely why you didn't.'

His eyebrows drew closer.

'Do you?'

'It's the same reason every other man has ever lied to me.' She folded her arms, looking at him, her gaze steady and cool. 'And it worked.' She gave a small, cold laugh but there was no humour in her eyes. 'You got me into bed.'

The words slammed into him, ringing in his ears. His stupid decision to live a lie had confirmed to Maddie everything she'd ever believed to be true and cost him the best thing that had ever happened to him. What apology could begin to touch the damage he'd done?

Without thinking, he stood, drawn to her, somehow hoping that being near her might help him to make her understand—not that he was at all sure he deserved her understanding.

'Don't come any closer,' she warned, her voice quietly hard. 'I trusted you and you knew it, but you still lied. I told you things about me that I've never shared with anyone else because I thought we were friends.' Her eyes shimmered, not with tears but with fury held back by sheer will. 'Do you know why I've never shared them before?' Her voice fractured, just slightly, then hardened again. 'Because I don't hand over pieces of myself lightly. And you…you took them from me as if they meant nothing.'

He raked his hands through his hair, his chest tightening. This was unbearable—seeing her hurt, knowing it was because of him.

But he didn't flinch.

He deserved every word—everything she wanted to fire at him he would take.

Instinctively he reached for her, wanting only to comfort her as he'd done before, but she stiffened and he stilled. 'Clearly…' she swept her arm out towards the house '…you haven't the least idea what it feels like to be born with nothing; to grow up without parents, a home; to have a bag always packed ready to be moved on from place to place; to be bullied, laughed at; to wonder what was so wrong with you that your own mother didn't want you. And I'm glad about that, Will, I genuinely am because that shouldn't happen to anyone. But it did happen to me and even though, in my head, I know it wasn't my fault, somehow, for some reason, I still blame myself…and I'm ashamed.'

His heart ached for her. He wanted to draw her to him and hold her, love her until the pain of her past disappeared. He opened his mouth to speak but she silenced him, her palm towards him.

'I'd never shared any of that before,' she continued, her eyes shining with angry tears, 'because I learned a long time ago not to trust anyone. It became a habit I couldn't break. But then I met you.'

'I'm glad you shared it with me, Maddie...' icy blue eyes bored into his '...because it brought us closer.'

She swallowed, faltering.

'At the time, I was glad too,' she replied, more softly. 'It was a relief—as though I was lighter. And you didn't judge me. You just accepted it. It was empowering, freeing, validating. But now I realise you never shared anything back. In fact, you actively hid everything from me. I trusted you, Will. I thought we were friends.'

'We were...are. We're more than friends, Maddie.'

She shrugged.

'That was just sex. It was an arrangement we made. Friends with benefits, I think you said.'

Will closed his eyes. How much more could he regret everything—wish he'd done it differently?

'That may have been how it started, Maddie, but...' He drew in a breath. This was it—if he wanted any chance to put things right, he had to tear down every wall he'd built around himself, fight for her. And to do that he needed to open up—find the key to the padlock, unlock it, place his heart in her hands—risk everything. 'But it became much more than that...for me.'

Wary blue eyes searched his as though she was trying to work out if there was truth in his words. She had to see it. She'd become so much more than he could ever have imagined—much more than he'd ever intended or thought possible.

'I fell in love with you, Maddie.'

Her brow creased just enough to hint at confusion before she lifted her chin, survival instinct and practised defiance refusing to let her put her guard down.

'But still I wasn't good enough for you to take home to your family.'

It was as though she'd slapped him.

'What?'

'You were ashamed of me. I expect I'm a far cry from your ex-wife or any of the other women you've taken home to meet your family. I'm not classy, sophisticated or stylish; I don't have the right accent, or a private education, I didn't study Classics, art or literature; I certainly don't have parents to be proud of—I don't fit in and I get it. I just wish you'd had the decency to have been honest with me from the start. But I guess I don't deserve respect either.'

Will took a half-step back, as if her words were a hand that had shoved him hard in the chest.

Ashamed?

'No, no, that's not what it is. That's not who you are to me. I've never been ashamed of you—far from it, Maddie.' His voice cracked on her name as though it physically hurt him to have her look at him that way.

'Don't worry, Will.' Her voice was quiet, her eyes flicking away. 'It wouldn't be the first time a man's only been interested in me for a good time—I'm kind of getting used to it.'

He froze, recoiling from her words, wanting to know more and, at the same time, not sure he could bear it. *What had happened to her? Who had it been who'd hurt her? How could he?*

'That's not how it is, Maddie.'

Her eyes snapped back to his, searching them as though trying to strip his soul bare, to see if there was anything in him worth trusting. Was she deciding whether to believe him or bracing herself for the pain of being wrong again?

'I'm not that person…whoever he was.'

'Andrew,' she replied, her voice tight. 'He was wealthy—you know the sort, houses and apartments all over the world; expensive cars; speedboats…' She swallowed. 'A family I wasn't good enough to take home to.'

He looked at her, at the woman who'd made him smile

again, who'd made him understand what love really was, and his heart splintered. Her eyes were full of hurt, and defiance, and her bravery, standing there, holding herself together, killed him. He'd wanted to protect her and all he'd done was become another person she needed protecting *from*.

'You're the most amazing woman I've ever met. I'm not ashamed of *you*, Maddie, I'm ashamed of *me*.'

It was time to tell the truth…everything. She deserved nothing less and it might just save something from the train wreck hiding from his shame had caused.

CHAPTER SEVENTEEN

MADDIE KNEW SHE'D left him in no doubt as to how she felt. She had intended to—there was no point in not telling him the truth, was there? His lies had hurt but what had really broken her was the shame—his shame of her. It shouldn't matter—they were only friends, nothing more. But it did matter—it mattered because it took her back, to her harsh, unforgiving childhood, to all the times others had treated her in the same way. To a time before she'd realised that survival could lead to strength and that she could build a life on her own terms.

'I'm sorry, Maddie. I wish I could turn the clock back,' Will continued, his eyes on hers as though they were searching her soul, her heart skipping a beat despite herself, as it always did when he looked at her. 'But as I can't, all I can do is explain why I kept all this from you.'

She wanted to look away. But she couldn't. His eyes held her. They were so familiar now but she didn't know what lay behind them, did she? She didn't know him as she'd thought she had. She didn't know him at all.

'Let me guess.' Her voice was cold. 'Is it because you knew I'd grown up in poverty and been used by wealthy men and, surprise, surprise, therefore distrusted them? So, in order to stand a chance of sleeping together, you lied about your own wealth—hiding it in case it ruined your chances?' She lifted her chin. 'Deny it if you like, Will, but it'll come as no great shock that I'm very unlikely to believe a word you say.'

But she did want him to deny it. Because if she was right, and that was the truth, it hurt like hell.

Will ran his hand through his hair and across the back of his neck.

Deny it, Will.
Please.
I don't want to be right about this.

But there was no other explanation, was there?

'It's difficult to know how to say this to you,' Will began, 'because we both had such a different start in life and you've been through so much. It feels ridiculous to say this but it's the truth.'

He drew in a long breath as though steeling himself.

'I was very lucky to have been born into all this. I have two loving parents, a brood of amazing siblings and I've never wanted for anything. I know this is nothing in comparison to what you've been through, Maddie, but I've never really known who's been around me because of me. When you're wealthy, you don't really know who your real friends are. Are people there because they like you or because of what you can give them, do for them?'

'I suppose I can see that, yes,' said Maddie slowly. Did he have another explanation after all? One that didn't involve him being ashamed of her?

'So I wanted to see what would happen if no one knew the truth about me. I wanted to see what it would be like to know that the people who were my friends were friends because of me and not because of my money.'

'So I was part of an experiment? It seems a bit drastic to leave your job and move all the way up to York to live a secret life where no one knows the truth about you. Did friends let you down so badly that it led to such a charade?'

He was searching her eyes again, his gaze penetrating deep into her soul, to the questions lying deep within her. She needed answers. She needed to know if he'd lied to her because she meant nothing to him or if there was another explanation—one that didn't reduce her to someone who didn't matter.

'You weren't an experiment, Maddie. Yes, there were a few friends who just wanted access to the family for business and contacts, for preferential deals, jobs, that sort of thing. That I can deal with. It's disappointing but par for the course really.'

There was something else.

'You're still hiding something.'

Will nodded and she saw his Adam's apple slide in his throat.

'What is it? What was it that made you want to deny all this? Why did you come to York and want to keep secrets, live a lie?'

He had a loving family he was clearly close to—something she'd only been able to dream about, invent fairy tales about. There was a part of her—maybe the child inside who'd gone to sleep every night hoping she might wake up and find her mother wanted her after all—that couldn't help but envy all he'd had. There was something else—something deeper, something he wanted to hide.

He came to stand next to her, leaning against a wooden beam, opposite her—only a couple of feet away but miles apart. The air between them crackled with everything as yet unspoken. She allowed herself to meet his gaze, the intensity of his deep blue eyes, unwavering, holding her.

'Scarlett.'

'Your ex-wife?'

'She married me for my money.'

Maddie went cold.

'You *know* that?' she asked.

There was raw pain in his eyes.

'She told me herself.'

Something in her chest twisted and her anger wavered. Will carried on.

'She lied to me for years. She knew from the outset that I'd always wanted a family—*really* wanted one—so she said she did too but all along she had no intention of having one. She stayed on the pill but cried every month when she wasn't pregnant.' He gave a hollow laugh. 'They were crocodile tears. It turns out she didn't want to risk losing her figure. She loved the lifestyle, the houses, the holidays, the credit cards she didn't need to worry about paying off. But she never loved me. I know it sounds crazy to say it and I know I'm lucky and I'm absolutely not looking for pity, but having money isn't everything. There are more important things in life.'

He paused, dropping his gaze for a moment before lifting his eyes, once more finding her own.

'It's humiliating to admit—God, it kills me to say it out loud. But I want you to know the truth. I'm not ashamed of you, Maddie. I love you. And I wish I'd told you all this from the start.'

She took a slow breath as his words flowed over her, slowly sinking in. She wanted to take away some of his pain. Because, despite everything, she still cared.

'I'm so sorry, Will. I had no idea.'

There was shouting in the distance. Will glanced in the direction of the house. His brother Hamish was standing there, his hands cupping his mouth, shouting Will's name again followed by the words 'birthday cake'. Will raised his hand in acknowledgment and Hamish gave a thumbs up, turned and began to walk back.

'I have to go and cut the cake while everyone gives me a rousing but very out-of-tune rendition of "Happy Birthday". Will you come?'

She couldn't walk away now, could she? Not after he'd opened up like that. She still hated how he'd treated her but she wasn't heartless.

'Well, apparently, it's a lemon cake, so... I guess.' Maddie turned towards the staircase but Will caught her hand, holding it, making her turn back around to face him.

'Are we still friends?' His eyes searched hers—hope and regret fused together in their dark blue depths. She looked at him.

The truth lay bare now.

He wasn't ashamed of her. He'd lied to protect himself. She got that.

He'd said he loved her too.

A few hours ago, her heart would have soared. But not now. His truth might have saved their friendship—it was too soon to even begin to work that out. But it had killed anything more.

'I need to let all this sink in,' she replied, slipping her fingers from his. She held his gaze. 'Let's just…see what happens.'

Will closed his eyes. Just for a moment. When he opened them again, she knew that hadn't been what he'd wanted to hear. But it was all she could give right then. She turned, heading down the wooden stairs. Maybe, once she'd gathered her thoughts, made sense of everything he'd said, she'd be able to work out where they stood.

But not yet.

The only thing she did know was that even if they could remain friends, they'd never be anything more. Not knowing what she knew now.

Will lived in a world she'd loathed all her life, didn't trust and didn't feel comfortable in. He wasn't ashamed of her but she'd never be accepted in the circles he moved in. The friends-with-benefits thing had been amazing but falling in love with him had been a mistake. He lived in a world she could never play a part in. So now all she had to do was fall out of love with him and the quicker she did that, the better.

CHAPTER EIGHTEEN

'THAT'S THE VERY best drawing of me I've ever seen, thank you, Lily,' said Will to the four-year-old who sat on her father's hip, smiling shyly.

'You can put it on the wall,' said Lily, pointing to the wall of pictures drawn and painted by the patients on the paediatric ward, 'so you 'member me.'

'I will,' he replied, 'and I'll definitely remember you, thank you.'

'Thanks for everything, Dr Lawrence,' said Lily's father, shaking Will's hand. 'We'll remember you too.' He poked his daughter lightly on the tummy. 'Come on, let's get you back home.'

Will watched them leave the ward. Lily had been dangerously ill when she'd been admitted a few days ago. Her diagnosis had been made quickly, type one diabetes, and treatment had worked well. It was always difficult to give a long-term diagnosis to a family but Lily and her parents had taken everything on board, learned about carbs, insulin, injections and everything that went with it quickly and he was certain they would be fine.

What he was less certain of was his own fineness. It had been good to open up to Maddie at the tree house. He'd planned to tell her the truth…gradually, in his own time. But, thanks to his brothers and their sudden and dramatic arrival in the helicopter, the truth hadn't come out in a carefully controlled way but in a spectacular and devastating rush. He'd been so afraid of losing her by saying too much and yet he'd almost lost her by not saying it soon enough. But honesty hadn't proved to be the answer. It had softened the anger of betrayal that his lies had caused in Maddie and seemed to have allowed their friendship to survive, for now, but it had destroyed any hope that he'd had that their friendship had developed into something more.

He wasn't the man for her. They'd grown up in different worlds and although that didn't matter at all to him, he knew it did to Maddie. She'd learned to distrust people who had money and he'd just confirmed to her that she was right to. And even though he'd tried to explain his reasons for lying to her and even though she'd accepted and understood them, in her eyes he was just another wealthy man who'd lied to her. His far-too-late-in-the-day honesty had been forced out of him in time to perhaps save their friendship, but it had been way too late to hope now that he and Maddie could ever be any more than friends.

She distrusted wealth. She didn't feel comfortable in it. Even though she had a good job now with a decent salary, she still lived as though she wasn't sure where the next penny was coming from. Her house was small and sparsely furnished like her office at work; she preferred thrifty cafes to fancy restaurants and if she bought anything new to wear, it would only be for a special occasion and then it would come from a high-street shop.

They were worlds apart and she'd never want anything to do with his, as had been proven in the days since his birthday. Their work relationship had survived and perhaps they could be friends of a sort, but Maddie had put a distance between them, one that had made clear what she wanted to be—good colleagues; maybe friends…nothing more.

***

The view from the wall window in Will's apartment, which looked out over the river and the beautiful gothic cathedral in the distance, was truly stunning. It had sold the apartment to him all those months ago when he'd been looking for his sanctuary. What had completed it had been when Maddie had been there.

He missed her.

Seeing her at work nearly every day wasn't a substitute.

He wasn't even sure she wanted still to be friends.

But being her friend wasn't enough anyway.

He'd thought he'd known what emptiness felt like. When Scarlett had stalked out of his life after he'd confronted her, he'd thought she'd taken his heart with her, but this…life without Maddie in it as she had been was something else. There was a void in his chest, in his soul, a feeling that he'd experienced the best of life and never would again.

His fingers hovered over the 'Book flight' option on the screen on his laptop. Running away—his go-to when things got tough. Seeing Maddie every day was both a much-needed tonic and agonising at the same time. Not touching her, not taking her into his arms, not stealing a moment when no one else was around to drop a kiss onto her lips, was torture.

So near and yet, so far.

Finally telling her the truth had been liberating and had maybe saved their friendship from certain ruin but it had also meant that friends was the most they could ever be. And he wasn't at all sure that, now he'd had a taste of life with Maddie, he could ever be satisfied with being just good friends, even if she agreed they could be. Pushing the laptop off his knees so it slid onto the sofa, he stood and walked to the window, his palms on the frame.

If she felt they could be friends again, could he live with being nothing else to her? Could he smile, make small talk, sit beside her and never touch her? Could he watch her live a life that didn't include him?

He knew the answer.

He'd known it all along—maybe even before the Parisian picnic when the thought of her having babies with another man had made everything inside him come to a sudden, chilling stop.

So what was standing in their way?

His fist clenched into a ball and he banged it against the window frame.

Money!

Most people dreamt of wealth but what good had it done him? Costing him a marriage had been one thing—he never should have married Scarlett in the first place—but now he'd lost Maddie because of it. A hollow laugh came from somewhere deep in his throat.

Scarlett had wanted him for his money and Maddie didn't want him because of it. How ironic. And a thought struck him so suddenly and forcefully, it was as though he'd been felled with a punch he hadn't seen coming.

If money was the reason Maddie had walked away, why didn't he show her that it could do good? That it didn't have to corrupt, exploit or demean—that it could heal. His medical tech company wasn't just turning a healthy profit, it was saving lives, transforming lives. He hadn't even mentioned that to her. And what if he showed her what else wealth could do? For something close to her heart.

The mentoring scheme.

They could set it up as a charity, get other medical professionals to join them, mentor loads more kids and even give grants to support them with university and cost-of-living fees. Imagine it. Maddie had to love the idea…surely.

He needed her to see that money wasn't always a weapon,

used for evil means—it didn't have to represent power, greed or control. Not in the right hands.

It could be used for good. He was using it for good. He had to show her that wealth didn't have to divide them—it could connect them. It could be used for something real, something that mattered.

He wanted to give her back something the world she'd grown up in had taken from her—the belief that not everything powerful had to hurt.

CHAPTER NINETEEN

'I DON'T WANT to pry,' said Aisha, following Maddie into the coffee room.

'But?' said Maddie with a wry smile as she filled the kettle.

'But,' her friend continued, 'it's been a week now since Dr Gorgeous whisked you away in his helicopter, declared himself to be a zillionaire and introduced you to his family and bizarrely you haven't been the same since. And I don't mean in a good way.'

'Decaff?' asked Maddie, spooning a heap into her own mug.

'Don't change the subject. Yes, please.'

Maddie added milk and boiled water, giving both drinks a stir before handing one to Aisha, who uncrossed her folded arms but didn't soften her questioning stare.

'Most people round here would have thought their birthdays and Christmas had been rolled into one for the next hundred years to have that gigantic revelation. So why have you been as quiet as a library ever since?'

Maddie sipped at her coffee, eyeing her friend over the top of her mug.

'Come on, Maddie. What's the craic?'

Maddie sighed. Aisha was right. Since the party and finding out that Will—she could still barely believe it, even now—was a multimillionaire who owned a huge medical tech company, she and Will had agreed that they were still friends but things had changed so much between them that they were friends in name only. They still saw each other at work and still worked well together, nothing had changed there, but, other than that, their relationship was unrecognisable. The connection had gone. Those moments of recognition, of subconscious shared thoughts, the closeness. She missed that. Not having that part of him had left a void within her she couldn't begin to work out how to fill.

'We're still friends. Nothing's changed.'

Aisha snorted.

'Catch yerself on, Maddie. You two were never just friends. Do you think I'm a complete eejit?'

Maddie straightened up indignantly.

'What do you mean?'

'For a start you look at each other as though the rest of the world doesn't exist. Secondly, since he started working here, you've had a rosy glow to your cheeks that I don't think I've seen on you before and, thirdly, since the helicopter episode, you're both walking around as though you've lost a gold coin. What can be so bad about a drop-dead gorgeous multi-millionaire falling in love with you and taking you back to the family mansion to introduce you to his family?'

Maddie stared at her friend.

'Don't look all innocent,' Aisha continued, pursing her lips. 'He looks at you as though he wants to devour and protect you all at the same time.'

Maddie placed her mug on the table. She knew that look he had. She missed it. She'd have to get used to missing it.

'He's way out of my league.'

Aisha's pager beeped and she glanced down at it with a grimace.

'Got to go, I'm afraid, but I'll say this first—you need to cop on, Maddie McArthur. Dr Gorgeous could have the pick of the crop in this hospital, and they don't even know about the helicopter, the country estate and the millions in the bank, but I'm telling you, that bang-on man only has eyes for you.'

Aisha closed the coffee room door behind her softly, leaving Maddie alone. Things had changed dramatically between her and Will since the discovery of his wealth—the time they spent together, the warmth, the laughter, the stolen glances. Her heart rate responded to the recollection of the kisses they'd seized in empty storerooms, the evenings and mornings they'd fallen asleep and awoken together, the whole days in bed. He'd been there in other ways too, hadn't he? When she'd received her letter from the bone marrow registry, when she'd found herself pouring out the story of her past to him. He'd been there, he'd listened, he'd understood... and she'd fallen in love with him.

With *him*.

And then it struck her.

His wealth hadn't come into it in any way, shape or form.

She'd fallen in love with the man. She'd known nothing of his wealth. And now she *did* know, what had changed?

He was the same thoughtful, kind, empathic, compassionate man she'd lost her heart to in the first place...the same man who'd looked her in the eye and told her he loved her.

So why couldn't they have a future together?

Because he lived in a world she knew nothing of. A world of privilege—a world she had no way of knowing how to fake her way through. How could they have a future if she couldn't be a part of that? She'd be an outsider, like a shadow trailing behind, living in constant fear of being found out, laughed at, rejected.

They loved each other. That was achingly true. But it didn't silence the voice in her head that kept telling her she didn't belong in his world.

He lived in it so effortlessly, would have done all his life. But she'd always watched that kind of life from a distance, knowing it wasn't meant for her. And he'd held his heart out to her as though none of that mattered. But how could it not?

It wasn't her love for him or his for her that she doubted. She doubted herself.

She had to get back to the ward. Will had been on the early shift and would have left by now. Part of her welcomed that.

Another part would miss him.

Straightening her ponytail, she swiped her security card and was met by Sister Lou who, on seeing her, fished in her pocket and handed her a white envelope.

'Will asked me to give you this,' she said. 'You need to read it right away, apparently.' She shrugged her shoulders and headed off down the ward.

Maddie stared at the envelope, turning it over. There was one word written on it in his neat, cursive handwriting...

Maddie

She glanced around, half expecting to see him, but the ward was quiet, most of the children were asleep and the staff were busy settling the others down or already settling down themselves with admin. She sat down at the nurses' station, slipping her finger under the fold of the envelope, pulling out the sheet of what looked like handmade writing paper.

I'm sorry. I never meant to hurt you.

I was an idiot.

Go to the drawer at the nurses' station—second one down.

Maddie opened the drawer where she was sitting. There was another envelope the same as the first, again with her name written on it. She pulled it out, opened it and unfolded the paper inside.

You're the best friend I've ever had.

Go to the cupboard in the clinical room where the gauze is kept.

Maddie followed the instruction, opening the cupboard. A smile began to curve her lips as she saw the third envelope, pulled it open and read the note.

Life without you just isn't the same.

Go to the scrubs cupboard.

The scrubs cupboard—where she'd first looked at him properly and wondered what lay beneath the white shirt and tailored trousers. She began to make her way to it, her pace quickening with each step. Where was this all leading? When had Will done all this? She opened the door to the cupboard, the light coming on automatically, her heart thudding in her chest. She found the envelope, ripping it open, her eyes scanning the note.

I miss you.

The next note is in our office—you'll see it.

Maddie swallowed. She missed him too. And she hadn't stopped loving him.
And he was still the same man.
He wasn't Andrew.
Not everyone with money was cruel. Not everyone who flaunted it was empty. Her long-held prejudice had clouded her judgement.
The problem was neither his lies nor his wealth.

The problem was her.

She'd lived all her life being told she wasn't good enough for people like him, for the very world he came from—so far from her own. Told she was an embarrassment, that she'd never amount to anything. She'd believed it—digested every word. Why wouldn't she? It was all she'd ever known—she'd had nothing else to measure the words by back then. But things had changed. She'd changed. She wasn't that scared little girl any more. The world she'd been brought up in hadn't broken her—it had revealed strength.

Opening the door to their office, she turned on the light. Their desks were as they always were. His covered in papers, family photos, coloured Post-it notes with reminders on them—hers, empty save for the envelope she'd been directed to find. She sat down in her chair, opened the note and read the words.

You are good enough, Maddie.

If you want the last note, come to me. I'm outside under the oak tree waiting.

You are good enough.

She read the words again. Did she believe them? She drew in a breath, lifting her chin.

She'd defied the odds.

Not just survived, but achieved something worthwhile, meaningful; she was making a positive difference to young people's lives—showing them the way when she'd walked her own paths in darkness.

Was it time to lay the ghosts of her past to rest?

She hoped that what had happened to her never happened to anyone else, but her past had shaped her into the woman she'd become—given her the strength, determination and defiance to overcome and succeed. And despite the words and voices that still echoed in her head, she knew she could finally hold her head high, look in the mirror and say:

I'm good enough.

Because she was. She always had been. And it was time to start living like it.

She looked at all the notes on the desk.

Should she go to the oak tree?

She'd never been able to resist him, had she? Even though they were from completely different worlds, there'd always been that irresistible pull between them. From the very beginning, it had been drawing them inexorably together, aligning them on a path that had led to here, to now.

The decision was hers.

Remain firmly rooted in the past where safety lay—where she couldn't be hurt and rejected, where the voices of ghosts spoke more loudly than the voices around her now, louder than Will's voice.

Or go to the oak tree.

To Will—who'd been so badly hurt; who was sorry; who wasn't ashamed of her; who loved her…for who she was, despite knowing the truth.

She folded each handwritten note and placed them into her drawer, turned off the light, opened the door and made her way to the garden.

She'd never been able to resist his pull.

The garden was in darkness save for the tiny lanterns glowing softly, strung from the branches of the trees. A tall, dark well-built figure stood as she approached.

'I wasn't sure you'd come.'

'I couldn't resist.'

'I mean every word, Maddie.'

'You mentioned a final note.'

He smiled.

'I was hoping that would entice you.'

'Oh, it did.' She returned his smile as he handed her an envelope. She slipped her finger under its seal, pulling out the note.

For richer, for poorer,

I love you Maddie McArthur

She looked up at him from under her lashes, knowing what that had always done to him, watching as his eyes darkened and that slow smile curved his lips.

'Being your friend was the best thing that ever happened to me, Maddie,' he whispered. 'Thinking I'd lost your friendship was the worst. I always want to be your friend but I want much more. I want the chance to make you happy, be there for you, love you.'

He reached for her, grazing his finger along her jawline, tucking the escaped lock of hair back behind her ear in that way he did that made her breath catch. It was such a small but now familiar gesture, one that was quietly tender and loaded with deep affection. It wasn't a grand declaration with a fanfare or fireworks—just a look, a touch, the quiet understanding between two people who cared deeply…who'd been through so much and found each other.

Friends.

Lovers.

Soulmates.

She lifted onto her toes and found his lips, kissing them lightly.

'I'd like to be more than friends too,' she whispered. 'Much more.' She smiled at him—the most handsome man on the planet and the kindest, most thoughtful one too. One who loved her as she deserved to be loved…for richer or poorer.

EPILOGUE

Looking out of the window of the sleek black limousine that had brought them into the centre of Paris from the airport, Maddie gazed in wonder as the famous sights each came into view—the towering Arc de Triomphe, the long, straight length of the Champs-Élysées to Place de la Concorde, stopping on Place Vendôme outside the Ritz Paris.

Will gave her hand a squeeze, drawing her gaze from the timeless elegance of the legendary hotel and into his eyes.

'Are you sure about this, Maddie? You can change your mind, you know. I can fly us back home if you prefer.'

Maddie smiled. Will's suggestion that they spend the first anniversary of their meeting having lunch in Paris showed just how far they'd come in the last twelve months. A year ago, the idea had represented a world so different from her own—a world where people with money could walk right over people without, a world where those with wealth could hurt and abuse those who had nothing with impunity. But her world view had been shaped by a past that hadn't been balanced. Growing up in care and in poverty had skewed her way of thinking about people who had wealth. Meeting Will had changed all that.

'I think I'll be okay,' she assured him with a smile. 'Anyway, I bought a new dress—I have to get some use out of it now.'

Will laughed.

'My little thrift fiend.'

'Agreeing to lunch at the Ritz Paris isn't thrifty,' she replied.

'It's a special occasion. Come on, let's go in.'

An immaculately uniformed doorman opened her door.

'Bonjour, madame.'

'Bonjour,' she replied, taking Will's arm, her heart rate beginning to climb in time-honoured fashion in circumstances such as this. Not that she'd ever been near such a hotel before, but places like it had always filled her with feelings of inadequacy. Will gave her arm a squeeze and placed his hand in the small of her back as he led her through the white porticoed doorway, into the blue-and-gold-carpeted lobby. He looked so handsome in his dark blue suit, crisp white shirt and the silk tie she'd bought him as a gift for their 'meetiversary'. He was greeted by name by the concierge, who spoke in French explaining that the room was ready and lunch would be served when Will requested it.

As she walked through the elegant lobby and down through the main gallery foyer with Will's hand on her back, Maddie's nerves abated. Will had shown her that she was good enough to belong in a place like this, that her past was part of who she was but was behind her. His unflinching support when she'd been deciding on whether to make contact with her stem cell recipient had allowed her to make the right decision. Meeting her half-sister and subsequently her birth mother had been daunting but uplifting. Her childhood fairy tales about her arrival into the world hadn't turned out to be entirely correct, but her mother hadn't given her up of her own volition. Her mother had been only fifteen when she'd given birth to Maddie and it had been Maddie's grandmother who'd taken it upon herself to take baby Maddie in the middle of the night and leave her on the steps of the hospital. Maddie's own mother had been so young and unable to do anything when she'd discovered what her mother had done. They had decided to remain in touch and were slowly building a relationship between them.

'Is this table okay?' said Will.

Maddie looked around the large terrace.

'It's the only table.'

Will pulled out a chair and she sat down.

'I wanted an intimate lunch,' he replied, sitting down opposite her, 'as it's a special day.'

'Monsieur Lawrence booked the entire terrace,' explained the concierge. 'I hope you enjoy. *Bon appétit.*'

Maddie stared at the concierge as he left and then at Will, narrowing her eyes.

'It's one thing booking a table at the Ritz Paris, but the whole restaurant?'

'Allow me this indulgence for our special day. Champagne?' Will lifted the bottle from the silver bucket, the ice chinking as he did so.

'What sort is it?' Maddie tilted her chin, her eyebrow arching imperiously, but even though she tried pressing her lips together, she was unable to prevent a smile curving her lips. 'I'm not having any of the cheap stuff.'

'The best they have, which means the very best there is… We've much to celebrate today.'

'Then how can I refuse?' Maddie pushed her champagne flute towards him. They did have much to celebrate. It was hard to believe that it had been a whole year since the day Will had walked onto the paediatric A & E with a desperately ill child in his arms. Little had she known then that the man she'd thought had been the child's father would turn out to be the man she'd fall in love with…the man who would show her that she could lower her defences, that she didn't need to hide who she was and where she'd come from…that she was good enough…good enough even to drink the best champagne in one of the world's most exclusive hotels and only feel a little bit like an impostor.

'I was hoping you wouldn't. A toast.' He lifted his glass, Maddie following suit. 'To a year of us and many more to come.'

Maddie chinked her glass against his, repeating his words, taking a sip and setting her glass down again. Many more years to come sounded blissful.

'Another toast,' said Will, his flute still held in front of him. Maddie looked surprised. 'To the MentorMed foundation, which as from today is officially registered at Companies House.'

Maddie's jaw dropped.

'Already?'

Will nodded, looking like the cat that got the cream. 'We're all official.'

'I didn't think that would go through for weeks yet.'

Will had insisted on putting some of his money into creating a foundation that would support young people from disadvantaged backgrounds who wanted to study medicine. He and Maddie would be joint chief executives. Maddie had assured him that he really didn't need to give his money away so that she'd be with him, but he'd said that once the idea had occurred to him, he wanted to do it anyway because he believed in it.

'Sometimes it helps to know the right people and as long as you use that advantage for good, I think it's legitimate.' Will grinned as they chinked glasses and Maddie sat back in her chair.

'That's amazing,' she said, beaming. 'A double celebration.'

Will set his glass down on the white-clothed table and met her gaze, his eyes holding hers in that curious, searching, suddenly a little more serious way he had sometimes.

'Actually, I was hoping for a triple celebration.'

Maddie blinked. What else did they have to celebrate today? None of their students were sitting entrance exams or waiting for university offers to come in. Was there something with a patient?

'The last twelve months have been the happiest of my life, Maddie,' he began, his eyes softening. 'I never imagined that coming to York would lead me to finding the love of my life…but I did.'

Maddie watched him as he got to his feet, her heart beginning to thud harder in her chest. *A triple celebration?*

'You've changed everything.' He got down on one knee and Maddie felt tears prickling behind her eyes. 'You're not just the woman I love—you're my best friend, my safe place, my greatest adventure. I love your kindness, your strength, your playfulness, your generosity…and your beautiful vulnerability. With you I can truly be myself. You've seen me, completely, and loved me anyway. You loved me for who I am and I love you for exactly who you are. With you I've found something real—something true. And my truth now is simple…'

He slipped his hand into his jacket pocket, pulling out a small black velvet box, opening it to reveal the most exquisite solitaire diamond ring. 'I want you for ever. Maddie, will you marry me?'

Maddie's hand went to her mouth. Time seemed to have slowed right down. How had this happened…to her… Maddie, the foundling, the girl who'd never been good enough now the woman who was loved by the most amazing, genuine, wonderful man she'd ever met? He was right—they'd fallen in love with each other for exactly who each of them was. Did she want to spend the rest of her life with this man?

'Yes.' There was no question she did.

His eyes, serious and earnest as he'd said the words that

would change their lives, misted and sparkled all at once as he blinked back his own tears and smiled as he lifted the ring from its cushion, took her hand and slipped it onto her finger.

'I love you, Maddie McArthur.'

'I love you too.' But the words barely had chance to leave her lips as he stood, pulling her up, drawing her into his arms and sealing the moment with a breathtaking kiss.

'Will you forgive me for all this?' said Will, still holding her and glancing around the elegant, opulent terrace of the Ritz.

'The private jet, luxury limousine, private dining at one of the world's most famous and exclusive hotels…lunch in Paris?' Her eyes held a challenge, her brow arched, but she couldn't disguise a smile.

'It was in a good cause.' He attempted a sheepish look but his eyes were full of mischief.

'It's almost exactly as I'd daydreamed it would be,' she replied.

'Almost?'

'Almost—because I could never have daydreamed that I'd be with someone quite as wonderful as you.'

And Maddie knew she was right. Her daydreams might have taken her to Paris before, but never with a man that she loved and trusted with all her heart and never with one who she knew for certain loved her just as much.

* * * * *

If you enjoyed this story, check out these other great reads from Colette Cooper

Wedding Fling to Forever
Nurse's Twin Baby Surprise
Both available now!

BUMP IN THEIR ITALIAN FLING

KATE MacGUIRE

MILLS & BOON

In memory of my dad, who forever
defended my right to read whatever I wanted.

CHAPTER ONE

ELEVATOR DOORS SLID open with a soft ping to reveal an upscale lobby with thick, cream-colored carpet and paneled walls that gleamed under soft lighting from stylish wall sconces.

Miranda easily found the lounge across from the hotel's elevator. Its glass doors were open, beckoning her inside. As she entered, the dim, warm lighting made her feel as though she was being welcomed into a cozy cocoon, far away from the disaster of her day.

Miranda slid onto a bar stool, tucking her clasp purse beside her on the bar. Its polished marble stretched the length of the room and gleamed under the glow of glass shelves stocked with top-tier spirits. A bartender in a crisp white shirt and black vest nodded to acknowledge her while drying glasses with a soft white towel.

He approached with a warm, professional smile. "Good evening, ma'am. Welcome to the Regent Lounge. What's your pleasure?"

The subtle elegance of the lounge was working its magic. Miranda relaxed for the first time that day and realized how famished she was. She had planned on having dinner on her overnight flight to Milan, but mechanical problems had stranded her in New York City. By the time she'd navigated the long reservation line to book a next-day flight, realized her luggage had mistakenly been dispatched to a different flight and finally waved down a cranky taxi driver, room service had long since closed, leaving her famished and exhausted.

Miranda sighed. "White wine, please. Whatever you recommend."

"Of course," he replied, suggesting an expensive option.

"That sounds good," she said, even though she had no idea if it actually was. Her wine knowledge was limited to whatever was available at Mulligan's, the hole-in-the-wall Irish pub where she and her colleagues often went to unwind after long shifts at Harborview Children's Hospital in Boston where Miranda worked as a pediatric neurosurgeon.

This lounge was worlds away from that noisy, crowded pub. Here, the conversation hummed softly, occasionally punctuating the hushed atmosphere, so that it felt like a library. She asked the bartender if the kitchen was still open, trying not to sound desperate despite her growing hunger.

"Yes, ma'am," he said. "Would you like to see a menu?"

"That would be lovely," she replied.

As she perused the late-night bites menu, her phone buzzed. Opening her texting app, her eyes landed on a message she had been ignoring all day. It was from her ex-husband—the subject line read, Surprise! followed by We're having a… before the rest of the message was cut off.

Her ex-husband's audacity left her speechless. The ink on their divorce agreement was barely dry, and he had already relegated her to group text status. And for something like this…

She wished she felt angry. The kind of white-hot, all-encompassing rage that would shield her from his cruelty, but she didn't. Knowing he was celebrating the impending birth of a baby he'd conceived with his scrub nurse slash mistress while Miranda had been undergoing two years of IVF treatments…well, it just cut her to the very bone.

She scrolled past it and opened a new text from her sister, Scarlett.

How's New York?

Miranda typed a quick reply. No clue. Just grabbing a bite downstairs in the hotel lounge before bed.

Her sister's response made Miranda chuckle. Woo-hoo, you go Party Girl! Just try to get home before dawn, 'k?

If only you were here to see my sexy nightwear.

Let me guess. Pink flannel with skiing kittens?

You know me so well.

Scarlett sent a gif of an adorable toddler smacking her head. Oy vey!

If you had the day I've just had, you'd be diving into flannel jammies too.

Scarlett sent a question emoji. Miranda hesitated before deciding to spill the news.

I got a text from Bradford. It's the gender reveal for their baby.

The silence from her sister was both out of character

and palatable. Miranda could just imagine the string of expletives her sister was likely hurling at her kitchen walls.

Well, screw him, her sister eventually replied. Who needs him? Though I can't believe he'd be so cruel as to include you in a group text.

Same.

Miranda aimed to sound casual, as if it didn't affect her. But the truth was it hurt so much, she could hardly breathe.

The bartender returned with her wine and a late-night appetizer of spiced chicken lettuce cups that smelled divine. She dug in, ignoring her phone for the moment, savoring the food as it eased the tension in her body.

She was about to devour the last lettuce cup when she finally looked up and noticed him—a man sitting across the bar. How had she missed him earlier? Dark hair, soft waves and glossy brown eyes that locked on to hers with an intensity that made her freeze mid-bite.

He wore a white shirt, unbuttoned at the collar, with his tie loosened. A whiskey tumbler sat near his hand, half-filled with deep amber liquor. His rolled-up sleeves revealed strong forearms, nut-brown skin and broad hands. Miranda had a bit of a hand fetish, and his were particularly striking—strong, confident and sure.

He didn't break eye contact. Miranda swallowed her bite, feeling a flush creep into her cheeks. She managed a half smile before quickly looking away, pretending to focus on her phone.

Her sister had texted again. Where'd you go?

Dinner, she typed back. She took a photo of her meal for good measure. Because she knew Scarlett would ask.

Looks delicious.

Her fingers hovered over the keyboard. She shouldn't tell her sister about the man. It would be like sprinkling catnip on a kitten's favorite toy.

But she couldn't help it. There's a guy across the bar staring at me.

Creepy stare or I-want-to-devour-you-babydoll stare?

Miranda risked another glance. The babydoll one.

Picture! Now!

No. That's rude and intrusive.

You gotta describe him at least! Spare no detail!

Reluctantly, Miranda did. Mid-to-late 30s, maybe 40. Dark, intense eyes. Big bold watch. She hesitated, then let her fingers fly. His jawline could cut glass.

Oh, my gosh, he sounds delicious. Go talk to him! her sister urged.

Miranda glanced up again. He was now scrolling through his phone, casually eating his meal. As if sensing her attention, he looked up and smiled—an utterly disarming, drop-dead, get-over-here-little-sister smile.

Her eyes darted back to her plate, her heart pounding. I don't think that is a good idea.

Miranda Hawthorne, you buy him a drink. Operation Revenge Affair starts now!

That was what Scarlett had dubbed Miranda's trip to Milan. After the messy divorce, Scarlett just wanted Miranda to find the sexiest Italian hottie in all of Milan and have herself a wild fling. She'd even promised to make sure that Bradford saw any scandalous pictures on social media.

But the very thought of it made Miranda's stomach flip. While Scarlett was fueled by caffeine and bouts of righteous rage, Miranda was the quiet, sensitive sister. Not even Scarlett knew how much Bradford had hurt her.

All she wanted from Milan was a chance to escape the looks of pity from the nurses. The relentless hospital gossip. And the anxiety of never knowing when she would turn a corner and see Bradford headed her way.

She wished she could leave Boston, but that wasn't an option. At least not while her mother was doing so well in her memory-care home. All she could do was hope that if Bradford was as brilliant an interventional radiologist as he loved to boast, one day he might get an offer to work somewhere else. Preferably five thousand miles away.

For now, she and Bradford were professional colleagues, along with his new wife, who used to be Miranda's scrub nurse and friend. Soon, their new baby would arrive, all circling about in Miranda's orbit. The future looked so bleak, it made Miranda feel sick sometimes. How could she possibly grieve the loss of her marriage and her hope of having a family when she had to see the person who had hurt her most in the world almost every damn day?

So no, she didn't need a *revenge affair* or *eye candy* or any of the other revenge fantasies her sister so desperately wished for her. She needed a real escape. A place where she could lick her wounds and heal from the hurt and humiliation of the past two years.

And it was time to make a serious life pivot. Maybe it just

wasn't in the cards for her to have a family of her own. But hundreds of children came to Harborview every year to see her. These were her children now. They deserved her best.

Still, she couldn't resist stealing another glance in the stranger's direction.

This time, his smile was even more mischievous. Like he knew exactly what she was thinking.

The shiver of excitement she felt at realizing this man had set his sights on her was undeniable. Terrifying, too, to be honest. What would she even say? Flirting, sexy banter—not her comfort zone at all.

Her fingers flew across her phone's screen. No thanks. Operation Go to Bed with a Good Book is more my speed.

Scarlett's response was swift. At least you got the first part right... But Scarlett didn't argue back. Miranda heaved a grateful sigh. She loved her sister, but Scarlett could be awfully pushy sometimes.

Somewhere behind the bar, Miranda heard a phone ringing. The bartender answered, glanced in her direction, said something, then laughed. He hung up the phone, filled a tumbler with ice cubes and bourbon and walked it over to the man across the bar. She caught their exchange out of the corner of her eye. When she saw the bartender nudge his chin in her direction, a warning bell made her belly cramp.

The man accepted the drink, then tipped the glass her way and mouthed *thank you*.

Her heart sank. She grabbed her phone. What did you do?

Scarlett sent a string of laughing emojis. Someone had to get this show started.

"Damn it," Miranda whispered. How embarrassing—the hot guy now thought she was hitting on him. The best thing she could do now was pay her bill and get out of there before she humiliated herself any more.

Miranda signaled for the check, then glanced across the bar. Mercifully, the man's seat was empty. Relief surged through her body. Good—he probably didn't want any part of this nonsense, either.

Still, she felt a tinge of disappointment. It had been fun playing flirty eye games with him across the bar.

She slid off her stool and turned to go when she practically ran smack into a solid wall of athletic chest. Partially revealed by an unbuttoned crisp white shirt and loosened tie.

"Thanks for the drink," the man said, indicating the tumbler in his hand. His voice was soft black velvet, haunting steel guitar and deep Shiatsu massage. And drizzled with a melodic, lilting Mediterranean accent.

Have mercy.

"You're welcome," she managed.

He gestured to the seat beside her. "May I?"

Every cell in her body urged her to make her excuses and leave, but her mutinous mouth just had to get involved. "Of course."

Of course, she said. Like she was no stranger to talking to drop-dead male model look-alikes with Mediterranean accents. *What the hell am I doing here?*

Her exasperation must have shown because he asked, "Is everything all right?"

Oh, gosh, she needed to *chill out*, as her nieces sometimes said. She was too nervous and distracted. What would Scarlett do if she were here? She'd be gorgeous, flirty and fun.

"Absolutely!" she said, trying to sound gorgeous, flirty and fun. But the dramatic hand wave she threw in for good effect nearly knocked her wineglass right off the bar.

"Oh, damn," she muttered, lunging for the glass and saving it just before it tipped off the bar.

That was the last straw. It all caught up with her at once. Her missed flight, her impossible situation at home and her sister's meddling hit her like a wrecking ball, and then she was blurting the truth to a total stranger.

She laughed softly. "No. Not really."

Then she was hit with such a strong yearning to be anywhere else than here. No, that wasn't true. She very much wanted to be leaving Boston. Maybe she just wanted to be someone else. Someone who wouldn't knock her drink off the bar and who knew what to do with this insanely hot man who was studying her with furrowed brows.

Who was she kidding? Her sister had teed her up for the perfect flirty exchange and she was making an absolute mess of it. She gave up and just said the next thing that crossed her mind.

"Have you ever wished you could be someone else, just for a night? Like, live someone else's life for a change?"

Because that was what she really wanted, at least for a night. Not to be the clueless wife of a philander. Not to dedicate years of her life and body to a dream that could never be hers. Not to be the fool who believed the lies her ex had doled out like candy.

To her surprise, he didn't laugh. Instead, he cocked his head, interested. "A made-up life or the turn not taken?"

Confused, she shook her head. "The turn not taken?"

"Oh, how do you Americans say? You reach a spoon in the road and you must choose which way to go?"

A smile warmed her face for the first time that day. "You mean a fork in the road?"

Now he was the one who looked confused. "Why would someone leave a fork in the road?"

"Or a spoon, for that matter?"

His laugh was so charming, so deliciously masculine. Their strange conversation, the frustrating day and this gorgeous man were all melding into a potent brew that left her no option but to laugh, too.

But that spontaneous laugh was impossibly followed by a sob that came too fast for her to choke back. The pain of the past and the frustration of the present blended with this gorgeous man and his tempting accent and that big nautical watch that showed off his thick wrists—her second fetish—and…oh, cripes, it was all so much.

Life was just too damn much sometimes.

She stared down at her drink, willing herself to get it together. She hoped he hadn't noticed her tearfulness or if he had, would think it was just from mirth.

She cleared her throat. "I know what you meant to say. The phrase is actually 'a fork in the road,' and it refers to a point where the path splits in two. It would make more sense to say a Y in the road."

She gestured with her hands, one veering right and the other left. "But I think you mean the road not taken. As in, if you choose the path that veers left, you may spend your life wondering about the road that went right."

He studied her with a piercing, perceptive gaze. "An unwinnable battle," he mused. "No matter which path you choose."

"True."

Something shifted in his gaze. "Well, in that case," he said, the lilting syllables rolling after each other like pearls, "yes, I have wished to live a different life. Many times."

Something in his tone made her slow down. She stopped trying to remember the details of this flirty, late-night chat so she could entertain her sister later.

His cryptic reply drew her in, sparking a deep curiosity

she couldn't ignore. It wasn't just that he was gorgeous—it was the way he seemed to peer right into her and see all the roads she had not taken.

Dante gazed down at her face and recognized it, too—some spark of connection between them. An understanding that seemed born of pain not easily forgotten. Or forgiven.

He slid into the chair next to her as she moved her purse aside. He indicated her empty wineglass. "May I?"

She nodded and Dante signaled the bartender.

"So," Dante said, "who *would* you like to be for the night?"

The beautiful woman looked confused until she remembered their earlier conversation. She laughed softly. "You're not serious."

"But I am!" Dante protested. "Look at us, a couple of strangers sharing a brief moment in time before the universe whisks us off to destinations unknown." He glanced at his watch. "The lounge closes in fifty minutes. So, why not be exactly who we want to be—just for an hour?"

She hesitated, her eyes searching his face. "Oh, why not?" She rubbed her chin thoughtfully before speaking. "All right. My name is Amelia Earhart, and I'm a world-class pilot."

"Amelia," Dante said, offering his hand. "Very pleased to meet you."

Her hand slid into his, soft and warm, and it stirred something protective in him, as if he were cradling a fragile bird.

He reluctantly released her when she pulled away. "And what brings you to New York City, Amelia?" he asked.

She smiled, glancing down at her empty plate. "Oh, just a layover. I'm on my way to the Bermuda Triangle, don't you know?"

"Make sure you have enough fuel this time," he teased.

She laughed. "I will definitely do that. What about you, Mr...?"

Dante paused, considering his options. Who would he like to be for just one night? Anyone whose last name wasn't "Ricci" would be a good start.

"Paul," he answered as he glanced around the bar for some hint of his alter ego's employment. His gaze landed on a stack of napkins near the bartender. "I'm a napkin salesman."

She arched her brow, pretending to be impressed.

"Don't mock." He waggled his finger. "Napkins are a staple good, in demand no matter how the economy is doing."

"Can't argue that." She sipped her wine, her glass glistening with condensation from the chilled Riesling. "So, what brings you to New York City, Paul? Or is New York home for you?"

He didn't want to mention Milan, or even Italy. Not now when he was miles from home and gazing into the eyes of a beautiful woman, beyond the reach of all that haunted him there.

"Actually," Dante admitted after a pause, "I am here for a friend's wedding."

"Ah, a New York wedding in the fall. That will be beautiful."

"Indeed. But then, aren't all weddings beautiful?" Dante drained the last of his drink and set the tumbler on the bar. Ice clinked softly against the glass.

"I tried to talk him out of it."

"Out of what?"

"The wedding. Getting married. All of it."

"Really?" Her expression was one of genuine surprise. "Is that for real?"

He wagged his finger again. "Remember, for one hour, we get to be and say whatever we want."

"That's true," she said, grinning. "All right, I'll play. Why did you want to talk your friend out of getting married?"

"Because it's destined to fail."

"Really? You're sure about that?" She was trying to stay playful, but he didn't miss the fleeting shadow that darkened her eyes.

Oh, yes, he was sure. He'd seen firsthand how families could look so happy on the outside but be miserable behind closed doors. The Ricci family had never truly accepted or loved him, but that didn't stop them from insisting he fit into their public image of a perfect family.

He had no choice but to comply whenever the paparazzi were around. His mother had died in a terrible car accident, which forced Vittorio Ricci, the patriarch of Milan's most influential medical dynasty, to adopt him, the illegitimate son of one of Vittorio's many mistresses.

Without the Riccis, he'd be out on the street. So he played his role well. Stood between his half brothers, flashed a brilliant smile and looked happy. The cameras always rewarded him with a flurry of clicks.

But inside, he was screaming. *Can't you see the truth? Can you see how unhappy this family is? Everyone here hates each other!*

"Oh, yes," Dante replied, his voice unwavering. "Quite sure."

"I don't know," she said, her tone thoughtful. "My parents celebrated their fiftieth wedding anniversary just a few months before my father died."

"Yes, but did they hate each other?"

Her shocked reaction told him that whatever she said next would be real, not part of the game.

"Not at all! Everyone said they were like newlyweds."

Dante leaned back with a sigh. "That's nice for them. Rare, though. I don't know—it just doesn't work out, in my opinion. It can't. People change too much. What they want when they're twenty is different from what they want at forty, and it's completely different at sixty. It's unrealistic to make commitments that span decades."

His thoughts drifted to his father. When Dante was young, his father had a simple explanation for his frequent affairs: People change. They just don't want the same things from one year to the next, and that was why he had lied and deceived and tore his family apart, taking his mother's sensitive heart with him.

Amelia tilted her head. "What did your friend say?"

Dante spun his now-empty whiskey tumbler between his palms. "Well, as luck would have it, my friend is a marriage therapist. He told me pretty much what you'd expect a marriage therapist to say."

"Which was?" she asked, leaning into his space.

"He said most people will have two, maybe three significant relationships in their lives. If they're lucky, all will be with the same person."

Amelia looked down at her plate with a small, knowing smile. "Yeah, I think that's true."

"Was that your parents' secret?" Dante asked.

"Maybe," Amelia replied softly. "They just had this… magic and sparkle energy. I'd see it whenever one of them left the room and came back—even if it had only been a few minutes. The other would perk up, like a dehydrated houseplant that had just been watered. They needed each other in a way that wasn't ugly or toxic. And they were happy."

Dante studied her expression, the wistfulness there. "Are you looking for some magic and sparkle, Ms. Earhart?"

She smiled at her new name for the night. A mysterious smile that made him desperately wish she'd say no. How perfect would it be if she were just like him? A busy professional who knew how to compartmentalize wants from needs, desires from disasters.

Amelia shrugged, her gaze dropping briefly. "Sure. I think everyone wants a little magic in their life."

But then her expression darkened. "Not everyone can have it, though."

"Why not?" Dante pressed.

"I don't know. Sometimes you just have to be practical, right? Some marriages are full of magic and sparkle and glitter and joy. But others…well, they're more like a—" she searched her memory bank "—a vacuum cleaner! Like, maybe it's not a marriage with all the bells and whistles and fireworks. But the marriage *works*. It gets things done. It's…functional!"

"Functional?" He repeated the word slowly, marveling at its blandness.

"You're making fun of me now."

"Not at all. I was just thinking…maybe it's different for you Americans, but *if* I ever got married and had a family—and I won't—I really don't think I'd want my wife to compare me to a vacuum cleaner."

She laughed and swatted him on the arm. It surprised him, that spontaneous gesture full of playful energy. He found he rather liked it.

"That's not what I meant! I just…" She finally stopped

laughing and gazed into her wineglass. "Never mind. The day's been too long…"

"You're married, aren't you?" The way she spoke, her thoughts were too…*specific* to be random musings. His gaze flicked to her hand—no wedding ring, but that didn't mean anything. Plenty of people were in committed relationships without the legalities of marriage.

Her voice softened. "Not anymore."

"What happened?" he asked gently, knowing he was venturing beyond the bounds of their lighthearted game. But something in him burned to know *Amelia* beyond the limits of their casual flirting.

Amelia cleared her throat, pushed her plate away slightly and crossed her arms on the bar. "I thought it was okay. I thought we were functional. But I didn't know everything that was going on. As it turns out, my now ex-husband… He had different passions. For someone else."

She looked away, brushing nonexistent lint from her sweatshirt. But not quickly enough—Dante caught the sharp edge of hurt in her eyes and the defensive brace of her shoulders.

"I'm sorry," he breathed.

Amelia turned back to him, forcing a smile. "Hey, this is a game, right? It's not supposed to be so serious." Her gaze sharpened as she changed the topic. "So, I'm guessing you don't see marriage in your future?"

Dante hesitated. Losing his mother as a teenager had left a wound that had festered for years. He'd eventually acted out, seeking distraction in wild parties, fast cars and a string of meaningless relationships with women who were as wild and reckless as he was. The paparazzi had dubbed him *Il Principe del Piacere* "The Prince of Pleasure," and photos of his reckless youth—from trashed hotel rooms to court appearances and totaled cars—were immortalized in the tabloids, much to his family's embarrassment.

He'd known he was dishonoring his mother's memory and he'd vowed to do better. He'd studied hard, made up for lost time and was eventually accepted into medical school.

But no matter how much he accomplished, he couldn't seem to shake his reputation as the spoiled, rich playboy son of Vittorio Ricci.

In the end, maybe the paparazzi had done him a favor. No woman who sought a serious future was interested in him. Which meant he never had to worry about breaking anyone's heart as Vittorio had.

Dante didn't know if a broken moral compass was hereditary, but he preferred to play it safe and let his bad reputation do the hard work of guarding his heart—and anyone else's—from ruin.

Dante returned his focus to Amelia, pushing aside his own thoughts. This wasn't about him—not yet.

"Who can say what the future will bring?" Dante said with a shrug. "So far, she has brought far too much work for me to have time for love."

"What about you? I know you've been married—any children?"

What should have been a fairly standard question seemed to land like a gut punch. Her expression of shock and pain was so visceral, he immediately regretted asking.

Amelia recovered quickly, but the napkin she'd been smoothing on the bar was now twisted in her hands.

"No, we didn't have any children."

It was impossible to miss or ignore the pain in her eyes. He was a stranger—he knew he shouldn't meddle or interfere. But everything about this woman compelled him to connect with her in some way.

"Hey, listen," he said, leaning forward. "We've only known each other for about eight minutes, but if you feel like talking about it, well, sometimes it's easier to open up to strangers than friends. Right?"

She considered this for a moment, then gave a small, sad laugh. "You're right. Why not? We'll never see each other again, right?"

"Right." Like an unripe berry, the word left a bitter taste in his mouth.

She exhaled. "My ex-husband and I got married and we started trying for a baby right away. Eventually, we tried IVF. Seven rounds. Seven rounds of hope and heartbreak. Then, on the day I found out our final attempt had failed…"

She paused, her voice thick with emotion.

"I also found out my husband had been having an affair for two years. With his…assistant."

Dante sat back, stunned.

"She worked with him," Amelia continued, her voice tight. "At the same place where I work. So we all knew each other, and it still happened."

He thought of Vittorio, how his betrayals had shattered his mother.

"I'm so—" he began, but Amelia interrupted.

"That's not the worst of it," she said. She grabbed her phone, powered it on and thrust it toward him. "Here. I can't even bring myself to read this. Would you do it?"

Dante took the phone and opened the message. It was a group text announcing that the sender and his new wife were expecting a baby boy around Christmas.

He froze. "This isn't your ex, is it?" he asked carefully.

"Yeah." Amelia's laugh was hollow. "You're probably wondering about my taste in men."

"No, I would never…"

"Well, *I* am," she interrupted. "I don't know what's wrong with me. We met in college as undergrads. He cheated on me back then, too—with his anatomy lab partner, no less. What a cliché, right?

"I thought I'd forgotten him completely until, years later, my dating app matched us. I thought, why not say hi? Just to be friendly."

She gave a wry smile. "One text led to another, then lunch, then a baseball game. Before I knew it…"

"You gave him a second chance."

She shrugged. "He swore he had grown up and changed. And I wanted to believe him."

There it was again. The change that broke hearts and destroyed lives.

"No magic or sparkle, I take it?" He kept his tone gentle, so she would know he wasn't teasing.

She shook her head. "Definitely not. But by my thirtieth birthday, I had given up hope of being swept off my feet. That's when I thought, maybe we don't all get the magic and the sparkle and the glitter and the joy that my parents had. Maybe we get something…pretty good. Why couldn't that be enough?"

Because it always ends like this.

"Hey," he said softly. "I know I've only known you for all of thirteen minutes, but for whatever it's worth, I think you deserve all the magic, and the sparkle, and the glitter and the joy that your heart can handle."

For one night—maybe tonight—he knew he could give her all that and more.

She looked up at him with big hazel eyes that made his heart hurt. "Thanks, Paul the Napkin Salesman. And for whatever it's worth, I think you deserve several grand love affairs with one loyal lover, if that's what you want."

He had to admit that sounded pretty wonderful. But he wasn't going to hold his breath. If love was meant to be, it would have to find him first.

Still, he had to admit that he wouldn't mind waking up to her beautiful face for the next hundred years or so. The air between them shifted. Something between them deepened, a silent tension tightening like an invisible cord. Her lips were soft, inviting and tantalizingly close. He couldn't stop looking at her face, luminous in its simplicity. Her long, caramel-brown hair fell in soft, natural waves around her face.

Why did this night feel so different? Because she didn't know who he was. Here, in New York, he wasn't the son of Vittorio Ricci or Milan's spoiled Prince of Pleasure. He was just an average guy in an anonymous hotel lounge flirting with a beautiful woman over drinks.

And the beautiful woman wasn't sticking around because of his name, reputation, or bank account. She just wanted to be with *him*.

That realization hit like a freight train. It was exhilarating—and terrifying.

His heart pounded as he leaned toward her, drawn like a magnet. He hesitated as an old instinct flared. In Milan, he'd have to worry about the paparazzi capturing every private moment, every stolen kiss. But not here. Nobody was watching. Nobody cared.

And then he saw the expression in her eyes. Damn, it was everything—vulnerability, curiosity and something else he couldn't quite name but wanted desperately to believe in. To *possess*.

She wanted him. *Just as he was.*

Without another thought, he leaned in and kissed her.

CHAPTER TWO

As Paul leaned in, everything around Miranda seemed to fade. No more background chatter, no worries about missed flights. It should have felt awkward, being this close to a virtual stranger. Instead, all she could wonder was how long had it been since someone had looked at her like *that*? Her mind whispered warnings, but her heart silenced them, too seduced by the intensity in his gaze.

The first touch of his lips was gentle. Soft, so it felt more like a question than a demand. Miranda's breath caught, her heart pounding as her body moved to his, enticed like a bee to nectar. His kiss was slow, sweet torture, testing her with a tenderness that made her chest ache.

Her hand hovered, unmoored from her wineglass, not sure where to land, until it found his shoulder. The slow sensuality of this kiss whispered of delicious possibilities and unraveled her with its relentless pursuit.

When he drew back slightly, unfairly taking that kiss away, she realized she had already leaned forward, chasing their delicate connection, hungry for more.

They froze like that for several long seconds. His dark, tousled hair framed his prominent cheekbones, strong jawline and a mouth that was curved in a sexy smile. It was his eyes, though, that did her in—intense, espresso-brown eyes that seemed to see through her every defense. Her pulse was a steady drumbeat in her ears as she waited and waited and waited for something she couldn't put into words.

Then, without saying a word, they both moved at once, closing the gap between them. All the gentleness of the first kiss disappeared like smoke. This kiss was fire and need, desire and pure, unadulterated lust. Miranda reached for his collar, pulling him closer, and felt his hand sliding to her waist. The world slipped away, leaving her with nothing but her hunger for him.

She broke off the kiss to catch her breath, regain her bearings. He stared at her for a long minute, looking as off balance as she felt.

Then he leaned forward, conspiratorially. "Listen, I know we've known each other for like, an hour? But if you'd like to continue our chat in my room…"

Then he was pushing something to her on the bar. A small paper sleeve that held the key card to his room. Room 321 was handwritten on the front.

She looked at him, her mind racing to keep up.

"If I never see you again, Miss Amelia Earhart, I will understand. Thank you for a bewitching evening."

Before she could react or respond, he leaned forward to kiss her again—a simple, chaste kiss—before he whispered in her ear, "But I hope you will come. Because I would love to give you a night of magic and sparkle…"

Then he was gone.

Leaving Miranda alone with her thoughts…and his room key. She plucked the plastic card from the sleeve, ran her finger down its edge.

She wasn't going to do this, was she? This was crazy. She barely knew the man! It would be reckless and risky. Something she would *never* do.

Which maybe was why she *should* do it? She had spent

a lifetime of being Little Miss Responsibility. What had that gotten her? Always taking the high road only seemed to lead to a lonely cliff that overlooked a pit of despair.

It would be just one night of throwing caution to the wind! If she didn't deserve this, who did? If not now, then when?

She slid the card back in its sleeve, tucked her purse under her arm and headed for the elevator, her stomach fluttering with butterflies.

Ten minutes later, she rapped lightly on room 321. A few nervous seconds later and the door opened. He held it for her and she slipped inside. She had no idea what to do next. Make small talk? Shimmy out of her clothes?

All these thoughts jumbled about in her head as she navigated the small hallway that led to the bedroom area. But before she made it past the bathroom, she heard the door click shut as he caught her by the wrist.

He tugged her back, so that she was pressed into his chest. "I wasn't sure you'd come."

His mouth crashed down on hers, revealing a passion she had barely tasted when they were in the lounge. Her surprise gave way to a new fire that licked its way up her body, starting at her core and radiating out to heat all of her limbs so that she felt she might burn up on the spot.

Some door of her heart—no, her libido—that she had kept shut and double-bolt locked now swung wide-open. His lips were soft, his olive-hued smooth skin a soft caress against her cheek.

But that mouth—his damn mouth…

"I had to think about it," she breathed between kisses. "For about ten seconds."

Another kiss, this one rough and needy and far from polite. He cupped her face with both hands, drawing her closer, and she felt such a ferocious desire race through her body, it made her head roll back.

Her hands moved from his shoulders to his chest, hungry to feel his skin, frustrated to find a stiff-starched shirt instead. She undid the buttons frantically, until she could slip her hands underneath and slide the shirt from his shoulders.

He roughly groaned her name, which wasn't her name at all. And how freeing was that? Tonight she didn't have to be Miranda, the surgeon too caught up in her work to notice her husband having a two-year-long affair. For a few hours, she could leave the painful past behind and be whomever she wanted to be.

Soon, he was slipping her out of her clothes, his lips never leaving hers, until she was down to her sensible black cotton bikini panties and matching lace camisole.

A little voice implored her to slow down; this was moving much too fast.

But she simply did not care. That kiss and his passion had done more to kill her inhibitions than any wine she had ever tasted.

He muttered something in Italian, then, "Amelia, you are pure temptation wrapped in perfection."

His hands on her hips held her in place, so that his gaze could roam over her body. A wave of self-consciousness rose like a cold ocean wave, threatening to douse the fire his kisses had ignited.

It had been a very long time since she had felt beautiful, or even whole. Years of failed IVF treatments, and the disappointment that Bradford had never tried to hide, had left her feeling broken beyond repair.

She couldn't help it. She pulled away, reflexively crossing her arms, building a fortress between her and the man she knew as Paul. Maybe this was a mistake. Even if she would never see him again, he could see her *now*, and the way he looked at her made her feel like she was already stripped bare.

Paul caught her arms, gently tugged them away from her body. "No, Amelia. Not tonight. Not with me."

Just one hour had become just one night, but the rules were the same. They were never going to see each other again. She could be anyone she wanted to be, at least for a few hours.

Paul waited, his hands lightly clasping her arms, waiting for some sign of *yes*.

Miranda would never say yes. But Amelia would. Tonight she was Amelia.

"Okay," she breathed.

A slow smile warmed his face. Not mischievous, like at the bar, but knowing, as if he had read every thought that had brought her to this place.

He reached out, his fingers finding the lacy edge of her camisole. He lifted it slowly, holding it over her head so she could slip her arms out, one by one.

She was almost naked now. The room was cold, and her nipples beaded from the air-conditioning.

He reached out slowly, almost reverently, to thumb her lower lip. Traced a trail to her collarbone where he rolled his finger pads over the delicate bones, then trailed downward to find the stiff nubs of her nipples. He lingered there, then glanced up to meet her gaze.

She felt exposed, but he also somehow made her feel safe. Even when his fingers trailed lower still, finding her rib cage and abdomen, rigid with anticipation. His fingers lingered there longest, stroking the soft curve of her belly.

The most vulnerable part of her body. The part that had let her down, maybe even killed her marriage.

But his touch said otherwise. *Not damaged. Not broken. Beautiful.*

Her muscles slowly relaxed under his touch. His lips found hers again, warming her mouth as he danced her backward to the bed. She melted into that kiss, her body going pliant as he guided her, then unzipped his trousers and kicked off his shoes. When he joined her, she felt his rigid length pressed against her belly.

That was her last logical thought of the night. Paul deepened his kiss as his fingers slipped under her panties to find her center. Never had she been so aroused, so insanely out of her mind with desire. His fingers pushed inside her, exploring her as his tongue explored her mouth. It drove her crazy with desire. She had never wanted someone to make love to her this badly. Not ever.

She moaned against his lips, willing him to take her fully. Instead, the scoundrel held back, his fingers masterfully stroking her need even higher.

She had no room to think. No ability to weigh the pros and cons of what she was doing in Paul's hotel room.

Just want. Raw, naked, primal need. A want so strong, it might be a bullet train hurling her toward her own destruction, for all she knew.

But if this was how she was going to go out, so be it.

But then he was breaking off the kiss again—maddening!—and apologizing for something. What on earth could it be?

"I'll just be a moment," he muttered, slipping his shirt back on. "I thought I had packed everything, but I brought a different suitcase, and..."

Condoms. He was planning to leave her alone, in this state, while he went to the hotel's gift shop.

She sat up and drew her knees to her. "Okay," she said. "But of course, I can't get pregnant. And I've been tested for everything under the sun as part of my reproductive treatment."

He paused buttoning his shirt. "Okay. Well, I had a full physical just before this trip."

"All's good?"

"Perfect. Still, I'm more than happy to get protection if you like."

"No. I'd much rather you get back to kissing me like you were."

Paul paused before a huge smile warmed his face. "My pleasure, *bella donna*."

His shirt disappeared and he was back, drawing her into his arms. His mouth found hers and everything melted away. All she could see and taste was him. She felt utterly devoured by his hungry mouth and it only made her more crazy.

He broke off the kiss again, frustrating her, but only to wrap her legs around his waist. Her panties were in the way, and she was about to tell him so, but he tugged them aside, making room for…

Then he swore softly against her mouth as he finally took her completely. Miranda's vision went blurry as she felt her core pulse around the length of him. This coupling was unlike anything she had ever experienced in her life. This was a man who wanted her—just her. He wanted her body and her touch and her sex with no expectations at all. Not even the expectation of knowing her real name.

Miranda leaned forward to lightly bite his shoulder, unable to contain all the passion he had ignited. But Paul remained rigid, holding himself back. His breathing was harsh, ragged, and she could feel tight cords of muscle running the length of his back.

"Paul?"

Her core tightened as she raised her head.

His face was contorted. "Dammit, Amelia. I wanted this to be so good for you. But I just can't…"

And that was it. One minute Paul was a stoic statue, fighting to stay in control.

The next he was a powerful athlete, taking her with long, powerful strokes. He drove into her hard, almost to the point of brutal. But it felt *so* good. Paul didn't make love to her like she was fragile or broken. To him, her body was an instrument of pleasure. Able to feel, and give, this kind of passion.

Her core tightened, a knot of pleasure making her arch her back, flutter her eyes closed. She hovered in the delicious in-between space, balanced on a knife's edge of bliss. All she could do was grip his shoulders and hope she didn't fall away forever.

But when he pressed his face into her neck, when she felt his hot breath as he crooned to her in Italian, she couldn't hold on anymore.

She fell and fell and fell like a falling star, exploding in the ancient night sky.

Far away, she heard Paul's guttural cry as his body seized into hers. She wrapped her arms around his back, felt the slick of his sweat on her skin. Thought blissful thoughts of nothingness while passion had its way.

How long did they lie like that? His body heavy and solid on hers, a thick silence in the air, punctuated only by the sound of their panting breaths and thundering heartbeats.

Finally, he rolled to his side, and they simply stared at each other.

Something in his gaze made her wonder if they were feeling the same thing.

What the hell just happened here?

A familiar dance of resuscitation flowed around Dante as he quickly assessed his three-year-old patient. The emergency room team worked in choreographed efficiency around him, securing a breathing tube and placing the intravenous lines that would be needed during surgery.

Dante's gaze landed on the large wad of gauze that the ambulance medics had hastily applied on scene after the car accident. The toddler had significant head trauma, and his right pupil was larger than his left—a clear sign of brain pressure.

Nurses and medics hurried in and out of the room, bringing bulging IV bags of blood or saline and syringes of medication to stabilize the child's dangerously low blood pressure.

"Do we know where the parents are?" Dante asked, but no one answered. An operating room had just opened up. Chaos followed him and the team as they wheeled the child to surgery.

"We're hanging trauma blood," Matteo, a longtime anesthesiology colleague, called out.

"Let's prep," Dante told his team. "But just the head."

In nonurgent cases, prepping and draping were a methodical and orderly process, with each piece of equipment carefully placed exactly where Dante would need it. But with a toddler's life hanging in the balance, his team worked lightning fast. After cleaning and preparing the wound, they draped just the top of the toddler's head. Cords and wires, suction tubes and drills became a tangled mess in the frantic rush to save the boy's life.

"Pressure's tanking!" the anesthesiologist called out. "You need to stop the bleeding now!"

Dante focused on the scene in front of him. Hundreds of tiny blood vessels on the boy's brain surface had been damaged and were bleeding profusely. The dura was torn to the skull's edge, though, thankfully, the sinus remained intact. But before he could do anything to help this boy, he had to stop the rapid blood loss.

"We'll start on the skin and work our way in," Dante said, placing a surgical sponge to pack off the worst of the bleeding. He and his team quickly cauterized the scalp vessels one by one, applying specialized plastic clips to compress and seal them.

With the bleeding somewhat controlled, they shifted their focus to carefully sculpting the damaged skull to prepare for a future implant. Direct pressure on the brain's surface temporarily held the damaged vessels at bay.

"Forty over ten!" the anesthesiologist shouted. "Do you have control of the bleeding yet?"

"Yes," Dante answered. "We're at a holding point for now. Catch up and let me know when I can continue."

Surgery could often be a delicate dance like this. Dante and his team had to wait while the anesthesiologist stabilized the boy's blood pressure.

Matteo administered trauma blood and concentrated products to reverse clotting issues, gradually restoring the boy's blood pressure and heart rate to safer levels.

"We're better now," Matteo called out. "Go for it."

Dante and his team resumed their meticulous work, repairing blood vessels one by one with surgical cautery and tiny titanium clips. Eventually, they reached a point where no further repairs could be performed that day.

The team placed an intracranial pressure monitor—a one-millimeter wire inserted into the brain—to track pressure as the boy recovered in the pediatric ICU. Further surgeries to repair the skull and address additional brain damage would be planned once the boy grew stronger.

"That's it for today," Dante announced. "Strong work, everyone." He directed the comment to the scrub nurse, a new member of the team. She smiled at him in a way that felt flirtatious, but Dante quickly looked away to shut that down. He might be *Il Principe del Piacere* in Milanese society, but in the operating room, he was Dr. Dante Ricci. Nothing happened here that didn't benefit his patients.

Drained after the grueling six-hour surgery, Dante longed to return to his office, type up the case notes and resume preparation for his team's first fetal surgery, a case that would require the collective skills of more than thirty surgeons and specialists.

The timing of the consultant's arrival from the United States could not be better. She was a world-renowned pediatric neurosurgeon from Harborview Children's Hospital, with decades of expertise and groundbreaking work in fetal spina bifida surgery. Her willingness to mentor his newly formed neurosurgery team had given Dante the confidence to accept this complex case.

As he stepped out of the operating room, the chief of surgery greeted him in the hallway. "Beautiful job on that boy, Dante. Really brilliant work."

Dante removed his scrub cap and thanked him. He loved working in this part of the hospital, far from where his father, the chief of cardiology, held sway. Dante had refused to follow in his father's footsteps, not just to escape the shadow of his influence but because he had fallen in love with the intricacies and high stakes of pediatric neurosurgery.

"The American consultant arrived this afternoon," the chief said. "We've been showing her around the hospital and hoped she'd meet your team, but of course, you were otherwise engaged. Can you stop by the conference room to meet her?"

The last thing Dante wanted was to socialize after such an exhausting day, but he couldn't refuse the request. Besides, he was eager to meet the neurosurgeon who would mentor his team through the complicated case.

"Of course," he said, debating whether to change into his usual suit and tie he kept in his office for meetings with parents and administrators. Ultimately, he decided to go in his scrubs.

The conference room was humming with activity and conversations. Several people milled around—members of the pediatrics department, the operating room staff, the emergency department and, of course, neurosurgery. All were eager to meet the new consultant and gain some much-needed wisdom before the hospital's newly accredited pediatric neurosurgery department flew solo. She would be on staff for the next eight weeks, helping with surgeries, consulting on complex cases and offering advanced training to staff.

He recognized everyone in the room except one woman, whose back was turned to him. Her long, caramel beachy waves stirred something deep within him—waves just like Amelia's. His gaze scanned the length of her body, finding curves that were just like Amelia's, too. But that couldn't be. It just wasn't possible.

Until she turned to face him.

Her eyes widened in shock as she recognized him.

My God, it's you. Here she was, right here in Milan. The woman who had haunted his dreams had somehow found her way into his world, into his hospital, his *conference room.*

It was impossible to see her and not remember the night that had rocked him to his core. He'd had the pleasure of dating many beautiful women in his life, but none had lingered in his memory the way *Amelia* had.

Of course, that was partially by design. His reputation in Milan, bolstered by relentless paparazzi coverage, ensured that serious relationships were never a risk. No woman ever went out with him expecting more than a fabulous night at Milan's hottest clubs or perhaps a weekend at an exclusive resort. His ill-deserved but unshakable reputation protected him from his deepest fear: making promises to a woman he loved and breaking them years later, just like his father had.

People change, his father had told him, over and over, until Dante believed it.

But now he had met *Amelia.* And the passionate hours they had spent together in New York had haunted his thoughts ever since. She was the first woman who had ever tempted him to push for more.

Amelia—no, Miranda, he corrected himself—licked her lips, her eyes wide like a deer in headlights. She was probably thinking the same thing he was—their little fling in New York should stay private. He had enough trouble with prying eyes; Miranda didn't need to be part of all that.

He quickly stepped forward, hand outstretched.

"Doctor Hawthorne. I'm so pleased to finally make your acquaintance."

A flicker of relief crossed her face as she realized he wasn't going to reveal their secret tryst.

"Likewise, Doctor Ricci," she replied smoothly. "I've been regaled with stories of your surgical proficiency all afternoon."

He chuckled. "Well, I'm sure that's a bit overblown. However, I'm looking forward to working with you over the next few weeks. I appreciate you lending us your expertise. We can only hope to achieve half the fame and recognition you've brought to Harborview Children's."

They were still shaking hands, their gazes locked, when words suddenly failed them. A discreet cough from someone in the room broke the moment. Miranda glanced down at their still-clasped hands and quickly let go.

"I have no doubt that Saint Joseph's will have a top-tier pediatric neurosurgery program of its own in no time."

Dante let go of her hand just as quickly, hoping she couldn't see the truth in his eyes—how deeply he'd been affected by her ever since they parted.

After they had made love in New York, Dante had fallen asleep next to her, holding her close, matching his breath to hers until he'd drifted into a deep slumber. So deep, in fact, that he had almost missed his alarm. When he had woken up, his mind defaulted to his usual routine: how to end things gracefully. Usually a casual, "Thanks for a lovely time, we really ought to look each other up sometime," did the job, both knowing full well they would never cross paths again. His partner usually happily accepted the exit ramp he offered, and they both went their separate ways. No harm, no foul.

But as he had lain there, watching the break of day slowly illuminate the impersonal hotel room, he felt something unfamiliar. Something that made him want to cancel his plans in New York and spend the weekend with her instead.

Somehow, he had found the strength to get up, leaving her warm body tucked in a nest of sheets and pillows. He had hoped a warm shower and some fancy hotel soap would restore his equilibrium, but the craving to linger with her just wouldn't go away. He had to admit that something about her was different. Hearing her stories of heartbreak, feeling her unhealed wounds through their connection—it had stirred something protective in him.

But a relationship was impossible. Ridiculous. His life didn't allow for such things. He didn't *want* such things.

Still, a small voice had pestered him. *What about breakfast, dummy? That's a few degrees shy of marriage.*

That small voice was right—he was being ridiculous. His heart had soared at the prospect of stealing one last hour with her. "Amelia," he had called out from the shower. "Wake up, sleepyhead. Let's grab some breakfast before your flight."

But there had been no response. Maybe the bathroom door was closed, and she couldn't hear him. But when he had pulled the shower curtain aside, he saw the door was wide-open. He had called out again, louder this time.

Still no response, but he had heard something. Something that had sounded a lot like a door clicking shut. His heart sank.

He had taken his time finishing his shower, toweling off, dressing for the day. All so he could delay the moment he returned to the room and found what he expected. The bed—empty. Her shoes, clothes, bag—all gone. Just a note by the bed, hastily scrawled. *Thank you…for everything.*

And that was the end of *Amelia*. She was gone.

The conference room eventually thinned out as staff returned to their departments, leaving Dante, Miranda and their chief alone to talk.

"You two should have dinner," the chief suggested. "You'll be working closely over the next few weeks, especially on the spina bifida case."

Miranda cast a furtive glance at Dante. "Thank you, sir, but I think I just need to rest before we begin tomorrow."

The chief would not be deterred.

"Coffee, then. Dante, take her to the *Aperitivo al Crepuscolo*. I think she'd love it."

Dante smiled. "Twilight Bites," he translated for Miranda. "A café that opens late and serves coffee, appetizers and other light fare."

The prospect of being alone with her again was irresistible, even if confusing memories from New York lingered.

"That is, if you'd care to join me, Doctor Hawthorne?"

"Of course," she replied with a smile, though fatigue etched lines around her eyes. Clearly, she was still feeling the effects of jet lag. Coming straight from the airport into work had pushed his own travel fatigue into the background. Despite that, her smile was genuine, and Dante felt the pull of her all over again.

Miranda waited while Dante changed out of his scrubs, and then they made the short walk from the hotel to the café in the plaza.

"I don't really know how to order in Italian," Miranda confessed when they reached the coffee shop.

"No worries," Dante said with a smile. "I'll take care of everything."

He ordered her a simple coffee, similar to what she would have back in the States, along with a plate of sweet pastries.

When they sat down, Miranda shrugged off her coat and folded her arms on the table.

"I owe you an apology."

He held up his hand. "No, you absolutely do not."

"I didn't mean to run out on you. I just…"

"Had a flight to catch?" he offered, a line he'd used plenty of times himself.

"No, no, it wasn't that. I just… Well, it's complicated."

Dante raised an eyebrow, his expression inviting her to continue.

Miranda sighed. "The truth is that my sole intention when I went to the lounge was to have a late dinner and a nice glass of wine before I went to bed. Meeting you was a surprise—a very pleasant surprise."

"Likewise," Dante said softly.

Miranda's lips curved into a faint smile. "I'm still sorry for standing you up the next morning."

"No apology is needed," Dante assured her. "We were playing a game, Miranda—or shall I call you Amelia?"

She laughed lightly. "No, I think we left Amelia and Paul back in New York."

"Exactly. Back there, it was a game. One night, we got to be whoever we wanted to be. And the next morning, the game was over. You went back to your life, and I went back to mine."

Inside, Dante couldn't help but hope she hadn't heard him calling out to her from the shower that morning. It wasn't as if inviting her to breakfast would have been catastrophic, but keeping his emotions in check was essential. He hadn't expected to see her again, but her sudden appearance in Milan felt like a gift from the gods. For the next two months, she was here—available, touchable, kissable.

It couldn't be forever, of course. He knew that. But still, it could be really good.

Dante made a whisking motion, as if waving away a fly. "Goodbye, Amelia. Goodbye, Paul. It's just us now—Miranda and Dante in Milan."

"In Milan for *work*," she reminded him.

"*So* much work," he agreed with a grin. "But what is that phrase you Americans are so fond of? All work and no play makes Jack a very dull boy?"

Her eyes sparkled. "Yes, we do say that from time to time."

"Well, let's talk about the work first, then. The spina bifida surgery is scheduled for two weeks from now," Dante told her. "But the parents have lots of questions. They'd like to meet the consultant who's going to help their baby."

"Of course," Miranda said, picking up her phone. They quickly found a time to meet with the family. Dante told her that while the parents spoke some English he would translate for them. Then they coordinated their calendars for a series of meetings, simulated surgical training and planning.

Dante tossed his phone on the table. "You see? We got the work done. Now, let's talk about the play."

He reached into his jacket pocket and withdrew two tickets, sliding them across the table.

"What are these?" she asked, picking them up with interest.

"Tickets to the Italian Grand Prix," he said. "I bought them so I could show our new consultant around Milan before we dove into the hard work. That was before I knew the consultant was you." His voice softened. "You can imagine my delight at seeing you today."

Miranda looked down at the tickets, her cheeks flushing. "Absolutely! I'd love to go."

Dante would have liked nothing more than to take her hand, press a kiss to her knuckles and savor the moment. But movement near the window caught his attention.

His stomach dropped. Not now, he thought. Not here. Not with her.

There was a pop and a flash, and Dante knew instantly what it meant. The paparazzi had followed him—again.

Miranda's back was to the window, and if he was lucky, she wouldn't notice. Paparazzi could be so unpredictable. Sometimes they left him alone for weeks, and then, suddenly, they'd reappear. Most of their photos never made it to print, but they were an ever-present annoyance.

An annoyance he'd rather Miranda didn't have to deal with.

So he'd have to work harder to keep his social, and hopefully romantic, life as private as possible—for Miranda's sake and his own.

CHAPTER THREE

MIRANDA WAS IN an exceptionally good mood as she headed to the hospital. Her thoughts drifted to Dante and what it meant to be reunited with him in Milan. Seeing him again had stirred a whirlwind of emotions within her.

Too many emotions, if she were honest. That was why she had left his hotel room without saying goodbye back in New York.

When she had woken up to the sound of Dante in the shower, memories of the previous evening slowly percolated through the haze of sleep. She had no regrets, but she had been overwhelmed by the spark of their connection. What had started as a casual flirting in the hotel lounge had evolved into something decidedly...more. With Dante, she felt seen and understood in a way that both healed and unnerved her.

Then he had made things so much worse by inviting her to breakfast! The prospect of prolonging their time together had sent a jolt through her entire being. There was nothing she wanted more than to stay with this mysterious, sexy Italian man who seemed to be piecing her back together. She almost said yes, but she'd stopped herself.

She wasn't ready for this flurry of emotions. She was still processing everything that had happened in her marriage.

So she had slid out of bed and silently padded around

the room, retrieving her things, then hastily dressed so she could slip out of his hotel room without a word.

Being reunited with him in Milan had been a shock. Escaping him wasn't an option now. She had no idea how they would manage this complication, but their easy, natural connection over coffee had drawn her in once more. Who knew what the future held? All that mattered was that he had made her feel alive and whole.

Before heading in, she stopped at a coffee shop for an espresso and a quick breakfast to go. As she turned to leave, a stack of newspapers by the door caught her eye. To her shock, her picture was on the front page alongside Dante's. They had been photographed together at the *Aperitivo al Crepuscolo* where they had reconnected.

She froze, picked up a copy and stared in disbelief. The article was, of course, written in Italian, a language she couldn't read. She paid for the newspaper, tucked it under her arm and hurried to the hospital, glancing at her watch. She and Dante were scheduled to meet with the parents-to-be of the baby with spina bifida in half an hour. Not much time, but she had to see him and get an explanation.

But his office was empty. A passing nurse noticed her distress and greeted her warmly in Italian before switching to English. "*Buongiorno, dottoressa.* May I help you?"

"Where is Dante…er, Doctor Ricci?" Miranda asked.

"I believe he's in a planning meeting," the nurse replied. "Is there something I can assist you with?"

Miranda hesitated before opening the newspaper and pushing it toward the nurse. "What does this say? Why is my picture in the paper?"

The nurse scanned the article, her eyes widening slightly as she read. Then, with an uncomfortable expression, she handed the newspaper back. "Madam," she said delicately, "it would be best if you spoke to Doctor Ricci directly about this."

Frustrated, Miranda pressed further. "But he's not here, and you are. Please, tell me what it says."

The nurse relented with visible discomfort. "The headline reads *Milan's Prince of Pleasure Spotted with Mysterious American Beauty—New Romance Brewing*?"

"The Prince of Pleasure?" Miranda repeated, confused. "What does that mean?"

The nurse explained hesitantly. "Doctor Ricci is well-known in Milan for his…romantic escapades. Because his family is very influential, he has always been in the public eye. The paparazzi love him. They believe you are his new love interest, and they'll likely start speculating about how long your relationship will last. But don't let it bother you, *dottoressa*. This is just what the media does."

With that, the nurse excused herself, leaving Miranda with more questions than answers. Who exactly was Dante Ricci? Why was he called the Prince of Pleasure? What the hell had her sappy, confused heart gotten her into?

Miranda checked her watch—ten minutes until her meeting with the family. Just enough time. She rushed to her office, threw her briefcase into the corner and slammed her chair against the desk as she fired up her computer. Quickly, she searched the internet for Dante Ricci.

The results left her stunned. Headline after headline appeared, revealing the controversial past of Dante Ricci. She used a web browser to translate the articles from Italian to English. Among the stories were scandalous accounts: "Spoiled Playboy Son Trashes Another Hotel Room," "Dante Ricci Spends Red-Hot Weekend with a Movie Star," and "Young Actress Heartbroken After Dante Ricci Dumps Her."

Photograph after photograph confirmed the stories: Dante on yachts, at movie premieres, in restaurants, on beaches, always with stunning women—each seemingly more beautiful than the last. Miranda sat frozen, her emotions churning.

Her watch beeped, jolting her back to the present. Five minutes until she had to present a composed, competent version of herself to the young and probably frightened parents of her spina bifida patient.

She pushed away from her desk, overwhelmed by a wave of disbelief. Never in a million years had she imagined that the sweet, caring man she'd met in New York was actually the reckless, spoiled son of a privileged family.

He didn't owe her a single, solitary thing. She knew that. But what she was feeling had little to do with Dante and everything to do with old feelings resurfacing—painful, raw memories of knowing she had been the fool. For two years, she had believed she had the best husband in the world. All her friends had said so, especially considering how much stress infertility could put on a marriage.

She had been wrong then, and she was wrong now. Dante didn't care about her. He hadn't cared in New York. They had just had a casual, meaningless fling in New York, and his attempt to act like it meant more made him just like her ex. A chameleon who could expertly become exactly what she needed in the moment, but whose true self remained hidden. Until she needed him.

A nurse poked her head into the office. "*Dottoressa*, the family is waiting."

"Yes, of course," Miranda replied, forcing herself to focus.

She took a deep breath. These parents needed her full attention. Meeting with a pediatric neurosurgeon was one of the worst moments of a parent's life. It was time for her to get her head straight, to channel her surgeon's mind and to forget about Dante.

She stopped by the restroom to freshen her lipstick, ensuring her appearance was professional. Then she headed to the conference room, where Dante was already sitting with the family, an array of documents and ultrasound scans spread across the table.

The moment Miranda entered, Dante's face lit up with delight. He stood with a brilliant smile, stepping forward with both hands outstretched, ready to clasp her hands in his. But Miranda artfully dodged him with a brisk, formal greeting.

"*Buongiorno*, Doctor Ricci. Very pleased to see you this morning."

Dante hesitated, then quickly introduced her to the parents. They were a modest family with two young children at home. Despite financial hardship, they had managed to raise the funds needed for travel and hotel costs for the surgery that would hopefully give their baby a full, healthy life.

Miranda took her seat, her posture rigid. Dante sat beside her, his warm gaze lingering on her for longer than necessary. She avoided eye contact, determined to keep her focus on the family.

She greeted the parents with a calm, professional demeanor. "I'm very pleased to meet you both, though I'm sorry it's under these circumstances," she began. "As you know, *Signora* Romano, the surgery has been scheduled for two weeks from now, when you'll be twenty-three weeks along. This is the optimal time for repairing the defect in your baby's spine."

Dante translated her words into Italian and the parents exchanged nervous glances before voicing their concerns.

"I don't understand," the mother said, her voice trembling. "The pregnancy was going so well. How could this happen?"

Miranda had heard similar questions countless times. It was the nature of her work—confused parents struggling to make sense of how their child could be healthy and active one day, and in mortal danger the next.

She explained gently, "Spina bifida is often linked to a folic acid deficiency. Some women's bodies don't produce enough, which affects the development of the fetal spinal cord. No one did anything wrong."

Dante stepped in, his voice steady and reassuring, switching between Italian and English to ensure that both parties understood. "In spina bifida, the spinal cord doesn't close completely during development, leaving the spinal canal exposed after birth."

He continued to explain every detail of what the medical team knew so far. He was an excellent partner, Miranda had to admit. His explanations were clear and comforting. Together, they described the benefits of fetal surgery, emphasizing its potential to significantly improve the baby's quality of life.

"There are risks, however," Miranda added. "Preterm birth is more likely after fetal surgery, and that comes with its own complications."

"And there are risks to the mother as well," Dante said. "Excessive bleeding, placental rupture, or uterine rupture later in the pregnancy."

Mr. Romano reached across the table to grasp his wife's hand, his expression protective yet resolute. "We understand the risks," he said in Italian, his voice firm.

Dante translated again, and for the first time, Miranda met his eyes. The sincerity in his gaze made her chest tighten with conflicting emotions.

"They trust our team," Dante said softly, his expression earnest.

Miranda swallowed hard. This was a sobering reminder of the stakes—the risks were high, and the surgery demanded the very best from everyone involved. She could not let her personal feelings cloud her judgment.

Just being near him was distracting. The scent of his cologne, the sight of his hands—hands that had done incredible things to her in New York. Just thinking about it made her blush. It was emotional, unprofessional and entirely unacceptable.

When the meeting ended, the parents stood to leave, insisting on giving Miranda and Dante hugs. They were optimistic, radiating confidence that everything would go perfectly. Miranda desperately hoped they were right.

She was about to follow the parents out of the conference room when Dante called out, "*Dottoressa* Hawthorne, a moment?"

Miranda froze in her tracks and closed her eyes. She had no desire to stay in the conference room, but she owed him this conversation. Slowly, she turned, her body stiff with tension.

"Is everything all right?" he asked, his tone uneasy.

Dante's expression was pure concern, the same vulnerability she'd seen in him back in New York. How did some people manage to fake looking so earnest and caring?

He gestured for her to sit. Reluctantly, she took a seat across from him at the table.

"I'm quite well, Doctor Ricci. Thank you for asking," she said, her tone formal. "But I do have a matter we need to discuss."

Her posture was rigid, her words brisk. Dante seemed

to take note of all of it, and his expression reflected his confusion.

Miranda reached into her pocket, pulling out the tickets. She slid them across the table to him.

"I am very sorry, but I cannot attend this race with you."

Dante frowned, looking down at the tickets and back at her face.

"Why not? I thought it would be fun."

"I'm sure it would be," Miranda said, keeping her tone cool. "But I think it's best if we keep things professional."

She pushed her chair back, preparing to leave, but Dante's voice stopped her.

"Miranda, wait!" His frustration was clear. "What's wrong? What's changed? Yesterday, at the aperitif, we were having a wonderful time reconnecting. And now it feels like we're enemies."

Miranda didn't want to engage, but she reached into her briefcase and pulled out a folded newspaper. She placed it on the table and pushed it toward him.

"I think what's changed is this," she said.

Dante opened the newspaper to the front page, and his expression fell.

"I didn't understand why my picture is in the paper, Dante, let alone on the front page. So, I asked your nurse. She told me this is a society paper—not serious journalism—the kind of thing that gets left in coffee shops—coffee shops frequented by hospital employees."

Dante sighed, leaning back in his chair. "Please, let me explain."

Miranda leaned back to listen, but her walls went up. How many times had Bradford told her the very same thing? He could explain. She didn't understand. She was overreacting.

No, no one was going to gaslight her like that ever again.

"My mother died when I was young. I didn't handle it well. I acted out and got into some trouble." He shrugged. "Ever since then, the paparazzi has taken a ridiculous interest in my personal and social life.

"Still…" He drew the paper to him, then tossed it in the trash. "It must have been a slow gossip day for the press to try to make our coffee date seem like a scandalous affair."

"Look," she said, her tone a little sharper. "New York was fun, but we're in Milan. I came here for work, not… whatever this is." She gestured at the trash can. "We're about to operate on Mrs. Romano and her unborn baby. Can you imagine how vulnerable she feels right now? We literally have both of their lives in our hands. This isn't the time for distractions. Let New York stay in New York. Milan is for work."

She pushed the tickets back to him. "Thank you for the invitation, but from now on, we're keeping things professional. That's what's best for the Romano family and all the other patients in this department."

She grabbed her bag with trembling hands and stood. Without giving Dante a chance to respond, she walked out of the room, praying he wouldn't stop her again. She wasn't sure how much longer she could maintain the facade of a woman who had made up her mind.

Miranda stood alone in the operating room, staring at the space where the surgery would take place in just a few days. The surgical training mannequin—dubbed "Maria" by the Italian team—lay on the gurney. Back in Boston, Miranda's team had always referred to their training mannequin as "Victoria." The name change felt symbolic of her new surroundings, though it didn't make her feel any more at home.

"Well, Maria," she said aloud, her voice echoing in the empty room, "shall we go through this one more time?"

She approached the gurney, glancing over the high-tech training tools. Maria was an obstetrics mannequin, so her belly was rounded and could accommodate a range of fetal mannequins at various stages of development. Maria was most often used by obstetric residents practicing their delivery skills, but she had been an invaluable partner in helping Miranda coach the new Italian team through the upcoming fetal surgery.

Although this would be St. Joseph's first spina bifida case, Miranda had assembled a world-class team to collaborate with the Italian staff. In addition to Miranda and Dante, the only pediatric neurosurgeons, the specialized six-member surgical team would include a maternal-fetal specialist, an OB surgeon, an anesthesiologist, a cardiologist and two veteran scrub nurses. With the addition of anesthesiology techs, OR techs and circulating nurses, the Romano family had a veritable army of medical professionals fighting for their baby.

But despite all the expertise in the room, Miranda knew there were considerable risks to the mother. The only way she knew how to offset those risks was to practice, over and over. So she had driven the team hard all week, calling them back to the simulation room day after day, determined their performance would be seamless.

As the surgery approached, unease gnawed at her. Working in a new place, with unfamiliar faces and systems, was a challenge that made it harder to relax and trust that all would go well.

Alone in the room, she began narrating the procedure to herself, mentally assigning each team member their role and reviewing the critical steps. Stiff muscles forced her to stop and stretch a bit, but she found no relief. Surgery practice, just like surgery, could be long and grueling. She often had to hold her body in unnatural positions for long periods of time.

She really needed to schedule a swim for the weekend. An hour in the lap pool would unkink the tight muscles in her neck and prepare her for the long surgery ahead. But when she called the private club where she had been scheduling her thrice-weekly swimming sessions, the attendant informed her that the club would be closed for a private event that weekend.

"*Grazie*," she murmured before disconnecting. This was a complication she didn't need. Surely, there was another club somewhere in Milan that could accommodate her, but when on earth would she have the time to research that?

"Dammit," she said out loud, turning back to Maria. Only to find she wasn't alone anymore. Dante had somehow entered the surgery suite without her noticing.

Her body involuntarily stiffened. She had been working hard on keeping her distance from Dante and when that wasn't possible, keeping her composure. It wasn't easy. Everything about that man was deeply physical and sexy.

Worse yet, she had caught him looking at her sometimes, which unnerved her even more. He had tried to flag her down after a meeting, but she pretended she didn't hear him because she didn't trust herself to resist him if they were alone.

And now they were alone. In the basement of the hospital.

"Doctor Ricci, I didn't see you." Wow, when did her voice start quivering like that? "I am, um, almost done here."

"Take your time." He leaned back against a table and

crossed his arms over his chest. Watching her with the same knowing, irresistible smile that had caught her attention back in New York.

Being alone with him was a bad idea.

"No worries!" She began flying around the room, looking for her coat, laptop, purse…oh, dammit, where was her purse? "I'm just…practicing and double-checking…because…surgery…few more days…"

She continued to dart about the room, babbling about who knows what, while he calmly watched her as if she were a specimen in a laboratory experiment of his own design.

Then he languidly pushed away from the table and walked over to a bookshelf.

"Looking for this?"

Her purse dangled from his finger.

She forced a laugh, trying to act like everything was normal. Like she wasn't reduced to the verbal skills of a middle schooler every time he was around. "That's it!"

She crossed the room to retrieve her purse, which put her close to him. Too close. Close enough she could smell his cologne, see gold flecks in his espresso-brown eyes.

Just grab your damn purse and go.

"Well, thanks. Guess I'll just…"

"Have I disturbed you, *dottoressa*?"

His gaze scanned her features, assessing every inch of her face. Unbidden, memories surfaced of his intense expression as he had edged her camisole up her torso, inch by delicious inch. He had made her feel like a treasured gift he had wanted to unwrap ever so slowly, just so he could savor the pleasure.

Ugh! These were exactly the sort of thoughts that had buzzed about like annoying gnats whenever he was nearby.

If he was on the opposite side of the hospital, she could work with a clear, calm mind. If he was within five hundred feet, she could barely form a coherent sentence.

"I can leave if you like."

"What?" Her cheeks flared with heat from her musings. "Don't be silly. I was just…"

"Hanging out with Maria?" He jerked his head in the direction of the mannequin.

It helped a little, his brevity. Gave her a reason to slow down and smile.

"Yeah, just us girls hanging out on a Friday night." She sighed and ran her fingers through her hair. "It's a challenging surgery. I wanted to run through the steps one more time."

He leaned forward, bracing his hands against the gurney where Maria waited patiently for another round of practice surgery.

Miranda wished he wouldn't stand like that. The pose made his forearms flex in ways that were…distracting.

"Yeah, me, too," he said.

Miranda was a beat too late when she finally tore her gaze from his hands and the way the steel gurney made his tendons flex. "What?"

"That's what I came here for, too. To run through my part… I mean, *our* part."

A hint of strain in his tone finally got her thoughts out of the bedroom and back to the moment. That was when she saw that along with his sexy, mischievous smirk was a trace of tension in the small muscles around his eyes.

"No, you're right. The defect repair will be all you. I'm just here to help."

He nodded and smiled, but it felt forced and a little unnatural. It might have been the first time she had seen

Dante less than fully confident. It was enough to trigger the doctor in her to make a much-needed appearance.

"Um, I could stick around if you want. Run through the procedure one more time?"

His expression remained carefully composed, but there was a subtle shift—a faint flicker in his eyes, a quiet exhale. Then, with a measured nod, he accepted her offer without yielding an inch of his pride. "Only if it wouldn't be an inconvenience."

"Of course not." And she meant it. Whatever start they had had in New York, this was what she'd come to Milan for. To *work* with Dante and his new neurosurgical team.

Miranda put her things away while Dante got the training mannequin and the second-term fetus ready for another session.

Miranda flipped on the monitor. Dante took his place across from her.

"Once mom has been deeply sedated, the maternal-fetal specialist will determine the baby's position with ultrasound." She had spoken the words out loud so many times, she could recite them in her sleep.

Dante played the role of the OB specialist, so they could get the flow of the surgery right.

Miranda followed along, making the incisions that the OB surgeon would make so the surgical team could reach the fetus.

Dante carefully moved the training fetus into a tummy-down position. "We only need her back to come up into the world."

"Right." Miranda checked the heart monitor that would be manned by a cardiologist during surgery. "Baby's heartbeat looks nice and strong. You ready?"

Dante nodded, then adjusted his binocular eyepieces

and picked up a scalpel. He began the intricate work of separating skin from the nerve tissue that belonged in the spinal canal.

"Hold up a second," Miranda said, moving around the table to his side. "Slow down as you approach the defect. The skin tissue there may be underdeveloped or damaged from exposure to the amniotic fluid. We have to be very careful."

She leaned in close, put her gloved hand over Dante's to guide his movement. "Small strokes, nice and slow," she murmured.

Touching him, even through latex gloves, was enough to break her concentration. Suddenly, she was far too aware of Dante. How his lashes, thick and black, fringed his dark brown eyes. How his navy blue scrubs hugged his body just right, subtly outlining his athletic build. How his forearms flexed as he worked slowly and deliberately.

Unnerved, Miranda pulled away, desperate to regain her equilibrium. This was surgical practice for Pete's sake, not some lounge in a hotel whose name she couldn't remember anymore.

As Dante navigated the fragile roadmap of spinal nerve and tissues, Miranda grabbed a saline bottle and irrigated tissue. Anything to keep her mind where it belonged.

"Good," Miranda murmured when Dante was finished. "Textbook perfect, if you ask me."

The tiny wrinkles that appeared above his mask told her he was pleased with the compliment. She stepped away from the table, signaling he was fully in charge now. Dante got to work closing muscle and skin tissue on the fetus and then Maria, his sutures perfectly uniform.

"*Voila*," she told him as they tucked Maria under clean

blankets. "You just completed your first fetal spina bifida closure surgery."

"My first *training* spina bifida closure." He tugged his mask off. Shadows of doubt still clouded his eyes. She couldn't blame him. Fetal surgery was not for the faint of heart.

"Hey," she assured him. "You just climbed the mountain. Monday's surgery is when we plant the flag."

"*Grazie*," he said, placing his hands over his heart. God, but he could be endearing sometimes. "It will be an honor to operate with you."

They got to work cleaning up the surgical area and mannequins, readying the area for anyone else who needed to practice before the big day. Miranda had just opened her laptop to update her training notes when Dante stepped into her field of vision.

"You know, I couldn't help but overhear your phone call when I came in. My family home is not far from the hospital. We have a heated pool. You're welcome to use it anytime."

Miranda froze for a moment. The vibe between them was different now. Not flirty like in New York. But not professional like their surgical practice. Something different.

"That's very kind of you, Doctor Ricci."

"Dante. *Per favore*."

"Okay... Dante. But I don't think that would be a good idea."

"Because of what happened with the newspaper?"

She hesitated before she fibbed. "Yes, because of that."

Yes, it had been unnerving, seeing her photo on the front page of a newspaper. But that wasn't all of it. Not by a long shot.

She wasn't angry with Dante—because he didn't owe

her a thing! They'd had a casual, sexy hookup in New York—no big deal. If the man wanted to live his life in the fast lane, that was 100 percent his business.

No, the problem was *her*. Somehow, she had managed to convince herself that they'd had a connection in New York. That she *knew* him in some way that transcended their fleeting encounter.

But coming to Milan to discover how wrong her impressions had been...well, that had slammed her right back to the night she'd discovered Bradford wasn't the man she thought he was. Not even close.

See, the problem with Bradford's betrayal wasn't just that he'd lied. It was that he had custom-built a reality just for her. It made her doubt every moment of their five years together. Had he ever loved her? Or had every moment been about the persona he wanted others to believe: that he was a perfect, long-suffering doting husband who stood by his wife's side as she tried—and failed—to give their marriage the baby he claimed he so desperately wanted?

She'd never really known the real Bradford, and it had broken her heart to realize she had been living a lie.

So that front-page news story had been another painful reminder of life's one bitter truth. Whether she knew Dante for a night or a decade, it was impossible to trust herself to believe she knew him at all.

She slung her purse over her shoulder, tugging out the waves that were trapped under the strap. "Thanks, anyway. I better get going..."

He caught her by the arm as she moved to pass him. "Miranda, hold up a sec."

She paused, surprised. His expression was earnest.

"Listen, I'm really sorry that went down like that. The paparazzi...well, they just love the 'spoiled rich boy' image and they pull it out anytime they need to sell more tabloids."

She held up her hands to stop him. "Dante, it's fine. You don't owe me any explanations."

He caught her hands lightly in his own. "I know. But you traveled halfway across the world to help our team, only to get caught up in paparazzi drama."

"Don't worry about it. Coming to Milan is my job."

"But it's more than that…to me. See, it's only because you agreed to mentor our team that I agreed to accept the spina bifida case. If—no, when—our team successfully completes this surgery, we'll undoubtedly receive more referrals for complicated pediatric neurosurgeries. And it might even inspire our hospital board to make my position as interim chief of pediatric neurosurgery more permanent."

"Ah," she said, understanding Dante's long-term goals. "I'd be happy to put in a good word for you when I leave, if you think it will help."

"You've done so much just by coming here, *dottoressa*. That's why I would consider it a great honor if you would reconsider attending the Grand Prix with me. It's just… my way of saying thank you."

Miranda hesitated. It would be so much smarter for them to keep their distance.

Thank you so much for the generous invitation, but I simply must decline.

That was what she meant to say. But her feckless, foolish heart got in the way.

"Sure, Dante. I'd love to."

CHAPTER FOUR

Dante paced his dining room as his personal chef laid out a simple breakfast of poached eggs and toast. He had had far too much espresso that morning and felt jittery and ill at ease.

Antonio, his house manager, waited patiently at the dining room table, a sheaf of papers in front of him. The papers outlined the agenda Dante had meticulously planned ever since Miranda had agreed to attend the Italian Grand Prix event with him.

"Let's review it again. Last time, I promise!" Dante said.

Antonio appeared slightly strained but maintained his composure. "Of course, sir. It would be my pleasure."

The day would start with Dante and his driver picking Miranda up from her rented villa. They would travel in style to a private airport where Dante had chartered a helicopter for the day. He had scheduled an early departure so that there would be plenty of time to take a scenic trip to the racetrack, complete with roses and champagne. The helicopter would land at a private airport near the city of Monza, where the racetrack was located. A private car would then whisk them off to the Monza track and deliver them at the door of the exclusive Paddock Club, where they would spend the afternoon enjoying premium hospitality with unparalleled views of the Formula 1 action.

Dante pored over the agenda, still feeling ill at ease. "Did I miss anything, Antonio? You would tell me if I did, wouldn't you?"

Antonio shook his head. "Oh no, sir. I think you've quite outdone yourself this time."

Antonio was no stranger to helping Dante plan creative, unforgettable dates. Thanks to his flair and attention to detail, Dante's reputation as the ultimate bachelor playboy was legendary in Milan.

But this date was different. Dante yearned to re-create the electric connection he had felt with Miranda in New York. They had gotten off to a bad start with the paparazzi in Milan, but with any luck, channeling all of his charm and resources into an unforgettable afternoon would sweep Miranda off her feet and back into his bed.

With every detail double-checked, Dante went upstairs to his bedroom to get ready. Antonio had laid out his clothing—as usual, his choices were the perfect mix of upscale yet casual. As he finished dressing, Antonio knocked on the door.

"Your driver is ready, sir."

"*Grazie.*" Dante took one last look in the mirror. He splashed a bit of cologne on his neck, then descended the staircase to the foyer and stepped into a luxury sedan.

On the way to Miranda's villa, he nervously tapped his knee. Miranda wasn't like the actresses and influencers he had dated in the past, who shared his goal of keeping romantic connections easy and superficial. They had wanted camera-worthy moments they could post on their social media, and he had wanted a few hours of feeling some semblance of love and affection. With Miranda, he wasn't entirely sure what the key was to her heart.

Magic and sparkle. That was what she had said her parents had. What she had hoped to have in her own life—until she'd settled for a man who had all the romantic charm of a vacuum cleaner.

Well, Dante was not about to be relegated to the "functional" category of male partners. If the lady wanted magic and sparkle, he would deliver that plus fireworks and meteor showers, if need be.

One last splurge should do the trick. He found the private number for the motorsport manager who represented several of Italy's top F1 racing talents. He knew he was leveraging the Ricci name for his own benefit—something he usually avoided at all costs. But he couldn't afford to leave a single detail to chance.

The car stopped in front of Miranda's villa, a charming, elegant Italian abode with a small garden. Dante opted to knock on the door himself instead of sending his driver.

"*Buongiorno*, *Signor* Ricci," she greeted him with a smile, clearly pleased with the Italian she had mastered.

"Likewise, *Dottoressa* Hawthorne," he replied, feeling momentarily unsteady. The American doctor, stunning even on her worst day, was absolutely breathtaking in a red polka-dot dress paired with matching sandals and sun hat. Her hair cascaded in waves, and her hazel eyes sparkled.

Her eyes widened when she saw his chauffeured car. "To the racetrack?"

"Not exactly," he said with a smile.

As they drove to the airport, he offered her champagne from a chilled compartment. Miranda pronounced the champagne delicious and asked Dante to point out landmarks as they passed.

Everything was off to a smashing start.

When they arrived at the private airport, she was taken aback. "Why are we here?"

"Trust me, *Signora* Hawthorne," he said, helping her from the car. He led her to the helicopter, which surprised her even more.

"Is this how everyone gets to Monza?" she teased.

"Not everyone. Just us," he teased back.

The helicopter ride was just as luxurious as he'd hoped, with breathtaking views and thoughtful touches, like champagne and strawberries. Dante pointed out landmarks below, excited to share this experience. Was she impressed with the exclusivity of the day? He certainly hoped so.

As soon as Miranda and Dante stepped out of the car, a tsunami of energy and noise enveloped them. Engines roared, mingling with the sharp tang of fuel and rubber, creating a symphony of sights and smells that stirred both excitement and awe.

Flags of every color snapped in the breeze, while throngs of passionate fans in team colors passed them, their shouts and laughter filling the air.

Dante guided Miranda to the Paddock Club, where they would have a bird's-eye view of the pit lanes and the teams as they performed crucial operations during the race. The glittering hospitality suites reflected the sun, and the scent of freshly grilled gourmet food mixed with the petroleum smell of race-car fuel.

Dante pulled out Miranda's chair. "I hope you're pleased," he said, watching her reaction.

She took in the luxurious accommodations and the attentive server, already standing at Dante's elbow. "It's quite incredible, Dante."

The afternoon unfolded just as Dante had planned. They started with an elaborate lunch, and he introduced her to the Michelin-starred chef responsible for the day's exquisite menu. Miranda sampled dishes that were as much art as food, each bite paired with fine wine and conversation with the exclusive guests of the club.

From there, Dante seamlessly maneuvered her into conversations with Italy's most influential figures—actors, entrepreneurs and politicians—effortlessly charming them all while keeping her close at his side.

When they left the club to visit the pit lanes, the atmosphere intensified as mechanics and managers moved in a blur of flashing colors and shouted commands.

But the grand finale was leading her to an actual Formula 1 car.

"Go on, have a seat," he coaxed with a grin as he held the door open for her.

"Oh, okay," she said, taking a seat where, in less than an hour, the real F1 driver would push the car to death-defying speeds in a quest to bring home the trophy. She ran her hands over the sleek steering wheel, but her expression seemed distant, even a bit overwhelmed.

Dante thought that maybe there had been a shift in her demeanor, and he faltered for a moment. Had he misread Miranda when he planned this date? No, that wasn't possible. He had spared no expense or effort in planning the perfect date for her to experience a unique Italian tradition. Surely, her apparent reserve was just his imagination.

Dante's phone rang and he glanced at the caller ID.

"I'm sorry, Miranda. It's the hospital. I'll be right back."

He stepped away, trying to find a quieter spot where he could confer with the resident doctor on a difficult case they had been managing. When he finally finished and returned to the pit lanes, Miranda was nowhere in sight.

Dante moved swiftly through the bustling pit lanes, his eyes scanning the crowd for any sign of her. The roar of engines and the rhythmic hiss of air guns filled the air, making it difficult to concentrate. He stopped by a group of mechanics, his voice urgent yet polite.

"*Scusami, hai visto una donna alta con i capelli castani?*" he asked, gesturing with his hand to describe her height. When they shook their heads, he pressed on, weaving through the chaos with determination.

"*Per favore, è molto importante,*" he added, stopping another passerby, this time a young woman in a team jacket. She paused, shaking her head apologetically, and Dante muttered a soft *grazie* before continuing his search. His worry deepened as he moved past the gleaming F1 cars and beyond the noise and chaos of the pits, hoping to find her before she slipped too far away.

At the edge of the pit lanes, he spotted a narrow walking path winding its way through the lush greenery of the park that surrounded the Monza racetrack. The path, dappled with sunlight filtering through the tall trees, seemed like a quiet escape from the frenzy of the race.

He paused, considering the possibility—Miranda had grown more reserved as the day went on. Perhaps she had been overwhelmed by the energy of the event?

Dante stepped up his pace and followed the path. He scanned both sides of the park, looking for any sign of her familiar silhouette among the trees.

He had gone quite deep into the park when he finally spotted her on a stone bridge that crossed a small lake where ducks swam about in lazy circles. She had kicked off her shoes and was eating a gelato while she watched the ducks.

"Hey," he said, joining her on the bridge. He felt his shoulders drop an inch with relief at having found her.

"Hey, yourself," she said, smiling back. She looked noticeably more serene here in the quiet park.

He shrugged off his jacket and laid it across the bridge railing. "Are you lost, *signora*?"

She lightly elbowed him in the ribs. He still liked that, this peculiar American custom of light abuse as a sign of affection.

"No. It's just nice here. Quiet and cool."

He turned around, so his back was to the bridge rail and he could take in her beautiful features.

"Would you like to go back to watch the race?"

She tongued the last of her gelato from the spoon, a more provocative gesture than she probably intended.

"Maybe in a bit. I'm enjoying this."

She tossed her gelato cup in the trash, then bent to swoop her sandals up by the straps. She followed the path deeper into the woods, away from the racetrack, and Dante followed like a love-struck puppy.

After a long minute, he finally blurted what was on his mind. "You hated today, didn't you?"

She didn't answer right away, instead wandering farther down the shaded path. Her bare feet were soundless on the walkway as the woods became thicker and cooler.

Miranda gazed upward at the canopy above their heads, where sunlight filtered through the leaves in shimmering golden streams. Dante followed her line of sight, noticing how the vibrant green leaves swayed gently in the breeze, casting shifting patterns of light and shadow on the forest floor.

High above, birds flitted between branches, their soft chirps the only sound in the stillness. For the first time that day, Dante felt his soul slow down to match the beauty and pace of this raw, unguarded moment in nature. Was this what Miranda was seeking when she left the chaos of the racetrack?

Was this what she had been seeking when she came to Milan?

Finally, she returned her gaze to him, sizing him up with a thoughtful look. "No, I didn't hate it. Not exactly."

"But you didn't love it," he pressed.

She returned to walking the path, and he stepped up his pace so he could fall in line with her.

"It was an amazing date, Dante. Very interesting and impressive. I guess I just prefer quieter spaces like this sometimes." She looked up at him and smiled. "Actually, that's not true. I always prefer being in nature. I feel sheltered by the trees, like they're keeping watch over me. But we can go back to the race, if you want."

He realized that would be a mistake; she would only be going for him. "No, I don't think that's necessary. Let's just enjoy the park," he said.

They walked in companionable silence while he wrestled with feelings of disappointment. Not only had he not connected with Miranda as he'd hoped, he also felt like he might have pushed her even further away.

They walked the circuitous route back to the racetrack. There was no point in watching the race, so he texted the driver and arranged for an early return trip to Milan.

As they waited, he racked his brain, trying to figure out what went wrong.

The luxury car pulled up alongside them. Finally, frustrated, he asked, "Miranda, why was this so much easier in New York? Was it because we were playing a game?"

She paused, her hand on the car door handle, considering the question.

"Perhaps," she said. She gazed past the car, to the racetrack and beyond, then shifted her focus to him. Her answer was honest, and that was why it hurt a little.

"Or maybe Amelia just liked Paul better," she said.

* * *

Miranda loved it when the operating room was like this. Despite the large team she had assembled, the operating room was relatively quiet, everyone working in synergy. Just as she had planned.

A wall-mounted video monitor showed the tips of their instruments as she and Dante worked in unison. A slow steady beeping from the heart monitors—one for *Signora* Romano and one for her baby—was reassuring. Everyone was doing well.

Which was damn near a miracle. Despite all the practice Miranda had insisted on, this surgery had been a challenge from the start. The OB surgeon had done her best to help them reach the fetus, but the fetus kept rotating away so that her back—the area they needed to operate on—was hidden from view.

Miranda huddled with Dante, trying to figure out a solution. She had tried all the standard movements to bring the fetus back into view, but it just wasn't working. The surgical site kept slipping away from where they could reach it.

"Here, let me try something." The OB specialist attempted to roll the fetus from the right side while Miranda guided its position.

None of Miranda's marathon practice sessions had planned for such a rough start. From the moment the team wheeled mom into the OR, it had been a challenge. Her blood pressure had been up and down all morning. Matteo, the anesthesiologist, did his best, giving her various medications to adjust her pressure while the pediatric cardiologist closely watched the fetal heart monitor, calling out issues as they came and went.

After a very rough start to the day, it seemed like they were finally ready to do what they'd come here for. The neural tissue was right there on the surface, ready to be separated and settled back into the spinal canal.

Miranda made eye contact with Dante over their masks. "The placode is in position, Doctor Ricci." She handed him miniature scissors and forceps. Tiny instruments for a tiny fetus.

Dante nodded. His brow furrowed as he focused on his tasks. But he had barely gotten started when alarms started ringing from behind the drapes.

Matteo's voice rang out calm and clear. "Just a blood pressure spike. We're treating it."

Right on cue, the pediatric cardiologist echoed, "We've got a filling defect showing here." A sign of early blood loss, source unknown.

And then the placode rolled away from them again.

"Dammit," Dante hissed.

"We'll get her," the OB said. Together, she and Miranda worked to rotate the fetus back into position.

And then, suddenly and inexplicably, there was blood. *So* much blood washing over Miranda's fingers, filling the uterus within seconds.

"Abruption!" the OB shouted. Miranda's and Dante's gazes met, and time seemed to hitch for a few long seconds.

Then everything started moving very fast. The OB surgeon called out directives, nurses and techs flew in all directions, alarms went crazy and Miranda and Dante continued to hold the fetus in position until someone yelled for them to get the hell out of the way because ready or not, this baby needed to be delivered *now*!

Miranda stepped away from the table, watching in shocked horror as the team worked frantically to deliver the preterm fetus.

Placental abruption was one of the most lethal risks of

performing fetal surgery. If the placenta pulled away from the uterine wall, the baby lost its lifeline. The team had no choice. They had to deliver her, even though it meant Baby Romano was going to lose her entire third trimester of development.

Gloved hands shifted and then an infant appeared, sprawled doll-like and carefully cradled in gloved hands.

Then, just as quickly as she appeared, the baby was gone, whisked off in a blanket to a team of neonatologists. Urgent voices called back and forth across the OR as one team worked on the baby and another on the mom.

I need a syringe of epi now!
Careful, let's get her in the warmer.
Suction! I can't see what's bleeding!

This was beyond anything that Miranda dealt with in neurosurgery. There wasn't a damn thing she or Dante could do to help now. Miranda's gaze raked wildly across the room, taking in everything all at once.

And found Dante's coffee-brown eyes, watching her over his mask. His eyes were full of questions and confusion.

She wanted to tell him it wasn't his fault. This was the risk that came with fetal surgery. She knew that—the family knew that—and now Dante knew it, too.

Eventually, the team stopped the bleeding. Mom and newborn were stable for the moment, but they would be closely monitored for the next few days. The room went calm. No alarms, no pushing blood, no furious chatter.

Miranda led Dante to the isolette, where the newborn was being carefully observed.

"You need to finish the surgery," she told Dante. He glanced her way, still in shock, and she understood. It was hard to imagine doing anything after the chaos that had brought their surgery to a standstill. But Baby Romano needed them now.

She squeezed his arm. "You've got this."

They left the OR to rescrub, then changed into clean gowns and gloves. Soon, their hands were working together, closing each layer and bringing them together with tiny sutures. When they were done, the nurses swaddled the newborn in a clean blanket and nestled her back in the isolette.

Miranda and Dante stood back as the team split, half following the baby to the pediatric ICU while the other half followed mom.

The chief of surgery poked his head past the door. "Press conference in five, you two. Let's go."

Ugh. The last thing she wanted to deal with right now was the press. But she knew she didn't have a choice. This was St. Joseph's first fetal surgery, and the public deserved an update.

The auditorium buzzed with tension as journalists and camera crews crammed into the lecture auditorium at St. Joseph's Hospital. Her team of surgical hotshots sat at long conference tables flanking a podium.

Miranda took her place at the podium, her hands clenched tightly around the edges of the lectern. As team lead, it was her job to answer the media's questions about the surgery. But she didn't really want to be here. It had been a long day where just about everything that could go wrong, did. And now she was going to have to answer for those complications in a very public way.

All she could hope was that the Italian media wasn't as accusatory as the American press could be.

She squinted her eyes against the camera flashes. "Good afternoon, and thank you for being here," Miranda began, her voice steady despite the tightness in her chest. "I'm sure you have a lot of questions about today's surgery—I'll be happy to address those in a minute. But first, I want to assure everyone that both the mother and the baby are stable and under close observation. Their recovery is our top priority."

Before she could continue, a reporter from *Corriere della Sera* shot up. "Doctor Hawthorne, you were invited to lead the hospital's first fetal surgery because of your reputation. How do you explain the complications that nearly resulted in the mother's death? Was this a case of overconfidence?"

Miranda's jaw tightened. So much for her hope that this conference would go well.

She forced a smile. "Every surgery carries risks, especially pioneering procedures like fetal spina bifida repair. I'm very proud of my team—some of the finest surgeons from Italy and beyond—who worked so tirelessly to mitigate those risks."

"Yet, the mother nearly bled out on the table," countered a correspondent from *ANSA*. "What do you say to critics who claim that your team was inadequately prepared?"

The cameras flashed relentlessly, their white-hot light making the suffocating room even more warm and oppressive. Out of the corner of her eye, she could see Dante shifting uncomfortably in his seat, his fingers tapping a restless rhythm on his thigh. His jaw was tight, his gaze darting between her and the reporters as if he was debating whether to intervene. She willed him to stay silent. With any luck, the press would wrap up their questions and move on to new targets.

"Our team performed extensive simulations leading up to the procedure," Miranda replied, her voice firm but even. "Despite this, unforeseen complications arose. The maternal-fetal specialist and anesthesiologist—both leaders in their fields—acted decisively to stabilize the patient. Their quick actions saved her life."

Another reporter chimed in. "Doctor Hawthorne, how do you respond to accusations that you were more focused on building your reputation than ensuring patient safety?"

The aggressive question cut through the air like a whip, and before Miranda could summon a response, Dante was on his feet. The scrape of his chair against the floor drew every eye in the room as he strode to her side, his presence commanding even without the authority of the podium.

His voice was steady but charged with emotion. "That's quite enough," he said, his accent sharpening the edges of his words.

"The last thing Doctor Hawthorne is concerned about is building her reputation. She doesn't need to worry about that because her well-deserved reputation is stellar. She would never put anything ahead of patient safety. That's why Mrs. Romano and her baby are still with us.

"Now, if you want the truth, ask real questions, not ones meant to provoke headlines."

As Dante's words cut through the room, Miranda felt an unfamiliar warmth bloom in her chest. For years, during the quiet despair of her marriage, she had felt vulnerable and unprotected. But with Dante standing at her side, she felt the startling and unfamiliar comfort of having someone in her corner—both as a colleague and as something far more personal.

"One last question," Dante said, leaning forward on the podium as if daring the reporters to start a fight.

A woman from *Il Giornale* stood. "With all due respect, Doctor Hawthorne, the optics don't look good. An

American surgeon flying in to lead a groundbreaking surgery that goes awry? Do you regret taking on this case?"

Miranda exhaled slowly as she considered the question. Did she regret coming to Milan? She had come here hoping for some space and grace to figure out the next chapter of her life. To grieve the loss of her marriage, her innocence and her hopes for a baby of her own.

Instead, she had fallen for some guy named Paul in New York. And then met his alter ego in Milan. A confusing man so far—equal parts attentive lover and showy playboy. But just when she was ready to dismiss Milan's Prince of Pleasure, he went and did something like this. Now she wasn't sure she knew the man at all.

"I regret the distress this has caused the patient and her family. But no, I do not regret coming to Milan." She felt Dante's hand find her back, his thumb gently stroking her spine. She took that as a positive sign that he did not regret inviting her here, either.

And then, mercifully, the ordeal was over. The hospital's director stepped to her side. "Ladies and gentlemen, that will be all for today," he announced, his voice brooking no argument. "Saint Joseph's stands behind Doctor Hawthorne and the entire surgical team. We thank you for your questions and your concern for our patients."

As reporters shouted out more questions, and camera bulbs flashed, Dante pulled her away from the podium.

"That's enough of that nonsense," he muttered, tucking her hand in his as he tugged her away from the reporters and back to the locker room.

It was quiet there, the hum of fluorescent lights the only sound as Miranda leaned against the cool metal of the lockers. "You okay?"

She opened her eyes and saw Dante sitting across from

her, his expression a mix of lingering frustration from the press conference and something softer, just for her.

She nodded and pushed away from the locker to gather her things. The day had been beyond challenging, and she was more than ready to escape to her villa for a simple dinner, if she didn't fall into an exhausted sleep first.

"It was a difficult surgery with a serious complication. Questions are to be expected."

"Questions are fine. Accusations are not."

She closed her locker and turned back to him. "Don't worry about it. If Saint Joseph's is going to become a top-tier site for pediatric neurosurgery, you'll be matching wits with the press plenty."

She slung her bag over her shoulder and headed for the exit. Then she stopped and turned back to Dante.

"Thank you, though, for having my back in there. It was…nice."

Wordlessly, he reached into his pocket, then pressed a small, worn key into her palm. "For your swims," he said, his voice low, as if the key carried more weight than its size suggested. "I will text you the address of my family's home."

She stared at it for a long moment, remembering the first time he'd offered—how she'd refused because she wanted to keep their boundaries clear.

But now, in the aftermath of a stormy day, she saw the invitation for what it was.

"Thank you," she said softly.

Then she wrapped her fingers around the key. Accepting it. And taking another chance with him.

CHAPTER FIVE

DANTE ADJUSTED THE eyepiece of his telescope until the Milky Way came into clear view. Its clean white glow stretched across the heavens, dotted with constellations like Pegasus and Cygnus. He was just about to search for the warm hues of Mars and Jupiter when he heard the distinctive rasp of a wrought iron gate opening.

He had a visitor. *Finally.*

For the past week, ever since the disastrous press conference, Dante had hoped Miranda would accept his invitation. That she would come to the house. Use the key. Find peace and quiet away from the hospital and the press. Be with him.

The surgery and press conference had taken its toll on her. She had been quieter, smiled less, as she'd continued to mentor his team.

It had taken its toll on him as well. The Romano family was doing well, thank goodness, though Baby Romano would need many weeks to grow strong in the NICU. But he had to admit, despite his experience with years of high-stakes neurosurgery, it had shocked him how fast things could go from perfectly fine to mortally dangerous in fetal surgery.

He cocked his head, listening, as the gate creaked closed and locked with a metallic click. Miranda would be in the garden by now. Crossing the perfectly manicured lawn that bordered an oversize infinity pool. He had asked the staff to clean the already pristine pool every day, on the chance that she might come.

She would not be able to see him from the pool area. He was around the corner, tucked away on a secluded wooden deck where a state-of-the-art telescope had been mounted under a retractable awning for unobstructed stargazing.

His mind struggled with his choices. Should he leave her to swim alone in peace? Or join her with hopes she would welcome his company?

Then he realized he hadn't stocked the pool house with fresh, clean towels. What a funny detail to overlook. Especially for a man who never left details to chance. Funny, too, how he had felt the urge to stargaze every night since he pressed that gate key into Miranda's hand. It was the perfect spot to hear a clandestine guest make her entrance.

He slipped into the house to commandeer several fluffy white towels. And spotted a bottle of red wine on the kitchen counter.

Would that be too obvious?

Heavens no. Not in Milan, where wine was an integral part of catching up with friends or relaxing after work.

Miranda was settling her things on a lounge chair when Dante rounded the corner. He cleared his throat so he wouldn't frighten her.

"Dantè! I didn't know you were here."

"*Buona sera, bellissima*," he said as he crisscrossed the outdoor space, turning on lights that illuminated the garden and pool area. "*La giornata è stata lunga, ma vederti migliora tutto.*"

She smiled. "I'm afraid my Italian is too new for all that, Dante."

"I said, good evening, beautiful. The day was long, but seeing you makes everything better."

She smiled, making his world shift. "It's good to see you, too."

Dante gave her a quick bow. "Let me know if you need anything else, Miranda. I'm just a shout away."

Miranda watched him leave, a towel pressed to her chest, biting her lip.

He had almost made it back to the house when she called out.

"Doctor Ricci, really? What kind of doctor lets a girl drink and swim alone?" Her tone was playful. Even a little provocative.

Dante's breath caught as his pulse quickened. The unmistakable tease in her tone sent a ripple of heat through him, and he felt a magnetic pull toward her. His brain seemed to simultaneously freeze and race at the same time. This felt like an invitation, one he should be able to easily accept since this was what he had wanted when he pressed that key into her hand.

But now…he wasn't certain of his next move. What an unfamiliar dilemma. What did she want from him? New York had been effortless, but the Grand Prix had been a romantic disaster. His only hint? That she'd liked Paul better.

He walked back to her, taking his time. "I didn't want to impose on your solitude."

She gave him a sexy, mysterious smile. "Maybe I've had enough solitude, Dante."

She slipped out of her gauzy cover-up, revealing a sleek black bikini that showed off an athletic frame shaped by hours of swimming practice. Dante's throat went dry, his eyes tracing the sculpted lines of her figure. A flicker of heat ignited deep in his chest. She was a stunning blend of strength and sensuality.

To reach the pool steps, she had to pass directly in front of him. Had to tease him with the scent of vanilla and coconut from her shampoo. Had to entice him with the strong curves of her shoulders, the long slope of her back. He held his breath as she descended the pool steps one at a time, the water lapping at her body until she ducked under the water.

Dante slowly let out his breath, feeling desire stir within him, undeniable and magnetic. It was as if every step she took was deliberate, meant to tease and torture him. If that indeed was her intent, her efforts were working. Amazingly well.

Eventually, she emerged, laughing, from below the water's surface. Her wet hair cascaded down her back. "My gosh, Dante. It's warmer in here than it is outside!"

That was no accident. Dante had monitored the water temperature twice a day, just in case she had accepted his invitation.

She took her time exploring the pool. Her strokes were slow and lazy, until she eventually flipped to float on her back. Water droplets pooled in the shallow depression between her breasts, reflecting the soft glow cast by the garden lamps that bordered the pool.

A flash of light near her navel reminded him of her belly button piercing. A small stainless-steel ball that had felt smooth and cool when he had flicked his tongue over it.

The memory made him shudder with longing.

She must have noticed. "It's cold outside, Dante. Join me—I won't bite!"

He would love nothing more than to join her and pick up where they'd left off in New York. But what was the key to finding Amelia again? He burned to understand, to figure it out.

To figure *her* out.

She was so beautiful—and mysterious. A beautiful, complicated, wondrous challenge.

That was it, wasn't it? Uncharted territory meant navigating without a map. He would have to draw the map himself, untangling her secrets by following his instincts and learning from mistakes.

So be it, then. *Challenge accepted,* bellissima. *Somehow, I will make you mine.*

"But I don't have a swimsuit," he pointed out. Of course he had several in the house, but damn if he was going to break the spell of whatever this was by leaving.

She shrugged. "Strip to your underwear, then. It's practically the same."

Practically, yes, but also so different. He hesitated long enough that she smiled and splashed water his way. How he loved that side of her, eager to tease and provoke.

"I won't look." She turned away so he could slip out of his pants and into the pool. It seemed like a silly formality after their passionate night in New York. But Paul and Amelia were long gone now. Miranda and Dante were still strangers in many ways.

She turned around and her teasing smile made him glad he was mostly under water. Then she slipped under the water again, like a mermaid he couldn't contain. He was almost getting concerned when he felt something brush his leg. Solid muscle first, then the tickle of her hair. She emerged from the water, much closer to him now. Close enough to touch—or kiss.

Beads of water clung to her skin, and her proximity hit him like a shock wave—the power in her swimmer's frame, the provocative parting of her lips—it left him momentarily breathless. For a man who prided himself on his self-control, he found that Miranda had an uncanny ability to unsettle him in the most delicious ways.

"You know what the nurses say about you, don't you?" She cocked her head, a coy challenge.

He knew it wouldn't be good, but he couldn't help it. He had to ask. "What do they say?"

"Well, my Italian is quite basic, but when they welcomed me to the ward, I think it went something like... *Ricorda solo, se il suo cognome e Ricci, il suo nome potrebbe anche essere Guai.*"

Dante forced a dry chuckle.

"Is it true? That if I meet a man and his last name is Ricci, his first name is surely Trouble?"

Good grief, there it was again. The joke his life had become, to everyone but him. The wealthiest family in all of Milan, forced to adopt the son of the patriarch's mistress. Paparazzi selling his misfortune for profit. And random colleagues gleefully perpetuating the myths he hated, yet needed to make sure he never became a man like Vittorio.

Because if it wasn't for his reputation as Milan's Prince of Pleasure, Dante would have no love in his life at all.

"People say a lot of things, Miranda."

She stood before him, her fingers tracing small circles in the water. He knew she was waiting for more.

Maybe this was what she had found with Paul in New York. Their little game had allowed them to deliberately lie to each other, which somehow made it safe to tell the truths they kept hidden from the world. If she had not been Amelia, would she have revealed the heartbreak of her marriage? Allowed him to feel that hurt in her body when they made love? He highly doubted it.

He took a deep breath as he cast his gaze over her shoulder, to the starry sky he had been studying before she arrived. "It was true of me—a long time ago."

Her eyebrows briefly arched as she nodded. A subtle sign to continue.

"My mother died when I was almost twelve years old. I didn't know that the man she was seeing was Vittorio Ricci, patriarch of one of Milan's wealthiest families. She was one of Vittorio's many mistresses, and her death put my father in a very awkward position. He had no choice but to adopt me into his family, where I was, as you can imagine, not exactly welcomed."

Miranda's gaze softened, as her playful demeanor gave way to a quiet empathy.

"There was no opportunity to truly grieve the loss of my mother. No one in that house wanted to hear her name or see my grief. Her funeral was quick and perfunctory, and she was buried far from the city, where I had no chance to visit and mourn."

Miranda's hand flew to her mouth, her eyes widening with the weight of his words. "Dante, that's awful."

Dante felt her hand find his, weaving her fingers into his. Her eyes were earnest and intensely focused on him, and he felt the intention coursing from her heart to his. *You are not alone with this.*

"I bore the burden as well as any child can, but by the time I was a teenager, the pain was too great. I began acting out in ways that were horribly self-destructive and, to be honest, embarrassing to me now."

"Many have done the same," she breathed.

"True," he conceded. "But most do not have the paparazzi constantly underfoot. My reckless years provided endless fodder to sell their stupid tabloids. And now, despite all that I have done to repair the damage and honor my mother's memory…"

"They just can't let that story go," she finished for him.

"No, they can't."

Dante looked at her, then at his fingers intertwined with hers. Something shifted deep inside him. She wasn't just the woman whose beauty had bewitched him when he'd first caught sight of her in New York. She was becoming someone who made him feel seen, understood and unexpectedly whole.

Maybe she felt it, too, because she stepped closer to him, slipping her arms around his waist. "I never believed it was true," she whispered. "That you were trouble."

His heart hitched at her confession. "But you don't even know me."

She glanced up, her sharp chin tilted in an adorable, defiant challenge. "Oh, really? Well, here's what I *do* know. I know you are always early because you value people's time. I know you leave no detail to chance." She cocked her head. "And, I have it on good authority that you sneak up to the NICU to check on the Romano baby at least twice a day."

A deep ache bloomed in Dante's chest, a mixture of awe and vulnerability, as he realized that Miranda saw him completely and was still here in his arms.

"Well, I just want to make sure that she is…"

"*And*," she continued, "that you feed her when her parents can't be there." Miranda's lips curved into a knowing smile, soft and teasing.

"Damn hospital gossip," he muttered.

But his mind wasn't on the hospital at all. His pulse quickened as the soothing balm of her understanding settled his soul. For once, he felt no need to guard himself, or hide behind the persona that had been created by others. He could be himself with her in a way that felt both exhilarating and terrifying.

Dante pulled her close, feeling the heat of her body against his as his arms wrapped around her. Her face tilted up toward his, her eyes shining with a silent, irresistible invitation.

"Miranda…"

"Mmm-hmm," she breathed.

"How much longer will you be in Milan?"

A hint of shadow darkened her eyes, then was gone. "Twenty-seven days."

Almost four weeks—a long time for two people who knew how to make the most of a single night.

"Dante? If you could be anyone you wanted for the next twenty-seven days, who would *you* be?"

Did she even have to ask? Wasn't the answer obvious in the heat that coursed through his body? Could she not feel the ache in his pounding heart?

He bent his head to hers, knowing words would make a mess of what was in his heart. He let his mouth and hands show her what he wanted.

Her soft lips gently parted for him, and he tasted red wine and temptation on her breath. Her skin felt cool under his feverish touch. This is what he wanted—to grasp this fleeting chance to be hers for as long as Milan—and she—would allow.

She broke off their kiss, her breath coming in rapid, shallow pants. "Twenty-seven days," she repeated.

"Twenty-seven days," he confirmed.

They both knew this could only be temporary. Miranda's life was in Boston, and he would never risk her heart on the permanence of love.

But twenty-seven days could still be something neither of them would forget.

* * *

Miranda arched her back, crying out as her body finally succumbed to Dante's endless teasing. For almost an hour, he'd kept her teetering on the knife edge of bliss before finally granting her the sweet release she craved. Wave after wave of pleasure swept through her body, making her toes curl and her fingers fist the sweaty sheets.

With a flip of the covers, Dante reappeared, his eyes glinting wickedly. She didn't want to tell him how good he was at *that*, but he was good. Maestro-level good.

Dante spooned himself around her, nuzzling her neck as she slowly floated back to earth. Every single muscle in her body had melted into a pool of blissed-out relaxation. She was utterly at peace with herself and the world.

She rolled to face him, tracking the salacious curves of his wicked grin with her thumb. How had she gotten so lucky? When she'd come to Milan, all she had wanted was to find a quiet place to nurse her broken heart and a chance to make peace with her losses. Then she'd gotten stranded in New York and now she had so much more.

Dammit. She would have to tell her sister she'd been right all along. A revenge affair had turned out to be exactly what she'd needed to put memories of Bradford in the rearview mirror where they belonged.

Except this didn't feel like revenge. Or an affair. More like finding a hundred dollar bill in a winter coat. Something unexpected and wonderful.

He curved his arm around her rib cage, pulling her closer. "One more week," he whispered against her neck.

Her heart took a little plunge. "One more week," she echoed.

It was a little game they played now. A way to remind

themselves and each other to treasure every hour until she returned home.

It was a bittersweet thought, returning home. She looked forward to getting back to the job and family she loved. But Bradford was still waiting, along with his group texts and occasional hallway ambushes at work.

And the reality that his baby would be here in just a few months.

Ugh. Boston was complicated. Milan was simple.

She sighed, snuggled into Dante. She didn't want to think about any of that until it was time to board the plane. Why ruin her last week in Milan with reality?

Dante's watch alarm went off. He groaned.

She reached up to curl her fingers into the thick waves at the nape of his neck. "Shh. Don't go."

He used a knuckle to tilt her chin up, so he could kiss the tip of her nose. "I have to. Staff meeting with the chief."

She wanted to complain but kept it in check. They were both grown-ups. Work was forever. This thing between them was not.

He kissed her two more times, then got out of the bed with a grumpy sigh.

She watched from the bed as he gathered the clothing he had shed just an hour before. He was such a gorgeous, interesting, sexy man. Leaving him behind in Milan wasn't going to be easy.

He kissed her twice and promised to get back as soon as he could. The door clicked shut behind him and she was alone.

She sighed and tucked an arm behind her head. She should get busy packing for her trip home. That would be a wise way for her to spend this rare night off from her work at the hospital.

But the packing looked no more inviting after she had taken a shower. She slipped into leggings and a soft T-shirt, then wandered the villa. She would miss this little Italian hideout and its well-tended garden. Having a constant supply of fresh herbs and pretty cut flowers had inspired her to start planning a garden of her own when she returned to Boston.

Eventually, she found herself flipping through recipes in a cookbook someone had left behind in her rented villa. All the recipes were in Italian, but with the help of a translation app on her phone, she was able to find a few that felt doable.

A light dinner of tomato bruschetta and lemon risotto for her and Dante to enjoy in the garden was a much better idea than packing suitcases and making to-do lists. The tiramisu looked pretty delicious, too. She added its ingredients to her shopping list, then slipped on her shoes so she could walk to the little market near her villa.

As soon as she stepped beyond the villa's wrought iron gate, the sleek energy of Milan met her with a vibrant hum. Her narrow cobblestone street was framed by tall, elegant buildings in warm ochres and creams, their shutters flung open to capture the last of the day's waning light. Young drivers on Vespa scooters—Milan's iconic vehicles—wove around pedestrians who were darting into boutiques and bakeries before they closed for the day. If she was lucky, one might stay open long enough for her to purchase a loaf of *pane toscano* for dinner. The crusty unsalted bread would be a perfect counterbalance to the creamy lemon risotto she had planned.

The small grocer sat tucked between two modern storefronts, its display overflowing with artfully arranged fresh produce, colorful bouquets of flowers and bottles of deep red wine glinting in the sunlight.

She took her time shopping, crossing each item off her list, before heading for the register. But the aisles were narrow and her bag bumped a display in the personal care department, knocking a few boxes to the floor. She stooped to pick them up.

Tampons, she thought. These were boxes of tampons.

Her brow furrowed as a hazy memory from weeks ago bubbled to the surface of her mind. How she had forgotten to pack tampons and made a mental note to buy some when she was settled.

But she hadn't bought any since she had been here. She hadn't had the need.

Hastily, she ran some mental calculations.

Oh, wow. Her period was late. *Really* late.

A million thoughts jammed her head all at once. At first, pure unadulterated joy. Could it be that after all this time, she was finally…?

Then cold reality slapped her hope back down. There was no way she was pregnant. Two years of failed IVF treatments had proved that she couldn't have a baby. It was impossible.

Well, maybe not *impossible*. She and Bradford has endured dozens of tests before starting IVF, trying to find some reason they hadn't been able to conceive on their own. "Unexplained infertility" was the only answer they ever got. And she knew from her endless research that even after multiple unsuccessful rounds of infertility, some couples were able to conceive naturally on their own, sometimes years later.

But still, there was a good chance this was something else. Early menopause or a hormonal imbalance or maybe something scary, like a tumor that was confusing her body.

She pushed the fear aside. She would call the hospital's gynecologist first thing in the morning. For now, she grabbed two pregnancy tests, just so she could tell the receptionist she had ruled out the obvious suspect when she made her appointment.

She walked home slowly, her shopping bag heavy on her arm. She no longer cared about bruschetta or tiramisu, but she made dinner anyway, to give herself something to do. She was no stranger to this dance she called "Pregnancy Test Procrastination." When she was trying to get pregnant, the only thing more devastating than the little minus sign on the test was getting official confirmation of her nonpregnancy status when her period showed up. Delaying that pregnancy test as long as possible let her enjoy just a few more hours of living in the land of *maybe it will work out this time*.

This was a little different, but the hesitation was the same. Only this time she was certain she would get a minus sign. Which meant something was wrong with her body—maybe scary wrong. Delaying taking the test this time let her live just a longer in the there's-nothing-to-worry-about state of delusion.

When the lemon risotto was done, she put it in the oven to keep it warm. Then sighed and accepted her fate. There was no point in delaying the inevitable. She went to the bathroom and brought both tests.

Three minutes later, a shocked half scream escaped her lips. She clamped a hand over her mouth and stared in disbelief. This couldn't be.

So she repeated the test with the second. And sat in silence, holding the plastic stick for who knows how long.

She might have stayed like that all night if she hadn't heard a door open, then slam shut.

"Miranda! *Dove sei, amore*?"

For as long as she walked this earth, she would never get tired of how Dante said her name. *Mee-ran-dah.* He made her name feel like a song. A part of her—such a strong part—wanted to fling open the door, fly into his arms and share the most amazing news of her life. *She was pregnant!*

But that would be a really terrible idea.

If I ever get married and have a child—and I won't—

If his last name is Ricci, his first name is surely Trouble.

And most potent of all, Dante's own warning: *Don't count on me, Miranda. I'll only disappoint you.*

This was exactly the sort of news he had spent his entire life avoiding. Dante had been perfectly transparent about his boundaries from the first night they met in New York. It was only she who had imagined a connection between them. A fantasy she couldn't afford to indulge anymore.

Okay, no big deal—it was just time to pivot. So what if her plan to become a mother wasn't unfolding as she thought it would? That had been the story of her life for the past year!

But it was time to take charge, set the course and let Dante know he was off the hook. Prince of Pleasure or not, Dante was a decent man who wouldn't abandon her to deal with this pregnancy all alone. He'd meet his obligations— and she didn't want that. Being someone's burden wasn't her idea of a good life. And Dante didn't have anything to offer her beyond meeting his obligations as a man who had knocked her up by accident.

No, thank you.

After Bradford, the last thing she would ever give up was her dignity. She had family in Boston, an excellent job, plenty of money. She could do this alone. She didn't need to beg Dante for anything. He could get back to the life he loved so much with no worries about being trapped by fatherhood or her expectations.

She tossed both tests in the trash can and smoothed her shirt. Studied her reflection in the mirror. Her lips curved in a small, shy smile. She was still in shock that after two years of trying, she was finally pregnant.

A light knock at the door, then Dante calling her name, soft and gentle. *"Amore mio, stai bene?"*

She paused at the door, her hand on the knob. And leaned her forehead against the door between them. The urge to tell him everything in her heart and hope for the best was so very strong. But it was pure foolishness, too. From their first encounter in New York, Dante had told her who he was. She had to stop this strange habit of seeing a connection where there was none.

She needed to do this quickly, before she changed her mind or lost her resolve and started crying tears of joy, confusing Dante into thinking that she needed or expected anything from him.

She flung the door open, startling Dante into stepping backward.

"Ciao!" she said with forced enthusiasm. "How was your meeting?"

"Good," he said, his gaze raking her face. "All good? You were in the bathroom a long time, *amore mio*. And what smells so delicious?"

"I am good!" she replied, forcing mirth in her tone. "And I have news. I'm pregnant!"

She beelined for the kitchen and, after a stunned few seconds, Dante followed. She grabbed a few small containers and began filling them with portions of the risotto and bruschetta. He remained in her peripheral vision, his mouth ajar but speechless.

"Everything's fine! I'm fine, you're fine—presumably the pregnancy is fine, too. It was a surprise, I'll tell you that. After two years of IVF, I didn't think this could happen!"

She pulled the tiramisu from the refrigerator and placed a generous slice in a to-go container. Then stacked all the containers in a cloth bag and pressed it to Dante's chest.

"You don't have anything to worry about, Dante. I've got this all under control. The news is a surprise, yes, but I've been preparing for a baby for years, no lie. I've got a supportive family, wonderful job, health insurance and money. You can take a deep breath and relax, because I'm okay! I won't need anything from you to raise this baby. Now, when it comes to covering college costs, well, then yes, we probably should talk." She forced a little lighthearted chuckle for brevity.

She took him by the elbow and steered him to the door. "Anytime you want to see your child, Dante, that's just fine. I'm sure we can work out an international custody agreement when I'm back in the States. I had a coworker who divorced and his wife moved to Europe. They figured out how to share custody and I'm sure we can, too. That is if that's even something you're interested in."

She opened the door to the courtyard. Beyond the gate, she could hear cars zipping past, someone yelling for the bus to wait.

"Now, I have a lot of packing to do for my trip back home, so it's probably good for you to go home tonight. I'll see you tomorrow at the hospital, okay?"

Dante stumbled into her courtyard, still gripping the bag she had given him. Then he turned back to her, his gaze raking her face, searching for signs of who knew what. She gave him what she hoped was a giant, reassuring smile, then went to close the door.

But Dante put out his arm to stop her. "Wait," he said, his brows furrowed. "*Non capisco.* You're pregnant? Miranda, what does this all mean?"

Miranda sighed and leaned against the door frame. "It means that I am going to have the baby I've always wanted. And you are still free to live the life *you've* always wanted." She didn't want this to end badly, so she reached out, caught his hand, squeezed it with her own. "It means everything is okay, Dante. I promise."

He lingered for another minute. "And this is what you want?"

She nodded, hard. "It is."

Still, his eyes remained locked on hers. She willed herself to be still, not give anything away. Then he sighed, deep and hard.

"D'accordo."

"D'accordo," she echoed.

She watched as he turned and walked away. Watched him pass through the gate. Watched until she couldn't see his wavy dark hair as he dodged bicyclists and dogs. Watched until she was alone again.

CHAPTER SIX

"Based on the scans, I believe it's a midline glioma. Surgical resection isn't viable without risking significant deficits, so I'd recommend targeted radiation therapy to manage the symptoms." Serena pressed her lips tight together, clearly nervous as she waited for Miranda's reaction.

Miranda nodded vigorously. "Exactly right. And your reasoning is solid—balancing intervention with quality of life is key here."

Serena clutched her tablet computer to her chest and beamed. It made Miranda feel good to know that during her short time at St. Joseph's, she'd been able to help young surgeons like Serena find their stride on the new team. Serena—all the surgeons, really—were more than ready to function as a team when she left in a few days.

But leaving wasn't what was on her mind at the moment. She flipped off her tablet, hoping to send a subtle signal to her protégé that their meeting had concluded.

"Will you be attending grand rounds, Doctor Hawthorne?" Serena asked. "I can't wait to see how 3D printing and virtual reality will be used in pre-operative surgical planning!"

Miranda's heart sank. Under normal circumstances, she would join Serena in nerding out on technological advancements in pediatric neurosurgery. But today was not a normal day, and she really wanted to be alone.

"Yes, I am," she replied with forced enthusiasm. "Just have to get some coffee first. Save me a seat?"

Thankfully, Serena didn't offer to wait for her. Miranda watched until Serena had turned the corner and was out of view before she left her office. She beelined past the break room—where the coffee was—straight to the ladies' restroom.

Please oh please oh please...let everything be okay.

The simple phrase had been her mantra all morning. She repeated it with every step, as if she could bring normalcy back into her day through her sheer force of will. The ladies' room was mercifully empty. But...

Damn damn damn damn...

Miranda's head dropped as she tried her hardest not to cry.

The spotting had started early that morning. At first, she hadn't freaked out. She was a doctor. She knew healthy pregnancies could include some spotting, especially during the first trimester, when the hormone shifts could be so wild.

But this spotting had gone on for hours. Denial wasn't going to help.

She texted her apologies to her colleagues for missing the meeting. Then looked up the OB on call and left a message with her paging service.

While waiting, she paced the length of the small restroom. *You're such a silly goose. You're going to wait forever until she can squeeze in a quick call between patients. Then she'll tell you to relax and make an appointment to see her in a week. Just to put your mind at ease.*

Instead, the OB called her back almost immediately.

After asking a few questions, she said, "Miranda, listen to me. I want you to go straight to Emergency Care, all right?"

Her soothing tone made Miranda even more nervous. How many times had she used the same tone with her patients, trying not to frighten them, while wanting to scream This Is An Emergency!

"I'll meet you there as soon as I can," she assured Miranda.

Miranda hung up, then stared at her image in the mirror. Was this the last time she would see herself as an expectant mother?

Then she grabbed her coat and ran.

An hour later, Miranda was wrapped in a blue hospital gown, sitting on the edge of a narrow, uncomfortable gurney. A nurse named Alessia had drawn her blood, recorded her health history and taken her vitals.

She drew the curtain around Miranda's gurney, giving her a semblance of privacy. "Doctor Bianchi has ordered an ultrasound," she told Miranda in a kind voice. "A tech should be by soon." Then she squeezed Miranda's shoulder. "In the meantime, just try to relax."

Miranda returned her smile, just to be friendly, but inside she was practically screaming *are you kidding me?* How could she possibly relax when the one thing she had wanted most in the world might be taken from her?

There wasn't enough room to pace properly and she didn't have enough bandwidth to read an ebook or keep up with her emails.

She could call her sister. Scarlett was always so strong and sure of what to do at times like this.

But Miranda was afraid she'd dissolve into ugly tears as soon as she heard her sister's voice. She couldn't do that here. These doctors and nurses were her colleagues.

Waiting, waiting, waiting. She would think after seven rounds of IVF, she would have her black belt at waiting.

But it didn't seem to get any easier with practice.

I wish Dante were here.

The thought was random and unbidden. But so powerfully true that she found herself fighting to suppress an involuntary sob.

She and Dante had kept their distance ever since she had told him she was pregnant at the villa. During the day, he was unfailingly polite and professional, though he seemed to be doing his best to work on cases apart from hers. He had texted her a few times. Are you okay? Feeling well? Do you need anything? Should we talk?

She had done her best to assure him that all was good. He could carry on with his life just as he had before she came to Milan. In two more days, she would be on a plane back to Boston, and they could both get on with their lives.

It was what she wanted. It was what *he* wanted. So why was she choking back sobs in the emergency room?

She felt so alone in this place. Surrounded by people talking, laughing, barking orders, whispering—all in a language she didn't understand. All she wanted now was warmth and comfort and something that felt safe like home.

But she wouldn't call Dante. He had made it clear from the start what his boundaries were around relationships. She very much doubted that emergency rooms and ultrasounds fit in with his vision.

She just had to deal with things like this alone.

But then…

Would he want to know?

She honestly didn't know. Ever since the test went positive, she had been running the show. She'd kept Dante at arm's length because she knew he didn't want any part of relationships, marriage, family. He had told her so from the very start.

But they had things to work out. Did he want to see his child? Or just pay child support?

She didn't know and honestly, she hadn't been ready to ask yet. She had so much to adjust to. Becoming a mother when she thought she couldn't—and returning to Boston with all of its heartache and challenges.

She just hadn't been ready to hear how much—or little—Dante wanted to be in her life. So she had pushed him away. There would be plenty of time to work out the details when she was home. Maybe once she left Milan, it wouldn't hurt so much.

But what now? Did she owe him a heads-up that something might be wrong?

Maybe she should text him to be safe.

FYI—I'm in Emergency Services due to light bleeding. Ultrasound results pending.

She reread her message before hitting Send. It looked more like a patient handoff than a note between two lovers. No hint of sobbing woman at all. Good.

She hit Send and tried to lose herself in one of the free games her phone kept adding without her permission. But nothing held her interest. She just had to fidget and cough and check her watch five thousand times.

Her throat felt tight with tension, and butterflies in her belly made her feel restless and agitated.

And then the curtain was ripped aside. Miranda looked up, hopeful it was the ultrasound tech and not another phlebotomist eager for her blood.

But no. It was Dante who burst past the curtain. His chest was heaving and his tie was askew. His gaze found hers, relief and worry battling in his expression, as he scanned the machines that surrounded her.

"Hey," she said in surprise.

Forcing a shaky smile, he approached her. "Hey, yourself."

"You okay? You're sweating."

He nodded. "I was running. Are *you* okay?"

Before she could answer, a short woman with an apple-shaped face appeared, pushing a cart past Dante.

"Pretty tight quarters in here!" she chirped. "But we'll make it work."

Dante grabbed her hand, his eyes darker than she had ever seen them. "Should I stay?"

There wasn't any time to talk. To figure out what their boundaries were now. There was just Dante's warm hands enfolded around hers, making her feel so much better now that he was here.

She nodded, not trusting herself to speak. Her fingers found his, laced their way through them. He squeezed back hard, and all the lies she had been telling herself melted into the ethos.

I've got you.

He made her feel like she could finally relax.

"Ready?" the tech asked.

Dante squeezed. She nodded.

Miranda felt the tech squeeze warm gel onto her belly, then the press of the ultrasound wand across the contours of her still-flat abdomen.

The ultrasound tech worked efficiently, making no comments or chitchat. She just swooped and tapped at her keyboard, capturing and labeling images for the OB to analyze.

Miranda knew better than to ask for information. The tech wasn't allowed to tell her anything.

She could ask Dante to take a look, but then he would have to leave her side to see the monitor. And she didn't want to let go of his hand.

But she also didn't want to know. Not yet.

If it was going to be bad news, she wanted to enjoy these last moments of feeling happy.

The tech smiled and closed her equipment. "Your doctor should be by soon with the results."

Then she was gone, and Miranda had to start the waiting game all over again. At least this time she wasn't alone.

But for long minutes, they didn't say anything. It was too hard to bridge the distance of all that hadn't been said since she'd learned that she was pregnant.

Miranda realized they were still holding hands. She moved to release her grip, but he held on for a second longer before letting her fingers slip through his.

"I'm sorry if I messed up your day. You didn't have to…"

He pressed his hand to his forehead, his head bowing under its weight. "Miranda, enough." His voice was thick, laced with something heavy that was impossible to decipher.

"What? What's wrong?"

"You texted that you were in the emergency room. Did you really expect me to yawn and carry on with my day?"

"I just wasn't sure if you wanted to know."

He shook his head, muttered something in Italian. "I don't understand, Miranda. Is this some sort of American thing?"

"What?"

"This—indifference! How could you even imagine that I *wouldn't* want to know if you're sick or injured or have *any* need—large or small?"

"Because you didn't ask for any of this! Fatherhood, commitments, responsibilities…and I get it! I'm not asking for anything from you. I just don't know…what you want from me."

Dante went very quiet. His jaw tightened, and his eyes flickered with something raw as they searched hers.

"Miranda."

She felt her brow contract. "Yes?"

"When you…"

But before he could finish his question, Dr. Bianchi tugged the curtain aside.

"I have good news!" she said.

Despite the big smile on her face, Miranda felt trapped in confusion. She just couldn't process all that was happening fast enough.

"So, everything is…"

"Perfect! Your baby's heartbeat is beating at a nice one hundred forty beats per minute. The placenta looks great, and all of your vitals look fine, too. You are eight weeks along in a very healthy pregnancy, Miranda."

"And the spotting?"

The OB navigated through Miranda's file on her tablet. "Nothing to worry about. Just a small subchorionic hemorrhage that probably happened during the implantation process. It should resolve on its own, but we'll give you some progesterone supplements to help." She powered off the tablet and smiled at Miranda. "But it would be good to take it easy for a few days. Just to be safe."

Miranda struggled to a sitting position. "But I have to move back to Boston in two days. I still have to pack and… Oh, my God, am I okay to fly?"

"No restrictions on flying or packing. But if you can get someone to help with the heavy stuff, that would be best."

Miranda opened her mouth to protest when Dante stepped forward, laying a warm hand on her arm.

"Do not worry, Doctor Bianchi. It will be my pleasure to make sure that Doctor Hawthorne gets all the assistance she needs."

Dante balanced two dessert plates on his arm, then used his free hand to carry the coffee mugs and dessert forks to the living room. He sidestepped open boxes of board games and stacks of books on his way to the couch where Miranda was reading.

He had done his best to find ways to keep Miranda's mind busy so she would let her body rest. It wasn't easy, that was for sure. The woman was like a worker bee with a never-ending to-do list motoring her from one task to another. It had taken all his creativity—and free time—to get her to sit still for a few hours.

But she was getting restless.

"What should we watch tonight?" he asked, sliding the dessert and coffee in front of her.

She closed her book with a sigh. "Sorry, Dante. No movie tonight. I really can't put off packing any longer!"

That was a trip he very much did not want her to take. He had managed to convince her to extend her time in Milan by a week, but she was adamant about returning to Boston in a few days. In Boston, she'd be 4,000 miles away. It was impossible to think of that distance without remembering the awful text that had set all this in motion.

He had gotten the message in the middle of a hospital administration meeting. Instantly, his body had turned hot with anxiety and an overwhelming need to be by her side. Which was the first moment of real clarity he'd had since Miranda told him she was pregnant. At first, he had been shocked and maybe even a little horrified. The last thing he wanted was to turn out like Vittorio, destined to break Miranda's heart because he wasn't made for a life of commitment.

So it had been a relief when Miranda told him she expected nothing from him. Or it *should* have been a relief. Instead, he was plagued by thoughts of her night and day. Was she well? Did she need anything?

But even odder was the realization that he was going to be a *father*. That brought a rush of memories—of how he had felt in Vittorio's home. An unwanted son whose very existence brought painful memories and shame to the Ricci family.

Would his child feel the same way? He had no doubt that Miranda would be a wonderful mother, but would his child still feel unwanted?

These thoughts had made it hard to keep his distance in the week since learning of the pregnancy, but he was trying hard to respect what Miranda wanted.

But that text message? No, he could not have left her to face that alone.

He had nearly broken his neck to get to the emergency department, pulling the curtain aside to find Miranda waiting, looking small and vulnerable in the hospital-issued cotton gown.

Thankfully, the ultrasound had put both of their minds at ease. But what if it hadn't? What if something went wrong? Unwanted images of how badly the spina bifida surgery had gone had haunted him for the past three days. There was no way he could risk her facing a catastrophe alone. Absolutely no way.

He sipped his coffee for courage and hoped his timing was right. "I don't suppose you might consider extending your work here in Milan? I am quite certain the hospital's medical director would be open to the idea."

That was no lie. He had already made a convincing case to his director and had the paperwork ready for her signature.

Miranda paused her fork midair, a bite-size piece of tiramisu wobbling gently on the tines. "That's very kind, Dante. But I have to say no. I have family waiting for me in Boston. And my job. Besides, your team is more than ready to run the pediatric neurosurgery department on their own. I'd only be in their way."

Oh, Lord, the last thing on his mind was work or his team.

She finished her bite of dessert, then sipped some coffee. "And let's be honest. I'm sure you'll be happy not to have to pretend anymore."

"Pretend what?"

"That this—" she waved her hand to indicate the mess in the room "—is you."

He genuinely did not understand what she was talking about.

She raised an eyebrow. "*Maybe it's different for you Americans, but if I ever got married—and I won't—I surely would not want my wife to describe me as a vacuum cleaner.*"

She was smiling and her tone was teasing, but the mirth didn't quite reach her eyes.

"Well, it's true. I wouldn't want my wife to describe me as…what did you call it?"

"Functional?"

"Right. Functional."

"And it's equally true that you don't want to get married. And this—" she indicated the room again "—looks a lot like a guy who has responsibilities to worry about.

"But you don't! Have to worry, that is. I have family back home, a good job and plenty of money to raise this baby. We just have to work out a custody agreement, and we can do that when I get back to Boston."

So this was why she hadn't called him from the hospital. Between the press ambushing her and the hospital gossip line, she saw him as everyone else did. The Prince of Pleasure—seducer of movie stars and models, avoider of All Things Serious and Real.

Only with her, it was worse. She was never going to think of him as someone she could count on. He was just some guy she'd met on her trip to Milan that got her pregnant, then carried on with his life.

Just like the paparazzi said he was.

Just like his father had been.

Good grief, the irony of it almost killed him. All these years of hiding behind a media-created persona, only to discover that when he found someone he really cared about, he couldn't convince her that she knew the real Dante. And that she could trust him.

He made a joke to keep the atmosphere light, then took their plates back to the kitchen so he could think while he loaded the dishwasher. He didn't know how to describe what they had. Definitely more than a workplace fling. But a forever thing? No, he didn't quite see that happening. They were both too committed to the vision of the futures they wanted for themselves.

But those futures were now inextricably linked by a tiny baby.

Couple or not, he wanted her to know she could count on him, no matter what. To be able to pick up the phone without hesitation. To know that he *wanted* to be there for her for any request, large or small.

But he wasn't the first guy to tell her this. That honor belonged to her first husband, who had promised to be everything she needed, then turned out to be anything but.

Words alone would fail him. If he wanted her to trust him, he couldn't just tell her that he was a man she could trust.

He would have to *show* her.

And that was impossible if she was 4,000 miles away.

With her planning to leave in a couple of days, he couldn't wait for the stars to align. He was going to have to align them himself.

He returned to the living room and found two suitcases already packed. Now she was on her hands and knees, rummaging through the hallway closet. "Almost done here," she called out. "Then maybe we can watch that movie."

"Sure," he said, retaking the lounge chair. "But can we talk about something first?"

She popped her head out of the closet, her gorgeous waves partially covering her face. Maybe his tone was more serious than he meant. "Everything okay?"

He steepled his hands. "Let me come to Boston with you."

She sat back on her heels, her expression flabbergasted. Maybe he should have practiced his delivery first.

Too late now. He galloped on. "I couldn't practice medicine, of course, not without a Massachusetts medical license. But my administration is willing to coordinate with Harborview Children's to create a fellowship or sponsorship opportunity. It would be an excellent way for me to continue gaining the skills that will be needed by our new pediatric neurosurgery department."

"But why would you do that?"

How to answer that without showing his hand? She would never agree to this if she knew his sole motivation was...*her*. "Well, figuring out the parameters of an international custody agreement is no small matter, *si*? I think it would be more productive if we could negotiate with an attorney in person, so we can avoid misunderstanding."

Good grief, he was making this all sound so ominous. She left the closet and crossed the room to sit next to him. He expected a fight, but she surprised him.

"We *do* have a lot of decisions to make over the next eighteen years."

"Exactly." He eagerly grasped at the flimsy excuse. "We might as well get things off to a good start."

"I don't know, Dante. That seems like a lot..."

"It's not! Really, it's no different that you coming to Milan to mentor our new neurosurgery department, right? Our team needed time to learn how to work together, and you made that possible. We would just be doing the same—for ourselves and our baby."

"Won't leaving now put your chances of becoming chief of pediatric neurosurgery at risk?"

Yes, it definitely would. His absence would leave a vacuum that another eager, young surgeon would be all too happy to fill. It should feel like an impossible decision, but it didn't. He wanted Miranda's trust far more than he wanted the new position.

But why did he want her trust so much? Sure, the emergency room visit had been frightening, but she was still planning to raise their child in the States. He wouldn't be able to be there every time she needed him. That was just the way things were going to be for them. So why go all the way to Boston to prove to her that he was more than the *Prince of Pleasure* she had heard about?

It's the baby. Babies change everything.

Yes, that was probably it. Nothing else really explained why he'd be willing to give up the best opportunity of his surgical career to follow Miranda to Boston.

He waved her off. "It's not a problem at all."

She looked at him long and hard, and he suspected she knew he was fibbing a bit. But there was a hint of something else in her expression. The slightest twinge of relief maybe?

"Okay," she said slowly. "But only if you are absolutely sure."

No white lies were needed here. "I am."

Relief flooded his body as he realized he wouldn't have to drop her off at the airport and hope for the best. He would be with her every step of the way. So long as he could figure out a way to draw "custody negotiations" out for nine months.

"Now, are we watching a movie or playing *Dominion: Age of Triumph*? Though I imagine you're afraid I'll topple your empire again."

She gave him one last appraising look and he knew it was a test. She was doing her best to size him up, to see if it was really safe to trust him.

He met her gaze with his own steady one. *Give me one chance, Miranda. That's all I need.*

Eventually, her serious expression relaxed into a smile as she reached for the controller. "Afraid? Nah. Watching you sweat is half the fun."

CHAPTER SEVEN

Alessandra Leone's office was the perfect blend of simple modernist design and old-world charm. Floor-to-ceiling windows bathed the room in natural light, illuminating sleek white furniture, a glass-topped desk and abstract artwork on the wall behind her desk. A massive bookshelf lined with law volumes and a single potted olive tree in the corner added a touch of warmth to the otherwise minimalist space.

"Doctor Baker said she was the best," Miranda whispered to Dante as they waited for the attorney to appear for their four o'clock appointment.

Dante loosened his tie and nodded. "That's good to hear."

Miranda nodded and drummed her thumbs on her chair. "See, Doctor Baker and his wife got a divorce last year, and then she got a job offer to work in France. It was complicated for sure, but Doctor Baker said that Alessandra found a way to work it all out."

Why, oh why was she prattling on so? It had been like this ever since Dante had come back to Boston with her. Everything was different, now that they were going to have a baby. This wasn't a fling anymore, which left them in a strange land of limbo. There was too much at stake to pretend this was just for fun, but they were far from a couple with a future.

They had lived in this uneasy space ever since he arrived a few days ago. Miranda was grateful when he'd offered to stay in the guest room. They had a lot of decisions to make over the next few weeks. She needed to be able to think clearly, and that was not easy when Dante was around. Impossible if he was in her bed.

Miranda was pouring herself a glass of cucumber water when Alessandra arrived. The attorney was poised and professional in a tailored charcoal-gray pantsuit with a silk cream blouse underneath, the faintest glimmer of a gold chain visible at her collar.

"So," Alessandra said, settling herself behind her desk. "Get me filled in. What are we trying to accomplish today?"

Miranda cast a quick glance in Dante's direction. They hadn't really discussed the particulars of sharing custody, but she was sure she had a pretty good idea of what a man who had tried to talk his friend out of marriage would want—maximum freedom, minimal responsibility.

"Thanks for meeting with us so quickly, Alessandra. So, Dante and I met in New York about two months ago. And now we're expecting a baby. Surprise!"

"Mazel tov," Alessandra said, steepling her fingers under her chin.

"But Dante lives in Milan, and I live here, in Boston. I think we just need to establish me as the custodial parent in Boston and outline financial expectations, that sort of thing."

"Actually," Dante said, leaning forward, "I would like shared custody of our child."

"Oh?" Alessandra scratched a few notes on her legal pad. "Do you have any objections to that, Miranda?"

"Well, no…" Miranda said. Of course, she didn't *object*

to Dante's wanting to see his child. She had fully expected he would visit from time to time. But shared custody... That had not been on her radar.

"Well, I'll be frank with both of you," Alessandra said, setting her pencil down. "These types of custody arrangements aren't easy. They can strain even the most amicable of partnerships. So, let's talk about expectations first. Miranda, how do you see this arrangement working?"

Miranda felt completely disoriented. How the heck was she supposed to share custody with Dante when he lived 4,000 miles away? She hadn't envisioned this possibility at all. Especially from a man who had told her he had no interest in ever getting married or having a family.

"I don't really know how this is supposed to work. I just want to give our baby a good life."

"And we will absolutely do that," Alessandra assured her. "Now, let's think about some of the bigger moments of life. Birthdays, holidays, that sort of thing. How will you handle the other parent not being there for these special moments?"

Miranda absolutely adored the holidays. She had never been one of those "less is more" types when it came to special occasions. For her, *more* was more. More baking, more planning, more wrapping, more friends, more family—just...more! And now she'd have a beautiful baby to spend those holidays with.

Except now she'd decorate for the holidays, only to spend some of them alone or at the hospital. Or spend them with a child who always felt something was missing, no matter how hard Miranda worked to make the holiday special.

"Um, I guess I would make sure our child had a chance to talk to Dante over video call or a phone call. Maybe he could mail his gifts early so she could open them at my house?"

Dante huffed and looked out the window. She could hardly blame him. The scenario she'd just described sounded terrible.

The room felt too warm, and Miranda felt lightheaded. Suddenly, all she wanted was to escape the confines of this too-perfect office and Alessandra's impossible questions.

"I'm sorry," she said, putting a hand up to stop Alessandra's next question. "But could we take a break? This is all…a lot to process."

Alessandra gave her an understanding nod. "Of course. Why don't we schedule a follow-up meeting later this week? That will give you two a chance to talk and figure out what you want."

Alessandra booked their next appointment in her calendar and sent them off.

Dante and Miranda stepped out of the attorney's office into a chilly, drizzly afternoon. The strong wind felt like a personal attack, and Miranda drew her coat tightly against her. Just then, a bicyclist in a bright yellow raincoat zipped by, his wheels cutting through a wide puddle. A spray of muddy water arced up, splattering her dress. Miranda froze, her breath catching in frustration as she stared at the damp, dirty streaks left behind. It felt like the world was conspiring against her when she was at her absolute lowest.

"Damn," she muttered.

Dante asked if she was all right, but she was in such a peevish mood, his concerned tone only irritated her more.

"Could we maybe just go for a walk?" She felt wound up and jittery and she needed to keep moving.

"Of course," Dante said, turning up his collar and jogging to catch up with her.

It was windy and cold—a miserable day for a walk. But Miranda didn't care. She welcomed the icy bites on her cheeks and the strong wind that felt like it was daring her to stop. Fighting the elements was a relief, something tangible to battle instead of the factors she had no control over.

Dante reached out, his hand a warm weight on her arm. She stopped her restless strides to look at him. He gently tugged her out of the wind into a narrow alley where the walls sheltered them from the weather.

"Miranda." His tone was soft, almost regretful. "I'm sorry about what happened back there. I didn't mean to ambush you. It's just…"

He hesitated, searching her face, his expression earnest and sincere. "I guess as the shock of all this wears off, I'm starting to see things more clearly. And realize what I want."

Miranda *had* felt ambushed in Alessandra's office, but that didn't mean she was angry with Dante. It was his right to see his child when he wanted, and that included sharing custody, no matter how complicated that might be to figure out. She just hadn't expected it.

"You're full of surprises, Dante. I guess I just thought…"

"I know. It's hard to imagine *Il Principe del Piacere* with a diaper bag slung over his shoulder, right?"

She smiled. "Exactly."

Dante used one hand to brace himself against the alley wall. "Listen, growing up a Ricci wasn't all glamour and privilege—not at all. My father was successful and charming, always the center of attention. And me? Well, I wasn't even supposed to be there. I was the secret child who'd invaded his perfect world, and nothing was ever the same for him after that. That made me a problem to be managed, not a son to be loved."

His gaze met hers, and she saw quiet determination in his eyes. "I carried that weight for years, but I will be damned if our child feels one second of wondering about their value. I will make sure that they always know how much I love them, no matter what. But I can't do that over email and video calls."

Miranda studied his profile in the dim light of the overcast afternoon. The raw honesty in his voice dampened her frustration. All this time, she had thought Dante was a man who lived for pleasure and fun. But now, seeing his unmistakable vulnerability, she felt something shift in her heart. Maybe she didn't know Dante as well as she thought she did. Maybe he was a lot more complex—and scarred—than he appeared.

"So, all this is hard on me, too," he told Miranda, waving a hand in the direction of the law offices they had just left.

That realization hit her hard in the gut. A realization that, like it or not, they were in this together, at least for the next eighteen years. Bonded not only by their baby, but also by the sacrifices that would need to be made on that baby's behalf.

"I know, Dante." Miranda wrapped her arms around herself, trying to find some comfort in the midst of the chaos they had created. "I guess I just dreamed of having a family life where everyone was together, every day. Sharing custody between two continents means I can only give half of what I have in my heart. Half the holidays, half the memories..." She tried hard to control the tremble in her lower lip, but she was losing control fast. Her voice broke as she said, "It's just a lot to think about when having a baby doesn't even feel real yet!"

The tears won, spilling over her lower lid and down her cheeks.

"Oh, Miranda," he murmured, then drew her into his embrace. His chest was warm and solid, and as hard as she was trying to keep herself together, feeling his arms wrap around her, his chin resting on her head, it was too much. It tipped her over the edge to a soft, vulnerable place where all she felt was hurt and confusion.

He gently tilted her chin until she met his gaze. "I don't know how this will all work, Miranda." His voice was soft, but steady with conviction. "But we *will* make it work. I promise."

Time seemed to freeze for a moment, the space between them shivering with something unspoken. She felt the sudden, urgent ache of wanting—wanting him to kiss her and turn this raw moment into something beautiful.

It had been like this ever since he had come to Boston. She knew it was best for them to keep their distance while they negotiated custody. But having him under her roof was like trying to sleep beside a lit match. Every time she heard his voice, memories of Milan flooded her body. The heat of his hands, the way he whispered in Italian in the dark. Putting him in the guest room was supposed to help her keep a cool head, but all she felt was the hot undertow of everything they had left unfinished. His eyes raked her face, filled with some dark emotion that mirrored her own. For a second, she thought he might give in. But instead, he stepped away from her, though it seemed like it took great effort. His focus shifted to something beyond her shoulder.

"Come with me," he said, taking her hand. "I think I know something that will make us both feel better."

Miranda held her ground, resisting his tug on her hand. "Oh, Dante. I just want to go home."

"Just give me ten minutes. If you still want to go home, we'll leave."

They crossed the street, splashing through puddles and dodging traffic, and stepped into one of the many charming shops in the historic Beacon Hill area. Miranda shook off her coat outside before hanging it on the store's coat rack.

Dante had brought her to a cozy children's boutique. Its warm lighting and quaint decor made it a welcoming contrast to the harsh October afternoon outside. An older woman with her silver-white hair drawn back in a ballerina bun welcomed them and encouraged them to ask for help if they needed it.

"Come on," Dante said. "Let's look around."

Miranda hung back again. "I don't know if I'm ready for this!"

Dante smiled, kissed her cheek. "Ten minutes, that's all."

They wandered the aisles for a few minutes, taking in the staggering array of devices and gadgets that were needed to raise a tiny infant to school age. Miranda was starting to wonder why on earth Dante thought this would make her feel better. It made everything feel even more overwhelming!

In the diapering aisle, a cellophane package caught Dante's interest. "Pee Pee TeePee," he read out loud. "What the heck are these? They look like tiny party hats."

Miranda took the package and read the instructions. "Oh! These are for baby boys. To keep them from, you know, sprinkling you during a diaper change."

Dante took the package back, looking genuinely impressed. "Wow, I did not even think about that aspect of parenting. You're right, Miranda. What the hell have we done?"

Miranda chuckled a little as he put the package back.

"We're not going to need these, though. We're having a girl."

She dropped her jaw in mock surprise. "How can you say that? We won't know for sure until the next ultrasound."

He shrugged. "Just a feeling."

In the next aisle, Dante picked out a thin box. "Glow-in-the-dark star wall decals—perfect for tiny astronomers and their overachieving parents." He arched an eyebrow. "Wow, never too early to start piling on the parental pressure, huh?" He tossed the package into their basket. "Now, where are those quantum physics flashcards?"

Miranda found herself smiling for the first time that day. Dante was right—this little side trip was boosting her mood, just a little.

In the back of the store, they found several nursery displays set up. Dante wandered around, stopping at a cherry-wood crib with an elaborate ruffled canopy.

He picked up the tag. "The Royal Slumber Suite," he read aloud.

"Right," Miranda replied, deciding to join in the fun. "Because nothing says 'low-maintenance baby' like a crib that requires a staff of butlers."

"Right you are. Onward, then."

They looked at several more nursery displays, getting increasingly caught up in their teasing and joking. There was the high-tech Lullaby Luxe 3000 that came with speakers and AI. The Glamour Baby Supreme featured tufted velvet side panels and an integrated music system. While the Urban Edge Sleeper with its sleek minimalist design and LED lights could be customized to create a "city-edge" effect.

By the time Dante had finished riffing on all the displays, Miranda could hardly speak, she was laughing so hard.

Dante paused, putting his hands on his hips to scan all the displays. "I don't know, Miranda. Maybe we should just open a drawer in a dresser and put her in there. I'm pretty sure that's how my *nonneto* got his start in life."

"Yeah, well, things have changed since your grandpa's time. We've got to find *something* that will work!"

Then she spied a display they hadn't seen yet. It was the colors that attracted her first—sage green, warm beige and hints of earthy browns.

"Come on, let's check this one out." This time, she was the one to lead him by the hand to the nursery display in the back. It was a simple design. Just a handcrafted wooden crib atop a fluffy cream-colored rug. Miranda played with the felt woodland creatures on the mobile—foxes, rabbits and owls—while she read the crib's tag.

"Woodland Retreat… This one's nice, don't you think?"

The setup included a cozy rocking chair with a knitted throw in one corner, paired with a small wooden side table holding a vintage-style lamp. Soft, textured rugs and a few woven baskets filled with essentials completed the space, while a bookshelf housed classic children's tales and whimsical plush toys.

Dante dropped into the rocking chair and perused the space. "I like it. It's calming, like the woods." He glanced her way and cocked his head. "What do you think? Does this make everything seem more real now…in a good way?"

He reached out his hand to her. If she wanted, she could take his hand and let him pull her onto his lap. The soft light from the vintage lamp highlighted the angles of his handsome face. It was an indulgence—she knew that—but she let herself imagine that this was the nursery in her house, and Dante was there, too. She could see him rocking their baby back to sleep in the wee hours of the morning. Then slipping back into bed with her, tucking her body against his as he nuzzled her neck.

If only it could be so. Maybe if they were younger and had met in college, it would have worked out. Before Dante's family had soured him and before she had tried to make the impossible work with Bradford.

They weren't a couple of young lovers in their twenties. Life had given them some baggage and scars. And heaped responsibilities on their shoulders. They were too far along in their lives and careers to pretend that they could throw caution to the wind and trust that love would be enough.

In some ways, it would be reckless to even try. What they had between them now was good. Dante knew how to cheer her up when she was feeling down. She understood what the demands of his career required, because she shared them.

No harm had come between them. No regrets or thoughtless words. No hurt. Just camaraderie and respect and their shared passion for giving their child the best life possible.

A love affair gone wrong could destroy all that. It could lead to bitterness that would taint their relationship and affect their child, no matter how much they tried to keep her out of it.

Her... Geez, now he had her thinking about their baby as a girl.

She took his hand and gave it a squeeze. A nice, friendly platonic squeeze.

"Yes," she told him. "Everything is feeling a lot more real now."

* * *

Dante's cell phone buzzed in his pocket as he leaned over a patient's bed in the brightly lit recovery room. Sofia was still fast asleep from her surgery, her well-loved giraffe tucked under one arm, as he reviewed her surgical notes. She had come through the delicate embolization of her arteriovenous malformation with flying colors, but Dante wanted to make sure she was stable before he left her side.

His phone vibrated again. He took a quick glance—Dr. Hawthorne, OR6. Immediately.

Dante took one last look at his tiny patient. "All will be well, *piccolina*," he whispered.

Dante found Miranda in the scrub room of OR6, methodically scrubbing her hands under the steady stream of the faucet. A few wisps of her caramel-brown hair had escaped her surgical cap, framing her face with damp curls.

She began briefing him as soon as he entered the scrub room, too deep in thought about the case to even say hello. "I wanted you to be here for this, in case you see a patient like this in Milan. We've got a twelve-year-old girl. Presented at ER with a severe headache that had progressed to vomiting and collapse. CT confirmed a subarachnoid hemorrhage. Angio shows a ruptured aneurysm on the anterior communicating artery." She glanced his way, her hazel eyes unreadable. "She's got just two options. Either we clip that aneurysm in the OR right now, or we have interventional radiology do a coil."

Dante finished scrubbing and reached for a towel to try. What would he choose if this case came through his OR? The radiologist could quickly place tiny, soft wire fragments into the aneurysm using blood vessels that were already accessed during the angiogram. The tiny wires would promote a clot within the aneurysm while the normal blood vessel would stay intact. It would be quick and far less invasive than surgery.

But there was also the risk of an incomplete occlusion, which meant the girl could be back in the ER in a few weeks or months needing surgery anyway. Or the aneurysm could burst and maybe end her young life.

Miranda seemed to look right through him as she considered their options. "She's twelve," she murmured, thinking out loud. "She needs something durable."

The OR nurse manager poked her head into the scrub room. "Doctor Hawthorne, the on-call interventional radiologist is on his way."

Miranda was still deep in thought. "Who is it?"

The nurse manager hesitated for a moment. "The other Doctor Hawthorne."

Dante noticed as Miranda's fingers stilled for a moment, the towel crumpled slightly in her grip. He saw her sharp inhale, the tightening of her jaw before she forced a nod.

"Fine," she said in a measured tone.

Her gaze briefly fell on Dante, the tension radiating from her body impossible to miss. But she didn't invite conversation, so he followed her to the surgical suite's prep station.

Her gloved finger traced the cerebral angiogram displayed on the monitor. "The neck of this thing is broad," she said in a clipped tone. "Coiling could be tricky. We risk coils protruding into the parent artery."

Before Dante could respond, the OR door swung open with unnecessary force. In strode a short, muscular man with an air of unshakable confidence. His polished bald head and his sharp, angular features gave him a look of pinched severity.

Dante took in the doctor's smug smile, the surgical cap

stuffed into the pocket of his scrubs and the pristine white of his lab coat. The "other Dr. Hawthorne" reference had already alerted him that this was Miranda's ex-husband. But it was the man's hawkish scan of the room, as if he was surveying his domain and everyone within it, that truly confirmed his suspicions.

"Well, well, Doctor Hawthorne," Bradford said with a grin that didn't reach his eyes. "Heard you needed my help to get out of a surgical pickle!"

Miranda's surgical mask kept much of her expression hidden, but Dante couldn't miss the steely tone in her reply. "Actually, I just requested a consult from the interventional radiologist on call. Which happened to be you."

Bradford swept to the monitor and gave the scans a perfunctory review. "Well, we're going to coil this, of course," he said with an air of authority. "I can get this done in under an hour with minimal risk. She'll be home in a few days." He rubbed his hands together in gleeful anticipation. "Let's get started."

Dante felt his jaw clench with irritation at the man's arrogance. Bradford wasn't the lead surgeon here. Miranda was. Dante would be happy to remind Bradford of that fact, but this wasn't his hospital or his colleague. It was Miranda's, and she was more than capable of handling the situation.

Miranda stayed calmer than he felt. "We're not doing anything without a full consult, Bradford."

Bradford's eyes widened. "Consult's over, Miranda. All that's left is for you to decide if you want to waste more time debating, or get this thing done."

Dante's chest tightened. Who the hell did this guy think he was? He shot a quick glance at Miranda, noticing how her fingers curled into fists at her sides. Bradford was getting under her skin, but she was doing her best to stay calm and cool.

"Normally, I would agree with you, Bradford. But look at this aneurysm!" She scrolled through the screens, pointing out the two lobes sized like blueberries. "There's no guarantee you can coil the entire thing. And that means there's a risk it could rupture again. If I do surgery—yes, it's more invasive and carries all the mortality risk that neurosurgery always does. But can we agree that a craniotomy would reduce her risk of rerupture to essentially... zero?"

Bradford hesitated, his expression darkening. "No," he muttered, the admission clearly irritating him. "Clipping is more definitive."

Dante's lips twitched into a small, satisfied smile. Miranda nodded and that seemed to set Bradford off.

"Dammit, Miranda. Why did you bother paging me if you weren't going to follow my direction? I was in the middle of a golf game with a perfect under par score!"

Follow his direction? Did he think she was a puppy? Dante struggled to hold his tongue. But Bradford saved him the trouble by turning on his heel and storming out.

"Charming," Dante said, watching Bradford's retreat. The OR nurse smiled behind her mask, making her eyes crinkle.

Miranda seemed stunned at the outburst, too, staring at the flapping OR door for a few seconds before she remembered where she was. She began giving directives to the nurse manager, summarizing the team she would need to complete the girl's surgery. Her jaw was tight and her shoulders were high with tension from the encounter. Dante yearned to reach out and touch her in some way, to let her know that she wasn't alone.

Instead, he settled for a simple, professional assessment. "Good call, Doctor Hawthorne."

Miranda didn't respond, but she gave him the faintest nod to show him she had heard him.

Dante's cell vibrated in his pocket again. He glanced at the screen and frowned.

"I've got to check on a patient," he told Miranda, reluctant to leave her. But she was already focused on planning for the girl's surgery.

"No worries. I've got this," she assured him, her tone brisk and professional. Her hands were busy organizing the tools she would need, but he saw a flicker of something soft in her gaze when she glanced his way.

Dante hesitated at the door, dropping his voice just enough to keep their conversation private.

"Don't forget the four o'clock," he said, keeping his tone light.

Miranda's hands paused working for just a moment before resuming their steady pace. "Wouldn't miss it," she responded, her tone giving nothing away.

To anyone in the room, four o'clock could mean anything. A meeting, a family consult, a lecture. But they both knew it was their four o'clock ultrasound scan, when they would finally learn if they were having a son or daughter. Dante permitted himself a small, secret smile before slipping out of the room.

Dante made a quick stop in the locker room to grab a protein bar from the supply he kept stashed in his locker. The sound of footsteps and humming drew his attention. Bradford strode into the room, his scrubs replaced by a polo shirt and tailored slacks. The golf shoes he set on the bench completed the ensemble.

"Doctor Ricci!" Bradford's tone was overly friendly as

he set a pair of designer sunglasses on his head. "Taking a break from the OR? Miranda does have a way of burning people out with her intensity."

Dante chewed slowly, trying to give himself time to think before he responded. But even after he swallowed, he still thought Bradford was a jerk.

"At least she's professional under pressure," Dante said carefully. "Especially in the presence of colleagues."

His words hung in the air, the weight of their insult unmistakable.

Bradford's smirk faltered, then flickered to irritation. "What do you even know about Miranda Hawthorne?" he challenged. "You're just a visiting doctor from Italy. You hardly know her!"

He paused as he considered Dante, then his eyes narrowed and his thin lips curved into a harsh smile. "Unless you are a souvenir Miranda brought back from her trip to Europe?" He chuckled then, shaking his head as he slammed his locker shut. "Well, good luck with that, sporto. Miranda's all work, no play. You'll find out soon enough—just like I did."

Dante's fingers tightened around what was left of the protein bar. He desperately wanted to defend Miranda and take Bradford down a notch. But he knew he'd likely make more trouble for Miranda if he did that, then leave her to deal with the aftermath when he returned to Milan.

It surprised him how protective he felt toward Miranda. Bradford would be an irritating guy under any circumstances, but Dante found his attacks on Miranda to be intolerable. Everything in him wanted to put Bradford in his place so that he'd never annoy Miranda again, but that was a pipe dream. Bradford lived and worked in

Boston—Miranda was going to have to deal with him long after Dante returned to Milan.

Maybe it had been a mistake to come here. All he had wanted was to be close if Miranda needed him during these early months of pregnancy. But being here made him want to be here for more. He wanted to do anything he could to make Miranda's life better. And if he couldn't solve her problems, he wanted to be by her side through every one of them.

He had thought it would be easy to return to Milan, but now he was seeing it wouldn't be easy at all.

Bradford grabbed his bag and stormed out of the room without another word. Dante did his best to shake off the unpleasant encounter and focus on his patient, reassuring her worried parents before he slipped away to end his shift and change into his street clothes.

The timing was tight, but he could make it work. He had a quick appointment that Miranda didn't know about just yet. He'd have to keep an eye on the time so that he wasn't late for their four o'clock ultrasound.

Dante slipped out the hospital's side entrance and into the crisp air of a New England fall afternoon. Late-day sunlight streamed through the canopy of trees that were slowly losing their leaves. The smell of hot dogs from a street vendor mixed with a faint hint of oncoming rain, though the storm clouds gathering on the horizon seemed too distant to be much of a threat.

Dante pulled open the heavy wood door of Mulligan's. Comforting warmth and the smell of hot stew and baked soda bread welcomed him like a hug. The low murmur of conversation punctuated by bursts of laughter filled the space.

He spotted her immediately, as did most of the eligible men in the pub. Julia sat alone in a corner, her striking raven hair catching the light from the overhead stained-glass lamp. Her emerald green eyes lit up when she saw him. Dante felt a pang of nostalgia at seeing her again after all these years.

"Julia," he said, kissing her cheek before he took the chair next to her.

She touched his arm briefly, her manicured fingers cool against his sleeve. "It's been too long," she laughed softly. "But I am glad—no, I'm *honored*—that you called me for this."

They soon settled into the easy rhythm of old friends. They had been lovers long ago, back when Dante was in the height of his rebellious phase. Though their breakup had provided fodder for the paparazzi for weeks, off the page, it had been a much more mundane affair. They were never in love, so it had been easy to agree to go their separate ways while maintaining a friendship that had spanned nearly two decades.

Julia was now a sought-after jewelry designer, her talent in demand by the elite on multiple continents. She had just returned from a convention in New York, taking a special detour to Boston at Dante's request.

She reached beside her to retrieve an oversize portfolio case. "I brought a few designs I've done for other clients, to give you some ideas," she said.

Dante flipped through the images of mothers' rings she had designed for others. Every sketch was an exquisite celebration of motherhood and love.

And yet, he couldn't imagine any of the rings on Miranda's lovely hand.

"These are beautiful, Julia, but for some reason they don't feel quite right."

"Well, of course not," Julia snapped playfully. "Because none of these were designed *for* Miranda." She opened a sketch pad and tugged a pencil from behind her ear. "Tell me everything you know about this woman, so we can design the perfect ring for her."

Julia listened intently, asking questions and taking notes while Dante told her everything he had held in his heart since he met her.

"I know she's sensitive, but she doesn't like to show it. She'd rather hide behind her work, because she feels confident there. She's drawn to nature for peace and healing. She finds joy in very simple things. She's loyal to her friends and family. She *hates* to ask for help. And, well, she has a sexy, playful side that's pretty irresistible."

Julia burst out laughing. "Well, thanks, Dante, but I was thinking more along the lines of what is her birthstone and what metal do you think she would prefer?" She set down her pencil. "Listen, maybe this isn't any of my business, but are you sure you want me to design a mother's ring? And not, say…an engagement ring?"

Dante's head jerked up, her words catching him completely off guard. "What? No, it's…it's not like that!"

She picked up her pencil again. "Okay, Dante. If you say so!"

Dante opened his mouth to protest, but the words stuck in his throat. Julia's playful jab had hit him in some soft part of his heart he hadn't thought about in a very long time.

Was he in love with her? His thoughts spiraled and his chest tightened as he considered the weight of that thought.

Whatever he felt for her, it went way beyond the lust that had inspired their fling in New York.

What he felt for Miranda was something different. He liked that she showed him parts of herself she kept hidden from the world. He liked being there for her when she was vulnerable, like at the press conference or when Bradford's arrogance reared its ugly head. He liked how she sometimes leaned on him in quiet, unspoken ways. And he liked being able to anticipate her needs without her asking.

He exhaled slowly, memories of the Ricci family's fractured relationship haunting him. His father's carelessness had convinced him love was a risk he should never take. Dante had dutifully taken his father's words as a valid warning, but was it true? The pain, heartbreak and suffering his mother had endured—was it really the inevitable outcome of trusting her heart to another? And was he really the bearer of a family legacy that said he was destined to break Miranda's heart?

What evidence did he have that this prophecy was true…beyond Vittorio's words? Dante had been honorable and honest in every relationship he had had, no matter how brief or casual they had been.

And Vittorio's callous disregard for others could be seen in many areas of his life. He was arrogant to his medical students, dismissive of his female patients and abrasive to his colleagues. All reasons why Dante had known he would never choose cardiology as his specialty. He never wanted to work in the same arena as his father.

So if he wasn't like his father in love or work, how else was he different? And was he not his mother's son, too? She had been steady and generous, loyal and loving.

He had been reckless once, but that wasn't who he was

anymore. He had remade himself in every way, going to medical school and shaping himself into a serious surgeon.

Vittorio claimed that he couldn't change, but Dante already had. Maybe he had a bigger heart than Vittorio, capable of more love, loyalty, joy. Maybe he *deserved* those things more than Vittorio ever had.

But as Julia's words lingered between them like smoke rings, he realized how much he had already given to Miranda—and how much he had received. The thought of walking away now, leaving her behind to raise their child deal with Bradford and face the world alone, felt heavier than he expected. He had always thought his self-imposed rule of avoiding entanglements had protected him and others from pain.

But now it would seem that sticking to his rules would lead to pain, too—and maybe deny him the one person he truly wanted.

Dante glanced at his watch, and his heart skipped a beat.

"Dammit," he cursed under his breath. He shot to his feet and grabbed his jacket from the back of the chair. "Julia, I'm so sorry, but I have to go. I'll call you tomorrow—I promise." He gave her a hasty farewell kiss on the cheek, then bolted for the door.

Julia waved him off with a little smile. "Okay, Romeo. Let me know if you change your mind about that ring design!"

He barely registered her parting insult as he navigated the crowded pub and crashed through the door. Miranda was waiting and he was late—really late.

CHAPTER EIGHT

MIRANDA'S STILETTO HEEL rocked like a metronome as she waited at the OB's office. She was dimly aware of quiet conversation around her and the occasional jangle of a phone ringing, but she was more aware of how the minutes on the clock seemed to drag. Where the heck was Dante? He was almost an hour late!

It just didn't make sense. They had both been so excited about this appointment, even reminding each other before Dante left work. They were going to see their baby on screen again, and finally learn the gender. Dante had even wagered that if the baby was a girl, as he was sure she was, Miranda would have to buy him dinner at Mulligan's.

Her irritation gave way to a gnawing worry. What if something had happened? He could have gotten into a car accident on the way…or had an aneurysm…or maybe had amnesia from hitting his head?

Oh, these were crazy thoughts. She needed to calm down. And make a decision. The clinic staff had pushed her appointment back an hour to give Dante extra time to get there, but they couldn't wait forever. She glanced at her phone again, willing it to give some proof of life, so she knew what she should do. Reschedule the appointment, or go without him?

And then, improbably, her phone did exactly that. It buzzed in her hand as it delivered Dante's message.

On my way!

She stared at her phone in disbelief, trying to make sense of those three little words. He was almost an hour late, and that was all the explanation she was going to get?

Shock and relief soon gave way to a deep, unsettling and all-too-familiar feeling of unease. A feeling she thought she had left behind when she signed divorce papers to end her marriage with Bradford.

This was how it had started with him, too. At first, he had been so supportive and understanding or at least appeared that way. But as the months went by without a positive pregnancy test, he had slowly disappeared, first emotionally, then physically. He couldn't make this appointment because of work. Or that procedure because of a charity golf event he forgot to tell her about. Always late, or absent, then ghosting and gaslighting until she finally gave up and filed for divorce.

She tried to shake off the comparison. What happened with Bradford had nothing to do with Dante. But like an itch just out of reach, her unease refused to be banished.

"Doctor Hawthorne? Are we ready?" The medical assistant had approached without her noticing. She contemplated stalling a little longer, but at this point, she didn't really know what *on my way* meant in terms of Dante's time frame.

Miranda nodded. All she could do was hope that Dante got there in time. And if he didn't, well, the sooner she got used to parenting on her own, the better.

The nurse led Miranda down a narrow hallway, her cheerful monologue an almost comical contrast to the dark thoughts that refused to stop pestering her. Once in the exam room, the nurse handed her a folded gown and left to give her time to change.

Miranda felt numb and uncoordinated as she tried to navigate major engineering challenges like buttons and zippers. Alone in the sterile, quiet room, her anger began to grow. Not at Dante, but at herself. What was wrong with her? Why had she allowed herself to believe that she and Dante had some kind of special connection? That he owed her more than a three-word explanation when he was late?

Because he didn't! Dante wasn't in Boston for *her*. He was only here because of this surprise pregnancy. He was trying to do the right thing by their child, and she was grateful for that. But it had nothing to do with how he felt about her. He probably couldn't wait to get back to his life in Milan, where he was free to do as he pleased.

She blinked back tears, furious that she had allowed herself to imagine something that wasn't real. At this moment, she needed to be more rational and clear-sighted for the sake of her baby, not chase a connection with a man who had never promised her more than a night of anonymous fun in New York.

Miranda perched on the edge of the exam table, wishing she had brought socks to keep her bare feet warm. The nurse and ultrasound technician returned, all smiles and cheerful banter. Miranda played along, but inside, she just felt churned up and uneasy. She answered their health questions with detachment as they prepared her for the ultrasound.

Soon, the room filled with a rhythmic swishing sound. The technician pointed out tiny details of her baby's development, and Miranda was thrilled to see that her baby was growing healthy and strong. But an undercurrent of pain tainted her joy. Dante was missing this monumental moment.

When the technician asked if she wanted to know her

baby's gender, Miranda hesitated. Should she wait for him, or carry on alone?

Before she could answer, a sudden commotion in the hallway got her attention. Then a frantic knocking at the door, and when the tech swung the door open, he was there, his gaze darting around the room until he found her. He rushed to her, already full of apologies, and the thin veil of control she had on her emotions melted away.

She swallowed hard, trying to keep her feelings stuffed away, but the truth was staring her in the face. She hadn't been frustrated with Dante for being late—she had been hurt. Because she had wanted to share this special moment—*all* of her special moments—with him.

All she felt at seeing him was relief, and a strange surge of joy.

There was no use in denying it—at least not to herself. She had fallen for Dante a long time ago, probably back in Milan. But even as her heart exploded with joy at seeing him, her mind was still able to slam on the brakes.

Because falling for Dante didn't mean she could have him, not in the way she wanted. All it meant was that she would have to silently carry this bittersweet craving in her heart for a very long time.

In a flash, Dante was by her side. His hand found hers, and their fingers interlaced.

"I'm so sorry. I had an appointment after work and it ran much longer than I expected." Then there had been the traffic, and a parking garage that had been closed for construction. So he'd had to park ten blocks away and dash to the hospital.

His words faded away as his gaze drifted to the grainy black-and-white image on the ultrasound screen. He kissed her fingers before gracing her with a huge, joyful smile.

Miranda squeezed his hand back but tried to stay focused on the images instead of how his scent reminded her of cedarwood and leather. His quiet murmurs of amazement and sheer joy at seeing their baby made it hard to stay detached, though. His touch was so solid, making her feel anchored and safe, at least for the moment.

The technician adjusted the wand. "Would you like to know the gender?"

His grip tightened slightly, his eyes never leaving hers. "Ready to lose a bet, Doctor Hawthorne?"

She rolled her eyes. "We'll see."

The technician's smile widened as she turned the screen their way. "Congratulations, you are having a gorgeous little girl."

Dante's grin was so triumphant, it was hard not to laugh along with him. And then she had the strangest sensation of watching herself from afar. Seeing herself in a tiny exam room with a man she had met a few months ago who was now whooping with joy at the news they were having a daughter.

Was this really her life?

Have you ever wished—just for a moment—that you could have a different life?

Good grief, this was exactly the life she had always wanted. But she had found it on the road not taken. Turning left instead of right when she came to the spoon in the road.

The memory of their first night together made her smile. And that seemed to inspire him to impulsively bend down to kiss her.

She kissed him right back, like it was the most natural thing in the world.

"I want to celebrate," he said.

"Me, too," she breathed.

Ten minutes later, Miranda was dressed and met Dante in the clinic's lobby. Dante's smile was magical, like there was no one around but the two of them. He grabbed her hand like it was their habit now, and a warm feeling coursed through her body. She liked this familiarity between them—this feeling of *us*.

Dante found a booth near the back of the pub. Miranda waved hello to some of their hospital colleagues, then slid into the booth next to Dante.

A waiter in a white apron appeared at their table. "Good to see you again, sir," he said to Dante, before taking their order.

Miranda cocked her head when the waiter left. "You've been here before?" That surprised her because she had been planning to introduce Dante to her favorite pub ever since he came to Boston, but it hadn't worked out with their demanding schedules.

But Dante never answered. Tuesday was trivia night at the pub, and the MC seemed to have his microphone set rather high. She wasn't sure Dante had even heard her.

Before she could try again, their drinks appeared. Dante proposed a toast to their good fortune of having a daughter, and she affirmed with a hearty *hear, hear* before they clinked glasses and by the time they ordered dinner, she forgot all about asking Dante when he had been here.

Dante set his glass down, a foamy mustache clinging to his upper lip from the stout beer. He licked it away with a quick swipe of his tongue, and Miranda had to curl her fingers under the table to resist reacting to the effortlessly sexy gesture. Damn pregnancy hormones.

"You know, Dante," she said with an arched eyebrow, "if you ever get tired of neurosurgery, you might consider a future in beer commercials. That move was pretty cinematic."

Dante leaned back, his arms stretching the length of the booth, and flashing that easy grin of his that never failed to make her heart stumble. "You just want another reason to stare at me."

He wasn't wrong, but she had to save face. "You flatter yourself," she shot back before sipping her nonalcoholic beer.

He chuckled, but the playful spark in his eyes dimmed as he straightened. His demeanor changed as he fiddled with his glass, and Miranda noted the tightness in his jaw and how he seemed to be avoiding her gaze.

"I got an email from my supervisor in Milan," he began, his tone quieter now.

"Oh?" Her heart sank, knowing whatever he was about to say wasn't good.

"He wants to know when he can expect my return." His fingers drummed a restless rhythm on the table, a contrast to his outwardly calm facade. "He's willing to be flexible, but he can't wait forever."

"No, of course not," she agreed. She was proud of how calm and reasonable she sounded. As if she had expected this all along and negotiating his exit was just a formality.

"So, when do you think you will go?"

It was insane the way she half expected him to say, *never. I love it here in Boston and I've put in my notice so that I can stay here.* What a dumb thing to think. Of course he was going to return to Milan. There had never been any expectation otherwise. She had just hoped she would have him a little longer.

"Well, we have that meeting with the attorney on Friday to finalize the details of the custody agreement. Once that's resolved…"

"There's really no reason for you to stay," she finished, hating the tendrils of wistfulness that laced her tone.

"No, I guess not."

Dante's gaze locked on hers, steady and unflinching. His dark eyes were intense in a way that sent a shiver down her spine, and she felt as though he was searching for something in her expression.

"But I think we should make the most of our time together before I leave."

Dante's words hung in the air, rich and suggestive, like a drizzle of warm honey. She couldn't read his gaze, but the slight shift in his tone and his trademark smirk sent a ripple of heat through her body. Her pulse quickened as she scrambled to understand what he meant. The way he spoke and looked at her, it felt like a sexy invitation. But she wasn't sure if it was her imagination running wild again, fueled by the magnetic pull he always seemed to have on her.

"What did you have in mind?" she asked, trying to keep the breathless edge out of her tone.

"A weekend away, just you and me," Dante said, his lips curving into a slow, sexy smile. "Like New York, but more intentional."

Her stomach fluttered at the suggestion in his tone, sending a warmth spreading through her chest. His expression was intense, and she felt like he was waiting for her to catch up to a plan he hadn't said out loud.

"Okay," she answered slowly, keeping her voice steady despite the uncertainty that tightened her throat. Her thoughts were jumping way ahead of her, flooding her with possibilities that made her feel both excited and unsure.

"We could leave Friday, after our meeting with the attorney. Then, when we return—" he looked down at his beer, thumbing condensation away "—I'll let Milan know my decision."

Those words felt charged with unspoken meaning. Did he mean he would let Milan know his return date? Or was there a hint of something else?

Miranda couldn't deny the magnetic pull she felt at the prospect of one last weekend alone with Dante. They had maintained a strictly platonic relationship while Dante was in Boston, so they could focus on navigating their new roles as coparents.

It hadn't been easy, dodging his gaze at breakfast. Trying not to notice when he came out of the shower with just a towel wrapped around his waist, his damp hair and bare chest making her heart thud in her own chest. Now he was inviting her for a weekend away and she wasn't sure what intimidated her more—falling back into his arms or having to stop when he left for Milan.

Because a weekend alone with Dante would *not* make it easier to say goodbye. Her body craved him in a way that made her heart hurt. She felt powerless when he was around, and she'd be lying to herself if she tried to believe that this weekend would "get things out of her system."

Spending the weekend together would be like throwing a match on a huge pile of dry kindling. She was going to burn up in his arms and only want more.

Because this wasn't a fling anymore, and it wasn't just Dante's obligations as the father of her child, either. Something was growing between them. Camaraderie and attraction, partnership and support. But was it strong enough to last? To build a life on?

And did he feel this connection, too?

"Yes," she murmured, her voice soft but steady. "I think that would be a good way to end things."

Dante's gaze lingered on hers, his faint smile unreadable. "Yes, it could be that."

Which left her wondering what else this weekend could be.

The scent of lavender and eucalyptus drifted around Miranda as expert hands massaged away all her worries and cares. Soft candlelight danced on the walls of the dimly lit massage room, gently flickering off polished wood beams, remnants of the building's past life as a working farm.

Miranda opened one eye to take in the nature scene beyond the window of the massage room. The window had been cracked open, and a light breeze made the lace curtains dance.

"This place is pure perfection," she murmured. "How did you find it?"

Dante opened his eyes to meet her gaze. Like her, he was naked beneath the warm, lemon-scented towels the massage therapists had draped over their lower torsos. His arms were folded under his head, showing off the sloped planes of his back.

He shrugged, making the round, hard muscles of his shoulders rise and fall. "Just did a little research, asked around."

A strong wave of need washed over her. It was not easy being this close to him when he was naked, slick with sandalwood-scented massage oil and right next to her.

"Well, it's amazing," she said, her mouth dry with lust.

And it was. Early Saturday morning, they had left the city in her SUV. As they had left the bustle of Boston behind, the cityscape melted into rolling green hills and winding roads flanked by towering maples just beginning to blush with autumn.

He hadn't told her where they were going—only what to pack. Casual clothes for hanging out. A warm jacket and hat for hiking. A nice dress for dinner. She could pack a book if she wanted, but they had a library there if she wanted to discover something new, and that had certainly piqued her interest.

When they had turned off the main road, the landscape had transformed into a picturesque New England retreat. The Hearth & Harvest Bed and Breakfast was a former farm that had been converted to an upscale spa retreat. Its centerpiece was a grand barn with weathered beams and a roof glinting faintly in the autumn sun. Rows of golden mums and deep orange pumpkins flanked the gravel drive as they approached a renovated farmhouse with a wraparound porch adorned with rocking chairs and lanterns.

"I'm glad you like it," he said, his tone languid and sensuous. His brown eyes were appraising her, making her wonder how much of her lust he could read on her face. Somehow, that only intensified the buzzing in her core.

Her senses had been awakened by the long, relaxing couple's massage he had scheduled for their arrival. So awakened that she would love nothing more than to lead him back to her room, snatch off that towel and devour every inch of his body as she had in Milan.

"I thought this might be more to your liking than F1 racing."

She smiled at the memory of their first date in Milan. Yes, she liked this version of Dante much better. Maybe too much. Sometimes she felt he had somehow put a spell on her, making her feel she was on the verge of losing all control when he was near.

But she feared what she felt for Dante went much deeper than lust.

It wasn't just the pregnancy or a contract that linked them now. He was like a fever she couldn't escape. She felt whole when he was by her side. And unafraid to face whatever was coming next. Surprise babies, demanding work—even Bradford—life was a lot less stressful when Dante was around.

She had decided in the days before the trip that she couldn't just let him go back to Milan as if the past months had meant nothing. If there was ever a man she'd be willing to risk her fragile heart with, it was Dante.

As the last notes of the instrumental music came to a close, her massage therapist finished her treatment and laid another warm towel over Miranda's back.

"When you're ready, you can get dressed and return to the lobby. We'll meet you there."

After dressing and tipping their therapists, Dante and Miranda walked slowly back to the carriage house that had been renovated to accommodate a dozen guest rooms, all themed with New England motifs. Casually and without thought, he reached for her hand, warming it against the autumn chill.

Her body felt lax and languid after the massage, every muscle relaxed and placid. But beneath the calm, a steady hum of need pulsed in her belly. So when they retreated to the quiet of their room, it felt natural, inevitable even, to close the door and slip into his arms.

She tilted her chin, teasing him with a soft smile. "That wasn't exactly fair, you know. Torturing me with a long, sinful massage while you're naked and just out of reach?"

His smile was a sexy promise. "I just wanted us to unwind and relax."

His breath felt like silk against her cheek.

"Are you relaxed now, *cara mia*?"

"Very," she whispered.

She felt his hand in her hair, then her clip was released, and her long waves spilled over her bare shoulders. His eyes went dark then, and he murmured something in Italian, the words soft and reverent. She felt like something precious in his arms; then he bent his head and claimed her mouth.

The heat of his kiss stole her breath away. It was instinctive to part her lips for him; she was desperate to taste him after all those long nights of craving him in silence. For weeks, they had been platonic roommates when all she had wanted was this—slipping into his arms and finally surrendering to her desires.

Weeks of denial rose inside her like a tsunami, rushing hot through her veins. She pressed closer to him, knowing she was powerless to stop what her body had been begging for.

His hands moved from her hair down her body, making her feel like a statue being shaped by the hands of a brilliant artist. His fingers found her belly and lingered there, reminding her of their first encounter in New York. She had felt broken then, but Dante had made her feel beautiful. She felt his breath on her neck just before he trailed kisses across her skin while he held her camisole up so she could slip out of it again. She felt no shame this time. She could be naked with him in every way. Because she trusted him with everything—her body, her heart, her vulnerability. He had proven, again and again, that she was safe in his arms.

But there was longing in his eyes and a shadow that made her wonder if he felt safe, too. Was it possible he yearned for more than this farewell weekend? This wasn't like their time together in Milan, when their lovemaking was only meant to be a fling—just fun and games. Everything was different now. They would be forever linked by their baby, even if they weren't together.

But was goodbye their destiny?

There was no way to know, and words felt hopelessly wrong in this moment.

Maybe she could show him with her body that he was safe here, too. And very wanted.

But did their story have to end with *goodbye*? Was there some small, quiet, aching part of him that wanted to stay, too?

Dante's kisses trailed down her chest, the curve of her breasts, until she felt a sharp little sting when he nipped her nipples with his teeth the way she liked. She sighed and relaxed in his arms, lost in the unique blend of pain and pleasure that had been their relationship since the night they'd met in New York.

She felt his hands run the length of her back, tracing its curves, until he found her hips, clasping them roughly, then turned her so her back was against his chest. Their eyes met in the mirror above the antique dressing table. She felt utterly pinned by his intense focus, unable to tear her gaze away. He left a trail of goose bumps as his fingers lightly grazed her body, going ever lower still until he found her mad with desire for him.

He groaned against her neck, an ancient, primal sound, then hooked her panties with his thumbs and slid them off her legs. Their gaze reconnected in the mirror, and she gave him the faintest of nods. *Yours*, is what she wanted to say. Her body and heart, pain and hopes—they were all his for the taking. She was ready to take a chance on love again, because this time she wouldn't be settling. There was nothing about Dante that felt functional or like a compromise. The way he made her feel was pure magic and sparkle.

Dante paused for just a moment before grasping her hips so that she braced herself on the dressing table. A deep, guttural cry escaped her lips as he claimed her completely. The antique table rocked under her hands with an audible thud against the wall, and she was vaguely concerned that they were too loud for the intimate confines of a bed-and-breakfast inn.

But she could barely breathe, she wanted him so much. All she could do was watch his eyes as they went dark and unfocused, her pleasure heightened by seeing how her body brought him such bliss. His deep, angled strokes, his grip on her hips, drove her to a maddeningly delirious state, and she almost gasped out what was in her heart.

At last, he closed his eyes completely, fingers pressed into her flesh, finding the deepest parts of her. One hand found her hair, wrapping the strands around his fingers, then gently tugging her back so he could kiss her neck.

She should feel vulnerable, being pinned like this, her neck bared to attack. But she had never felt safer in her life. Dante was making love to her with all that he had. She felt his warmth and strength everywhere—holding her up, driving her on—until she closed her eyes in her last act of surrender.

Tension coiled deep in her core as her moans became synced with the rhythms of Dante's thrusts as he pushed her closer and closer to the edge.

Then he released her hair and pulled her tight against his chest. Shouted her name as her breath caught for a second before she felt a rushing sensation, like she was standing too close to a passing train. Waves of pleasure coursed through her body, making her knees buckle and her eyes tear.

* * *

She was done. Or rather, utterly undone. Dante had broken through every defense, overcome all resistance. Had somehow taken up residence in her heart and even if he moved to the moon, she was never going to be the same again.

Their ragged breaths eventually slowed. She sagged against his chest, and he held her there, his eyes closed as he smoothed the hair at her temple with his thumb.

It was almost overwhelming to tell him her new truth. *I love you, completely.* It would be a relief, really, to let the words tumble from her lips. Whatever happened next… happened.

But she didn't want him to question her feelings. To blame passion or have any doubts.

She wanted him to know exactly how she felt; then he could decide what happened next.

He took a quick shower first, stepping out with droplets still clinging to his skin. He left the water running for her—a small, tender gesture that made her heart tighten.

She slipped beneath the spray, letting the heat soak into her muscles as she lathered her hair, her mind turning over the words she knew she needed to say. This wasn't something she could just drop on him out of the blue, or whisper casually in the dark. These words mattered too much.

"Dante?" she called softly, her pulse quickening as she rinsed the soap from her skin.

"Mmm-hmm?"

She heard the quick, rhythmic taps of his razor as he cleared away the shaving foam.

"Could we change our dinner plans tonight? Maybe order room service and eat on the terrace? It should be plenty warm enough with all the outdoor heaters they have here."

For a moment, silence. Then Dante's question, his tone tight and crisp. "Is something wrong?"

"No, I just want to talk to you about something. A little privacy would be nice."

More silence. Clearly, this idea didn't please him.

"Never mind, it's fine, I just thought…"

Humiliation made her cheeks grow even warmer in the steamy shower stall. Obviously, she had misread their relationship…again.

But when he pulled back the shower curtain, his gaze was earnest and sincere. "I want to talk to you, too, Miranda. That's why I planned a small, intimate dinner…"

He was interrupted by the shrill ring of the antique telephone in their room.

"Hold that thought," he told her, then the shower curtain slipped back in place. From beyond the bathroom, she could hear him thank someone for the good news.

He yanked the shower curtain aside again. "There's a package downstairs that I need to sign for, then I'm going to make sure everything is just right for our dinner plans tonight. We can talk after dinner, okay?"

She forced a smile. "Sounds lovely, Dante."

He scanned her wet face, then caught it between his dry hands and pulled her close for a kiss. His lips warmed hers for several long seconds, until she relaxed under his touch and kissed him back. When he finally broke it off, he continued to frame her face, his gaze searching hers. She felt a flutter of hope in her chest.

"Seven o'clock," he told her.

"Seven o'clock," she repeated, savoring the scent of sandalwood on his skin, the warmth of his hands on her face.

And then he was gone.

Miranda finished her shower and took her time dressing for dinner. The long, hot shower had only deepened her relaxation after the massage, making her feel languid and sexy. She slipped on her black cocktail dress and shoes, then applied her makeup and arranged her hair into a French knot. When done, she studied her reflection in the mirror.

Just what exactly are you planning to propose? That he extend his trip for a few more weeks? Stay forever?

She sighed, then applied a layer of Crimson Kiss, her favorite lipstick. Maybe it was best to just tell him what was in her heart. That against her better judgment, she had fallen for him. That even though there were a hundred reasons to be sensible, she couldn't deny that she no longer wanted to be without him.

Miranda made the short walk to the farmhouse, thinking Dante had planned dinner at the small, intimate restaurant there. But instead, he had planned an exquisitely intimate dinner in the little reading room with its shelves of weathered books and overstuffed armchairs.

Rain pattered against the wide-paned windows, blurring the view of the darkened garden beyond. A crackling fire in the stone hearth filled the room with warmth and the faint, woody scent of burning cedar. A small table was set for two, draped in white linen and adorned with flickering candles. Miranda felt like she was stepping into a dream.

"Wow," Miranda said as she slid into her chair. "I'm impressed."

And she was. She was also surprised at Dante's nervousness. Unlike Milan, when he had been the model of confidence as he escorted her around the raceway, he seemed self-conscious and anxious as they made small talk.

Servers soon appeared to deliver herbed cheese crostini and lobster rolls. Miranda nibbled on her appetizer, watching Dante fuss with his lobster roll until it slipped from his plate to the floor.

"Dammit," he muttered.

She handed him a napkin for cleanup, then tilted her head. "Are you okay?"

He sighed and squared his shoulders. "Not exactly."

She leaned in conspiratorially. "Listen, I know we've only known each other for like, a few months and then we went and made a baby and all. But sometimes it's easier to talk with strangers about hard things, you know?"

His mouth curved in a soft smile at her reference to their first night in New York.

"It's about returning to Milan. I didn't expect the hospital to ask me back so soon. I thought I had more time."

Yeah, me, too.

"And that's a problem?" She didn't mean to add that hopeful little lilt on the last syllable.

He looked down at the table, brushed away some imaginary crumbs. "Yeah, I think it might be. I think we ought to talk about all the options we have, Miranda. That is—" he looked up, uncharacteristically shy "—if you're interested in other options?"

Miranda's heart soared and it took a great deal of self-control not to fly across the table and plant herself in Dante's lap.

She smoothed away imaginary crumbs. "I would like to talk about other options. Very much."

Dante's expression broke out into a warm, expansive smile. "Well, that's good. That's…quite excellent actually."

A server appeared to clear their appetizer plates. "Dinner will be ready shortly, Doctor Ricci. Would you like another glass of wine while you wait?"

Dante nodded and the server filled both of their glasses

with a nonalcoholic wine that Dante had brought from Boston. For the second time since she had met Dante, she wondered how she had gotten so lucky. What should have been a simple work trip and emotional retreat had turned into so much more. Even more than the Operation Revenge Affair her sister had wanted for her.

Dante reached across the table to take her hand, and she returned his squeeze. Then she heard her cell phone buzz. Every cell in her body wanted to ignore the call so she could be immersed in this perfect moment with Dante. But it could be her new intern, nervous about a test result or symptom, and she'd rather be safe than sorry.

"Sorry," she muttered apologetically. "Let me just check this."

To her dismay, it was a text from Bradford. What on earth did he want? They didn't even work in the same department.

She would have been happy to toss her phone back into her purse and forget all about him, but the first few words of his text message made her pause.

Your Italian "friend" sure gets around…

Miranda bit her lip as she wondered what the heck that meant. Didn't Bradford have enough to keep him busy? She knew she should ignore it—everything Bradford did or said was designed to hurt her in some way. He was just making trouble.

Yeah…but what kind of trouble?

Curiosity won out and she opened the text.

Bradford's text included a link to a news article. She opened it and found a picture of Dante sitting very close to a stunning raven-haired beauty. The woman had her head thrown back in a full-throated laugh, while Dante's head bent toward hers. Conspiratorial. Intimate.

As curious as that was, it was even more curious to realize that the booth that Dante and the woman were sharing looked very familiar. Dark, worn leather booth. Dim lighting. Shelves filled with sports memorabilia.

This was Mulligan's, the little pub near the hospital. Which meant this picture had been taken sometime while Dante was in Boston.

Beneath the photo was some text. Milan's Favorite Bad Boy Reconnects with Old Flame in Boston... What's Going On?

What indeed? Miranda wondered. She read the short blip of a news story under the photo, if you could call the nonsense *news*. All she got from it was that Dante and his companion had once dated. That they'd reconnected in Boston.

And this was why Dante had been late to her ultrasound appointment.

"Everything all right?"

Dante's tone was warm, not really expecting a serious response.

She looked up at him and time seemed to still for a moment. Her mind tried really hard to connect the dots in a way that wouldn't break her heart.

But in the end, denial yielded to reality.

The hurt rushed in, hard and fast. What the hell had she done? Had she been so desperate for love after her messy divorce that she had sold her soul to the first man who'd thrown her some crumbs of affection?

Was this the price of wanting more? Shame, humiliation, defeat yet again?

Only it was so much worse this time. Because she'd

gone into this with eyes wide-open. She had been amply warned about who Dante was. Yet, she had willingly sacrificed her pride, her worth, her dignity, just to have a taste of something that felt like love.

She gasped against the sharp ache in her chest. She felt as if she'd been dealt the final knockout blow in a boxing match where she had been outmatched before she had even stepped into the ring.

An hour ago, he had made her feel like the most important woman in the world. But just a few days ago, he was doing the same for an ex-lover.

Was this how it was for some people? Chameleons who could just lie and pretend to be whatever you needed them to be?

Dante's shoulders stiffened as he read her expression. "What is it? What's wrong?"

Wordlessly, she handed him the phone. It was safer than trying to speak.

His face fell as his brows furrowed.

"Miranda, wait. This isn't what you…"

No, no, no, no. No!

She was *not* going to accept gaslighting again. Or let anyone convince her that her thoughts were incoherent and untrustworthy.

"No!" she practically shouted. "You don't get to do that!"

She stood up so fast, her chair knocked to the floor behind her. A server moved forward to help but then froze, her gaze ping-ponging between them.

Dante slowly rose to his feet. He moved slowly and carefully, like he was trying not to spook her. "Let's go outside, Miranda, so we can talk."

"No more talk!" Her hands were shaking, and her legs

felt like Jell-O. All she wanted was to get out of that room, that farm, that city, hell, maybe even the whole damn state.

Away from second chances and charming devils like Dante. Back to what she could trust: her life, her family, her work.

She released her grip on the edge of the table to press her fingers into her temple where a monstrous migraine was brewing. Foolish! Why had she been so damn foolish?

She tossed her napkin on the table and told the server to call her a cab.

"Miranda, I'd be happy to take you home."

"No! I don't want you to drive me home. I don't want you to follow me when I leave this restaurant. I just want you to leave me alone, okay?"

She ran out of the farmhouse, dashed across the cobblestone courtyard to her room. Packing was a mad affair. She just grabbed what she could and vowed to buy replacements for anything she left behind.

Then she dashed back out into the rain, still in her cocktail dress and heels, her wet hair plastered to her head. So she could wave down the cab driver and tell him to please, please, please take her home.

CHAPTER NINE

DANTE FELT BOTH dread and determination as he pulled into Miranda's driveway and switched off the ignition. Her small home, an understated Craftsman in an older neighborhood near the hospital, sat in the fading light. Its darkened windows and the absence of her porch light cast an unwelcoming stillness over her home.

It was the day after their terrible fight at the bed-and-breakfast inn. He had hoped that giving her a little space would help her cool off, but the silence that stretched between them was as unwelcoming as her dark, cold home. Other than replying to his text that yes, she had gotten home safely, his phone had remained quiet. No teasing messages, no phone call to say she was ready to talk.

He stared at her front porch. Long shadows stretched over the wide steps where they had argued about the best color for the nursery. Was that just a few days ago? She had been right, of course. The delicate lilac she'd chosen was the perfect choice for the nursery's Woodlands and Garden theme.

The sight of a large box leaning against the porch rail caught his eye—the crib had arrived. Assembling it was supposed to be a fun task they would do together. But the prospect of doing anything together seemed further away than ever.

He used the key she had given him to let himself inside. Somehow, despite their shared history, the act felt strangely intrusive. He wrestled the box across the threshold into her living room, where the shelves were stuffed with books. In the kitchen beyond, he could see the recipe she had taped to the cabinet from their last dinner together. Chicken Cordon Bleu with herbed new potatoes. It had been delicious.

He set the box down in the nursery, the smallest bedroom at the end of the hall, and took a deep breath. The new shelves he had installed were adorned with woodland creatures she had meticulously chosen. It made him pause a moment, to take it all in.

Dante never thought his life would include any of this. He had resigned himself to a solitary existence, convinced marriage and children were risks he could never take. He had seen the damage his father left behind, the shattered women who had loved him. Dante never wanted to be the source of that kind of pain for anyone else.

But then Miranda happened. And the baby.

She didn't just breach his carefully guarded walls—she'd obliterated them. It had been terrifying at first—the weight of the unknown, new responsibilities on his shoulders.

But standing here now, surrounded by the small, tangible signs of a life they were building together, he felt something he hadn't allowed himself to hope for: clarity. This was what he wanted. *She* was what he wanted. A family. A future. A love that felt unbreakable—if only she would let it be.

He rolled up his sleeves and got to work on the crib, tightening screws and aligning panels. Anything to keep his hands busy and his mind off the ache in his chest.

The front door opened, then closed. His heartbeat picked

up as adrenaline flooded his system. He just hoped he could make things right with her.

"Hey," Miranda said softly. Her voice was devoid of the anger that had made her eyes blaze the day before. But her face was pale, with dark shadows under her eyes, as if she had found sleep as elusive as he had.

"Hey, yourself." He kept his voice low, as if he might startle her into flight.

Her gaze scanned the room, taking in the half-completed project. Wordlessly, she draped her jacket on the back of the rocking chair and dropped to her knees. She looked over the instructions, then reached for a screwdriver.

Okay, this wasn't what he'd expected. But he didn't push for more. He just let the rhythm of work ease them back into some kind of camaraderie.

They worked in silence for several long minutes, the tension between them palpable. He felt such a strong need to speak, to explain everything, but he didn't know how to begin.

"Miranda," he said finally, breaking the silence. "About that picture…"

"There's no need," she interrupted, her hands holding the wood frame in place. "I couldn't sleep, so I followed the story online. I know her name is Julia. That you two dated long ago. And that she had come to Boston as a favor to her good friend. Because you asked her to design an engagement ring for the woman you want to marry."

Relief flooded through his body. She understood everything then. But it was a big move, asking someone to marry you.

"I know it seems fast, Miranda. And there's no expiration date on the offer. I just wanted you to know how I feel. I can wait forever if that's what you need."

He reached into his pocket and touched the box he had been carrying since it had been delivered to the bed-and-breakfast. This wasn't the real ring; that would take a few weeks for Julia to design and deliver. But she had created a prototype for him, so he would have something tangible to give Miranda when he asked her to take a chance on him—for life.

If she understood what that picture meant, why did it feel like everything was so wrong?

They finished the crib in silence, adding the fitted sheet, positioning the crib in the corner and draping a soft blanket over the rail. His final touch was adding the mobile that he had bought in a little shop in Milan. Delicate stars and moons spun gently above the crib.

Miranda stood by Dante's side. "It's perfect."

Then she slipped her hand in his and led him to the guest room. Somehow, he knew before she opened the door what he would find.

Two suitcases, packed and lined up with military precision by the door.

His stomach sank. "You packed my things."

"Yes." Her voice was steady, but her gaze was direct.

"Why? I thought you understood what happened."

She pulled away from him to lean against the hallway wall. She slipped her hands deep into the pockets of her cardigan sweater, looking away.

"Dante, when I saw that picture of you with Julia, my mind immediately went to the worst possible places. It never occurred to me to give you a chance to explain. I didn't even ask any questions!" Her gaze returned to him, her voice trembling with vulnerability. "My first thought was to protect myself. To accuse you and to run. And that's not about you—that's about me."

"Miranda…"

She held up a hand to stop him. "Let me finish. I went to Milan because I needed to heal after my divorce and I really thought I had. But with the way I reacted when I saw you with Julia… Now I'm wondering if some wounds just cut too deep."

"No, Miranda, that's not true. You're stronger than this. *We're* stronger than this."

She shook her head, tears brimming in her eyes. "All this time I've been worried about you, thinking you couldn't change from the man you once were. Turns out it's *me* who can't change. I just can't give up the fear of being deceived again. It's always there, under the surface, making me question every good thing between us.

"You deserve someone who loves you for who *you* are, Dante. Not someone who's always waiting for you to prove them wrong. I don't think I can be that person for you."

His heart broke and he wanted to fight back and prove her wrong. This was just a rough spot for them. They could work through it. He could get her to believe in them again, if she would just give him a little time.

But the pain etched in her face, the conviction in her voice—he knew he was sunk before he even had a chance to try.

"This isn't what I want."

"Me neither," she admitted. "But it's what's right. We have a baby coming, and she is what matters most. We can't risk destroying what is good between us. We must be two mature coparents who can put our baby's needs ahead of our own. Let's…just keep it at that."

She turned away from him to hide her tears. More than anything in the world, he wanted to pull her into him. Kiss and hold her until all these bad feelings subsided and all she could see and feel was how much he loved her.

But she couldn't give him what he most wanted: to be loved for who he was.

And she couldn't accept what he most wanted to give her: the peace of knowing that he would never hurt her as she feared.

Dante stared at her back for several long seconds, letting the weight of their impasse settle on his heart. Then he lifted his suitcases and headed for the front door.

He paused in the doorway and looked back at her one last time.

"Take care of yourself, Miranda."

"You, too," she whispered.

The cold night air nipped at his nose and cheeks. He didn't bother turning up his collar or zipping his coat shut.

He just closed the door and accepted the life he couldn't seem to outrun.

Miranda's phone buzzed on the bench next to her. For the second time that day, she was changing into a clean pair of scrubs. The glow of her cell phone screen felt eerie and ominous in the dim light of the hospital locker room.

Her stomach cramped when she read the message.

Urgent: 16M, severe head trauma from MVC. OR3. ETA 5min. Neuro consult needed STAT.

Without hesitation, she slipped a scrub top over her head, then strode to the OR.

Head trauma could mean a lot of things. She ran through the possibilities, planning what she would need for each scenario.

Ensure massive transfusion protocol is activated. Cardiology will manage blood pressure with vasopressors, but I need to know his coagulation status. Use fresh frozen plasma if need be. Have suction and vascular clips ready for hemorrhaging. Prepare for vessel ligation or repair.

Every step she rehearsed in her mind felt urgent. Her pulse was steady, but her mind was a flurry of hyperfocused determination. Severe head trauma could be a life-or-death situation, and she wanted to use every resource she had to give this boy a fighting chance.

As soon as Miranda entered the OR, she knew the teenager was in danger. Her team hadn't waited for her assessment or instructions; they already had the surgical trays open and the OR prepped for surgery.

Her resident was bent over the teenager, one hand pressed hard against the boy's head. The gauze he held was already soaked with blood.

Instantly, Miranda's heart rate picked up and she felt the familiar prickle of goose bumps down her back as her body flooded with adrenaline. Her body was preparing to fight or flee, but there would be no fleeing today. She was going to have to fight with everything she had to save this patient.

"What do I need to know, people?"

Without waiting for a reply, she raced to the scrub room to prep for surgery. Her scrub nurse followed close behind, giving her a concise briefing.

"Sixteen-year-old male with severe head trauma from a car accident. Vitals are unstable—blood pressure is eighty over fifty, heart rate one-twenty and he's showing signs of hypovolemic shock. Imaging revealed a large epidural hematoma with a midline shift and active bleeding from a sheared intracranial vessel. Pupils are unequal and sluggish. Anesthesiology has his airway managed and he's being stabilized with fluid and blood products. OR is prepped for an emergency craniotomy to control the hemorrhage and relieve pressure."

"Excellent," Miranda murmured, soaping her arms to the elbow with an antimicrobial scrub. Harborview had assembled the very best surgical team for the emergency surgery, and from the look of things, this boy needed nothing less.

Miranda waited impatiently while her scrub nurse tied her gown and mask in place, then took her spot with the team. But it took her less than a minute to realize their chances of saving this boy were very slim. The accident had sheared a major blood vessel in his brain. Despite her resident's desperate attempt to manually stop the bleeding, the blood loss was already catastrophic.

Miranda swore heartily and got to work. Her only hope was to get the bleeding under control. She began blindly placing aneurysm clips wherever she could get a glimpse of the damaged vessel, trying to stem the bleeding. It was no use, though. The bleeding was too massive and when the boy's brain began to swell aggressively, Miranda knew he could not survive.

She stepped away from the table and looked at her team. "There's nothing more we can do here—let's close up and get him to the PICU so his family can say goodbye."

She winced when she realized she had just given them an order, as if they were still performing surgery. In a softer tone, she thanked the team and asked the anesthesiologist to make sure the teenager was comfortable for whatever time he had left.

For several minutes, they worked in grim silence. Miranda knew everyone was sharing the same feeling of crushing defeat. Losing any patient was tough, but children and teenagers were just so heartbreaking. When he had woken up that morning, the boy had had his entire life ahead of him. Now it was gone in the blink of an eye.

Miranda accompanied the boy to the PICU but left as the family began to file in. She had learned long ago that her presence was no comfort to a grieving family at times like this. She was just a reminder of what could not be. The family needed each other now, and their shared love for a boy who was going to leave the earth far too soon.

When Miranda returned to the OR, her team was working in a heavy, oppressive silence. Trays of used equipment were removed and new equipment had been set out for the next patient. Miranda had checked the schedule and knew it was an eight-year-old girl with life-limiting headaches caused by a congenital brain malformation. A successful surgery could bring her life back to normal.

Miranda cleared her throat. "Hey, everyone?"

There was no need to raise her voice. Everyone could hear her just fine in a room that felt more like a tomb than an OR.

Eight solemn sets of eyes looked her way.

"He had the very best team," Miranda began, trying to keep the wobble in her voice in check.

Her scrub nurse quickly looked away, trying to hide the tears that spilled onto her mask.

"We had the best equipment and the best resources. And you all did your jobs to absolute perfection. But sometimes, none of that matters."

Words from a long-ago mentor crossed the valley of time, coming back to her in exactly the same way she had heard them when she was a junior doctor struggling with a tough loss.

"We cannot save every person in this OR. All we can do is try."

She swallowed hard, hoping her words would bring solace to a team that had nothing to regret or doubt.

"There is a little girl in holding right now and she really needs us. We can make her life better when we are done."

Her team seemed frozen, still not grasping for the emotional life preserver she was offering.

"I can promise you this—in the process of healing this girl, we will heal ourselves just enough to move on from this."

Everyone remained still for a few more seconds as Miranda's words lingered in the air. Then they began to stir, slow and hesitant at first. One by one, they resumed their tasks—restocking supplies, adjusting monitors and disinfecting surfaces—prepping the room for the next patient who deserved their best.

The adrenaline rush of trying to save the teenage boy wore off and Miranda felt exhaustion flood her body, making her limbs feel heavy and sluggish. She yanked off her scrub cap and left the OR to change into clean scrubs for the next surgery, using the break to hide behind her locker where her tears would not be noticed.

At the end of the day, she had traded her scrub cap for a swim cap and slipped into the cold, clear water of her health club's lap pool. It was late on a Tuesday night, and she mostly had the pool to herself.

The cold water was an icy shock that jolted her mind into clarity. She struck out with smooth strokes, the familiar resistance of the water welcoming her like an old friend.

As her arms cut through the water in crisp, perfect rhythm, her breathing settled into the steady cadence of the freestyle she had mastered years ago when she swam for her college's swim team. Every lap was like a meditation, forcing her to focus only on the mechanics of her body and the comforting repetition of motion.

Tension that had coiled in her chest since the surgery began to ease, replaced by a faint burning ache in her muscles.

But she wasn't sure that the tension she carried in her body was solely from today's surgeries. These heavy limbs and achy muscles had been with her ever since Dante had come to her house after their disastrous weekend at the bed-and-breakfast.

The breakup with Dante had left Miranda feeling hollowed out and empty. Sleep had been a joke. Her body was too restless with memories of how his warm body had felt beside hers, and she could swear his cologne still lingered on her pillows, despite changing the linens twice.

Food tasted like cardboard. It was only for her baby's sake that she forced herself to eat every day.

Even swimming—her sanctuary—couldn't drown out the ache that their breakup had left behind.

Dante had continued to work his shifts at Harborview, but they did their best to avoid each other. In a few days, he would return to Milan. The thought should have brought her some relief, but instead, it made everything so much worse.

Her words to her team echoed in her mind as she sliced through the water.

We cannot save every person in this OR. But there is a child in holding right now who needs us, and in the process of helping to heal her, we will heal ourselves.

She had meant those words to inspire her team's resilience, but now they felt like a personal challenge. What about her? Wasn't she clinging to the wreckage of her marriage, letting its ruins drag her down?

And by stubbornly holding on to her hurt, who else was she hurting? She had wanted to remind her team that they had responsibilities to many patients. That they couldn't afford to let the pain of losing the boy dampen their passion and skills for saving their next patient.

Her thoughts shifted to the grainy ultrasound images that were now stuck to her refrigerator. Her baby needed abundant doses of love and joy as she grew up. And the security of knowing that she always had family who would stand by her side through thick and thin.

Miranda had spent months grieving the wounds left behind by a man who had never really been there for her.

While keeping Dante at arm's length, because she didn't want to be disappointed or let down again.

Was she really going to push away the one man who had never let her down? Who had been willing to cross an ocean for her?

The realization of her own blindness over the past few months hit her with the force of a wave.

She pulled herself out of the water and dried off with a towel. In the locker room, she studied her reflection. She was more than a surgeon, more than an ex-wife, even more than a mother.

She was a woman who had a lot of love to give. And she deserved someone who could give her all the magic and sparkle and glitter and joy that her heart could handle.

Her cell phone buzzed against the bathroom counter where she was twisting her hair into a French knot. She picked it up, hoping as she had for the past week that it was Dante. That he might lob her a soft opening—a simple *hey* so she could text back *hey, yourself* and they could start talking again.

But it wasn't Dante; it was Alessandra's office sending her an auto-notification that Dante had signed the custody agreement. The ball was in her court now.

Her heart sank at the news. If Dante had accepted the custody agreement, it meant he had accepted his fate. He had accepted that things weren't going to work out for them, and he was ready to go back to Milan.

She dropped her hairbrush into her gym bag and stared at her image.

You're too late, Miranda. He's given up on you.

She could hardly blame him—she had let her fears drive him away.

The thought tightened her chest, but she pushed it aside, letting the words of wisdom she had shared with her team be her salvation, too.

We cannot save everyone in this OR, but we can try.

What worked in the OR could work in life, too. All she could do was show up, speak her truth, do her best. *She could try.*

Dante hadn't left for Milan yet. He was still here—somewhere—in Boston. And if she could find him, maybe she could undo the damage she had done when she let him go. Maybe she could convince him that she was ready to take a chance on love again—with him.

If she failed, well, she had faced plenty of loss and failure in her life. Whatever came next, she would face it with courage.

She navigated to her texting app and lobbed the ball into play.

Hey…

CHAPTER TEN

DANTE STARED AT his image in the mirror. Beads of sweat dotted his forehead and upper lip. His biceps quivered with exertion as he did another rep, then another and another. He had lost count of how many reps he had done. He didn't even care. All he wanted was the distraction that pain and effort offered.

If he pushed it much further, though, his muscles might give out on him. With a frustrated groan, he dropped the dumbbells on the floor with a tremendous clatter. He was glad he was alone in the tiny hotel gym.

Dante sat on the workout bench and pressed a towel to his face. Normally, he hated hotel gyms; they were too small and could be crowded. But he was grateful to have a place to burn off some energy.

He gazed out the window as his breathing slowed. It was mid-afternoon and the roads weren't yet crazed with traffic.

He had been at the hotel for about a week, ever since his disastrous weekend with Miranda in the country. At Dante's request, Harborview's scheduling coordinator had put them on staggered shifts. Dante thought Miranda would appreciate the space at work, and Dante liked knowing that Miranda was getting a full night's sleep while he worked the night shift.

But he wouldn't be able to extend his time in Boston for much longer. St. Joseph's chair of neurosurgery had emailed him nearly daily, gently pressing for a return date because he had been gone quite a long time, don't you think?

There really wasn't any reason to draw this out. With the custody agreement finalized, all that remained was for him to sign on the dotted line and schedule his return flight.

Dante checked his email, scrolled past yet another inquiry from his boss, and saw a new email—from Alessandra.

Action Needed: Please Review and Sign Hawthorne-Ricci Custody Agreement via SignEase

Dante's gut reflexively tightened. This is what he had been waiting for. And dreading.

He scrolled through the contract and found everything just as they had agreed. For the first two years of his daughter's life, Dante would come to the States twice a year for visits and bring the baby back to Italy for a month every summer. Unless she was still nursing, in which case all his visits would take place in Boston, or he could pay for Miranda and the baby to join him in Milan. He welcomed that idea, but it didn't seem terribly realistic with the demands of Miranda's surgical schedule.

When she was older, he and Miranda would alternate the holidays and her birthday. She would spend eight weeks with him in Milan every summer. He was free to visit her in the States so long as he provided advanced notice so the visit could be planned around her schoolwork and future activities.

Alessandra had assured him that this was a "living contract" that would be adjusted as things came up. Because things *would* come up, she assured him.

None of this was improving his already dark mood. But there wasn't anything he could do about it. Miranda wasn't reaching out, wasn't texting, wasn't even crossing paths with him at work.

He just needed to accept reality. This was their final agreement. The culmination of all that had happened between them since they met in New York.

His fabulous prize for taking a chance on love? Having a child who would know him mostly from a distance. No matter how hard he tried to forge a connection, there was only so much he could do from Milan. And losing the only woman who had ever wanted him to take a chance.

Unless he moved to Boston. That would change everything. Then he could see his child—and Miranda—every week.

Maybe he could think of these things in the future. But not now. The breakup was too fresh, the pain too raw, to think about making a major change in his life. And he doubted Miranda would welcome his presence in her life and work.

He reviewed the document one last time. He wished there were some error or unfinished business that could maybe slow this process down. It would give him more time to think of some way he might convince Miranda that they could be good together.

Where had everything gone so wrong? The picture with Julia, yes, but that was resolved. Miranda knew who Julia was and why they had been meeting.

So why was it so hard for Miranda to believe that he would be there for her? Was it really her past, or was it him?

Had he told her everything in his heart? That he was

ready to have two or three grand love affairs, all with her? That she had made him believe that some couples *could* be happy for a lifetime?

He wasn't sure he had told her all the things in his heart. Because he wasn't sure he had ever let go of his fear that he might hurt her in the end.

In my haste to protect her from a broken heart... I broke her heart.

Stubborn her. Stubborn him. Winning battles, but losing the war.

With a frustrated sigh, he opened the electronic document. Signature here, initials there. Page after page after page.

There. It was done. He hesitated for just a few more seconds. Once he hit Send, he would be accepting this version of life and family.

It would be okay. It had to be. He would find ways to let his child know she was the center of his world, even if he wasn't always in it.

And eventually, he would get over losing Miranda.

He hit Send.

He stalked back to his room, his mood as dark as midnight. His cell phone dinged again as he opened his hotel room door. As usual, his thoughts turned to Miranda, desperately hoping that she was reaching out to him, ready to talk.

But no, it was just his travel agent.

Just checking to see if you're ready to make your return trip home?

Technically, he still had a week left on his hospital sponsorship. But what was the point of sticking around? He had come here for Miranda's sake, and she had made it clear that she just wanted him to leave her alone.

Half-joking, he texted back: any flights out tonight?

Little dots jumped about, showing that his agent was texting a reply.

I could get you on the last flight out to New York. Overnight layover with a first flight out in the morning to Milan. Should I book you at The Regency again?

He was about to text back *just joking!* But when he thought about it, he couldn't come up with a good reason not to leave that night. Harborview Children's hardly relied on him; they had only created a sponsorship at Miranda's request. He was living in a hotel room, which was depressing as hell.

Miranda had made it clear that she didn't want him here. She had a family who could be there for her during the pregnancy. She didn't need him.

So why the hell not?

That works. But do not book me at The Regency. Anywhere but there.

There was no way he'd be able to walk back into the hotel where he had met Miranda. He was barely able to handle sharing a city with her.

It took him less than an hour to pack his belongings and wrap things up with Harborview Children's Human Resources Department.

As for Miranda, what should he do? Send her an email? Write her a formal letter? Say nothing and let her live in peace?

He muttered his frustration to himself as he zipped up his suitcase and lined it up by the door. He'd have plenty of time to figure that out as he waited at the airport.

Hi Dante, your itinerary is confirmed! Boston (BOS) → New York (JFK) → Milan (MXP). Check-in opens 24 hours before departure. Safe travels!

He had hours to go until check-in, but why wait? He could go to the airport and get some work done while he waited to board.

Dante returned his rental car and boarded the shuttle to the airport terminal, the hum of the engine and the faint chatter of other passengers barely registering in his mind. Every movement felt automatic, like checking off boxes on a list—return car, board shuttle, catch flight—yet each step felt like it was carrying him further into the darkness.

Heads up! Flight #2345 to New York now departs from Gate B12 instead of Gate A7. Please check the terminal screens or our app for updates.

Dante made it all the way to the airport before the weight of his decision crashed through his fog of denial. It wasn't until he was standing in the terminal, strangers moving all around him, that he felt the full weight of what he was about to do.

He was going to jump on a plane and leave the only woman who had ever loved him for who he was. The only woman who had made him take a chance on love. The only woman who had ever made him believe he deserved more than the superficial appearance of love.

His cell phone buzzed again, triggering that hope that maybe this time, it really was Miranda.

Want to travel in comfort? Upgrade to First Class for just $89! Limited seats available. Reply YES to confirm or visit our app to learn more.

Without any thought, he turned on his heel and bolted back toward the shuttle stop he had just left. It took forever for the next shuttle to arrive, then a half lifetime to get back to the rental counter. All he could think about was figuring out where Miranda was.

He had to find Miranda and try one more time. *But what if she...*

No, he couldn't let himself think about anything other than finding her.

Back in the car, with rain hammering the windshield, he gripped the steering wheel and navigated Boston's slick city streets. Desperate to reach her before it was too late.

His cell phone buzzed again and he seriously considered tossing it out the car window and into the rainy streets of Boston. If Miranda wasn't going to text, he didn't want to continue being tortured by his airline's automated texting service.

But curiosity got the best of him, and he pulled into a shopping center parking lot so he could check the message.

Hey...

He stared at the mysterious symbols for a long minute wondering if he was imagining the message. People could do that, he knew. Want something so much that they convinced themselves it had happened.

But even when he closed his texting app and reopened it, the words remained. It really was a message from Miranda.

Quickly, before the mirage—if it was that—disappeared, he texted back.

Hey, yourself...

Miranda pushed open the door to Mulligan's and was greeted with the familiar scent of fresh-baked bread and woodsy smoke. She paused in the doorway for a moment, the weight of the moment pressing down on her.

This wasn't just a meeting; it was a last chance to save something she wanted very much. She felt desperate and a little out of control, but she didn't care. Dante had come to her in a dozen ways over the past few months, putting his heart and even his career on the line for her. If they were to have any chance, she would have to do the same.

Her heart thudded painfully as her gaze swept the room. She recognized a few familiar faces, but it was Dante she wanted. What if he'd changed his mind since they exchanged texts? She wouldn't blame him if he didn't want to give her a second chance.

Finally, she spotted him, sitting at the bar, his back to her. Her breath caught as emotions crashed over her, one after another. Relief, longing, the sharp pang of uncertainty. He was looking devastating, as always, in a crisp white starched shirt, his nautical watch reflecting light from overhead lamps. It reminded her of when she'd first spotted him in New York—how she had thought he could have been a male model, he was so gorgeous.

Her nerves tingled with anxious energy at the sight of him. Every cell in her body was urging her to flee before she said something stupid and risked humiliating herself forever. What if her plan didn't work? She had practiced her speech a dozen times on the drive over, scrutinizing every word with painstaking attention, but now the words just felt weak and flimsy. Utterly inadequate for the moment ahead.

With a deep breath, she squared her shoulders and forced herself to move.

"Come on, you guys," she murmured, holding the door open for her coconspirators. She took a minute to review the plan one last time, making sure they were prepared for what would come next. Then she pointed to a dark corner in the back near the stockroom and told them to wait there for her signal.

The girls disappeared into the lively crowd of Mulligan's. Miranda took a deep, bracing breath and worked her way around tables and through clusters of patrons gathered around the bar. The warm glow of overhead lights reflected off polished wood and glass.

Miranda felt her neck prickle with nerves and anticipation. Her chest tightened with every step. Did Dante really want to see her? Or was this just a polite gesture on his part, so they could remain civil for the sake of their future parenting?

She stood behind him for longer than she intended, willing herself to reach out and touch him, say hello, whatever. But she felt paralyzed by the possibilities of all that could go wrong.

He must have sensed her presence, because he glanced over his shoulder and their eyes met. In that moment, everything around her—the bustling of the bar, bursts of laughter and the clink of glasses—all faded into the void. His gaze was steady, but his expression was hard to read. Still, it held her in place like an anchor in a storm. He had always been that anchor for her; she saw that now. From their very first night together, he had steadfastly helped her find her way through the pain and loss that had driven her to Milan. Always there when she needed him, no matter how fiercely she told herself she didn't need anyone.

"Hey," she managed to squeak.

He gave her a quick nod. That trademark chin tilt of his that always made her smile.

"Hey, yourself."

"May I sit here?" She indicated the bar stool next to him.

"Suit yourself," he said, tipping his beer back.

So now what? She felt as lost as she had that first night they met, when she took a chance and went to his room for the night. Should she jump right into an apology or make some small talk about the weather first? This was uncharted territory, and she didn't know which way to go.

She laid a hand softly on his arm and felt gratified when he didn't tense or pull away.

"Dante, I have been so wrong about you. So has the press and your family and maybe even you, too. You've shown me in so many ways that you are so much more than that. From the moment we met, you've been patient and completely trustworthy. There is no one else I'd want to raise our baby with.

"I'm sorry it's taken me so long to see what was right in front of me. I held on to the pain of the past, thinking it would protect me from being disappointed again. I was wrong, and I don't want to waste another minute being afraid. I want to dream again, take chances and believe in the future. That future might still be murky, but I want it to include you."

She paused to take a breath. Dante's gaze remained fixed on her, but his expression was guarded and hard to read.

"That is if you want your future to include me, too."

For a moment, Dante said nothing—just sat there, his gaze unreadable, his jaw tightening as if her confession had caught him somewhere between relief and regret. Then he gave a soft laugh, but it didn't quite reach his eyes. That laugh wrapped around her heart like a chill, leaving her to wonder if she'd just made a mistake. Maybe wanting forever with him was wanting too much.

Miranda's stomach tightened, the warmth of her confession draining away as she watched him shift his weight, running a hand through his damp hair like a man searching for the right escape. His eyes dropped to the bar, then flicked briefly back to hers—guarded now, as if he'd just rebuilt the walls she'd thought they had finally knocked down. Her throat went dry. Had she read this all wrong? Maybe he didn't want a future with her. Maybe he never had. The ache in her chest bloomed sharp and fast, and suddenly Mulligan's felt too small, too crowded, too raw with grief and regret. This was a horrible mistake, she thought, her pulse hot with humiliation. She needed to get out of there as fast as possible.

But as she turned to leave, Dante caught her by the wrist. His touch was electrifying and it made her stop in her tracks. She looked down at his hand, remembered how he had done this in New York, when she went to his room and didn't know what to do next. The memory washed over, equal parts heat and cool, soothing balm.

His expression softened as their gazes met. His jaw relaxed and something flickered in his eyes that sparked the tiniest glimmer of hope in her chest.

"Wait," he said.

Wait? Was that all he wanted? Of course, she would

wait. For a thousand years if need be. There was nowhere else she needed or wanted to be.

"Okay."

He exhaled, a low, shaky breath that seemed to carry the weight of the world.

"Miranda, you're not the only one who has made mistakes. I've made plenty, too—mostly, not speaking what was in my heart. I've spent so much time hiding behind clever words and charming escapes that I never told you how much you've affected me. You made me believe in something I thought was impossible. That love can last, and that it's worth holding on to. I'm not perfect, that's for sure. But I know I can change—and I want to—over and over again, decade after decade, with you."

"We could be evergreen," she whispered.

"We already are," he whispered back.

Then, from across the bar, there was a flash of light, then another.

Dante took immediate note. His jaw tightened and his eyes darted in the direction of the light flashes. His body stiffened as his fingers curled into fists.

"You have got to be kidding me. How the hell did those jerks know I was going to be here? What the hell? Are they following me now?"

He set his beer down hard on the bar, then moved to slide off his chair. "I think it's about time I have a word with these nimrods."

Miranda curved her hand over his arm. "I invited them."

Dante's brows arched in surprise while his mouth went slack as he processed her words. He searched her face for some clue, disbelief contorting his face into a pained expression of betrayal.

"Why the hell would you do that, Miranda? Haven't they ruined things for us enough already?"

"Give me a minute to explain, Dante. This isn't quite what you think."

She motioned for the girls to come out of the shadows. "Dante, meet Susanna and her friend, Michelle. Susanna is my niece and she covers the celebrity beat for her school newspaper. I have her and the photographer on loan from Willow View High School. I thought they might want first scoop on some hot celebrity gossip."

Susanna gave Dante a shy smile, her cheeks flushed with nervous excitement. Her friend furtively snapped another photo.

Dante's eyes narrowed as he tried to make sense of this unexpected news. "Okay, that's kind of cute. But why are they here? What's the hot gossip?"

"They are here because you have spent your entire life being defined by what others say about you. I think it's high time you get to make news of your own."

The school photographer hovered nearby, oblivious to the tension and emotion, her camera clicking incessantly.

"And the hot celebrity gossip might go something like *Mystery American Realizes She's Been an Idiot and Wants to Win Back the Heart of Milan's Prince of Pleasure*. Though these days, I think the Prince of Pleasure is about to become the Prince of Piggyback Rides."

Susanna was keenly attuned to the emotionally charged scene she had been assigned to cover. She stood in rapt attention; pencil poised over her reporter's notebook.

"You might want to make a note of that, Susanna. We are having a b-a-b-y."

Susanna and her photographer exchanged urgent whispers, then the photographer crouched low, her camera angled upward for the perfect shot.

A few people seated near them at the bar had taken note of the unusual activity. A hush settled the lively chatter around them, and several heads turned in their direction. Miranda could hear whispers behind her, while those nearby leaned in to catch fragments of her conversation.

A feeling of electric anticipation hovered in the air, a sense that everyone was holding their breath. Maybe it was just her imagination, but it really felt like everyone's attention was centered on Dante, waiting to see how he would respond.

Miranda felt a knot form in her stomach. This wasn't quite how she'd envisioned her plan unfolding. It was supposed to be a humorous, lighthearted plan to turn the paparazzi ambushes that had dominated his life into something funny that they could talk about for years to come. Instead, this was spiraling into something far more intense. Suddenly, she wasn't sure this was a good idea at all.

Dante's lack of mirth only confirmed her fears. He wasn't laughing, nor did he seem amused. His gaze was dark and his breath shallow and oh, my gosh, what a terrible thing to do to the man after all they had been through for the past few weeks.

"I'm sorry," she mumbled. "This was a mistake."

All she wanted to do was escape that stuffy bar and all the stares and Dante's stern expression. But before she could bolt for the door, Dante reached out and cupped her cheek, then drew her to him. The junior photographer's camera bulb went crazy when Dante's thumb brushed her cheekbone, and Miranda felt her heart explode into a million tiny pieces. She leaned forward, felt his breath mingle with hers as every doubt finally melted away.

Dante pressed his lips to her, soft at first, hesitant, still testing the edges of their love. It was a deliberate, unhurried kiss—a kiss she knew they had fought for and earned. Miranda's hands found his shoulders, anchoring herself to him and their future.

She was dimly aware of a smattering of applause around them, then the bartender declaring that the next round was on the house. But she could barely hear anything outside the pounding of her heart and Dante's steady breaths.

All she wanted was to stay wrapped up in Dante's arms, feel his heart beating with hers, safe in the quiet strength of his embrace. In that moment, she felt such a surge of gratitude. For all that was right in her world, but for all that had gone wrong, too. Because pain had made her take a chance—to go right instead of left when she reached the spoon in the road. And that road had led her to this moment—imperfect but so unexpected and real.

Whatever roads lay ahead—and all the spoons they encountered along the way—she and Dante would face them together, side by side.

EPILOGUE

THE GARDEN BEHIND Dante's childhood home in Milan had never looked more beautiful. Summer light filtered through the olive trees, casting dappled shadows over white tablecloths and colorful paper lanterns swaying in the warm breeze. Laughter echoed off the old stone walls, mingling with the faint chime of church bells from somewhere in the distance.

Miranda stood barefoot on the grass, watching Isabella clutch a piece of birthday cake in one tiny fist while smearing frosting across her sunhat with the other. Her daughter's dark curls peeked out from beneath the brim, and her chubby cheeks blushed with delight.

"A year old already," Miranda whispered in wonder.

Dante came up behind her, handing her a glass of wine before sliding an arm around her waist. "And already mastering chaos," he murmured against her ear, his lips brushing her skin in a way that still made her shiver.

"What's that?" she asked, eyeing the gift bag dangling from his arm.

"A little something for *la dottoressa*." He winked conspiratorially.

Miranda protested with a laugh. "Dante! She can barely say 'mama,' and you're already pushing med school?"

"She said 'papa' first," he reminded her with a grin.

"Only because you bribed her with gelato."

"Strategy," he said with a wicked grin. "An essential surgical skill."

She rolled her eyes but leaned into him, resting her head against his shoulder. He smelled like sunshine and aftershave, and his ever-present steadiness still felt like a miracle.

Dante crouched beside Isabella, offering her the gift bag. "*Per te, piccolina*," he whispered, his Italian soft and lilting.

Isabella tore at the tissue paper with both hands, but she needed her daddy's help to reveal a tiny plastic stethoscope and a set of toy medical instruments.

Miranda laughed, covering her mouth. "You're unbelievable," she teased. "Her first *Play Doctor* set?"

"Hey," he said with mock gravity. "Harvard Medical doesn't accept slackers."

Isabella babbled in agreement, thumping the plastic stethoscope against her chest and then trying to put it in her mouth.

Miranda shook her head, heart swelling. "Well, I hope you're ready to play the patient for the next ten years."

"Anytime you want," he whispered, brushing his lips against her temple.

Behind them, Dante's parents lingered near the olive tree, chatting with some of the neighbors who had stopped by. Isabella's laughter drifted over to them, and for a moment, Dante's stepmother couldn't hide the soft smile that made her eyes crinkle.

It had taken time to soften all the years of tension and misunderstanding between Dante and his adopted family. But Isabella had been the salve this family needed. Somehow, through the shared awe of watching her grow, something had shifted. Love had softened the edges of painful memories, rewriting old hurts with new joys.

Miranda swallowed the lump in her throat and turned toward Dante, cupping his face in her hand. "You've changed, you know."

"So have you."

They kissed softly, the kind of kiss that belonged to two people who had chosen each other again and again, even when it had been messy and hard.

They lived in Boston for most of the year now, both working at the children's hospital. Bradford had moved on to greener-and higher-paying pastures elsewhere, giving Miranda much-needed peace of mind at work.

But every summer, they came back to Milan, back to the olive trees and Dante's family and the parts of themselves that only bloomed in this place.

Miranda reached for Dante's hand, lacing her fingers through his. "Same time next summer?" she whispered.

"Wouldn't miss it for the world," he whispered back.

As the sun dipped lower, casting the garden in soft amber light, Isabella toppled onto her bottom with a happy squeal, plastic stethoscope still clutched in one tiny fist. Dante's stepmother scooped her up, spinning her gently in the air while Dante's father snapped a picture on his phone, grinning widely.

Miranda watched the scene unfold, her heart so full it almost hurt.

And in that golden moment, with Dante's arm around her and their daughter laughing beneath the bright blue Mediterranean sky, she knew this love she felt for Dante would always be. Sometimes it would surge strong in her heart; other times it might be a silent shadow that followed her everywhere. But it would always be there. This love would last.

* * * * *

If you enjoyed this story, check out these other great reads from Kate MacGuire.

City Doc for the Single Mum
Resisting the Off-Limits Paediatrician

Both available now!

MILLS & BOON®

Coming next month

EXPECTING IN THE ER
Tina Beckett

They got on the elevator, and he pressed the button for the second floor, which was where Mack's office was housed, and they rode up in silence. He didn't try to indulge in small talk or anything else until they reached the confines of his office, and he firmly closed the door and gestured to one of the two seats in front of his desk.

He sat behind his desk, feeling the need to keep barriers between them, including physical ones, to get the point across that they were separate beings with separate lives, despite what had happened in Boston.

'Well, it seems I am to welcome you back to the team.'

'I'm sorry, Mack. I was pretty sure you would have said no, if I had come to you directly with a request to come back to work.'

He nodded. 'Which brings up the question of why you want to come back.'

'Do I need a reason?'

'Frankly, yes. I'm sure it's not because I'm here.'

Her teeth came down on her lower lip for a minute before she answered. 'Not entirely, but it did weigh into the equation.'

'Lainey—'

'No, stop. Before you say anything, I didn't come back in hopes that we'd get back together. That's not what either of us wants. I think we've proved that point. But there is another player in this game. One I just found out about a couple of weeks ago.'

'I don't understand.'

She put her hands in her lap and leaned forward. 'I'm pregnant, Mack.'

Continue reading

EXPECTING IN THE ER
Tina Beckett

Available next month
millsandboon.co.uk

Copyright © 2026 Tina Beckett

COMING SOON!

We really hope you enjoyed reading this book. If you're looking for more romance be sure to head to the shops when new books are available on

Thursday 26th March

To see which titles are coming soon, please visit
millsandboon.co.uk/nextmonth

MILLS & BOON

FOUR BRAND NEW BOOKS FROM
MILLS & BOON MODERN

Indulge in desire, drama, and breathtaking romance – where passion knows no bounds!

OUT NOW

Eight Modern stories published every month, find them all at:

millsandboon.co.uk

TWO BRAND NEW BOOKS FROM
Love Always

Be prepared to be swept away to incredible worldwide destinations along with our strong, relatable heroines and intensely desirable heroes.

OUT NOW

Four Love Always stories published every month, find them all at:

millsandboon.co.uk

LET'S TALK
Romance

For exclusive extracts, competitions and special offers, find us online:

- **f** MillsandBoon
- **X** @MillsandBoon
- **◉** @MillsandBoonUK
- **♪** @MillsandBoonUK

Get in touch on 01413 063 232

For all the latest titles coming soon, visit
millsandboon.co.uk/nextmonth